PRAISE FOR THE SALT LINE

"*The Salt Line* is a 'literary thriller' that manages to fulfill each side of that phrase with admirable vigor. It's both gripping and emotionally resonant, both suspenseful and heartfelt. Holly Goddard Jones has a true storyteller's instinct for suspense, along with a deep gift for empathy. She'll make your heart race as you turn the pages, and then she'll crack it open a little before she's through."

—Scott Smith, author of ***The Ruins*** and ***A Simple Plan***

"With this intense, arrestingly vivid fever dream, Holly Goddard Jones fully realizes a completely original and wholly terrifying dystopian nightmare. Jones's wild, ventriloquist talent unfurls in this novel like never before. Each magnetic character in *The Salt Line* is boldly alive to the novel's world, at once monstrous, uncanny, and yet entirely ours."

—Claire Vaye Watkins, author of ***Gold Fame Citrus*** and ***Battleborn***

"Combining elements of sci-fi, thrillers and speculative fiction, *The Salt Line* is a page-turner. Ms. Goddard Jones . . . builds a believable world and generates tension effectively. The plot is action-driven, but an ensemble cast of characters keeps the story rooted in human emotions and motivations."

—***Pittsburgh Post-Gazette***

"*The Salt Line's* most poignant moments occur when the perceived impenetrability of certain protective barriers is undermined. . . . Jones' masterful use of suspense not only bends the style boundaries of dystopian lit, but it shows that the barriers we all often rely on can break."

—***Paste*** magazine

"Engrossing . . . *The Salt Line* is a well-written, literary novel. Making deft use of shifting third-person viewpoints, Jones creates complex and interesting characters. . . . These richly drawn characters and the world in which they struggle provide twists and turns that will draw in any reader brave enough to enter a grim and frightening world with killer ticks." —Greensboro *News & Record*

"Jones' darkly clever worldbuilding creates a nightmare that seems far from unthinkable. . . . It's *The Hunger Games* meets *The Godfather* meets Robin Cook, with female characters playing all the key roles. Hell, yeah." —***Kirkus Reviews*** (starred review)

"Social commentary and intense thrills rolled into one seamless story. Outwardly an adventure story, this suspenseful novel uses a thrilling premise to examine the fallout of abandoning universal freedoms in order to ensure collective safety."

—***Publishers Weekly***

"The mystery-like structure keeps the reader guessing as Jones switches seamlessly from evocative pastoral descriptions of North Carolina and Tennessee to action-packed scenes of violence. . . . At once dark, disturbing, and highly enjoyable, this is a timely novel bursting with ideas." —***Booklist***

"Terrifying and bold . . . A character-driven thriller with shocking plot twists, jaw-dropping revelations and splashes of horror, sci-fi and romance . . . Jones' unique riff on dystopian fiction as a platform for examining present-day concerns like climate change, immigration, technology and fundamental human rights offers plenty of surprises, but the most disarming aspect of *The Salt Line* is the unexpected tenderness expressed by its fully fleshed out, complicated characters who are fighting not just for their lives but for their very humanity. More than just a high-octane, speculative survivalist tale, *The Salt Line* is also a powerful meditation on humanity's fragility and resilience."

—***BookPage***

"Heartfelt and absorbing . . . A great thriller."

—***The Washington Book Review***

"[A] taut tale of survival and social commentary."

—***Locus*** magazine

"Well-developed . . . A slightly disturbing view of future earth with life threatened by something as small and common place as a tick, with some adventure, thrills and terrors along the way."

—***The Speculative Herald***

"A lot like what Golding might have produced had he diverged into a world of arachnids. And, it must be noted, nearly as well examined and executed."

—***Mountain Times*** (Western North Carolina)

ALSO BY HOLLY GODDARD JONES

The Next Time You See Me

Girl Trouble: Stories

The Salt Line

Holly Goddard Jones

G. P. PUTNAM'S SONS
NEW YORK

PUTNAM

G. P. Putnam's Sons
Publishers Since 1838
An imprint of Penguin Random House LLC
375 Hudson Street
New York, New York 10014

The Library of Congress has catalogued the G. P. Putnam's Sons hardcover edition as follows:

Names: Jones, Holly Goddard, author.
Title: The salt line : a novel / Holly Goddard Jones.
Description: New York : G. P. Putnam's Sons, 2017.
Identifiers: LCCN 2017001076 (print) | LCCN 2017006009 (ebook) | ISBN 9780735214316 (hardback) | ISBN 9780735214323 (eBook)
Subjects: | BISAC: FICTION / Literary. | FICTION / Science Fiction / Adventure. | GSAFD: Dystopias.
Classification: LCC PS3610.O6253 S25 2017 (print) | LCC PS3610.O6253 (ebook) | DDC 813/.6—dc23
LC record available at https://lccn.loc.gov/2017001076
p.   cm.

First G. P. Putnam's Sons hardcover edition / September 2017
First G. P. Putnam's Sons international edition / September 2017
First G. P. Putnam's Sons trade paperback edition / August 2018
G. P. Putnam's Sons trade paperback ISBN: 9780735214330

Printed in the United States of America
1 3 5 7 9 10 8 6 4 2

BOOK DESIGN BY AMANDA DEWEY

For Selby and Raina

Part One

The Salt Line

One

The burn was the first rite of passage. The brochures had warned them about this much.

It was Day 1 of the three-week training camp, 6:00 a.m. sharp, and Edie sat with Jesse on the gymnasium floor among a circle of sleep-slurred bodies, all of them clad in the regulation black athletic suit, their names piped across their hearts in silver-threaded cursive.

At a minute past the hour, according to the clock above the door, a man entered the gymnasium. He infiltrated their circle with the casual authority of someone in charge, pulled off his T-shirt, and lifted his arms above his head like a boxer who'd just knocked out his opponent with a single right-hand hook.

"Take a look at me, you dumb rich fucks," he said. Jesse leaned forward with bright-eyed interest, giddy, lapping it up, but a middle-aged Japanese couple, wearing matching fleece vests over their gym suits, flinched in affront. The man's stomach and back were polka-dotted, the marks perfectly round, perhaps a centimeter in diameter. The skin on his shins was tight and shiny, and the hair on his scalp grew in only sporadically. "I see some pretty ladies in the room." He looked at Edie for a moment, and she recoiled, as though her beauty were a thing to be ashamed of. "I see a lot of soft-looking men. I see a bunch of people with more money than sense, who think they're buying themselves some adventure, some street cred."

The speech had the cadence of spontaneity, but Edie could tell that it was one he'd delivered many times. Jesse's fawning acceptance surprised and disappointed her. He wouldn't like it if she rolled her eyes right now; he wouldn't mime laughter and nod knowingly, as he usually did.

"My name is Andy, and I'll be your guide and your coach and your shrink and your goddamn messiah for the next eight weeks. I have fifty-seven burns on my body. Each one hurt like a motherfucker." He stopped in front of a silver-haired woman wearing diamond earrings and held out his arm. He pointed at a thick red weal with a blunt forefinger. "Some of the burns are keloids, which means that they can expand into healthy tissue. I don't know why some turn out this way. Most of us have only the faintest notions of how our bodies will react to trauma. I imagine that goes double for a bunch of people who are willing to pay good money to put their lives at risk."

The man in the fleece vest was red-faced. He looked around the circle, hoping to find another person who shared his anger, but no one accommodated him.

"The average traveler will arrive at Quarantine 1 with at least one of these scars. I know you think you understand what this means, but let me make this very real to you." A projection appeared in the air to his left, dust winking in the column of light. The light coalesced into the shape of an insect, which rotated slowly. "The dread miner tick. You've lived your life in fear of it. Miner ticks are resourceful and very, very difficult to kill. Some scientists claim that they are capable of strategizing. This one time"—he was almost smiling now; he obviously liked telling this story—"I woke up, unzipped my tent, and saw something hanging on one of the seams. I thought a leaf had snagged on it, and I reached to pull it off, and that's when I saw that the leaf was actually a cluster of miner ticks." He paused so the significance of this could settle upon the ten people sitting on the floor around him like children at story hour. "They had chosen a spot—some place where there was a tiny fault in the material, not even visible to the human eye—and joined forces to work it open. Another couple of hours, and they might have."

Edie grabbed Jesse's hand before she could stop herself. He gave her a reassuring squeeze.

The projection zoomed in on the tick, so that the three-dimensional image hanging in the air was a couple of horrifying feet tall.

"An adult male miner tick will attach and feed but not burrow. A male tick bite will become inflamed, and there is some risk of disease, but male miner ticks weren't what drove us behind the Salt Line. Now females—"

The image changed, grew. A barbed protuberance extended from the head.

"The females are real bitches." There were some nervous titters. "The bite of a pregnant female miner tick releases a numbing agent, which allows her to work without detection. The burrowing appendage, which is called the horn, is corkscrew shaped. The female essentially drills into your skin, pulling her body behind her into the opening. This takes less than half a minute.

"By the time you feel the itching, the female miner tick has created a tiny cavity under your skin and settled into place. I cannot stress to you enough the importance of quick action here. Within a few minutes, the female will start releasing eggs into the cavity. The eggs are each the size of a pinprick. They can't move on their own, but they're covered in a fibrous coating, which makes them exceptionally sticky, like burrs. They spread out quickly and can even enter the bloodstream."

The woman with the diamond earrings had gotten very pale.

"If the itching stops, you're fucked. The female has died, and the eggs have scattered. Over the next several hours, the area around the bite will erupt in hundreds of pustules. Depending on where the eggs traveled, and if evacuation occurred near a vein, eruptions can occur all over the body, and even in vital organs. The itching will return and become almost unbearable. If you don't scratch the pustules open yourself to try to sooth the itch, the miner ticks will eventually tear their way out."

The giant tick vanished, and a time-lapse video took its place. There were a couple of gasps, though this was nothing most of the travelers hadn't already seen in their secondary school health classes or on internet shock feeds. There was a forearm with a single red bump. Then little bumps started popping up all around it, spreading down to the wrist and up to the bend in the elbow, the red heads turning taut and yellowish and then bursting open. Out of the oozing fluid crawled hundreds of tiny miner ticks. The arm never moved. Edie realized that the host must be sedated.

There was the unmistakable sound of someone's rising gorge, and then a young man—maybe even Edie's age, unlike most of the other people here—shot up from the circle and fled the gymnasium.

"Such infestations can be survived, and in fact, the infestation itself is painful and disfiguring but not necessarily life-threatening, unless eggs hatch in vulnerable tissue, as I mentioned before, or if there are multiple infestations that result in significant blood loss. The problem is that the female miners often carry blood-borne diseases. Ten percent of them have a juiced-up version of Rocky Mountain Spotted Fever, which is unpleasant but mostly treatable.

"But it's estimated that between forty and forty-five percent of female miner ticks carry Shreve's disease, which you've no doubt heard enough about to last you a lifetime. Shreve's is the big bad wolf in our story. Symptoms manifest within forty-eight hours of a successful infestation and include blurry vision, nausea, and loss of feeling in the limbs. The disease is fast and deadly. Total paralysis, then death. All in a matter of days."

He stopped and made another full circle, connecting eyes with each of the ten travelers. "That's why we have the Stamp. Some say it's archaic, or barbaric, but it doesn't change the fact that we've not been able to eradicate these goddamn ticks from the face of the earth, and we still haven't been able to create some kind of a foolproof defense against them, either, or an inoculation against Shreve's. The microsuits help but have a five percent failure rate. Lotions and sprays have minimal to nil effect."

He pulled a device out of his pocket. It was about the size of a cigar but stainless steel, with a little glass lip on one end and a button on the other. The projected image shifted into an animation of the device. "The Stamp is the single most effective tool we have against female miner ticks and miner tick infestations. As soon as you feel the itch, you place the mouth of the Stamp on the affected site"—he mimed on his own arm—"and depress the button." He made an exaggerated motion of his thumb but didn't press down. "You'll hear a click, like a flint getting struck. And then you'll feel some of the worst pain of your life. The Stamp thrusts a barbed hook through your skin, skewering the female miner tick, and then retracts it, capturing the tick in a chemical solution. Then a burner brands the wound, cauterizing it and killing any of the eggs in the perimeter, as well as disinfecting the blood-borne contagions the bitch might have left behind. The Stamp, my friends, has a ninety-nine-point-eight percent success rate if used within sixty seconds of initial burrowing."

He stopped, letting that last statement linger. Edie knew what was coming next, and she swallowed hard, feeling as if her windpipe had constricted to a mere thread of opening.

"You *will* have to use this device if you go on this journey beyond the Salt Line. The question isn't 'if'; it's 'when.' And that's why Outer Limits Excursions requires each of its travelers to submit to the Stamp before beginning training. We don't want to waste your time. And we don't want you wasting ours.

"If you walk out of here today, you can still get a ninety percent refund of your package price. The penalty covers Quarantine cancellation fees and the time it took me to give you this entertaining presentation." A few people smiled halfheartedly. "And if you decide you regret it down the line, you can reapply for a future excursion at a five percent discount." The projection disappeared, and Andy crossed his arms. "There's the door. The lovely Jessica is waiting in the front office with your paperwork, and she'll even make you a cappuccino for your drive home."

Edie sneaked a glance at Jesse. He was still hunched forward, still beaming. The Japanese couple in the matching vests had an intense whispered exchange.

"You may be wondering right now why you even came here in the first place," Andy said. "You may be thinking, 'Jesus Christ, why didn't I just buy that condo at the beach, or book a week at Casinolake? What in the hell was I thinking?'" He placed his hands on his hips, emanating a cocksure vigor at odds with the ravages of his many scars.

"Here's why." Now he put his palms together as if in prayer, a canned gesture, rehearsed as his speech. "You know there's a whole world out there we've run and hid from, because the going got a little tough. You know, for a few scars and a big wad of cash, that you can go see the things your great-great-grandparents took for granted, that are available to you now only in photographs or simulations. Sunrise from a rock precipice. A hawk circling over your head. Trout bellies in a mountain stream. You can listen to cold water dripping from the ceiling of a cave, and you can see deer flipping up their white tails at you before dashing between trees and out of sight. Right now, on this Fall Color Tour you've each paid a premium for, you can hike across hillsides covered in reds, golds, and oranges, the scale of which—I promise you—is like nothing you've ever seen before.

"I've risked my life and defaced my body because I believe those sights have value, and that connecting with nature—however dangerous it can be—is essential to the experience of being human." Edie, despite herself, felt a stirring of tender pride, so acute that tears prickled her eyes. "But this isn't for everyone. That's a fact. So please, if your instincts are telling you to take off, take off. No judgment here. I like people who know their own minds and their own limits.

"If you're ready for an adventure, though—if you want to know, for the first time, what it really means to be alive—stay." He held up the Stamp, wagged it a little. "There is no pleasure without pain."

Jesse started to clap. An excruciating second passed in which no one joined him, and then Edie remembered to move her hands, and most of the others followed suit.

Andy nodded along with the sputtering of last claps, then leveled his gaze, standing very still. There was a moment—a dozen seconds, twenty—of perfect silence.

"Anyone leaving?" he asked.

The travelers looked around at one another. Edie stared at the couple in the vests, then the young man who had run out of the room to throw up (he had returned, almost endearingly shamefaced, as Andy was finishing his demonstration of the Stamp), hoping—she realized—that someone would raise a hand, would declare "This is insane," and then maybe the rest of them would have the courage to stand up and agree. Maybe even Jesse could be convinced. But no one moved.

"Well, then." Andy grinned, brandishing the Stamp. "Who's first?"

This time last year, Edie was sleeping on a cot at her mother's bedside during the daylight hours—catching naps between nurse's visits and her mother's scattered moments of lucidity—and bartending each night from seven to three. The cancer's attack had been swift and ruthless: one day her mother was finishing another ten-hour shift at the industrial laundry facility where she worked, suffering from nothing more than low energy that she had understandably attributed to working long hours and getting older; a month later, she was bed-bound and guzzling bag after bag of "blood product," as the nurses always called it, the disease a web of secret insults in her middle—breast, lungs, lymph nodes, bones. Her insurance didn't cover generated tissue transplants, which were still deemed "experimental." So she lay in a hospital bed and suffered. "Don't let me die," she told Edie some days. "Take me home," she said on others. Edie, in a fog of exhaustion and grief, didn't know which version of her mother to trust. So she blinked as the doctors explained options to her, nodded along, approved each suggested procedure. Thinking: *I've got to give the universe time to fix this.* Thinking: *Every day I get with her is better than nothing.* Thinking: *I can't be the one to finish things. That can't be on me.*

At last, when the doctors assured Edie that everything had been tried and the only things keeping her mother alive were transfusions and blood pressure medication—Edie had pictured one of those car lot air-sock people, the kind that reached and waved when the fan was on and collapsed the second it was shut off—she had agreed to take her off life support. Thinking: *So this is what life support is.* She hadn't known, had pictured some anonymous machine, a throbbing robot heart. Thinking: *Maybe I can finally get some sleep tonight before my shift starts.*

But it had taken another six hours after that, the dying. Six more hours, the space between breaths speeding up at first, maddeningly, her mother grimacing and moving her tongue around in her mouth, as if tasting something foul, then jerking up her chin, then parting her lips for air, the gestures so determined that Edie allowed herself to wonder if the doctors were wrong, if her mother's will to live transcended the cancer that had seemed to be decimating her. But this, too, didn't last. The breaths slowed. The grimaces stopped. The nurse came in to tell Edie that her mother's heart rate had dropped to fifty, and it wouldn't be long now. Edie called in at work. Stefano told her OK, do what you got to do. She watched her mother and thought self-torturing thoughts, like: These are the hands that rubbed my back when I was sick and were always so smooth and cool, and this is the mouth that sung over the dishes each night in that clear pretty alto, and here are the brown eyes, behind closed lids, that will never again see me. Like that. And the nurse was right, not long after that she was gone.

She kissed her mother's forehead. She didn't say anything—her voice was hoarse from the six hours of plaintive whispering she'd done into her mother's ear—and drifted out of the hospital, drove across town, walked into O'Henry's, and tied a green apron around her waist.

"You sure you want to be here?" Stefano asked. It wasn't a tender question, but a practical one.

"I need the money," she said, and he nodded.

It was eleven, the clientele rowdy. She went to the computer to punch in an order and unbuttoned a couple of buttons on her blouse, feeling like a cliché, not even wearing one of her good bras. These guys didn't care, though. What she needed tonight was to not go back to the apartment she and her mother had shared until her hospitalization six weeks ago. What she needed tonight was to not see the "Happy Halloween!" wreath her mother had hung on the door, or the Our Lady of Guadalupe candle she kept on the dresser next to her rosary, or the stack of paperback romance novels by her recliner, books with titles like *Sultry Savannah Summer* and *A Lovers' Pact*. So when a man hit on her who met her three criteria for the night—not too old, not too disgusting, not too dodgy—she flirted back. And checked into a hotel room with him as soon as her shift ended.

This was her life for a while. This was how, a couple of months later, she brought home Jesse Haggard for the first time.

Edie owned only the most basic tablet, which operated at low speed and didn't sync with most wall monitors and speaker systems, and her life, even before her mother's illness, had been a slog of work and broken sleep. So she wasn't very current on popular culture, had only the vaguest notion of who Jesse Haggard was, and recognized him not at all that first night, even after they'd exchanged names. He was dressed like the men at O'Henry's always dressed—flannel shirt, jeans, lace-up work boots—and so she had no reason to guess that he rated thirty-seventh on the Atlantic Zone's list of Deep Pocketz, or that the webshow he served as a judge on, *Pop Sensation*, was such a phenomenon that Jesse had renegotiated his contract to the record-breaking tune of five hundred thousand credits an episode. She'd just found him cute and charming. When another bartender, Inez, had cornered her at work the next night to quiz her about what had happened—"Oh my God," she'd asked, "did you boink Jesse Haggard?"—and Edie had subsequently assembled the basic facts about his fame, her first impulse had actually been to not see him again, though he had scrawled his tablet's quickcode on an O'Henry's bar napkin, along with the message: *I had a great time. Let's have another.* Her grief was an all-consuming thing right now, a thing that couldn't accommodate the complications of keeping a pop-star lover, and she discovered that she did not much like his music, which Inez had proceeded to play on a loop throughout that night's shift, until Stefano threatened to throw her tablet into the trash compactor.

I've got this feeling and I don't want to hide it
This magic mission and I won't be denied, oh, no no
Not tonight is what you're trying to tell me
But this burnin' yearnin' make me go a little crazy
If this hunger's bad I don't wanna be good
'Cause it's the right night—the right night—for you

It was kind of a disturbing song, if you really listened to the words.

To his expressed delight but obvious consternation, Jesse proved over the ensuing weeks of boot camp to be just as unimpressive to the rest of the Outer Limits Excursions travelers as he had been, at first, to Edie. Most of them, aged well beyond the perimeter of Jesse's fan base, didn't recognize him, even when Jesse would pretend to just absentmindedly hum "Right Night for You," which had been picked up in a Burger Blitz marketing campaign. Those who did know who he was, or who figured it out, were, at best, amused by him, "pop star" being the most novel of novelties, a relic from another era almost, like those people who specialized in rebuilding electrical HVAC systems or the boutique gardeners who claimed they could trace their seeds' lineages back to the preindustrial age. "That's the young man who's a judge on that show," one of the men—a lawyer named Mickey Worthington—told his traveling partner, Lee Flannigan. "That singing contest."

"Oh, yeah!" Lee said. "What a hoot. I'll have to tell my daughter. She'll really think her old pop's cool now."

"A *hoot*," Jesse had grumbled that night in bed. "Better a hoot than a suit." Then he'd grabbed his tablet from the bedside table and scribbled some notes. "That's not bad, actually," he murmured.

Edie, of course, was practically invisible among these people who saw their financial bounty as proof of their superior intellects and talents. *What do you do?* they would ask her. Or: *Are you Jesse's wife?* Because her answer to the first question was essentially "nothing," and her answer to the second question was "no," she had been relegated to the status of accessory: Jesse's hanger-on, his groupie, his flavor of the month. She could see it in their eyes: *Poor girl. She'll go through this for him, come back with a shaved head and scars on those pretty arms, maybe even on that pretty face, and he'll drop her as soon as he gets bored.*

But they didn't know all of the story.

Boot camp passed in a blur—marathons of rigorous exercise; primer classes on topics such as "Three Foolproof Methods for Building a Fire" and "Edible Plants and Fungi of the Eastern Appalachians"; fabulous, plentiful meals served with good wine and beer (but never liquor) in the Canteen. Goals that had at first seemed unattainable were suddenly achieved, and Andy brightened with delight and pride. It was the army on a cruise ship. Hard work, obliteration of the self, fidelity to a group, but also the pleasures and the exclusivity that such wealthy men and women had come to see as their due. Edie's Stamp wound—she'd opted for the meaty upper buttock, where she'd once been administered her childhood vaccines—crusted into a scab, and then the scab fell off in the shower, leaving behind a wet-looking red maw.

She had learned, over meals or during water breaks, that the majority of the travelers in the group were venture capitalists of some kind, or lawyers who were cagey about the kind of law they practiced and the names of the clients they served. The young man who'd thrown up on the first day—a nice guy, quirky, with a fast smile and a self-deprecating sense of humor—turned out to be the creator and CEO of Pocketz, the social web cooperative for safe credit storage, savings, and transfers. "This guy is bigger than big," Edie tried to convince a dubious Jesse. "He basically changed the global economy."

Jesse, unimpressed, shrugged. "Fuck that. Pocketz is old-school. Everyone's going to switch to Bank On It in a couple years' time. I guarantee it."

One day about halfway into the training, as weightlifting ended and the travelers headed to their rooms to shower before dinner, Andy stopped her at the doorway. "Edie," he said. "Got a sec?"

Jesse, whose hero-worship of Andy had only compounded since that first day in the gymnasium, smiled eagerly. "She's doing great, isn't she?" he asked. "She's lifting eight more kilos than she was last week."

"Yeah," Andy said. "Super. You've really helped her. Hey, my man, would you try catching up with Tia and seeing if she needs a hand with the tent demo? I forgot to drag all of that stuff out of supply before the last sesh started."

"Uh, sure," Jesse said, his smile faltering a little. "See you back at the room, Edie?"

"Yeah," Edie said. She couldn't read the look on Andy's face, and a tremor of fear passed through her: *He knows.* Something flagged during the medical exam. *Don't be paranoid,* Jesse had told her. *Even if they could tell, and they can't, they have a lot of my money right now. No way they'd risk that.*

But *they* weren't Andy. And maybe Andy wanted his cut.

Jesse lingered in the hallway outside the weight room, and Andy smiled big, waving him off in an affable way. "We won't be a minute, dude. Go help Tia."

Edie watched him go. When she turned her gaze back to Andy, he was leaned against the door frame, smiling in a knowing way. He held out his Smokeless in offering.

She accepted it, feeling she had no choice, though she didn't smoke much. She was so drained of energy that the NicoClean went straight to her head.

"Your accent," Andy said. "It sounds very familiar."

Edie shrugged vaguely.

"My mom's from the Gulf Zone," Andy continued. "She got a vestment here forty years ago because she tested in the ninety-ninth percentile on the math AEs." He smiled crookedly. "You some kind of genius?"

Edie laughed sharply. "Hardly," she said.

"But you're from the Gulf."

She nodded.

"And now you're here," he mused. "I know you're a citizen. You couldn't get the papers for this excursion if you weren't."

She nodded again, thrown by this line of inquiry.

"I can tell you're not like them," he said, making a sharp gesture with his chin toward the living quarters. "You didn't buy your way to Atlantic Zone, nuh-uh. So tell me, Edie. What's your deal?"

Sweat was running down her face, and she blotted it with a towel. "No secret," she said casually. "My dad was an outer-zone contractor for a timber company. He caught a case of Shreve's and died when I was eight. There were accidental death benefits."

Andy sighed. "And now you're following Mr. Guitar out into the woods. My shrink would call that self-destructive behavior." His face grew serious. "Do you mind if I give you some advice?"

Edie checked the hallway for Jesse, wondering if he had gone on to Tia, as instructed, or if he lingered just around the corner and out of sight. "I have a feeling I'm going to hear it."

"Leave," he said. She looked back at Andy, startled, and he was nodding, hard. "It's his money, right? They'll refund him seventy-five percent of it. Drop in the bucket to him. You take off and let that dipshit have his little adventure, and maybe you'll even still be together on the other side of this. If you go, I guarantee you won't be."

"And why do you say that?"

"Because guys like that reveal themselves is why." Andy switched off his Smokeless and pocketed it. "You'll be carrying his ass, and you'll resent it."

"But I won't," Edie said. "Resent it, I mean. That's why I came. To look out for him."

Andy shook his head in a disgusted way. "It's a shame. What a waste." He started off toward the dining hall, and Edie grabbed his sleeve—emboldened, maybe, by her perplexed relief.

"Wait. I don't get it. What about this communing with nature stuff? This 'you're not human until you sleep under the stars' stuff?"

"I thought it would have been obvious to you, of all people."

Andy put out his forearms and made fists; the tight, scarred skin pulled into painful-looking little wrinkles. "I do what I've got to do to make a living. To feed my kids. Maybe once I was sold on that nature bullshit, but that goes away when you've been Stamped enough times. When you come home and your little boy's crying because you look like a goddamn monster."

Edie remembered her own terror when her father had returned from a month-long contract with two new Stamps on his face. "What about you," she said. "Do *you* want some advice?"

"Sure," he said sarcastically.

"Quit," she said. "Your kids need their father."

He broke eye contact for the first time. "As a matter of fact, this is my last tour."

"Really?"

"Yeah," he said. "And let me say this one more time—as a man who's seen his limit and is on his way out. Take off. You want thrills, go to the water park. You don't want to be on this excursion."

"I'm not abandoning him," Edie said.

"Well, honey, I hope he's worth it." Andy tipped an imaginary hat. "See you in the mess hall."

Was he worth it? Well, yes. Jesse had saved her life, sort of.

The math had been of the humiliating sort that you saw on webshows like *Outta Wedlock*.

Two weeks late.

Three different men, including Jesse, during what Edie had been able to calculate must have been her fertile window.

You had to be careful whom you talked to about these things. Edie had heard the stories. The pierced, tattooed broad who'd worked at your side for four years and never hesitated to slam the president when the news crawl by the Pabst clock churned out some new story about him—she might be the first one to report you to

Public Safety and Morals if you so much as made a little insinuation, floated a teensy hypothetical. In high school, Edie had known a girl whose parents sold both family cars to take a sudden vacation to Midwest Zone, though no one ever vacationed in Midwest Zone. There were the girls you saw on the news, dumped at emergency room bays or, worse, left in alleyways. Woke up handcuffed to their hospital beds. You were supposed to be able to find herbal abortion recipes on the dark web, but Edie had no idea how you even got on the dark web, and that was the sort of question you couldn't go around asking, either. Not if you liked your freedom.

She supposed she could pin it on Jesse, threaten to make a stink if he didn't claim it, or at least give her money enough to go away. There was a good chance it was his, anyway. But she liked him. He was sweet. And Edie wasn't built that way. She didn't want to be the kind of person who could treat people like that.

A while ago, she'd worked with a woman, a PU (pregnant and unwed), who found a sponsorship through LifeForce and actually made a tidy profit once the baby was born. This seemed, to Edie, like the best option. She had no money to raise a child. She had no desire to raise a child. And she wasn't going to be able to bartend once she was showing. Stefano couldn't legally fire her, and Edie thought he was a decent enough guy not to try, but he'd have the law on his side if he wanted to move her to the kitchen or something, and those jobs paid for shit.

She supposed that another sort of person—another sort of woman—would see the pregnancy as a blessing. As a reincarnation of her mother's spirit. Edie's mother would have thought this way. Her mother had been religious; her church's women's group sent casseroles to Edie's apartment throughout the hospitalization and did prayer circles over her mother's writhing body a couple times a week. Her mother had always told Edie that she was blessed she could raise her daughter in a place that was not just safe but moral—Atlantic Zone was safe *because* it was moral—and this had been Edie's father's gift to them, bought with his death, his noble, tragic sacrifice. Edie had never believed in any of this, or most of it. But she loved and respected her mother, and she hadn't fought with her. Not often.

But no, Edie was more inclined to see the pregnancy like she'd seen her mother's cancer: an invasion, unwelcome, to be survived and not embraced. It helped her, a little, to think of the pregnancy as a job. A hard job, like her father's six-month tours out-of-zone. You could do anything for nine months, for money. Her pregnancy would be contract work, a deployment.

She told herself this again, and again. She stopped answering when Jesse messaged her. This hurt, but it was easier, cleaner, than putting herself through his awkward reaction, the pain and humiliation of his rejection of her. She marked days on her calendar, careful to keep even these vague notations on print copies, never doing a search for LifeForce (or Caring Connection, or the Greatest Love) online. When she started showing—no sooner—she would walk into one of the clinics and start the process, let them tag and process and herd her, police what she ate and drank, her medications, the music she listened to, the webshows she watched. She would undergo the genetic screenings, the rigorous family history surveys. She had her looks going for her, but her mixed-race heritage might be a liability, as well as her mother's breast cancer, though a wealthy enough family could pay to have a gene like that shut off.

Then, one Saturday night, she came home from her shift—so tired she had barely been able to lift her bus pass to the scanner—and nearly stumbled over Jesse Haggard, who'd parked himself on the floor in front of her apartment door. She gasped and jumped back, fumbling for her pepper spray, and Jesse leaped to his feet, hands lifted in surrender, and said, "Shh shh shh, it's just me, Edie. It's Jesse. Shit, baby. I didn't mean to scare you."

"What are you doing here?" she asked, her heart booming in her ears. "Fuck, Jesse. You about gave me a heart attack."

"I didn't know how else to catch you. You haven't made it easy."

She shoved her key into the front lock, jiggled it in the funny way required to coax it open, and nudged the door with her hip. "Take a hint," she said.

He waited at the threshold. "Can I come in a minute?"

Edie shrugged.

"I won't linger. Promise. I just wanted to see you again and hear from you direct what's up. Then I'll go and leave you alone forever, if that's what you want. OK?"

Edie sighed. "Fine. Sit." She pointed at the couch. "I'm tired, Jesse, and I don't have the heart to dance around this. So I'm going to be blunt." She fell into her mother's rocking chair and sighed, lifting one heavy foot, unzipping her boot. Then the other. Her sock feet, as always after a shift, emerged from their sheathes wrinkled and damp, and she peeled her socks off with a sigh. "I'm pregnant." She saw him opening his mouth and put up a hand. "No. Let me finish. I don't know whose it is. I slept with a couple of guys around the same time you and I started seeing each other. I slept with one of them after that first time with you. I sleep around. That's what I do."

She paused here, unable to look at him. When he didn't jump in, she continued.

"Anyway, I'm dealing with it. So let's move on. You don't owe me anything."

Another silence, which she itched to fill—but she wasn't sure what was left to say. She chanced a look at him. He seemed . . . thoughtful. Not shocked or panicked. Not angry.

"I mean," he said, "do you want it? Like, to have it?"

"Of course I don't fucking want it," Edie snapped. "Of course I don't want to fucking have it. What goddamn choice do I have? I'm going to go to one of those agencies and sell it."

He cleared his throat. "You don't want to have it."

She felt a charge in the air—a sense that they were moving toward some new understanding. "I don't want to have it," she replied carefully.

"Because—you don't have to." He leaned over and rubbed his mouth. "This doesn't have to be a big thing is what I'm saying. I know people. It happens all the time."

"Has it happened to you?"

"Once," he said. "A few years ago."

"And you got it taken care of."

"It really wasn't a big deal."

She rocked in her mother's chair, absorbing all of this. The gulf between what was and wasn't a big deal, and for whom.

"I'd have to go somewhere? Out-of-zone?"

"Oh, hell no. It would happen right here."

"And this place—it's safe? I mean. Clean? Sterile?"

He laughed. "Sorry. I don't mean to make light of this. But yeah, of course. It's totally up-and-up. They just offer certain after-hours services."

"How much?" she said flatly.

He shook his head dismissively. "On me."

"It might not be yours."

"Or it might. If you want to feel better about this, it's a lot cheaper for me to help you now than to take the risk you change your mind later about raising it."

She started to cry. It was the first time she had cried since all of this—what she thought of as *all of this*—had started: her mother's sickness, her death, Edie's madness in the wake of the death, the dread news of the pregnancy. She cried hard, for all of it, and at some point Jesse put his hands on both of her upper arms, gingerly, and he said, "Shit. I didn't mean that. It's up to you. Of course it is, honey. I'm not trying to force this on you."

Now Edie laughed, just as hard as she'd been crying, and she mopped tears off her face with her shirttail. "That's not why I'm crying. Hell yes, I want this. Yes. I'm crying because I'm thinking about how lucky I am I fucked a rich guy."

He didn't reply right away—she supposed he wasn't sure what

tone to take, what was allowed—but then he said, "Glad to be of service," and she hugged him. He hugged her back, firmly, and kissed the top of her head. He returned to her bed that night, and then they fell asleep, exhausted, and when Edie lifted a swollen eyelid ten blissfully blank hours later, he was still there. His narrow back, ridge of spine. The tattoo of a golden eagle taking flight across his rib cage. *I think I could love this guy,* she told herself. *If love is what he wants from me.*

A few months later, Jesse heard about Outer Limits Excursions, and he became obsessed with this excursion-into-the-wild-beyond stuff. There had been a session musician named Neil—a guy Jesse's producer had hired to add a layer of classical guitar to a track on the new audio feed—and Jesse, who had never seen a Stamp in the flesh (or, as it were, on the flesh), was fascinated. Edie had been hanging out at all of the recording sessions by then ("Please stay, baby," Jesse would say in his insecure, yearning way, and his producer would scowl), and so she had seen firsthand the mix of boyish emotions that had crossed Jesse's face as Neil displayed the welts on his arm, stomach, neck, and ankle: the jealousy and crushing admiration, the thrill of possibility. "Experience of a bloody lifetime," this Neil guy kept repeating, and by the end of the day, he had gotten paid for as many hours of storytelling as guitar playing, as Jesse had him recite and repeat the entirety of his eight-week adventure. Three weeks of boot camp. Three beyond the Salt Line, in what had once been the Great Smoky Mountains National Park. Two weeks in Quarantines 1 and 2. Drinking water from pure mountain streams, eating rabbit charred over an open fire. An open, undisturbed sky crusted with millions of stars.

And then there were the tick stories, which Neil told with as much nostalgia as he did those of nature's majesty. *This one*—he'd point—*I got when I stripped down to bathe in a waterfall. Fucker was on me the second I pulled off my microsuit. This one*—he pointed again—*had stopped itching the second before I managed to use the Stamp, and I worried for days that I'd gotten to it too late.* Jesse nodded and prodded, and he kept saying, "Fucking rad," and Edie had gotten uneasy. *Shut up shut up shut up,* she wanted to snap at Neil. Because she knew enough by now about how Jesse's mind worked to guess how this would go. She had seen it the previous month, when Jesse had spotted a man outside a club who had pulled up on one of the new CO_2 motorbikes, and instead of just waiting to place an order for one at a dealer, Jesse had transferred the guy ten thousand credits on the spot, taken the key, and gotten Edie to drive his Zepplyn 8.0 home. Or how, at a rave, he'd accepted a Bullet from some weirdo stranger with eyelid rivets and popped it before Edie could protest. He had finished that night stripped naked and running down the side of the road, screaming, *"HEEEEEEEEEE!"* until he fell over in a ditch, unconscious.

He was an innocent. What he saw in himself as hot-bloodedness and boldness, a masculine thirst for thrills, was actually just a longing for acceptance and admiration, and a childlike confidence in the goodwill of others. It made Edie's heart break for him, and it made her feel that it was her duty, as the one person in his inner circle beside his parents who wouldn't indulge and lie to him if it meant getting an opportunity or a freebie, to look out for him. And she owed him. Didn't she? And so she had agreed to join him on this Outer Limits Excursion, though she knew all too well the dangers that awaited them on the other side of the Salt Line. The thought of one of those miner ticks burrowing under her smooth skin had awakened her every night of their strange stay in this sumptuous brick training facility, sweat popping on her brow, heart racing.

On the final day of boot camp, they shaved their heads. Edie twisted her long brown hair into a sloppy ponytail and took up a pair of scissors, then hacked above the rubber band until her hand ached and the last hairs finally gave way. There was a bulletin board where the women and some of the men hung their ponytails—"Wall of Manes," the placard read. Smiling, she added hers to the display, spearing it with a thumbtack, and the group clapped good-naturedly. Jesse snapped her picture and posted it to his feed before she could tell him not to. Edie could just imagine the comments that were pinging his alert box, the now-familiar assortment of insults and promises of sexual aggression and expressions of dismay from Jesse's adolescent female fans (and even some of his middle-aged ones).

Now her scalp was bristled with fine hairs, and she couldn't stop running her hands across it, listening to the rasp against her dry palms. Jesse, robbed of his cap of waves, looked a bit older, the angles of his cheekbones sharper, but still handsome. He was surveying the wall, all those flaccid tassels like the trophies of a hunter, and he must have sensed that Edie was rattled because he said, "It reassures me, actually."

"The hair wall?"

"Yeah." He pointed a few different places. "How many do you think are up there—a hundred or more? And they all came back."

"They didn't all come back," Edie said.

"They mostly all came back. And heart attacks? That could happen anywhere." He took her hand. "If anything, it makes me feel like—I don't know—it's not that big of a challenge. It's a little disappointing, even."

Edie laughed. "You're nuts."

"About you," he said, and he gave her a very full, sudden kiss. "Damn, honey, if I knew your head was going to be so pretty, I'd have suggested you shave it months ago."

"I don't look too militant?"

"You look fucking rock and roll is how you look." He kissed her again and then resumed his pacing, lace-up boots squeaking a little on the polished floors. They were waiting for Andy to come down and give them one last pep talk before lights-out, and the nervous energy in the gymnasium was so palpable that Edie vibrated with it.

The three-week training had sounded excessive, even dull, when she and Jesse were doing their research, but it had gone by in a blink. And Edie didn't feel ready. Her hair was on the wall, and the small, circular burn scar was on her ass, but she didn't feel ready.

The Andy who had revealed himself to Edie that day in the weight room had not made a reappearance since, and it was hard now, watching him work the room on this last night of boot camp, to believe he had even existed.

"Wow," he said with a laugh. "I sure see a lot of cue balls."

The travelers murmured and smiled, touching their heads self-consciously.

Andy's face grew serious, but his eyes twinkled. "I've got to tell you. I had serious doubts. If someone had told me three weeks ago that every single one of you would be Stamped and shaved and ready to load that bus at oh-six-hundred tomorrow, I'd have wagered otherwise. But you proved me wrong. You did good. Damn good."

Mickey Worthington's mouth tilted, and he folded his arms across his chest, nodding with satisfaction. Even the Japanese couple who'd begun boot camp in such a perpetual state of affront, Ken and Wendy Tanaka, seemed pleased. Jesse whooped and raised a cheer, which the rest quickly chimed in on.

Jesus, Edie thought. *We're a bunch of suckers.* But she felt her own tiny, reluctant swell of pride, too.

"I would be proud to lead this group anywhere," Andy said, setting off a second round of applause. Edie joined it halfheartedly and stared at Andy, willing him to meet her eyes, but he kept his focus elsewhere, bobbing his head in a modest way and finally lifting a hand to ask for silence.

"You won't sleep well tonight, probably, but try. The first few nights out there are always rough. You're going to feel aches in muscles and joints you didn't even know you had. You're going to feel hot and constricted in the micro-sleepsacks, which is why I urged you to start using them during boot camp, even though I realize how hard it is to give up comforts you know you're not going to have for much longer.

"Worse, though, is the fear, and the way that fear fucks with your head. You'll wake up dozens of times convinced something is crawling on you. It won't matter that I'm telling you now it's going to happen. It won't matter that the combination of the micro-sleepsack and micro-tent makes the risk of infiltration negligible. It will be so real to you that you'll sit up, snap on your light, and wake up your tent partner. And the second you finally slip off into real sleep, someone else will shout or switch on a light and bring you right back. You won't be happy campers these first few nights."

A hand shot up, and Andy nodded his acknowledgment.

It was the woman who'd worn diamond earrings on that first day. The earrings were, Edie supposed, now locked up with the rest of her valuables in her room safe. "Will you dispense sleeping pills?" she asked. It was stated explicitly in the tour company's brochure, and in the Traveler Contract they'd each had to sign, that weapons, most pharmaceuticals, liquids, and unpackaged food items were forbidden for travelers; the guide and his two assistants would control the stores for the safety of the group. There was a note of something in her voice—desperation, defensiveness—and Edie felt vaguely uneasy.

"I think you know the answer to that," Andy said, the glint in his eye extinguished. "No sedatives or mind-altering drugs on the excursion. It's better for you to wake up to something that isn't really there than to not wake up when something is. I can't stress enough the importance of that."

The woman—her name was Marta, and something about her quiet bearing gave Edie the sense that she must be the wife of a powerful man—blinked and pursed her lips. Andy seemed to take that as assent.

"Of course," he added with a laugh, "the company tends to turn a blind eye to the two or three bottles of whiskey I've got hidden away out there, and we all get a share out of that." He was being the good buddy again. This was a group of people for whom surrender of personal luxuries was cause for the deepest distrust—even when they had knowingly signed away their rights to those luxuries—and his job, Edie supposed, was to walk the very fine line between treating them as underlings and treating them as customers.

"Any other questions?"

An uneasy silence had fallen. The spell of camaraderie had been broken; Edie could see in the faces around her sudden doubts, regrets, a flash or two of panic. Even Jesse was looking at his hands, picking at a dry triangle of skin beside his thumbnail.

"I have never failed to bring every single one of my travelers back to Quarantine 1 alive and free of serious injury," Andy said. "In the four-year history of Outer Limits Excursions, only two deaths have occurred on any excursion: One was by heart attack. The other was a single incident of Shreve's, and though we hate to say this, by all accounts the person was infected because he failed to adhere to recommended best practices, even after repeated corrections from Outer Limits staff. So, one more time: What's our mantra?"

They were all looking down now, like a classroom full of students who'd failed to do the assigned reading.

"Come on," Andy said. "Humor me."

"Stay in suit, stay aware," Jesse said, raising his voice a bit.

Andy nodded. "What else?"

"Always have your Stamp," said Wes Feingold, the young man who'd thrown up that first day.

"*Always*," said Andy. "I'm not kidding. If you lose your Stamp, you'll be issued a replacement at a cost of one thousand credits. If you lose a second Stamp, the next one will cost you five thousand credits. The penalty is as harsh as it is not just because these are expensive pieces of equipment but also because for the next three weeks that Stamp is the most precious item in your possession. Always have it close at hand. And what else should you have close at hand?"

"Your buddy," said Anastasia, an athletic-looking woman in her late thirties or early forties. As if in illustration, she reached out and grasped the forearm of her husband, Berto.

"Bingo." Andy put his arms over his shoulders, as if he were trying to scratch an itch or give himself a hug. "There are places on the body that you can't reach on your own. Period. And if you're not within a dozen paces of a person when you're bitten in one of those places, you're screwed. I can't emphasize this enough: We are all in this together. When the moment comes to administer a Stamp, you can't flinch. You can't second-guess yourself. You just do it."

Edie's armpits dampened, and she could suddenly smell herself—a ripe, feral odor, a fear-sweat. She wasn't afraid of giving Jesse the Stamp, or of giving it to herself—but what about Jesse? Would he hesitate? If Edie felt the blossom of intense itching between her shoulder blades, the itching that Andy had assured them all was unmistakable, would Jesse quickly do what had to be done?

"The mantra," Andy said. "One more time—say it together."

The group of travelers mumbled through it: *Stay in suit, stay aware, keep your buddy close and your Stamp closer.*

"Who's ready for the time of their lives?"

Jesse, who seemed revived and reassured by the recitation of the mantra, cheered and waved his hands in the air. Edie stared at him, throat dry, her own hands still folded in her lap.

"All right then, folks. Nighty-night. Sleep tight."

He didn't finish the rhyme, but they all knew how it went.

Two

Marta Perrone was lying awake, eyes trained on a fine crack in the ceiling, long before the speakers started to emit the first soft strains of the "Sunrise Serenade." It was a cheerful, rousing, but not overly obnoxious instrumental number, heavy on the flute and piccolo, that increased in decibels as the ceiling lights brightened, so that—this according to the Outer Limits brochure—"waking is as stress-free as sliding into a warm bath." At 4:45 a.m., the automatic thermostat switched from its programmed sixty-eight degrees to seventy-two, and the floor tiles in Marta's private bathroom started to warm. The rhetoric of this strange, awful place—the way a command, such as the time to rise from bed, was softened with luxuries—was not unfamiliar to Marta. She had lived a life of sumptuous captivity.

She sat up and rubbed her face briskly. Her heart was pounding hard, the way it did the nights when she drank too much and stumbled from the bed to the bathroom, but Marta hadn't had anything to drink last night—not last night and not for the last three weeks. She put her feet on the floor, retrieved her silk robe from the nearby settee, and crossed the room to an electronic panel. She could silence "Sunrise Serenade" only from here, a bit of electronic bitchiness that made her want to put her fist through something. But her thoughts of violence never extended beyond the want, and so she went on to the bathroom, slid dutifully out of her robe and nightgown, and tried to enjoy what she knew would be her last hot shower for weeks. Despite the heat of the spray—her skin was stinging and pink—she could not stop shaking. She was more terrified than she had ever been in her life, and that was saying something, considering her life. For fifteen years now, she had not driven cars without first running a scan on the doors and ignition for explosives. For fifteen years, she had not been able to step out for lunch with a friend or attend her daily Pilates class without being followed—protected, her husband always insisted—by a 250-pound goon in a dark suit loose enough to hide the pieces strapped to his side and his calf. For fifteen years now, her husband had been the boss of the Atlantic Zone's organized crime clan, and she had learned all too well the fine print of her marital contract.

Toweling off, she was racked with a now-familiar churning in her gut, and she dropped to her knees in front of the toilet, lifting the lid just in time to expel the meager contents of her stomach.

Recovered, she stood in front of the bathroom mirror, stiffening with shock at the sight of her bald head. David would be horrified—he would make her get a wig until her hair had grown back in to a respectable length. And even Marta had to admit that this was not the best look for a woman of her age, that she, unlike the frankly stunning young woman with the ridiculous pop-singing boyfriend—mixed race, she must have been, with all of the gifts (luminous, vaguely Asiatic eyes, clear, nearly poreless light brown skin) such an ancestry might bestow—could no longer accentuate her beauty by radicalizing it (not that Marta had ever dared to radicalize her beauty, even in the bloom of youth). No, Marta's face was drawn, hollow-eyed; her eyebrows had thinned and lightened so much that there was nothing to temper the shock of her hairless dome, so that, if she blurred her eyes, the image was not of a woman but of a skull. Trembling, she uncapped a pot of Retylastic face cream—a fifty-gram container cost as much as a replacement Stamp—and applied dabs to her face and neck using the soft pad of her ring finger. Then sunblock (what a strange, almost lovely sensation, working the cold lotion into the skin of her scalp). Then she squeezed a tiny bit of antiseptic Scar-Rid into her Stamp wound, which she had opted to have branded in the meaty flesh of her upper arm, where a long-ago generation had been scarred by polio vaccinations. The disfigurement scared her the most—more than her uncertainty about how well she would be able to keep up with the other, mostly younger travelers; more than her anticipation of David's reaction upon her return; more, even, than the fear of death, though she would rather not meet her end in some slow, horrible way. Her only capital had ever been her looks, and later, her status as wife to David Perrone and mother to David Perrone's twin sons ("heir and a spare," David had joked—at least, she took it then as a joke—upon their birth). Age had taken away much of that capital, but she was still a handsome woman, a woman who was respectable on the arm of a man like David (no matter whom he kept out of sight and on the side), and she was loath to compromise that. Though there was a part of her that wondered what it would be like to come back to her husband visibly battle-marked. *Could you have done this?* her scars would say to him. *Could you have risked yourself this way?*

She packed quickly. All of her personal effects, excepting her microsuit and Stamp, had to fit into a small knapsack with a total weight of no more than thirty-five hundred grams; the knapsack also had to pass a security inspection, including X-rays and hand searches, to rule out the presence of forbidden items. Hanging her pack on a luggage scale, she started dropping in objects in descending order of importance: three changes of underwear, three changes of socks; a tube of sunblock; her Retylastic cream and Scar-Rid. That was just over two thousand grams. A canister of ibuprofen, which was permitted on the Outer Limits Excursions Rules and Regulations for Travelers. Three manufacturer-sealed pouches of antibiotic ointment, also permitted. These items were sold at the

Canteen, as was the small spray bottle of Critter-Rid, which was useless against the miner ticks but handy for the nonfatal but still annoying (and prevalent) chiggers and mosquitoes. She was now up to twenty-seven hundred grams.

The Outer Limits Excursions statement on weapons read as follows:

> Section 3.2: *OLE Inc. is a firm supporter of our constitutional right to bear arms. However, for the safety of our travelers, personal weapons—including but not limited to firearms, blade weapons, explosive devices, projectile weapons, chemical or pepper sprays, and any other instruments or devices designed to inflict harm on another living being—are prohibited. OLE staff members will carry only small utility blades and have thumbprint and password-controlled access to locked weapons vaults at various points on the excursion. These vaults store bows, shotguns, and rifles suitable for the hunting of game and accessible only for the purposes of controlled hunting parties as described in the relevant Excursion Package (if applicable).*
>
> *Travelers attempting to bring in weapons of any kind, or who use* OLE *weaponry in any manner other than that for which it has been designated, including hunting of out-of-season game, will be banished from the Excursion and issued a 25,000-credit fine. Criminal cases will be turned over to the proper authorities.*

The statement on Drugs, Alcohol, Tobacco, and Prescription Medication was equally restrictive:

> Section 3.5: *Because the safety of a Traveler requires first and foremost an alert mind, possession of alcohol and most controlled substances is prohibited on* OLE *Tours. The exceptions are certain prescription medications (prior approval must be sought through the* OLE *physician-in-residence), allowable only in quantities nec-*

essary for the duration of the Excursion, and over-the-counter anti-inflammatory and allergy medications that can be purchased through the Canteen. Leaf tobacco is not allowed; however, Smokeless and replacement NicoClean cells are also purchasable through the OLE Canteen in unrestricted quantities. Canteen purchases have an identifying bar code—any over-the-counter medications or Smokeless not bearing that bar code are forbidden.

And so Marta paused, stomach knotted, over the last items on her dresser top.

The first was a Smokeless, still sealed in its box—a box, her husband assured her, that was printed with the invisible bar code identifying it as an OLE Canteen purchase. The item inside the box looked exactly like a Smokeless, and it weighed, within a tenth of a gram, the same as a Smokeless, but it was not a Smokeless. It contained an illegal chemical called Quicksilver, which, if sprayed into an attacker's face at close range—a sprayer was built cleverly into the fake Smokeless, the valve only visible upon close scrutiny—caused unconsciousness within seconds. The length of that unconsciousness was highly variable: a few minutes, at least, but often much longer, and there were cases of brain damage and even death reported. "Don't smoke it by accident," David had said, barking harsh laughter, when he gave it to her.

The other item, packaged to look like a NicoClean replacement cell (complete, too, with Canteen bar code), was a fifteen-gram vial of Salt. "A little pick-me-up," David had said, and Marta accepted it with effusive thanks, knowing that these two going-away gifts had probably cost him a small fortune, and that the point for him was as much the extravagance as the usefulness of the presents themselves. He liked knowing he could cheat the system, that he had the money and the connections to make it easy. He also liked knowing that Marta had thirsts only he could quench, thirsts that kept her occupied and compliant, thin, dependent. The second-hardest thing she had ever done was quit Salt cold turkey; the hardest was hiding the fact she had quit from her husband and pretending, for six weeks now, that nothing had changed. She still accepted his "gifts," still emerged from the bathroom pretending to feel that clean, radiant calm way down deep into the whorls of her fingerprints, when she was actually so depressed, so tired, that simply coming to a stand felt like a chore. And her stomach was still so riotous, even now after six weeks, that getting most of a meal down was a misery, the aftermath often agony.

She had purchased an actual Smokeless and NicoClean replacement cell at the Canteen, thinking that she would need to get the purchase on record, and she thought now about putting those into her bag instead. She had been smoking since getting here—partly to establish a precedent for bringing the Smokeless past the checkpoint, partly to take some of the edge off her sudden break with not just the Salt but also booze—and she wouldn't mind having the option once they were out in the woods. A way to calm her nerves. She could lock the Quicksilver and vial of Salt in her room safe, along with her jewelry and her zonecard, and no one would be the wiser. But she hesitated.

She would feel safer with the Quicksilver. As for the Salt, perhaps she shouldn't tempt herself. But her gut told her to bring it, that it could never hurt to have something valuable on hand. A carrot as well as a stick. She'd learned, as the wife of David Perrone, that there was a time for both.

"I'm going to need you to go out of town for a while," David had told her. This was in September.

"Out of town?" she said vaguely. It was six o'clock, an hour before their dinner reservation, and they were both in the living room, sipping vodka tonics, each tuned to their feeds and not speaking much to the other. Scrolling with her thumb pad, then tapping the screen gently with a nail, she checked on the boys, Sal and Enzo, who were both in Wilmington, attending classes (they claimed) at the university. Sal was at the Sand Dollar Tavern, where he had already spent, she saw, a hundred credits on happy hour longnecks and appetizers. Sweet lord. And Enzo wasn't showing up on her feed at all, which only meant that he wasn't currently spending money—or maybe he was with Sal, and Sal was putting it all on his tab. *His* tab—well, his father's. *I hate how you watch every single little thing I do,* Sal had complained his freshman year, when Marta had called to express concern about the fact that he was at a gaming parlor when she knew he was supposed to be attending his Psych 100, and Marta had said, *Well, when you have your own Deep Pocketz, you can have all the freedom you want.*

"Not immediately," said David. "It'll take time for certain things to go into motion. A month or two. And not for long, just until things quiet down some."

Marta blinked and paused her feed. "Wait. What?"

"I'm just being overly cautious."

"Overly cautious about what?"

He exhaled, bull-like, through his nose. "Can you unplug for thirty seconds here? I'm trying to tell you that something has come up. We need to get you somewhere safe until my business is settled."

Marta swallowed the rest of her drink so fast that an ice cube went down her throat and slivered like a stone through her esophagus. "Wait. What about the boys?"

"I've been looking into it. Enzo's been hounding me about some semester abroad thing. Italy or England, but I'm leaning toward England. It's going to cost a fortune, but security's tight there, real tight, and the quarantines are stricter. And they have the Edu-Passes already, so we could have them there by the end of the month."

For a split second Marta felt a burst of hopefulness and joy—a break in the dark clouds that had been hanging over her since the boys left home for college three years ago. "I haven't been to England since I was a girl. There's so much in London I could show them."

David's face grew still, and his lip curled in that way she had grown to hate. "Marta."

"What?"

He shook his head with exasperation. "For one thing, I don't want everybody I care about in one place. That puts you all at greater risk. For another, I can't have you all going off to Europe at the same time without me. It would seem suspicious."

"So you're separating the boys?" The thought unnerved her.

"Of course not," David said. "I might as well cut their hearts out."

What about my heart? she thought of saying. Instead, in a voice edged with a wearisome (even to her) bitterness, she said, "But everyone gets along just fine without me."

"Oh, Jesus Christ. You know we couldn't get the paperwork to get you over there with them before November, anyway, and that would be too late to do any good."

"Never mind. Forget it. So where are you hauling me off to? Casinolake again?" There had been a time, just after the last boss died unexpectedly and David and another capo were each trying to take over the clan, when David had sent her and the twins quickly to Casinolake. It was a bad several weeks, hell with six-year-old boys whose only source for recreation was the hotel swimming pool. Casinolake was an adult vacation destination, a place where middle-aged men gathered in packs to gamble, play golf, drink whiskey, smoke cigars, and contract the services of prostitutes, and Marta could only guess that David had chosen it as a hideout for them because he had the management in a stranglehold, or because it seemed like such an implausible place to put away a wife and children for safe keeping. Whatever the reason, Marta had spent her shapeless days stewing with resentment, then vibrating with it; the minute the boys slipped into sleep each night she started downing liquor, wondering when their imprisonment would end, and how, and if the next knock on the door would be her husband or the hotel staff or someone who had been sent to do away with her. Then, when her legs tired, or the liquor had sedated her, she climbed into bed and played webshows on her tablet all night, one episode after another after another, moving dully between watching and dreaming and not knowing the next day which had been which.

I could kill him, she had thought a thousand times. And, *I'll divorce him*. Her anger had solidified by the end into a certainty, a plan; she would never put her sons through this again, she would never put *herself* through this again, and damn David for thinking he could ask it of them. But when David had finally arrived, victorious, to bring her and the children home, she had known instantly that things had changed irrevocably—that this was a man who would never suffer the indignity of being left, even if a part of him would be secretly glad to rid himself of her; a man who would kill her before he let her turn his sons, the heir and the spare, against him. In a way, she had been stuck at Casinolake ever since. Her prison had only gotten larger, and she was jingling and jangling with the same restless fury, a fury that made her want to walk grooves into the polished wood floors of their six-hundred-square-meter home. When the boys left for college her anxiety grew, and no amount of liquor was able to soothe it, and that was when she started using the drugs.

Now, here she was again. Some danger was on the horizon, and she couldn't even be with the boys if the worst were to happen. This time, she was alone.

"Not Casinolake," he said. "I have something else in mind. Something out-of-zone."

Her heart—it seemed to almost quiver rather than beat. "I thought you said it wasn't that bad."

"I said I was being overly cautious."

"Out-of-zone cautious?"

He rose, crossed the room to the banquette, and poured another finger of vodka into his highball glass. Then he held the glass so that the base sat flat on his palm, a funny affectation of his that stretched back to their earliest days together, when he was the scrawny, gawky young man she had fallen in love with, a man whose streak of cruel entitlement had only yet manifested as improbable confidence, charming then because it seemed so mismatched with his physical self. "It's good news, mostly. I have a major deal lined up. Something that's going to make us a lot of money. And it's legit money. One hundred percent legit."

Marta frowned. "What's the 'mostly' part?"

"I have to do something kind of bold to clench it. And when I do the thing I have to do, I want us all lying low for a little while."

"What's this thing you have to do?"

"Honey," he said, "you don't want to know."

He was right. She didn't.

Out-of-zone. She uncapped her necklace vial and took a bump—she hadn't planned on it that night, but Christ—and pondered the possibilities. Slum-ridden Gulf Zone, where even the better hotels were constantly getting shut down for tick infestations, and if the ticks didn't get you, the street gangs would? Midwest Zone was no better. New England had stricter quarantine sanctions than Atlantic Zone—Marta doubted that even David had the power to get her over there this year—and Pacific Zone, by every report, was still so drought-ridden and poisoned that drinking water sold for a hundred credits a liter. You saw the Pacificans in the feeds wearing micromasks everywhere, even to sit in their own homes, and Marta thought the worst sign of all was that the webshows out of the West Coast, which used to be the best, were in recent years poorly produced and unpredictably transmitted.

The thing was, you hoped like hell to be in a zone as clean and safe as Atlantic, and if by birth or luck or talent you got in one, you stayed put—because the rules kept changing, the quarantines and security measures kept getting revised, and everyone knew the story of at least one person who traveled interzone and got stuck somewhere for weeks, or months, or even forever. What if David sent her somewhere but couldn't get her back once the heat was off?

"What did you have in mind for me?" she said quietly.

"You remember that adventure touring company I invested in a few years back? Outer Limits Excursions?"

It took her a few beats to process this. First, just the words: *adventure touring company.* What that even meant. Then, the implication—

"Good lord, David. You can't be serious. You don't mean to—"

"Hear me out," David said harshly. "This is a completely professional outfit. They know what they're doing, and their rate getting people back home is nearly perfect."

"Nearly," Marta said jeeringly.

"It's VIP all the way. You wouldn't believe some of the people going on this trip. Wes Feingold. Wes Feingold's going on this trip. And if there's a rich little cocksucker you want to be standing near when the world goes to hell, he's the one."

She felt the sharp, strangling fingers of panic at her throat, making it hard to breathe. "I don't want to do this, David. I *can't* do this. I'm in my fifties. I don't . . . hike. I'm not in any kind of shape for that. I'd rather risk staying here than go on that trip."

He walked across the room to her, hard-soled shoes surprisingly light and silent on the tile floor, and grasped her chin between his thumb and the crook of his forefinger just hard enough to contort her neck uncomfortably. "This is not a choice. This is not about what you want. If I say you put on your hiking boots and start marching your way down to the Wall this very night, you do it. Do you even realize how lucky you are?"

Their eyes locked for an agonizingly slow moment, his thumbnail just creasing the skin on her chin, the vein running up along the edge of his nose pulsing visibly. He'd had three cosmetic procedures in the last eight years, most recently a face-lift and eye rejuvenation, and though the work was eerily good—he looked, in all the superficial ways, much as he had in his early forties, when he first became boss—there was a shadow of the older man under the surgeon's fine work. Did David see the same shadow when he looked at her? She had resisted all but the standard procedures (a person of her means would no sooner opt against an eye rejuv than she would neglect to wear sunscreen or take her metabolizers), and she had insisted on not coloring her graying hair, which may have been nothing more than piddling contrariness—a way to undercut David, to thwart his will, without seeming as if that were her object. But still, there were times when she looked in the mirror and didn't know herself, when it seemed that past and present had converged in her features, her haunted, fifty-four-year-old eyeballs framed by tight, plump new skin cells.

David let go of her chin, finally. His mouth pulled up a little in the corner. "So. Do we have an understanding?"

They did. Marta wasn't a hiker, maybe, or a twenty-five-year-old woman who could sleep eight hours without waking to relieve her bladder, but she knew a lost cause when she encountered one. She would go on the adventure tour.

She had never craved the great outdoors, never registered the nostalgia others felt for bygone days of national parks and waterfalls and hiking trails. She had spent her life in the cultivated, curated inner-zone landscapes of manicured and carefully monitored trees, flowers, and grasses, all genetically engineered to resist tick infestations, and when she wanted a break from the cement, she spent a weekend at the beach, or she took a walk in one of the several excellent city arboretums. The times she had gone to 3D-LUX theaters with Sal and Enzo so that they could watch films such as *The Late, Great Polar Bears* (the boys had left sobbing—why, she wondered, was this targeted at children?) or *Mountain Majesties: A*

Tour of Appalachia, she had felt not wonder or longing but oppression and vertigo. So many trees, so much variation in the landscape, whole chunks of sky blotted out by jagged precipices—she didn't know how people had ever been able to stand it. Even those startling, high-up views, with the landscape rolling away kilometers into the distance: it was too much. Perhaps she lacked imagination. Perhaps, for all her brooding over being a prisoner in her own home, she was too meekly content to be a prisoner of her safe province. So no, camping was not something she had ever in her life felt even the slightest interest in doing.

But on this morning of their journey across the Salt Line, she was strangely stirred—with excitement as well as fear. For the first time in her married life, she was not just out of David's sight but out from under his veil of influence. This, she thought, sliding into her microsuit and drawing the zipper up to her neck, was as close to freedom as she was ever going to get. She should make the best of it.

It was 5:30. She had time to stop by the Canteen for breakfast—Andy had insisted that they all make sure to eat something before leaving—but her stomach was still roiling and sensitive, and she didn't want to have to use the bus's chemical toilet on the three-hour drive to the first checkpoint. She poured a glass of water from the bathroom tap and contemplated the bottle of OLE-brand vitamin capsules she'd been issued and encouraged—even pressured, oddly—to take. They didn't sit well on her weak stomach, and she usually just threw them right up when her stomach was empty, as it was this morning. She supposed she'd successfully kept only a few down over the course of the three-week training, and she didn't see the point of stoking her nausea for no good reason. So she left the bottle on the bathroom counter.

From the size of the group already gathered in the gymnasium, and the expressions of queasy resignation on many of the faces, Marta guessed that she wasn't the only one to bypass the breakfast line. They were an absurd-looking assortment of adventurers, the cream-colored microsuits slim-fitting enough to intimately trace the shape of every body, hoods drawn up over chins and down to just above the eyebrows so that faces became small and saucerlike.

She looked around for her assigned "buddy," Wes Feingold. It was a ridiculous pairing, necessitated, perhaps, by the dearth of single travelers, though Marta hadn't ruled out David's influence here. She was traveling under a fake surname, Severs—for her protection, David had assured her—and presumably anonymous to at least the ground-level OLE crew, but he had his ways, just as he'd managed his trick with the Canteen bar codes. Wes was probably disappointed to be burdened with the company of a woman his own mother's age, but Marta couldn't help feeling pleased at the thought of partnering with a strong, able young man, like her sons; a young man who didn't have the option for the next three weeks of taking off to live on the other end of the zone and never calling to let her know how he was doing. He seemed serious and polite, and he had accomplished in his young life more than the most exceptional men and women of Marta's own age, much less his contemporaries. While Sal and Enzo were skipping class for the gaming parlors and buying rounds at the Sand Dollar, Wes was running one of the most important companies in the world.

Thinking of Pocketz, she felt the familiar itch to scan her feeds—even in the midst of her nervousness, she felt that itch. Here, too, she wasn't alone; others were checking their tablets one last time before they were confiscated, tapping out messages with their thumbs, a few of them engaged in energetic mimed discussions with people on their screens, the little bud communicators (which Marta's sons used often and easily but she couldn't get the hang of) just visible in the cup of their ears. Marta scrolled past Realstar, Friendz, Mi Familia (which was useless to her now that the boys were over eighteen and had the opt-out option), Soapville, and Almaknack, her right-hand thumb making practiced horizontal sweeps across the screen, until she got to Pocketz. The sight of the familiar interface, with its pleasant, tranquil graphics and the little swirling gold coins at the top of the page indicating new activity since her last log-on, affected her a bit like the Salt did, so that a pleasurable calm suddenly flooded her body. Tapping the coins, she was treated to the following list:

Salvador Perrone spent 47 credits at the Cock and Bull.
Explore **Share** **Dispute** Twelve hours ago, near London, UK

Salvador Perrone earned 2 punches toward free pint! at the Cock and Bull.
Explore **Share** **Dispute** Twelve hours ago, near London, UK

Lorenzo Perrone spent 30 credits at Cinema 12.
Explore **Share** **Dispute** Sixteen hours ago, near London, UK

She tapped Explore under Enzo's Cinema 12 debit.

Lorenzo Perrone purchased two adult tickets to see *Rubber Meets the Road III*.

The movie trailer started to play, an opening shot zooming in on the image of a heart-shaped, bikini-clad female bottom, framed by the open driver's-side window of a bright red CO_2 roadster. Sighing, Marta navigated away from the screen.

Finally, having saved it for last, she exited Pocketz and scrolled to her messages feed, heart pounding, hoping that sometime in their evening of movie watching and beer drinking the twins had thought of her, remembered what she was embarking upon this morning, and sent her something—anything—to let her know they cared. And . . . there was a flag up! A message!

It came from Enzo's account, and there was a video. She hit Play, walking a bit away from the group for privacy.

Her sons' grinning faces were side by side—above and behind them Marta could make out the gilt letters "nd Bull." "Hey, Mom!" they said in singsong sync, obviously drunk, but there they were, so handsome, Sal with his hair combed tightly into a ponytail (how long he had spent in front of the mirror as a high schooler, doing his best to smooth out every bump), Enzo, a bit shorter and stouter, hair parted rigidly and combed in a swoop to the side the way his father wore it. "We're so proud of you," Sal said, "going out and being a total badass in the woods."

"Yes," Enzo said, "so badass."

"And we love you, and we can't wait to see you again."

"Can't wait to see you, Mom," Enzo said.

"We're having the time of our life here."

"We thought of you at St. Paul's Cathedral, and we did the whispering dome and went to the cupola like you told us to—"

"—probably Tower of London next week—"

"—the new Buckingham Palace wing."

Someone called out rudely to them, and there was laughter. Enzo yelled over his shoulder, cheerfully enough, "Fuck you!"

"So anyway," Sal said, "have fun."

"Have fun," said Enzo.

"Love you," they repeated, blowing her kisses and waving, and then the message ended. Tears were rolling down her face.

"Oh," someone said from behind her, and she felt a hand, warm even through the glove, on her arm. "Oh, hey there, buddy. It's OK."

She quickly wiped her eyes, embarrassed. It was Wes Feingold.

"Sorry," Marta said. "This is harder than I realized it would be."

"No reason to be sorry," Wes said. He was a small man, no taller than Marta, with frizzy dark blond hair (pre-shave), chubby child's cheeks, and eyes that seemed to be blue, though he had such a squinty smile that she had never gotten a very good look at them. "Those were your sons?"

She nodded. "I—I didn't know for sure that they'd call. I couldn't get them to pick up yesterday."

"Yeah, it reminds me. I ought to call my own mom."

"For goodness' sake," Marta said, "don't leave her wondering. The only thing worse to me than the thought of making this trip is the thought of my boys doing it, and me not knowing the whole time how they are. Call her."

"Well," Wes said, still smiling in his affable, squinty way, "my mom's not like other moms. But you're right, got to make the gesture."

"She probably worries more than you know."

"Sure," he said, squinting and nodding. "She must."

An Outer Limits staff member—Tia, one of Andy's assistants—entered the gymnasium and clapped her hands briskly. "OK, folks. We're going to open the screening area, so go ahead and queue up when you're ready behind the red line"—she pointed—"on the south end of the gym. Please remember that we'll be collecting tablets and drawing up itemized manifests for everything in your packs, so if there's something you want back in your room safe, now's the time."

Marta dropped her chin against the rising flush in her cheeks. There it was again, the racing heart, and she wondered if she should run back to the room and stow the doctored Smokeless and Nico-Clean cartridge. If she failed to make it through security today, what would David do with her?

"Well, this is it," said Wes. "Ready, partner?"

"As I'm going to be," she said.

They joined the other travelers forming a line, and Marta chewed on the inside of her bottom lip until she tasted blood. "One of the things I'm actually most excited about," Wes was saying from what seemed like a great distance, "are the parts of the trip when we're on the road or passing through the old cities. I actually considered the

Ghost Towns of the Old Republic excursion, but I decided that this one offered a fuller experience, and the Rate It scores were higher. Plus, that quarantined chalet at the midpoint sounded good."

"It sure does," Marta said. Her grip on the pack strap was so tight that her fingers were going numb. What was the stupider risk—taking the Quicksilver or leaving it behind?

"One of my ancestors on my mother's side was actually a professor of sociology at a private college in Asheville, right as the outbreak started getting really bad. I found an address for him in the old web archives, and I'd love to go and get a look at it."

She was next in line now. She couldn't summon the courage to even stammer a reply.

"So wait," Wes said. "You sounded before like you didn't much want to do this. Why's that? Why are you forcing yourself?"

"Please place your tablet and pack on the conveyor belt and walk through the scanner," an Outer Limits staffer—a campus employee, not a guide—told Marta.

She laid down the requested items and tried to smile pleasantly, though her face felt out of her control, as if it were contorting into some ugly grimace, and she again thought about her shadow face, and she wondered which one the employee was now seeing. After she stepped through the scanner, another staffer waved her over.

"Hey, there," he said. He was waiting on the other end of the conveyor belt. "Having a good morning?"

"Pretty good," Marta said. A third employee was scrutinizing a screen, where Marta supposed a digital scan of her pack was displayed. The employee, a middle-aged black woman, pinched her fingers together in front of the screen, then twisted them left and right, frowning. Marta felt a twisting up inside her. Then the woman's fingers spread apart, as if she were making a hand sign for an explosion, and her features sagged with disinterest. The conveyor belt started to move again.

"OK," the employee on this end of the line said as Marta's pack and tablet stopped in front of him. He moved them aside to a table and lifted his gloved hands ceremonially, like a magician getting ready to introduce a trick. "The tablet, as you know, I have to take now, but it will be reissued to you the second you set foot in Quarantine 1 three weeks from today."

"I understand," Marta said.

"You don't have a camera to declare?"

"No, nothing like that." It hadn't occurred to Marta to take pictures of this journey, to memorialize it. Why would she? For whom?

He started pulling everything out of her pack and laying it side by side. He turned the pack inside out, gave it a quick shake, and started speaking into a microphone. "Manifest for Traveler Marta Severs," he said. "Ladies' microfiber briefs, three pairs," he said. "Ladies' microfiber undershirt, three. Tube socks, three pairs." He started running a scanner over Canteen items, setting off a little green light with the bug spray and the antibiotic ointment before grabbing the NicoClean canister that was actually the fifteen-gram vial of Salt. He passed the wand over it.

The light turned green.

"One canister of NicoClean," he recited, and she had to put a bracing hand against the edge of the table as every clenched muscle in her body suddenly loosened.

The Smokeless bar code also scanned without incident, and in another few moments, she had signed her name to the generated manifest, and the filled pack was back in her hands. She stared at it wonderingly. She had done it. She had gotten away with it.

The air outside was crisp, the morning sun bright and true in a way that promised a gorgeous day, and the air smelled of damp, fresh grass and a faraway note of burning wood. For the first time in years, she was completely sober, and it seemed to her that even the depression of withdrawing from the Salt had finally receded—she felt light in her limbs, strong, and clearheaded.

Then Wes approached her, and they stood side by side contemplating the large touring coach that would convey them past the Salt Line, the silence surprisingly companionable.

"I gave you the wrong impression before," Marta said. "When I acted like I didn't want to be here doing this."

"You did?"

"Yeah," Marta said. "It was just the nerves talking."

"Well, I'm glad to hear it." Wes lifted the crook of his left arm in an old-fashioned, gentlemanly way. "Shall we board?"

"Yes," said Marta. "Let's."

Three

The beginning of the idea for Pocketz had come to Wes Feingold when he was only fourteen years old, and his parents were the inspiration.

They were having their best friends, the Duncans, over to the house for dinner in a couple of days, and his mother was frantic, scanning so many different feeds that she had to transfer some from her tablet to the wall monitor in the kitchen.

"Lynn served grouper the last time we were over there, and this site is saying that it was selling that week for sixty credits a kilo. And the wine—do you remember the vintage, Dan?"

"It was a Malbec," Wes's father said.

"And it had a red and black label, I remember that much." Now his mother was using her thumb to deal out feed pages like playing cards, so that the kitchen monitor was cluttered two and three deep. "Crap. I think I found it."

"Let me see," Wes's father said.

She put this most recent page on top of the pile and expanded it using her thumb and forefinger. "Cara de Roca. One hundred fifty credits. Damn. Damn it."

Wes, who had been sitting at the counter working on his Advanced Calculus homework—he had already placed well beyond high school level in Calculus, Physics, and Chemistry, and so was taking distance courses for those subjects—looked up. This was a version of a conversation his parents had had hundreds of times in his life, but only today, for some reason, did it capture his interest. He studied the scatter of feed pages on the wall and then the stricken expressions on his parents' faces. There were hardly ever times when Wes failed to understand some intellectual principle (though fine art and literature tended, with only rare but powerful exceptions, to leave him cold), but this mystification at people's emotions, the fervency and utter lack of motivating logic behind so many of them, was familiar.

"You're upset because your friends served you fish and wine?" he asked.

"We're upset," his mother said, "because they served us expensive, hard-to-get fish and wine."

"What's wrong with that? It's nice of them, right?"

His mother exhaled harshly and rolled her eyes. "Oh, it's nice, all right."

When Wes cocked his head, still unable to process what had gotten his mother so upset, his father said, "Son, there's nice and then there's showing off."

"But you wouldn't have even known they were showing off," Wes said, "if you hadn't gone deliberately searching the feeds to see what they paid for things."

"Everybody does that, Wes. It's what you do. The Duncans wouldn't have served us grouper and Argentinean wine if they hadn't known we'd track the prices later." His mother—she was only in her late thirties on this day, though she'd seemed to Wes, then, both ancient and ageless—swept her blond bangs roughly out of her eyes and started jogging her foot against the rung of the bar stool she was sitting on. "OK, Dan, you've got to help me think here. We should have started planning this last week. We should have checked the feeds the moment we got back from dinner that night."

"I can get a nice Bordeaux from Lisa at work," Wes's father said.

"We served them that last time they were here." She tapped the tablet's stylus against her bottom lip. "What if we did something kind of whimsical, kind of off the wall. Like, OK, we do the Bordeaux again, but we get a bottle of port for after dinner?"

His father whistled. "That's a lot of dough."

"Dough?" Wes asked.

"Credits," his mother said vaguely. "Yeah. But if we do the port, I think it would be OK to go cheaper on the meal itself. I could do my fresh ravioli with the good farmer's cheese from Maple Street Market."

Wes found himself getting excited, the way he did on the rare occasions when a difficult mathematical proof suddenly yielded its solution to him. "Because the ravioli is labor-intensive," he said.

"Well, I suppose you could say that," his mother said.

He filed his homework feed and brought up the sketch pad on his own tablet, syncing with the wall monitor so that his doodles would be projected. He swept his mother's pages thoughtlessly to the side, and when she started to protest, he said, "*Shh, shh, shh.* Let me think a sec."

"Young man, I wasn't through with those feeds."

"I can get them right back," Wes said. He wrote on the top of the screen, in all caps, *COMPARATIVE VALUATION OF DINNERS.*

"Jesus Christ," his father muttered.

Then:

Variables

- Cost (C)
- Rarity (R)
- Novelty (N)
- Complexity (X)

"But there's perhaps another, secondary set of variables, and that's where it gets tricky," Wes said, scribbling. "Because complexity in one sense is valuable, but maybe also simplicity is valuable. In the case of the farmer's cheese, for instance. Mom, you called it good, and I agree it tastes good, but it's not all that rare or refined."

"It's made by local artisans," his mother said. "It's organic!"

"So that's another variable. I mean, it's funny to me, because you seem to think the wine they served was so great because it was from Argentina, but you think the cheese you're going to serve is so great because it's from here in Durham." He moved his initial notes to the left and started another column of secondary variables. "The derivations are going to be messy," he murmured apologetically. "But the general idea, it seems to me, is that the equation you're working on is Value of the Duncan Meal, in which the primary variables are Cost, in this case roughly 210 credits, not counting the sides and dessert and miscellaneous, and Rarity, because the fish and wine are hard to get, though of course Rarity is a variable that is already factored into Cost by the manufacturer of those particular products."

His mother and father exchanged bewildered looks.

"That's the thing about Cost as a variable: it takes into account so many other variables. But—" He paused. "Do you think you'll spend as much as the Duncans did?"

His mother shrugged impatiently. "I don't know, Wes. Probably not. We couldn't get our hands on a bottle of wine like that now if we tried."

"So—wow!—that's another variable, relating to cost but not overlapping perfectly with it. Something to do with exclusivity, accessibility." He was glowing now with good cheer, nodding vigorously over his notations. He hooked his thumbnail on his bottom front teeth, chomping down hard to catch his racing thoughts, and his mother swatted at his elbow to make him stop. "For some reason, the Duncans can get a hold of something you can't."

"I wouldn't say *that*," his father said.

"OK. What we're dealing with here, then, is a situation in which Cost, Rarity, and Exclusivity on the Duncans' side is, if I'm hearing you two correctly, getting balanced on your side by factors that aren't individually as valuable but that, in combination, eventually add up to comparable value, like the fact that Mom's going to use time and skill to make the fresh ravioli, and she's going to go to a local merchant for the cheese. So another factor seems to be not value but the extent to which the purchase adheres to Values, in the moral sense, though—fascinating—that only means anything if the Duncans happen to share your middle-class liberal values, or if you can at least make them feel, for the space of a dinner, that your liberal values are superior to theirs, whatever they are." Under "Societal Values," he listed Environmental, Civic, Economic, and Nutritional.

"What's totally crazy to me is how you're able to keep all of these different kinds of values in your head at once—how you can even value all of these things at the same time. If the farmer's cheese contributes to the meal's Societal Values, because the cheese is organic, and therefore healthier, and local, therefore better for the community and the environment, why would you even want to drink an Argentinean wine that has to be shipped thousands of miles?"

"Oh, Wes," his mother said miserably.

"And for that matter, if you're a person who cares about Societal Values in a liberal, middle-class way, why does it even matter to you if your meal is equal with the Duncans' meal? Why not just enjoy your friendships?"

His parents were glaring at him.

He hit Save on the sketch pad of lists and equations, filed them, and shrugged. "Anyway, I'm going to go play some *Land of Shadows* before dinner," he said, his mind, for now, already on to the next thing, which was whether or not he would be able to assemble enough Coin of the Realm to advance his clan to Level Sixteen before the coming Catastrophe that was being advertised in all of the *LoS* feeds.

But in the coming weeks, those equations he'd jotted down for his parents started to nag at him. This certainly had much to do with playing *Land of Shadows* and analyzing his own desire to accumulate Coin of the Realm, and how that Coin, the quantity of which was visible to any player who wanted to check his stats, affected his influence in that virtual world, granting him powers (spell casting, life after death, speed, swordsmanship) as he played. He watched his mother and father carefully, listening to their desires and complaints, noting that so much of what seemed to aggrieve them in life was tied to money: how there was never enough of it to live as they wished, and how the culture of its use was abstract and unspoken, with rules that everyone was expected to follow without ever having been taught them. Why? Why did people live like this when they could just live like the *Land of Shadows* players? The *LoS* feeds reported to Wes, usefully, information such as "Clansman Zor Greatship acquired 5,000 Coin of the Realm by battling Clansman Dagon Quicksilver" and "Clan Leader Mero Redfinch spent 250 Coin of the Realm to acquire a Lifeforce Restoration Spell." It helped Wes strategize, knowing that it might be useless for him to battle Mero Redfinch if Mero could just cast the Lifeforce Spell if he lost. And that time he let Lissa Pollywog borrow 500 Coin to purchase a Silver Shield, he set his feeds to alert him when Lissa had gone on to acquire enough Coin to repay him along with the 10 percent interest he'd charged. At that point, he could either retrieve the money from her account or negotiate new terms. Why did the real world not work like this? One day, he overheard his mother complaining about her sister, his aunt Meg, and how Meg had still not returned to her the eight hundred credits his mother had loaned her for a rent payment, even though she (his mother) knew that Meg had since gone on a clothes shopping spree and come home with, among other things, a very expensive pair of suede riding boots. If the real world were more like *Land of Shadows*, Wes thought, then his mother could have simply collected the credits as soon as Meg had earned them rather than muttering about Meg behind her back and all the while acting to her face like things between them were hunky-dory.

Programming was a bit of a hobby for him, and he had to submit an honors dissertation to be approved for early graduation, so in the next year he created the architecture for what would essentially become Pocketz Beta. The system was based on two core ideas: transparency, so that conspicuous consumption became regulated and systematized; and nearly fail-safe accountability, meaning that credit exchanges could happen person to person, without a lending institution acting as a go-between. Money was entirely virtual now, had been since well before Wes was even born, and so what point did banks serve, anyway? A credit was not a dollar. It was not substantiated, however arbitrarily, by some gold reserve in a vault. It was, he had learned that day of his parents' conversation about the Duncans, an abstraction, an emotion, potent as love and as impossible to harness or define. So why not create a system that made apparent those abstract qualities that gave a credit its power, that made plain who had the most Coin of the Realm and how they were willing to spend it? Why not make the unspoken rules spoken, and reveal rather than obscure the power dynamics driving value exchanges? If the child is spending the parent's money, the parent knows on what. If the debtor has the funds to repay the lender, the lender can reclaim what is owed. If more participants in the feed are spending credits on BoostJoose than Rola Cola, let that determine the relative credit value of energy sodas, at least until the trends shift. By the time Wes submitted his honors project, he had created, he believed, the framework for an economic utopia, an entirely self-regulated market system that resisted fraud and inflation and made apparent the true nature of Societal Values, however contradictory those values may prove to be.

"This is very inventive," his honors advisor, Professor McGregor, said. Her voice was brittle and nasal, her tone patronizing. "It's a clever idea, though perhaps a cynical one. You've taken the relationships out of social networking and left the ads."

"I think that's a gross simplification," Wes said.

She crooked an eyebrow.

"In fact," Wes said, "the system subverts advertising, at least in the current sense of the word. What's the more powerful argument for the value of a product: a manufacturer-financed image or video for how great it is, or the clear evidence that it's selling two to one over the competition?"

"Value is subjective," Professor McGregor said.

"Of course it is," said Wes. "That's the whole point of Pocketz."

She huffed. "OK. Let's move on. The project itself is fine—totally adequate for the purposes of an honors thesis."

"Adequate," Wes echoed.

"Adequate," Professor McGregor repeated. "But the Review of Literature is quite poor. You only mention five economists specifically—Smith, Mill, Veblen, Krugman, and Odhiambo. It reads a bit like an EncycloFeedia entry. In fact, when I conducted a search of some of the sentences in your Review of Lit, I found that you had cut and pasted whole paragraphs from your source materials, including EncycloFeedia."

Wes waited calmly for her to make her point.

"That's plagiarism, Mr. Feingold."

"So?"

She laughed disbelievingly. "You wrote in your Significance of Project section about 'Societal Values' and how those compare to value in a more general sense. Or, rather, how 'values'"—she made exaggerated air quotes—"influence value." She sipped from a mug of coffee like an actor using a prop. "Academic honesty is a Societal Value. Perhaps it's one that doesn't have much capital in certain circles of life, like the world of web feeds that you seem to want to be a part of, but here, at this school, it has premium worth. This place cares if you plagiarize your sources. And since this place has the task of determining whether or not you graduate with a high school diploma, which determines whether or not you will be able to go to university, our value becomes your value, at least temporarily."

"So what are you saying?" Wes asked.

"I'm saying that I want you to rewrite the Review of Literature and the Theoretical Framework portions of your thesis. You need at least ten more sources, and you certainly need a refresher on how to properly cite your sources. Here's a hint: if you didn't write the sentence, you better put it in quotation marks." She synced her tablet so that a calendar appeared on the wall beside Wes. "I'm thinking five months should be sufficient time, though I can give you longer if you think you need it. So . . . August fifteenth. You send me the doc by no later than noon that day. I read and get back to you by mid-September. And maybe we can still have you walking the line by the December ceremony. What do you think?"

"I think," said Wes, "that it's bullshit, and I could give a rat's ass about a high school diploma."

Her face and neck bloomed with red heat. "Excuse me?"

"What possible value could a certificate declaring me a high school graduate have if a person like you has the power to withhold it from me? I just brought you a system that's going to revolutionize the world, and you're concerned about whether or not I pulled some quotes from EncycloFeedia. It's fucking ridiculous."

Professor McGregor was practically shaking now with rage. In later years, Wes would register some guilt over this meeting. Not over the fact that he had, as she called it, plagiarized; the Review of Lit *was* bullshit busy work, he knew it and so did she, and the fact that she would delay his graduation over it revealed an appalling lack of vision. But he shouldn't have cursed, and he shouldn't have raised his voice. He should not have said, as he went on to, "In a few years' time I'm going to be rich and famous, and you're still going to be sitting in this room lording yourself over kids who are smarter than you are, because you know it's your last chance to do it. So keep your stupid degree. I'm out of here."

And, in the time it took him to gather his tablet and turn his back to her blotchy, ugly, shocked face, he was. When Pocketz went live the next year, and when the stock went public four years after that, the news stories always began with a version of the same theme: "High school dropout Wes Feingold," "Unlikely CEO Wes Feingold." It was a part of the myth now, and Wes thought sometimes that it would have been worth doing the revision, which would not have been all that hard anyway, just to live without hearing those qualifiers before his name. He wasn't some lucky idiot who screwed up his life and later stumbled upon success; he was simply beyond Professor McGregor's petty moralizing and worthless degree. But that didn't make for a good headline.

Ten years later and here he was, doing this crazy thing, this OLE Fall Color Tour, a trip valued at one hundred thousand credits. Now this was an expenditure that defied most rational theories about relative value. In a society that placed safety at its highest premium, that had withdrawn itself into zones, each with its own strategies for fighting or deflecting the advances of an epidemic of aggressive parasites, what did it mean for rich men and women like him to spend extravagantly on a trip right into the midst of that epidemic?

He had more credits than he could spend in his lifetime. Pocketz, as he anticipated, was operating now mostly on its own momentum, and the innovations he periodically made, such as refining the stock market Projectionz interface, gave him none of the thrill of engineering the system's initial structure. Nor had Pocketz changed the world in exactly the ways he had imagined it would. As a teenager he had theorized that systematizing conspicuous consumption would reduce the cultural capital of spending. Remove the mystery, make it so that his parents could have known before going over to the Duncans what was for dinner and exactly how much it cost, and maybe the credits spent wouldn't matter as much. Maybe, just maybe, the friendships would matter more, and value would be derived not from the selection of fish and booze but from the quality of conversation, the number of genuine laughs. That had been his hope. No, his premonition.

He was wrong, of course.

His board of directors had pressured him to move into interactive advertising. Someone goes to a movie, you hit Explore, and a trailer for *Rubber Meets the Road III* starts playing. Someone has dinner at Felipe's Mexican Cantina, you "explore," and the menu scrolls through your feed to the accompaniment of mariachi music. Your best friend Jake claims a coupon for a buy one, get one free latte at Pappy Chino's, and your feed offers you the same deal. It was the obvious evolution of the software, but it wasn't what Wes had in mind the day he stormed out of Professor McGregor's office. Nor had he imagined then what would eventually become the site's most popular feature, the daily roundup of Deep Pocketz and Big Spenderz, sortable by country, zone, city, and even personal friends list, though it was Wes himself who had suggested that some system of rewards, however trifling, might help to solidify the program's popularity. Now, each day the news feeds reported the top five in each national feed. Wes was ranked seventh in Deep Pocketz as of yesterday morning—his usual slot—and he usually didn't even rate in the top 100 of Big Spenderz, though booking the OLE tour a month ago had edged him briefly into the eighty-third slot.

He had tried for most of the last two years to design a new and better program. His mistake with Pocketz, he had decided, was relying on Cost as the reference variable—that is, measuring value against the existing system of credits instead of creating a brand-new virtual credit system with its own reference variables, such as Intellect, Morality, Creativity, Humor, and Spirituality. He thought it might be possible to commodify Societal Values, and therefore move them from the periphery to the center of value exchanges. Then, it wouldn't matter if a music track were illegally downloaded; you'd be paying for the musician's talent rather than the product of that talent.

But he couldn't make it work. The beta version of Virtuz, which he had test-run on a group of college sophomores, was a failure. "Boring," according to Wes's survey-processing software, was the most frequently used adjective in the discursive evaluations, followed by "confusing" and "useless." The test subjects hadn't liked the rewards system. The updates in the feed made them feel guilty and inadequate rather than inspired.

Betsy Chang volunteered 2 hours at Calabash County Soup Kitchen.
Explore **Share** **High-five** Two hours ago, near Wilmington, AtlZ

Ely Singleton wrote 986 words for Sociology 256.
Explore **Share** **High-five** 30 minutes ago, near Greensboro, AtlZ

When Wes complained to his girlfriend, Sonya, about the failure of the trial run, how it was indicative of the superficial nature of young people today, she had said, "Well, what on earth did you expect? It's a feed for Goody Two-Shoes. Hey, wait—that's what you should call it." She synced her tablet so he could see on the wall what she was writing: *Goody Two-Shooz*. She used the Fontastic! app to make the letters gold and sparkling, with halos tilted over the letters *G* and *S*. Then, mouth slanted in thought, she erased the halo over the *S*. "There you go," she said. "That's your logo."

Granted, they were having a rough go of it lately—and this wasn't the first time one or the other of them had snapped and said something nasty—but that stung.

"Well, if you felt that way all along, why didn't you say so?" Wes yelled, swiping her stupid logo out of sight.

"I did. Half a dozen times I said to you, 'This isn't how a virtue works.' That the minute you try to attach a precise value to it, you turn it into something that isn't a virtue. The whole system's a paradox, and I told you so, but you never listened."

Wes found himself pouting, childishly sullen. "You didn't say it in so many words."

She shook her head in a disgusted way, so that her chin-length, auburn hair swung back and forth. She was thirty, five years older than Wes, and a Pocketz employee, head of the team of graphic designers who came on last year to freshen up the main-feed interface and create subtle, pleasing avenues into what Wes had started calling the "ad opps." She had been his first real girlfriend—his first sexual partner—taking the initiative in almost every negotiation, from the night she asked him if he wanted to join her at Ozzy's for a beer ("I don't drink," he had said, and, unruffled, she replied, "Well, you can just watch me") to the night a week after that when she put his hand on her warm, full breast and asked him, "So, are we going to fuck or what?" Wes lived a life of precision and self-discipline. Each morning he washed down half a dozen vitamins with a glass of fiber-infused orange juice, had one bowl of plain oatmeal, and then went for his usual six-mile run before the urge came, like clockwork, for him to empty his bowels. He ate a strictly vegan diet, did not drink, did not smoke (even Smokeless), and abstained from refined sugars, caffeine, and gluten. Sonya, on the other hand, never exercised (though she was tireless in bed), drank daily, smoked leaf tobacco and pot, and subsisted on a diet of sugary cereals and vacuum-sealed cold-cut sandwiches that she purchased in bulk each weekend from Tesley's. Her favorite meal out was a rare steak, salty fries, and most (or all) of a bottle of red wine. She was Wes's only indulgence, his only bad habit, and Wes had assumed all this time that he, on the other hand, was the point of light in her life, the voice of reason. Her daily vitamin.

"Not in so many words," she muttered. They had been sitting at Wes's small kitchen table together, Wes with his oatmeal, Sonya with her bowl of Salty Caramel Crunch Nuggets and a tall mug of sludgy black coffee, and she stood and flipped the cover of her tablet closed. She went to the living room, grabbed her backpack from the credenza (where Wes always stowed it, since her habit was to simply sling it into Wes's recliner, or on his coffee table, or in the middle of the floor, where anyone could trip on it), and shoved her tablet roughly into it.

"What are you doing?" Wes asked.

She was tall and lean but not scrawny, her hips a little on the wide side compared to the rest of her, good-sized hands and feet, toenails always painted some garish hue but never, somehow, freshly. He would have liked to paint her toenails for her, to work the color neatly into the tiniest corners, even on her funny-shaped pinkies, getting it exactly right; but he had not, in their eight months of courtship, had the courage to make the suggestion. She stalked around his living room in a cropped T-shirt and boxer shorts, hunting down her things: two balled-up socks, a lipstick, an old paperback mystery novel. Into the bag they went.

"You're leaving?" he asked, bewildered.

"Yup." She stuck her bottom lip out and huffed, blowing her hair out of her eyes. Wes looked at her cereal bowl, where what was left of her Crunch Nuggets was growing bloated and sodden in the milk, and he wondered if she planned to at least clean up after herself.

"Oh, Jesus H.," she said. She snatched the bowl out from in front of him and dumped its contents in the sink, then ran the garbage disposal without turning on the water first. "Better?" She disappeared into the bedroom, returned a few minutes later in a sweatshirt and jeans, and paused in the door between the kitchen and the living room, hands on her hips. "OK. I'm going."

Wes tried to process this. "For good?"

"Yeah," she said.

"Because you say I didn't listen to you about Virtuz?"

"I don't just *say*," she said, "but no, that's not the reason. Or all of it. I just realized that we've hit the wall."

"The wall," Wes repeated. This was how Sonya spoke: not *a* wall, but *the* wall, as if Wes ought to know what she was talking about, as if the thing they'd hit was looming ahead in the distance all along.

"The 'more work than fun' wall," Sonya said. "The, 'My boyfriend has a tablet instead of a heart' wall. So anyway, I'll see you at work."

"That's it?"

She stopped at the door. "What else would there be?"

"And you're still going to work at my company?"

She cast a level gaze at him. "Well, unless you're planning to fire me for not fucking you anymore."

"God, when you put it like *that*," Wes said.

"See you at work," she said again firmly. And as quickly and unceremoniously as she had entered his life, she left it.

"You could say I had a crisis," Wes was telling Marta on the touring bus as it rolled past still-familiar landscape. The Salt Line was at least a half-hour's drive away according to a map animation on the overhead monitor, but the Wall's vibration was already making its presence known, shivering the window glass, wiggling into the soles of his feet so that he had to start flexing his toes against numbness. "I needed a radical change in my life. I needed to do something no one expected me to." By *no one* he meant Sonya, of course, but he'd be damned if he'd say her name aloud, even to a person who had never met her, who knew nothing about how they'd come together and why they split.

"And you think it was the right choice?" Marta asked. She was a good listener, easy to confide in.

"Well, that remains to be seen, doesn't it?" He drummed a little rhythm on the tops of his thighs. "Wow. Feels weird not having my tablet."

She sighed. "For me, too."

"I can't even remember the last time I went without it," Wes said. "It must have been that brownout three years ago."

Marta shivered. "That was scary. The boys had just left for college. I couldn't reach them. I had no idea how they were." Her face sagged, as if she'd suddenly realized she was now in a version of the same position.

"Those 'free yourself from the tablet' nuts—you've got to wonder about them," Wes said. Marta had insisted he take the window seat, and so he stole a quick glance outside, wondering, like a little boy, *Are we there yet? Are we there yet?* So far there wasn't much to see. Thirty kilometers back, they'd passed a community of single-wide trailer homes: cars rusting into piles of weeds, laundry flapping on lines. No one outside, not even playing children. There had been no housing since. Ten or fifteen kilometers ago, he'd noticed that there weren't trees or shrubs any longer, and the October grasses had yellowed, but there were some fields of wildflowers—goldenrod, purple asters—to break up what was otherwise a level and almost wintry prospect but not an overtly dismaying one. Past the Wall, however, the situation would change. *We're talking a little bit "scorched earth" for the first couple of miles,* Andy had said. Nothing they hadn't seen on the feeds, more or less, but experiencing the thing in the flesh would be different. "It always struck me as a kind of bullshit proposition," Wes continued. "You know, willfully out of touch with how the world is. Like, if you're not going to use a tablet, I hope you're also going to grow your own veggies and never ride in a car or a train. Good luck with that."

His right-hand thumb was miming the tablet sweep stroke, and he tucked the hand under his thigh.

"I'm obviously biased. If I sold ice cream for a living, maybe I'd try to convince you it doesn't make you fat."

"I don't think that's a fair comparison," Marta said. "You're being hard on yourself."

"Well, maybe." He looked down, embarrassed—as if Sonya were watching him and smirking—by the conscious pose of his modesty. Sonya had, in the months since their breakup, become a kind of scolding, mocking voice in his head, and the pathetic part was that the voice comforted him. He liked it. "Anyway. I say all that because I have to admit that part of the appeal of this trip for me was going somewhere the signals don't reach. Three weeks of feed silence. Crazy, right?"

"I wouldn't call it crazy," Marta said.

"Like Captain Cluck swearing off fried chicken." He smiled ruefully. "There was this . . . person. This person I'd come to depend on. And then she didn't want me to depend on her anymore. At first, it didn't bother me much. I told myself it didn't. But I still had to work with her, and I'd see her in the office, and she'd act completely nonchalant. Not just like she was over me, but like there wasn't anything for her to get over in the first place."

Marta patted his microsuit-clad knee. "I'm sure that wasn't the case."

He lowered his voice, aware of a gradual silence that had settled in the seats around his and Marta's. In the quiet, the vibration coming off the TerraVibra—whose presence had been so creeping and gradual—was obvious, verging on overwhelming, and Wes used his middle fingers to knead the two points just in front of the hinge of his jaw. "She wouldn't talk to me, except work stuff. And then I checked my feeds even more than I usually do, thinking maybe she'd call or message. Or I'd see something to help me know what was going on with her."

"Did you?"

Wes was almost whispering now. "One night she spent twenty credits at a restaurant I used to take her to, this steak house. Mahogany. But so did this other guy at work, Timothy. Same place, same night. Same time for the charge."

"They could have just been friends," said Marta.

"That's what I thought," Wes said. "I considered it rationally. They're on the same design team. They each paid their own tickets. But a few nights later, they both rang up simultaneous charges at a bar. Then dinner again the next week. Then, the same night as the dinner, Pine Ridge Bed and Breakfast puts a two-hundred-credit hold on his account."

Marta didn't have a response to this. She gave him a pained, tight little smile, eyebrows drawn into a pitying peak.

"My first thought was to go over there." He barked a sharp laugh. "Yeah, me. The big man. I was going to confront them. Then I thought, well, maybe I'll just sit outside the hotel and see what I see. Maybe I'm wrong. Maybe I won't even see them leave together.

"Then—I don't even remember how it happened—I booked this trip. I just did it before I could even decide to do it, if that makes any sense. I had to get away from her, and I had to get away from the feeds. I was going to do something I'd regret if I didn't."

"That's quite a story," Marta said sincerely.

Well, it was a story. Some of the story. Not all of it.

"She said I had a tablet instead of a heart," Wes blurted out, voice thick with feeling, and that was when he heard muffled snickering in the seat one back and over from theirs.

Then there was a tiny, cheerful strumming sound. A ukulele, Wes thought, accompanied suddenly by a pleasant, raspy tenor:

That girl sure was a habit
I stalked her on my tablet
She was everything I need

So I feasted on her feed
Till I was bloated as a tick
And sure she sucked his dick
I just wish there was a Stamp
What could rid me of that tramp

A female voice hissed sharply, "Stop being an asshole, Jesse."

Wes stood, bracing himself with a hand against the back of his seat, in time to watch as Jesse Haggard finished his little ditty with a twangy riff on "Shave and a Haircut," biting his bottom lip comically for the last two notes. He was slumped, knees tucked up against the seatback in front of him, ukulele resting on his chest, and he opened his eyes, which had been pinched tight with affected earnestness, and grinned at Wes. "Good stuff, my man. Good stuff."

His girlfriend, Edie, looked stricken. "Oh, Wes. Please ignore him. He has a weird sense of humor."

Wes's mouth got very dry. He swallowed, blinking stupidly, and gripped the seat harder, afraid that his knees were about to turn to liquid. Edie's expression of embarrassed pity was harder to bear than the song had been. For three weeks now he had been noticing her, admiring her, and wondering why she'd paired off with someone like Jesse "Burger Blitz" Haggard, who couldn't even do a chin-up in the weight room without manfully grunting a plea for attention. The Timothys of the world, the Jesses—what did women see in them?

"Don't go and do something you'll regret now," Jesse said.

Every eye on the bus was on Wes. Marta grabbed his forearm, tried to pull him back into the seat. "Ignore him," she said. "He's a child." Andy, sensing some tension in the group, started back the middle aisle toward them, but then the bus hit a bump in the road, and he and Wes both swayed. There was another vibration now, strong enough to make Wes's teeth clank together, and Wes realized that the road had gotten rough and textured the way it did close to shoulders, so you knew if you were about to go into a ditch. The travelers turned their attention to the windows, craning their necks for a view of what lay ahead—Wes, too—and when Marta leaned against him and said, "What is it?" he replied, hoarsely, "It's the Wall."

"Back in your seats, folks," Andy said. "We've reached the Salt Line."

Four

Arguing with your boyfriend was bad, Edie thought. Arguing with your buddy, whose side you would not be able to leave for the next three weeks, was worse.

"Just lighten up," Jesse said. He was picking the same four- or five-note sequence out on his ukulele, barely brushing his thumb across the strings so that the sound wouldn't travel far. It was driving Edie nuts, especially since she was trying to concentrate on what was happening outside the bus. "If you can't have a sense of humor about yourself, you're fucked at life."

"You don't have a sense of humor about yourself," Edie hissed. "At all." The bus driver had restarted the engine, and a guard in an armor-reinforced, helmeted microsuit was waving them forward. She felt nauseated, and she didn't know how much of the sensation to attribute to her mortification, how much to the rhythmic churning of the air around the Wall, how much to her fear. Right now, the split seemed to be about even.

"That's not true." *Strumly strum strum strummmm.*

"It is," Edie said. "You moped for two days when the guys in the band laughed at your eyeliner."

Strumly strum strum. He'd pinched his eyes closed again, ignoring her.

"And at least you know those guys. You have a rapport with

them. Why on earth you'd want to start this trip out with bad blood between you and a virtual stranger is beyond me. With everything else to be worried about." She shook her head with irritated wonder. The bus darkened momentarily as they passed under the structure of the gate and guard station, the view just outside her window only a seamed concrete wall punctuated by intermittent flashing red lights before the bus was again flooded with hazy daylight. She had opened her mouth to say something else, something about how nice Wes seemed and how randomly cruel Jesse's actions were, when the words turned to dust in her mouth. She made a strangled sound of horror, and the muted strumming of the ukulele stopped.

"Oh my God," someone behind her said.

There was a popular but controversial picture book that kids Edie's and Jesse's age had been raised on called *The Shaman and the Salt Line*. Like so many stories meant for children, it was very grim, even frightening, but in a way that only increased its deep and abstract appeal, so that as a young girl Edie found herself reading it over and over again until the binding of the book finally fell apart and her mother had to duct-tape it. (They also had a tablet version with animations of the drawings, but those animations never had the same horrific fascination of the static, color-saturated illustrations of the print version, with its freeze-frames of faces contorted with anguish, terror, fury, and joy.)

The book began by describing a tribe of happy, carefree people who enjoyed the pleasures of both village and forest. "They were so full of love for one another," the author wrote, "that their numbers doubled and then tripled, and soon their little houses could not hold them." So the members of the tribe expanded their numbers deeper into the woods.

One day, a boy and a girl stopped their play to rest.

"I'm hungry," the girl said.

"Then I'll gather us some blueberries to eat," said the boy.

They ate until their bellies were pleasantly full, but then the girl noticed there were still blueberries left on the bushes. "We should eat those, too," she said.

"Why?" her friend asked.

"Because they're there and we can," said the girl. So they ate those blueberries as well.

The book went on to describe two other incidents of this kind among the tribe, each increasing in degree. A carpenter decided to cut down two trees instead of one, because "more is better than less, and because I can." A hunter killed two rabbits, though he was only hungry enough to eat one, because perhaps the extra meat would come in handy later on. When later came and the hunter wasn't in the mood for rabbit, he left the poor, discarded creature's body lying in the dirt, untouched. "I could kill it and so I did," the hunter said. "And there are plenty more rabbits where that one came from."

But then the forest, which had been so plentiful and yielding of its resources to the tribespeople, grew stingy and unaccommodating. The clear stream water turned bitter and sat uneasily on the stomach. The blueberries shriveled on the bush. The trees refused to yield to the ax, and the rabbits, when shot and skinned, offered up only the thinnest slivers of meat, which the starving children fought over brutally. There was at this point in the book a two-page illustration that more than once gave Edie nightmares: half a dozen children, three boys and three girls, each grabbing for a share of a shriveled leg of rabbit, mouths contorted with hunger and rage. Drool dangled from exposed teeth; a fork's tines skewered a grabbing hand.

The children were very, very wicked was the only line of description.

The once-happy tribespeople, withered by hunger and twisted with cold because they could no longer build shelter, or burn wood in their fires, became panicked, and they started waging war on one another, diminishing their numbers. One among them, an elderly woman who remembered the light of their earlier glory, fled in the night to seek out the shaman who lived on top of the mountain. If anyone could explain to the tribespeople what had set them on this path to ruin, it was he.

The shaman told her that the hunter, in killing and discarding the second rabbit, had earned the curse of its spirit. That curse—*Yeye ambaye ni zinazotumiwa teketezwa*, "He who consumes is consumed"—was carried out for the spirit by a demon, Vimelea, who could only be cast out of the human realm if the surviving tribespeople would withdraw back to their village, salt the earth in a perimeter around it, and vow only to venture into the woods when the greatest necessity required it.

Some of the tribe agreed to the shaman's plan; others dismissed it as folly. And so half the group returned with the old woman and the shaman to the village, and the shaman walked out from the village center until its central spire was barely visible. Then, ever keeping the village center just in sight on his left, he began his slow procession to mark the perimeter, laying down the line of salt and chanting the ceremonial words, *Sisi hutumia tu kile tunachotaka*, "We consume only what we need." When, many, many hours later, the ends of the Salt Line joined to make a circle, he rested. It was done.

The curse, for those within the village, was lifted. They grew healthy and plump once more, and their numbers increased, but never so much that they were forced to live outside the perimeter, or to take from the surrounding forest two things when one would suffice. Those who had not believed the shaman, however, continued to be subsumed by Vimelea's curse. Some tried, when no other option was left to them, to return to the village—but the salt that kept the demon out also kept them out, for the demon was inside them now, and all that was left for them was death.

In the forest, the water ran sweet, and the blueberries and rabbits came back in abundance. The last of the cursed tribespeople eventually disappeared, and their punishment was to live on eternally not as human spirits, but as tiny, crawling, bloodthirsty things, the lowest of the forest's low. Because they still carried within them a piece of the demon Vimelea, they would forever try, whenever one of their former tribespeople entered the forest, to steal back some of the life force they had lost the day they mocked the shaman. In this way, the villagers were reminded of the dangers of taking the forest for granted, and they never ventured long or far away from home. And they lived, safe within the Salt Line, happily ever after.

The Shaman and the Salt Line, whose pseudonymous author and illustrator, B. A. Trist, never made a public appearance, outraged everybody. The fundamentalist Christians complained that it advocated paganism. The atheists were angry that it subscribed to biblical, Noah and the Flood–style distinctions between good and evil. The liberals were bothered by the implication that inner Zoners were somehow morally superior to the unfortunate souls who were on the wrong side of the Salt Line in the zoned America's first dark days, and the conservatives disliked the book's Marxist "each according to his need" subtext, which was indoctrinating children as young as five into socialism. The environmentalists claimed that it painted a too-pretty picture of zone policy toward natural resources, given that outer-zone contract corporations such as Environ and the Valley Corporation continued to rely on poor labor sources, mostly from the Gulf and Midwest Zones, for logging, mining, drilling, manufacturing, and large-scale cattle factory operations, no longer answerable to most pre-zone regulatory policies. The academics critiqued its lazy (and inaccurate) appropriation of the Swahili language. And yet, despite these arguments—perhaps because of them—the book became ubiquitous. Every library had it, every elementary school classroom. If you went into your doctor's office and perused the low-built, brightly painted children's table, it would be there beside the Tabkins and the abacus and the pedestal with plastic rings of diminishing size. Most children, even Gulf children like Edie, owned it, and those children grew up with the notion of a literal line of salt before they were later told, by parents and schoolteachers, that the "Salt Line" protecting most zone perimeters were actually borders where, during the eradication, controlled chemical burnings had taken place, and so the earth was "salted" in the symbolic sense of having been purified, rendered uninhabitable. Then, over the course of a decade, the Wall was erected, and the Terra-Vibra soon followed, emanating its pulse fifty kilometers eastward, a layer of protection that no other zone, even New England, could boast.

Edie had long ago known better than to expect a literal line of salt, or even a less literal band of earth that had been treated with salt; the internet feeds had shown her plenty of grim pictures of long reaches of black earth, places where the old paved roads had boiled and run in bubbling eddies, at some point cooling and freezing in strange, almost beautiful formations. Andy himself had warned them, during one of the training sessions, that the first few outer-zone kilometers were "not pretty to look at."

But the sight meeting her gaze as far as she could make out from her window was not merely burned, empty earth, as she had expected. The world just past the Wall was a wasteland of garbage—a seemingly endless mountain of trash that emitted a sulfurous odor that she realized now she had been smelling for kilometers and attributing in the back of her mind to the bus, which ran on one of the new biofuels. A couple of bulldozers trundled sluggishly across the surface, pushing the pile of trash ever upward, away from the wall, so that it peaked perhaps a couple of kilometers off, at a ridge that blocked out the sight of anything that lay beyond it.

"I know this looks bad," Andy said from his position at the head of the bus.

"That's a fucking understatement!" an angry male voice called from behind Edie.

Jesse, tight as a guitar string beside her, sunk clutching fingers into her forearm but didn't speak. A panicked din rose in the bus, and another male voice, Lee Flannigan, it sounded like, called, "Turn this thing around! This was *not* disclosed!"

Andy murmured something to the driver, and the bus slowed to a stop. He stood stoically, hand raised as if he were a student waiting for the teacher to call on him. After a moment, the conversation ebbed.

"I'm going to talk briefly. If you don't like what I say, we can turn around, but I warn you that you'll have to go straight into Quarantine 2 for a week, regardless. So: May I speak?"

He received a surly silence in reply.

"What you see outside your windows lasts for another four-point-eight kilometers, and it stops as suddenly as it began. Your Outer Limits Excursion tour is exactly what you were promised it would be. There's a lot of beauty to experience if you'll trust me for just a little bit longer."

"Why didn't you just tell us it would be like this?" Marta asked.

"Honestly? Because this is unprecedented," Andy said. "Our usual route through the Wall along the old Blue Ridge Parkway corridor has been closed by the Atlantic Zone Department of Border Security for maintenance, and we don't know when the gate will reopen. We were, as of a week ago, granted permission to pass through this service entrance along the old I-40 corridor, which is normally only used for outer-zone contractors."

"Why?" Edie found herself asking.

Andy gave her a surprised look. "Why, what?"

"Why did they bother giving you permission? Why not just make you cancel the excursion and refund us our money?" She felt a flutter of embarrassment at her automatic use of the word "our"; she wondered if Jesse had noticed and, if he did, what he thought.

"Well, a couple of reasons. One is that two million credits had already been invested into this excursion by some of the zone's most influential and prominent citizens, and it's bad economics to interfere with a transaction of that scale, especially on the basis of what amounts to a trifling technical issue."

"Trifling," Mickey Worthington said. "You call this trifling."

"I do," Andy said. "What you're looking at is no secret. Congress passed legislation over thirteen years ago OK'ing the use of the outer-zone perimeter for waste disposal. This"—he thumbed out the window—"is nothing more than what you're producing. Your garbage collector hauls it off in a truck once a week. You knew it was going somewhere."

"It's just a shock," Wes Feingold said. "The scale of it." He had a hand over his nose and mouth. "The smell."

"It's an efficient solution to an ongoing problem," Andy said, "which is maintaining a perimeter that resists miner tick infiltration as well as border crossings by outer Zoners and zone refugees, mostly from Gulf. When this area was left empty, it required regular chemical treatment to prevent reforestation. Zone waste does the same job. The landfill ends up becoming a habitat for certain animals, of course, especially rodents, but many researchers argue that controlled habitats are as efficient a way to operate as eradicating the habitats entirely. And for whatever reason, the miner ticks seem not to like the rats very much. There's a science team stationed just south of here trying to figure out why that is—what we can learn from the rats."

What we can learn from the rats, Edie thought. Jesse would probably want to write that into a song later.

"It's good environmental policy, and it's good politics. In twenty years, this waste wall will extend along the western front of Atlantic Zone, a distance of almost sixteen hundred kilometers. The methane emissions are already helping to power the TerraVibra, which has resulted in considerable energy savings. I mean, listen. We're one of the most advantageously positioned zones in the country, with the Appalachian Mountains to our front and the ocean to our back." An ugly, almost angry expression flashed across his features, so quickly that Edie wondered if anyone else had seen it. "Other zones are not in such good shape."

"They're building fortifications," Wendy Tanaka said.

"Something like that," said Andy. "At any rate, this is one of the other reasons the excursion wasn't canceled. The folks controlling the Wall are banking that you'll like what you see, even if you don't really like what you see, if that makes any sense."

The murmuring now was more measured and subdued. Andy waited it out with patient aplomb.

"So what do you think?" he asked. "Do we keep going forward? Do you want to see what you pained and trained for?"

"Is this an all-or-nothing proposition?" Berto asked. "We all go or none of us?"

"Of course not," said Andy. "This is a recreational excursion. It won't be recreational if anyone is forced one way or the other. Though I will say that you of course have to be accompanied by your buddy, or able to pair off with a new buddy. And we need at least six travelers per guide, so if there's less interest than that, my going forward becomes unfeasible. I like you all"—he smiled in a wry way, eyebrows raised—"but even I don't operate purely out of the goodness of my heart. I'm sure you understand."

"And refunds?" Lee Flannigan asked.

"The trip itself hasn't changed. There are no promises in the contract about what your view on the bus ride in will be. But I imagine that OLE will be willing to work with you after Quarantine, training, and transportation fees have been subtracted from your total. I can't say an amount with any surety, but my guess would be at least half."

Edie, sneaking a sidelong look at Jesse, felt a surge of hope. He had removed his clutching hand from her forearm only to lock on to his own knee, and his complexion was grayish, as if he might be sick. They had been arguing already, which did not bode well for their ability to make it happily through three stressful, difficult weeks. OLE was already changing the terms on them, in a way that might not yet add up to much but could later, if the company was this willing to withhold information and play fast and loose with what they had implicitly, if not explicitly, promised. All signs pointed to leaving, and she remembered what Andy had told her that day in the weight room: *You take off and let that dipshit have his little adventure, and maybe you'll even still be together on the other side of this. If you go, I guarantee you won't be.*

She leaned over and whispered into Jesse's ear, "Hey. Let's just leave. OK? I don't feel good about this."

His eyebrows drew down in affront, but she could tell that she was saying what a part of him was yearning to hear. The trick would be to make him feel like he was quitting for her—acting out of a gentlemanly regard for her delicate feminine sensibility—and not out of his own fears. Frame it so he'd have a story to tell later on: *You should have seen this mountain of garbage . . . Not what they told us to expect . . . Edie was a mess . . . I didn't know if she'd be able to handle it.*

"I'm really scared," she said, and she was, but she hated herself a little. The calculated warble in her voice.

"Well, I don't know. Maybe. It's a lot of money to lose."

"We're on a bus full of lawyers," she said. "They wouldn't dare not refund you most of it, maybe all of it. And you," she added in a burst of inspiration, "have maybe the biggest profile of all of these people. If you threatened to publish something to your feed about how they treated us, what we saw out here . . ."

"It would be a big story." He was nodding.

"Let's just go," she pleaded. "OK?"

"Well," Jesse said. "If you're—"

That was when Wes Feingold called out loudly, "I'm still in."

"And your buddy?" Andy asked.

"Still in," said Marta.

Jesse's face contorted. He was almost ugly. Edie remembered his derision when Wes Feingold had run out of the gymnasium to throw up that first day, his subsequent dismissal of Pocketz. His mean song, she understood now, was a punishment for what Jesse perceived as Wes's two greatest insults: his power and influence on the one hand, power and influence that exceeded his own; and Wes's weakness on the other.

"Jesse," she warned, but his hand had already shot up, and he said, before Andy could even call on him, "We're going. Edie and I are going."

Andy looked at her. "Edie," he said. There was a pleading in his eyes. "Is that true?"

It had been easy these last ten months for her to deny, to herself and anyone else who insinuated it, that she was a groupie, that she had gone after Jesse Haggard, and stayed with him, because he was a well-known pop singer. She knew the truth of what they'd been through together, the ways he had supported her when another guy would have gone running. She knew something about his secret, kind heart, his vulnerability and longing to be loved. His fame, to her, was his greatest liability as a partner.

But even as she nodded her assent to Andy now, agreeing to see this through, she wondered. She had believed it love, but could it be love if Jesse was willing to disregard her own desires so completely?

She didn't know.

But if she insisted now on going back, and either left Jesse to find another buddy or put him in a position that made it impossible to stay—either way, essentially initiating a breakup—what did she have to go home to? She had quit her job. She had broken her lease to live with Jesse. Worst of all—and God, how she hated to admit this to herself—she had gotten used to the lifestyle. She had gotten used to not pouring drinks and fending off the advances of drunken, middle-aged men, and she had gotten used to not having to count every credit she spent in the last week of the month, and she had gotten used to good wine, fresh fish, VIP access, chocolate, honey for her tea, the safety of living on a street where break-ins weren't reported several times a week. She had come to depend on the variety and novelty of Jesse's lifestyle; it dulled the ache of her loneliness, let her forget, sometimes for hours on end, that both her father and her mother were now lost to her forever. None of these things had gotten her into bed with Jesse, but she found now that they made it hard for her to leave it—at least without some kind of plan in place.

And she did love him, she thought.

"Are you sure?" Andy asked. "I'm going to need you to say yes out loud if that's really your decision. And it *is* your decision—not anyone else's." He looked around. "That goes for everyone on this bus."

"Yes," Edie said. Jesse was trying to smile at her, but she refused to meet his gaze. "It's my decision."

In the end, they all decided to keep going.

And as promised, the view once the bus topped the rise and turned a corner, penetrating the wall of garbage, was everything the brochures had assured them it would be, the land spreading out generously ahead and then rising suddenly into mist-shrouded peaks, the closest mountains at this distance a muted orange, the more faraway ones charcoal-smudged and out of focus. Soon, Edie noticed, even the residual tremor of the TerraVibra had fallen completely away. The windows opened three inches and were protected by double screens, so Edie shoved hers down and leaned her temple against the glass, letting the fresh cool air rush into her nose and take away some of the lingering scent, or scent memory, from the landfill. She was suddenly exhausted and limp. She had been rigid with fear before, and getting past that first bad moment outside the gates had given her, she knew, a temporary and false sense of relief, a lulling certainty that she could close her eyes now, let the slight sway of the bus rock her to sleep, and not worry, for a time, about problematic boyfriends, great walls of trash, ticks.

But there was much to see outside her window. Well, strike that—what was compelling, actually, was the relative emptiness of the landscape compared to inside the zone, or at least the reaches of the zone beyond the perimeter of the TerraVibra, where you could hardly expect to pass, outside of the arboretums and parks, an empty lot, much less undeveloped kilometers populated by nothing but grass, trees, and rock. And the trees! The ones at home were mostly young, thirty or forty years on the top end, and though there were, in the parks, some of the larger species, the oaks and the cedars, the inner-zone trend was toward small, slim, and ornamental: Japanese maples, crepe myrtle, dogwoods, redbuds. The trees weren't to blame for the ticks, but there was a strong cultural distrust of woods and canopies, not to mention a limited amount of space for them. But these outer-zone trees climbed stories.

Also fascinating were the signs of the old life, the one that had been finally abandoned so many years ago, well before even her mother was born, when construction on the Atlantic Zone's perimeter was complete and the last group of refugees was granted entrance. Little things. Like road signs, large and green with bold white text, designed for view at a fast-passing distance: Old Fort, Black Mountain, Swannanoa, they sounded like storybook places, like places where the villagers and the shaman might have lived. And those blue signs with their simple declarations of "Food, Gas, Attractions," the little squares with logos reminding her of the home screen on her tablet—how strange was that? "Gas" and half a dozen places that sold it. No rations, no digital counters, no yearly fuel audit requiring drivers to keep track of kilometers traveled and the purpose of that travel (work, recreation, family, public service), then to calculate a taxable footprint based on the results. She knew that the old times weren't simpler, that the lack of foresight then was in part what had led to the necessity for strict regulation now, but it was amazing to ponder that freeness. And hard not to feel some jealousy of it.

"Look," Jesse said, pointing.

It was another green sign: "Exit 55, E Asheville/VA Hospital." Edie glanced at the overhead monitor and confirmed their progress; the little pulsing dot on the map that represented their bus was almost on top of the destination flag now. The bus didn't exit at the first sign, or the next couple, but it slowed as highway 25A approached. Edie's stomach sloshed uncomfortably as the bus veered right, onto the off-ramp. She pulled off her glove so that she could gnaw on her thumbnail.

Andy stood in the aisle, grasping the backs of two seats for balance. "We're approaching the first checkpoint. It's just a few minutes after nine o'clock, which means we've managed to stay on schedule. Our driver, Johnny, made up some time on the road. Give him a hand."

There were a few claps.

"We'll rest for an hour here, so double-check to make sure your watches are synced with the bus's clock." He pointed at the monitor. "Nine-oh-four. We want to be loaded and ready to go by ten after ten. If you're not on the bus by then, tardiness penalties go into effect. We would never leave a traveler behind, but we'll make it very expensive for you to waste our time. Got it?"

Heads bobbed.

"Tia and I will be handing out power bars and orange juice. Please dispose of your waste in the designated OLE trash cans around the checkpoint facility. They're bright red and marked with our logo. Hard to miss."

The bus pulled into an empty parking lot and stopped. The silence initiated by the shut-off engine was sudden and eerie.

"We monitor this site for ticks, but you should be on your guard and near your buddy from here on out. Don't panic, and don't psych yourself out, but remember the things I told you. You'll know the itch when you feel it. It's unmistakable." He gestured to the sprawling brown building on the driver's side of the bus. "This place was a restaurant, a kind of curiosity. We've got generators hooked up, and the bathrooms are converted to chemical toilets, so you can use the facilities more or less as you normally would, have your snack at the tables, look around the store. You *may not* remove or purchase items from the store. Think of it as a museum. We have video monitoring inside, and we'll be doing bag checks. No souvenirs."

Wes Feingold, shoulders hunched as he leaned in for a better look, raised a hand and said, "What's a cracker barrel?"

"Beats me," said Andy. "But this place was a restaurant with a little store attached, part of a big chain of them. For whatever reason, this location has held up pretty well, and the general store wasn't looted. I think you'll get a kick out of it."

They disembarked the bus sedately from front to back, no one rushing the aisle or holding up the line to pull things from the overhead bins, and, like schoolchildren, accepted from Andy and Tia their designated morning snacks. The foil pouch of juice with the plastic nozzle was the same brand Edie had carried in her kindergarten lunchbox. Comforting. She walked a few steps away from the pack to get a look around. Not much to see here. A chilly but fresh-smelling wind blew into her face, and she tugged her goggles down over her streaming eyes. The restaurant was situated on a rise, surrounded by a parking lot that appeared to have been recently resealed, as was the road leading from the interstate up to it. The air out here, beyond the Wall, was different. The word that sprang to Edie's mind, oddly, was *uncluttered*. No trace of smoke or of corn fuel. No cooking oil or perfume of a hundred different competing strains of cuisine. No musk of many bodies, bottled together in subway cars or tiny apartments or watering holes like O'Henry's. It was beautifully empty air, remarkable to Edie for its surprising neutrality.

There were a few standing structures down the opposite direction, away from the interstate, but they were empty, dilapidated; the overhanging roof on the thing that looked a bit like a fuel station had collapsed completely into a pile of rubble, and the windows on the attached structure were shattered. Edie felt an urge to walk down that way—she wondered what other damage she'd find, what story it would reconstruct—but now wasn't the time to wander. Or wonder. And Jesse was eyeing the relic of a restaurant with enthusiasm.

"Cracker Barrel Old Country Store," he read. The sign was faded but still fairly clear, brown print on a yellow backdrop. "What a goddamn riot."

He strode across the parking lot, and Edie hustled to keep up, but he stopped to hold the oak double doors open so she could pass through. "Milady," he said.

Edie sighed. *I love him,* she told herself. *I do. I do.*

The store inside smelled oppressively old and musty in contrast to outdoors, despite the evidence of regular and recent cleaning. There was a faint odor of burned wood and of something fleetingly but recognizably musky or uric—maybe the promised chemical toilets, maybe the lingering scent of the rats and raccoons that would have bedded down here in the years of the store's abandonment. Andy wasn't exaggerating, though; the store was remarkably well preserved. And remarkably . . . strange. Where to begin? Where to lay her eyes? There were obvious gaps in the wares, items that had been lifted over the years, or thrown away because of rot, or chewed up by animals, but still, everywhere she looked, junk: piled up on tables, strung by wire from the ceiling. A bicycle, marked Schwinn, dangled above her head; elsewhere hung other items, each random and not just old but used-looking: a battered aluminum fuel can, tennis rackets, a gas lamp, a rusted mailbox. Stuff that would have been antique by the early twenty-first century.

At eye level was the merchandise. The table facing the front door displayed a set of plates glazed with the old American flag pattern. Nearby was a pyramid of once-white boxes, each marked with the faded, peeling images of the product they contained: "Elegant Christmas Angel," the photographs depicting porcelain yellow-haired women wearing ruffled blue gowns, their faces blank and unsettling, red lips rounded like a sex doll's. A display of yellowing cardboard, slumped with dry rot, advertised "Music by Today's Top Artists Only $14.99," and Jesse, wagging his eyebrows at her, flipped through the slim square packages and read names and album titles aloud. "*Mercy on Me* by Alan James Flint. Never heard of him. Get a look at the costume."

"He was a country singer," said Edie, thinking of her father and the music he'd always played in his pickup truck. "That's the kind of thing they wore."

"Albums," Jesse said with a laugh. "Can you imagine? What an arbitrary way to put out songs." He flipped to another disc, mouth tucked around the nozzle of his juice pouch, and Edie wandered to the next table. More plates, though these were merely decorative, edges scalloped, resting on little gilded easels. They were printed with a portrait of a long-ago British royal family and their handsome children. She stared at the image until her vision blurred, imagining the person—the people—who would patronize a place like this, an Old Country Store, but also cared enough about the British monarchy to purchase a commemorative plate in their honor. It made her suddenly and inexplicably sad.

When she was sixteen, her high school class took a field trip to Washington, DC, to tour the old American capital landmarks, some museums, various memorials. The centerpiece of the trip was supposed to be the Memorial to the Lost Republic, a two-acre park, flanked on both ends by infinity pools symbolizing "the shining seas," with fifty sculptures, each completed by an artist from every state of the old republic. Edie and her classmates were given some nominal assignment—choose a sculpture, document it, describe it, analyze its significance—but most of them spent about five minutes taking pictures and jotting down notes in their tablets, then gathered in clumps out of the teacher's line of sight to talk and smoke. Edie and her best friend, Sasha, had staked out a good hiding spot behind the Kentucky sculpture, which was an abstract representation of the log cabin where Abraham Lincoln was born, and passed a joint back and forth. *The sculpture is significant,* Edie had gigglingly written in her report, *because it is shaped like a box and boxes contain things like important ideas and memories.* She got a B+.

She hadn't felt anything at the Memorial to the Lost Republic. The old United States was long gone—*c'est la vie*—and the people who had known the people who died in the epidemic or got shut out-of-zone were long gone, too, with the exception of a couple of senile old crones who were interviewed each year on the local news feeds. Only now, contemplating this cheap novelty plate, did Edie feel a stirring of what she was probably supposed to feel at the memorial. So many people gone. A whole way of life reduced to a roadside novelty.

She wasn't sure she wanted to look around anymore. She didn't know if she had the stomach for it.

"Jesse," she said. "Hey, I need to go to the toilet."

He was holding what looked like some kind of an old-fashioned puzzle: wooden, triangle-shaped. He moved a plastic peg from one hole to another, removed the peg he'd jumped, and paused, then cursed. He replaced the jumped peg and moved the other peg back to its original position. "Umm?"

"Bathroom," said Edie.

"I'll be right out here," Jesse said without looking up. He moved another peg. Edie noticed that his Stamp wasn't in its designated holster-pocket and was instead jutting out of the hip pocket of his microsuit. "Ten feet away. Just yell if you need me."

"You sure?"

"I'll be fine," he said. "Go do your business."

He'd missed the point again. But there were plenty of people nearby, and she didn't suppose that the chemical toilet would be tick central. She hoped not.

The bathroom smelled strongly of cinnamon deodorizer and, under that, the chemicals. The shit. It wasn't a place you'd want to linger, and so Edie made a beeline for the first empty stall, not registering, until she was unzipping and hanging her bottom over the toilet seat, that Anastasia, who had been examining the reflection of her bare stomach in the mirror over the sink, was not wearing her microsuit.

"Uh, Anastasia?" she said. "You OK out there?" She finished as quickly as she could and arranged her microsuit back into place, heart pounding. Lifting a shaking hand to her waist, she felt for the hard line of the Stamp in its pocket. "Anastasia?" she repeated.

"I'm fine," Anastasia said with a tone of casual distraction. When Edie snagged the Stamp and exited the stall, arm raised at the ready, Anastasia caught her eyes in the mirror and laughed. "Seriously. You can put that away."

"You're not wearing your suit." Edie let her arm drop. The suit made a pool around Anastasia's boot-clad feet; she hadn't even stepped out of it. Her boxer shorts were pulled down a little, exposing the ridges of her hip bones, and her tank top was rolled up to rest under her breasts.

"I gave the room a once-over," Anastasia said. She picked up something from the countertop and ripped it free from a paper sleeve. A syringe. "For all the difference it makes."

Edie hadn't talked to Anastasia much during the weeks of training. Why? Edie couldn't say, though she had hardly noticed at the time their disinterest in each other, had found it natural, unremarkable. But it was strange, in retrospect. Women were a minority in the excursion group. Anastasia, thirtysomething, was the woman closest in age to Edie. And yet, for some reason, these facts had driven a wedge between them rather than bonding them. Edie tried now to reconstruct her first impression of Anastasia, the flutter of quick observations and judgments that had snagged in her semiconsciousness before she had a chance to second-guess them. Initially, she'd been uneasy. Anastasia, with her athletic build and long honey-colored hair (the cruelest sacrifice to the shears, in Edie's opinion), had looked at a room's distance like a potential rival, the kind of woman Jesse might fix his gaze upon. Closer, that anxiety dissipated. Anastasia's age became more apparent in her freckled face, the lines around her mouth, an almost unnoticeable softness (to eyes less hungry for fault than Edie's) around her jawline. Her chin was too long, her chest too flat. So then it was superiority Edie felt. Confidence in her own beauty and youth. And finally, though she'd acknowledged no dislike at all, having nothing real to base it upon, she had sensed the falling away of it when Anastasia linked hands with Berto, leaving in its wake amiable indifference. *Married,* some part of her had noted. *Older than me. Not as pretty.* Unworthy of her jealousy. Unworthy of her notice. Maybe she was exaggerating, being hard on herself, but she burned now with the shame of it.

Shyly, Edie took a couple of small steps forward, still looking at the mirror and not directly at Anastasia. "Um. What are you doing?"

Anastasia pulled a plastic cap off the end of the needle with her teeth and spit it out on the bathroom floor. "Heroin," she said. Catching Edie's look in the mirror, she laughed and shook her head. "Fertility drugs. I'm having my eggs harvested right after we get back in-zone."

"OLE lets you bring those out here?"

"They didn't have any choice if they wanted my money." She lay the needle tip at an angle against her stomach, slid the point under the skin, and depressed the button, biting her lip with a little grimace. Then she pulled the needle free and sighed. "I'm almost forty. I can't go on hiatus for eight weeks."

"So why come at all?"

"You're just full of questions," Anastasia said.

"Well, it's the question I've been asking myself."

"And I bet my answer's the same as yours. My man." She said it in a jokey way, *my mayun*. "He wanted a last great adventure before I started chaining myself to the exam table. Well, really, so did I. To be fair. My preference would have been Iceland or something, but it's cool. He drew the long straw." She pitched the empty syringe into the wastebasket, hunched over, and grabbed the rumpled microsuit, wriggling into it and pulling the zipper to her chin. "Hood, you think?"

Edie touched her own head. "I'm not taking any chances." She realized, embarrassed, that she was even still wearing her goggles, but her embarrassment didn't motivate her to remove them.

Anastasia winked and donned the hood. Her amber eyebrows were just visible. "These things are ridiculous."

"Better than the alternative," Edie said.

"Are they? I'm dubious. But I suppose they can't hurt."

"So you must really want a baby," Edie said, abruptly, unable to stop herself. "To be putting yourself through all that."

The sly smile fell off Anastasia's face. "We've been trying for four years. It's a fucking nightmare. So yeah, I guess I want one. My advice, if you think you ever want to do it, is do it now, while you're young."

"I don't want children," Edie said. She ran water to wash her hands, thinking with a quiet fury about the unfairness of—well, everything. Everything.

"Even better," Anastasia said. "It's a shitty world, anyway. See you on the bus." She slipped out, and Edie cranked the paper towel dispenser, dazed, unaware until she'd done it that a pile had folded back on itself several times. Ripping the end loose, she dried her hands, remembering, for some reason, how excited her mother would always get when Edie took her out to Sunday supper, a treat they indulged in once or twice a month, depending on how good

Edie's tips had been. Her mother would spend the week up to the outing thinking through restaurant possibilities—did Edie think she'd want the Chinese buffet, or Positano's, or maybe that cute café downtown, where they'd once gotten the handsome waiter who brought them free dessert? (They never got that waiter or free dessert again; that had been a singular day, a magic that would never repeat itself.) The meals themselves always pleased her; never did she complain about the food, about bad service. It was all delicious, all delightful. She luxuriated in it the way a child would, and sometimes Edie would be grumpy enough to feel annoyed at her, but mostly, her mother's moods were infectious. Her mother had made Edie see the good in a shitty world.

She trashed the damp mound of paper.

Jesse was waiting just outside the door with his arms and ankles crossed, a pose of false calm that went rigid as soon as Edie exited. "What happened in there? You fall in?"

"My stomach was bothering me," Edie said, which was the right thing, because she knew he wouldn't press her. Ten months of dating, and he still ran the shower whenever he had to use the bathroom for a number two.

"You just had me worried is all." He pulled her close and kissed the top of her head, their microsuits making rasping sounds against each other.

"I'm fine," Edie said. "Everything's fine."

And that's when the screaming started outside the restaurant.

Five

Marta's husband's sudden interest in legitimacy was not actually so sudden, in retrospect, but it took her by surprise nonetheless. Oddly, it troubled her. She wasn't exactly thrilled with the turn her life had taken, as his wife—had never imagined, marrying him, that she was signing on to be the first lady of a crime boss—but in the world of Atlantic Zone's dark underbelly, its secret economies, his power at least had its limits. So, too, did his ambition. If David wanted to be *legit*, he must be seeing his way around those limits.

There were the parties he wanted her to host at the house, the dinners out to five-star restaurants where groups of four or six or eight, never more, perched around tables set on daises, or tucked into lavish back rooms. Men in fine suits. Silent, beautiful women in couture gowns. Marta knew who some of these men were. David's dealings with politicians weren't new; he'd long depended on greasing the right palms as a way to get the outer-zone contracts he needed for his business fronts, or to encourage legislation friendly to his business interests. But this public socializing was very new, and so, too, was David's manner in these meetings. He was polite, deferential—even obsequious. She had never seen him listen so intently without asserting his own strong opinion. She had never seen him *agree* so readily. And when he did speak, the things that came out of his mouth bore little resemblance to what he said at home, when he was alone with her, or when she overheard him conferring with his most trusted inner circle. At the parties and dinners, he said things like, "Well, all the science points to this tick thing getting worse before it gets better," and, "It's clear that the smart funding is going to the Wall." He said, "Now's the time to circle the wagons, not spread out. Gulfers and Midwesterners are already attempting border crossings. We have to shut all of that down while we still can." He nodded gravely when one suit bloviated at length about the importance of penalizing feticide like any first-degree murder, despite the fact that David had, Marta knew, taken care of a little problem Enzo got himself into out on the coast. He hadn't told her about doing this, much less asked for her advice or permission; she'd overheard a conversation between father and son during the boys' first Christmas vacation visit home from college. "You need to start wearing a goddamn raincoat," David had said. "I'm not paying to get another girl flushed. Do you understand what I'm saying? Need I spell out for you the alternatives?"

"No, Dad," Enzo muttered. "I mean, yeah. I understand. You don't have to spell out anything."

Was this when she started using the Salt? It was not long after, at any rate, when the boys packed their suitcases, lavished her with kisses and promises to call, and drove back to Wilmington to finish the academic year. Enzo, the younger twin (by three minutes), had once been *hers*, had told her everything: about his school crushes, the bullies, the embarrassing "sticky dreams," about the times his father scared him or shamed him. They were coconspirators. And now, what did she know? Enzo hadn't come to her with this problem. She couldn't have fixed it for him if he had. But still. It wasn't just that he'd had sex, or been careless, or even the abortion. It was that calm, cowed, *No, Dad*. He knew the alternatives. He accepted them, easily, as part of his reality, his privilege and burden as David Perrone's son. Marta had, all these years, convinced herself that the boys had been shielded, protected. They didn't know. They weren't tainted. She was a fool.

Now, at these dinners David wrote old-fashioned checks (required by law, for political donations over fifty thousand credits) in smiling, dramatic shows. And when he handed them over, he held them in his grasp for an overlong moment, still smiling, and extracted some promise: the golf game, the drink at the club, that weekend retreat to Casinolake. Driving home from these dinners, or closing the door on the last guest at their home, he would mostly sulk in brooding silence. Every now and then—over a final nightcap, or as he and Marta turned the sheets down on their bed—he'd let loose with some rant about "that fatass" or "that idiot," or he'd say, "Deek's wife's aged about a decade since the last time I saw her" or "Wonder who Sagong thinks he's fooling with that half-rate rejuv job." Empty, bitter insults. If Marta asked questions—"Why are you having to deal with him?" or "What did you say it was he does at the magistrate's office?"—he waved her off or ignored her entirely.

Then there was Helle. A year ago David had introduced her to Marta as "new to my staff, a consultant." More strange words out of his mouth: *staff, consultant*. The woman who extended a chiseled, long-fingered hand to Marta was fortyish, vaguely Nordic; she had bladelike cheekbones and dark blond hair, worn straight and cut blunt at the shoulders—broad, strong shoulders. Beautiful. Like a supermodel just past her prime. A lover, Marta assumed, put on the payroll as a way to keep her busy and flattered, or as a formal courtesy to Marta, so that her constant presence wouldn't serve as an outright humiliation. But as the weeks passed, Marta wondered. Maybe Helle was a lover, but she wasn't only that. She was doing actual work for David, though the nature of that work still wasn't entirely clear. Helle spoke to David the way only a few of his capos did: firmly, even roughly, at times. She got up in the middle of meals to take calls, came back, gave David a look: *You're going to want to hear this*. It was revealed, offhandedly, that she had worked until recently on the president's staff. *The president's*. "As in Glenn Nichols?" Marta had asked David, perplexed. "*That* president?"

David had shaken his head, exasperated. "Is there another?"

But, like the situation with Enzo, Marta was the last to know, the last to put two and two together. Still the fool. This evidence all mounted, and it wasn't until David announced the "legit" deal and Marta's impending trip beyond the Wall that she started to understand what all of this might be building toward. David didn't just want money. Or power. He wanted to be visible. He wanted a platform.

On the morning she was to begin the OLE training camp, David sent for a car and offered, magnanimously, to accompany her on the ride. "It will be nice to have a little quiet time together."

Marta, warily, had agreed.

The city, its familiar contours, rolled by outside her tinted window. It was early, not yet 6:00 a.m., and the streets were mostly empty in this posh area of town, and the only unshuttered businesses were the corner coffee shop, the Greek diner, and the bagel shop that David called "the Jews'": *Heading down to the Jews' for a bagel and lox. Want anything?* Today, they didn't stop. Marta's stomach was a cauldron of churning acid, and she popped another antacid, swallowing just enough water to get the pill past her throat. It slithered through her chest like a stone.

"I know what's running through your head right now."

"Do you?" Marta asked. She couldn't keep the sarcasm out of her voice.

"I do," David said. He was looking at his tablet as he talked, scrolling past feeds with his thumb. The orange-gold band on his right hand, emerald nestled in its center, glimmered. "You're thinking this is an exile. You're being shipped off. Discarded. You're thinking, 'David isn't taking care of me anymore.' Am I right?"

Marta shrugged. "Not exactly."

David ignored this. "The first thing you need to know is that

David is still taking care of you. David will always take care of you. Trust me. OK?"

Her forehead prickled with heat, and she reached into the open mouth of her purse to tweeze the edge of the plastic bag she'd brought. If she threw up, she'd blame the nerves. *But don't throw up,* she told herself.

"OK?" he repeated.

She nodded, closing her eyes against another wave of nausea.

"The second thing I want you to know, or think about, is this: I want you to see what you're doing, what I'm asking of you, as something other than an exile. Don't even see it as hiding out. It's a mission. It's a job you're doing to help out your husband, for your sons' sakes, and the implications of it could be huge for us."

Marta licked her dry lips and swallowed. "OK," she said.

"Now you're just trying to placate me." His light tone belied a strain of impatience. "I want you to really hear what I'm saying. This trip gets you out of town at a delicate time, and that's good. But it also means that you can do an important job for me. I want you to watch Wes Feingold. I want you to come back and tell me what you think of him. His interests, his weaknesses. Whatever you can find out."

She could have laughed. "You seem to think I have special skills," she said. "First I'm some kind of great outdoorswoman, and now I'm a spy."

"Well, you're being silly now. Because you're angry. And I understand that." He was being nice. Studiously so. Marta had a sense, after almost thirty years, of how far she could push David without blowback, and she knew he wouldn't want to start a fight with her now. Because he was so close to unloading her. Because he wanted something from her. "But you do have skills. You're a warm person. People want to talk to you. Why do you think I bring you to all of these business dinners?"

"Because I'm your wife?"

David laughed. "Well, that's no requirement. These guys bring girlfriends half the time, leave the wife at home."

Marta saw the threat as well as the flattery in what he said. "You could bring Helle."

"You think Helle's my girlfriend?"

Marta shrugged again. They had left the city now, were rolling past the first ring of housing complexes—old subdivisions, with names like the Estates at Mercy Glade and Timber Ridge Homes, now chopped into multitenant units—that extended west of Greensboro until petering out about a hundred kilometers from the border. Any closer, and the vibrations off the Wall would rattle your dental fillings. Or so Marta had heard. She'd never experienced this herself, had never driven even this far west of the city, but she supposed she soon would.

"Helle has many gifts, but I wouldn't count being warm and disarming among them. Also, she isn't my girlfriend."

"What a relief," Marta said flatly.

He was silent, and she sneaked a glance his way. He'd set the tablet on his lap and was now giving her his full attention.

"You're a smart woman, Marta. What is it you think I've been doing this year? What do you think has been happening?"

Marta pulled her hand from her purse, from the plastic bag she'd been tweezing, and picked at a nail. "You've set your sights on something. Something political."

"Not just something. Everything."

"What's that mean?"

"I don't do things halfway," David said. "David Perrone goes all in."

A moment passed between them, one of those awkward moments where Marta thought and discarded as absurd the obvious thing, *president*, and then tried to think of what else might be "everything," and as she did this mental work, and registered the expression on her husband's face—this man she'd taken almost thirty years to unknow—she saw, finally, that *president* was it.

"But . . . why?"

"Because I want it," David said. Then, almost as an afterthought: "I'd be good at it."

"What do you even believe in?" Marta asked.

This question seemed to catch him off guard. He went back to his tablet, punched in a message with his thumbs, stabbed Send. "This would be good for us," he said, still typing on his tablet. "For Sal and Enzo. I want them to inherit a legacy. Not just an estate. This is going to be it."

Marta shook her head in wonder. *President?*

"So stick close to this Feingold kid. Be his friend. Be his mommy. Come back with something I can use, OK?"

It had been years since Marta had gone on a long drive, her childhood since she'd been on a bus, and she had forgotten the way it felt to be more than a few rows from the front seat, the gentle, almost imperceptible rocking of the cab, the bouncing of the shocks each time the bus topped even a gentle rise in the road. Then the vibration off the Wall, and the smell of the landfill, and the steady stream of chatter from Wes, who was a dear—really, she was happy to listen to his sorrows, David's directive notwithstanding; flattered that he felt he could share them with her—but who was oblivious to her mounting nausea, so that Marta was almost grateful when that pop singer shamed him into silence with his silly song. The moment she was standing on solid ground again, she promised herself, she'd do better. But on the bus, sweat pricking at her temples and in the well of her clavicle, a finger of pain pressed into her sinuses, she wanted only silence.

So when the bus finally did pull into the parking lot outside the old restaurant, she told Wes to go on in without her—she'd follow when she had a moment to gather herself—bypassed Andy and Tia and their offerings of food and drink, and retreated behind the cover of the bus, where the newly laid blacktop stopped and the lawn (mown sometime in the not so distant past) began. Alone, finally, she started heaving, vomiting only water, then nothing, and then she sat back on her bottom, in the grass, and wiped her face with the sleeve of her microsuit, catching her breath.

A few minutes later, Wes found her. "Marta? You OK?"

She had rested her crossed arms on top of her knees, and her forehead against her forearms, and so she nodded down into the dark well her body had created. The gentle pressure of Wes's palm resting on the crown of her head was soothing. "Just carsick," she said. "I'm not off to a strong start, am I?"

"You need to rest and get something in your stomach," Wes said gently. "I'm surprised I'm not down there yakking with you. I'm a yakker, if you haven't noticed."

She remembered, lips twitching into a small smile, his race out of the gymnasium that first day of their training. "Well, I guess I shouldn't be wallowing down here on the ground." She looked up and offered Wes her hand. "Give me a lift?"

He pulled her to a stand, and they walked together back to the open expanse of the parking lot. "I know that Andy had some bottled waters along with the juice. Do you want one?"

"Sure," Marta said.

"Just hold tight. I'll be right back."

The irony, she would think later—and this was perhaps something to be grateful for—was that she was feeling good in this moment, almost as good as she'd felt a few hours ago, when she and Wes first boarded the bus. The nausea was gone. The air was fresh on her face. Her lower back and hips, which had been getting a little tight during the long drive, were warming up. She thought she might even have an appetite, finally.

And then she felt it. The sensation. Unmistakable, as promised.

It began with a pulse of heat, down on the back of her leg, the fleshy part of her calf. Then, the itch: an itch that sank in roots, unfurled tendrils, a growing thing that was in motion, as if blown by a breeze, or underwater, and something in the itch reached well beyond her leg and into the core of her, so that she felt it in her chest, her belly button, her sex, and her first clear and furious desire was to take the back of her leg and rake it across the rough pavement until it bled. Her breath hitched, then caught. She looked up. Wes was coming toward her with a bottled water. All she could do, it seemed, was widen her eyes at him, and she had time to think, *I'm going to just stand here and let this happen,* but then Wes seemed to understand, to inexplicably know, and he dropped the water and ran toward her, fumbling with his holster-pocket.

"Where?" he shouted.

Tears had started streaming down her face, but still, she couldn't speak. Couldn't breathe. She managed with a hand to motion, and Wes said, "Leg?" and she rasped, "Yes," and then her weight somehow was on her left knee and her palms, her right leg stretched out behind her as if she were at her Pilates class, doing lunges, and someone was holding her shoulders, rubbing the back of her neck. She felt her trouser leg being tugged up, a sudden slap of cold air on her exposed skin.

"Do you want me to—" A male voice.

"No," Wes said. "I've got it."

Then the pain. At first it was satisfying in a strange, vaguely shameful way: incinerating the itch, severing the tendrils that had reached into those other parts of her body, isolating the agony to this one point of flesh. But then it was as if her heart pumped a surge of blood across her body, a wave that passed hot salt through the burn, and then the agony was more intense, immeasurably worse than the initiation Stamp had been. Her entire leg throbbed hotly, the pain unlocking her voice, and she wailed, couldn't stop herself, then screamed, the scream breaking up after a long couple of moments into croupy sobs. She collapsed onto her side and pulled her injured leg toward her chest, rocking a little. Someone, a woman, was still patting her head, making a shushing sound. Tia, she thought it was.

"Oh, Marta," Wes was saying. "Marta, I'm so sorry."

She blindly put out a hand toward his voice, and when it grasped hers, squeezed it hard. "No," she said. "You did well. Thank you."

She could sense that a crowd had gathered around them. She understood why—if another had been the first, she would undoubtedly have been standing and staring stupidly, just like the others—but that did not make it less invasive and mortifying. "Please make them go away," she whispered to Wes, and he said, "Back off! Give her a minute!"

"Where the fuck did it get on her?" a man yelled. He sounded panicked.

"Where do you think?" said Andy.

"But you said this place is monitored for ticks," the pop singer said. Marta wasn't yet looking up, but she knew his voice—the entitled bravado and its underlying warble of fear.

"I also said to be on guard and be near your buddy," Andy said. "Wes, that was some fast and decisive action. Good job."

Wes bobbed his head in acknowledgment, face pink. Marta managed to smile at him.

Andy squatted down beside her, forearms resting on his knees. "Marta. How're we doing?"

"Better," she said.

"Tia will get some ointment and a bandage on it, and we can give you ibuprofen for the pain. So tell me, where did this happen?" An odd look flickered across his face. "This really shouldn't have happened," he murmured, more to himself than to her.

Marta pointed. "I went in the grass over there to throw up. I sat down for a minute."

Tia began dabbing the Stamp site with an alcohol-soaked swab, and Marta winced. "How about your suit?" Andy said. "This is an unusual first contact point. Did you have your pant leg tucked in? Socks and boots, the way we discussed?"

"I thought I did," Marta said. "But it could have pulled loose. It must have. I just don't know."

Andy patted her knee. "I'm not trying to give you a hard time. This was probably just bad luck, but if a burrowing can be avoided, we want to avoid it. So remember, tuck in. Check and double-check. You've gotten a hard first lesson."

Tia finished applying the bandage and tugged Marta's trouser leg down. "Like this," she said, pulling the microsock up over the leg opening, then re-lacing the boot so tightly that Marta felt like she was going to lose circulation to her foot. She grunted thanks.

Wes helped her up, and she brushed grit off her bottom self-consciously. The wound, bearing now the pressure of her standing weight, throbbed, but she tried to draw back her shoulders, reclaim a posture of dignity. If she still had hair, she would be brushing it carefully into place now.

If only David could see her, could know what his selfishness had already begun to cost her. *David will always take care of you,* he'd said. What a joke.

Wes's face was drawn with concern. "Do you want to go inside and sit? Go to the bathroom?" He had picked the bottle of water back up, and he handed it to her. "You should at least drink this."

"All right," Marta said. She uncapped the bottle with a trembling hand and took a long sip, then held it against her forehead. "My God, Wes. That was worse than I expected. That was much worse than the initiation Stamp."

"It was?"

She nodded. Felt her face crumple. "Oh, goodness. I thought I could do this. I don't know if I can do this again. I thought it would be better when I got through it the once, but it isn't. It's so much worse."

Wes didn't offer her a platitude in response.

Marta hugged him. Unlike Sal and Enzo, he was about her own height—she didn't have to stand on tiptoe to reach his shoulders—but there was something comforting and familiar about the awkwardness of his young man's embrace, the yeasty smell of perspiration on his neck, and she squeezed him fiercely. If she needed proof that God was looking out for her on this trip, it was this boy. Only now did she fully grasp the importance of a buddy—how much of your well-being you were handing over to that person.

Her heart finally slowing its insane rhythm, Marta pulled back. Wes would feel even more dragged down by her now, she thought. Oppressed by her need. But he grabbed both of her hands, smiling a little, and gave them a cheerful little shake. "You and me," he said, as if he'd read the tenor of her thoughts. "We're a team. It's going to be great. OK?"

Marta nodded weakly.

"No, seriously. It is. OK?"

"OK," Marta agreed.

"Then let's go check out this weird restaurant."

They started inside, cutting a path through the prying looks of their fellow travelers, but Marta felt better already. Stronger. She vowed to herself then that her allegiance would be to Wes, not to David, and she wouldn't do anything to betray him. She'd protect Wes with as much ferocity as she'd protect her own sons.

Six

Two a.m., according to the glow-in-the-dark dial on his watch, and Wes didn't feel the least bit sleepy. Even Marta, who had spent the first two hours after lights-out rolling over to her side, then her stomach, then her other side, with the steady regularity of a rotisserie chicken, was now breathing deeply beside him, inflatable pillow tucked between her right ear and her bent right arm, left arm curled up close and tight to her chest, as if she were cold. Wes pulled her blanket up over her shoulder. The tent, to him, was cozy, even a little stuffy, and his mattress, which Andy had cautioned against overinflating, was so thin that he could feel every bump in the ground unless he lay flat on his back and perfectly still. It was like trying to sleep floating in a swimming pool.

Across the campsite there were sighs, coughs. Sniffling—maybe allergies, maybe soft crying. He dozed a while, then jolted awake to a low-pitched gasp and a sudden blaze of light a dozen paces outside his tent. He waited, tense, Stamp clutched in his right hand.

"Oh," said a man's voice. There were a few hitching breaths. "Oh. Sorry."

It was that Jesse Haggard—he knew it. Of all the blowhard, cowardly assholes he could have drawn as company for a trip like this.

Marta groaned and rolled 180 degrees this time, so that she was facing Wes. "A bite?" she asked hoarsely.

"False alarm," said Wes.

She propped herself up on one palm and smooshed her face with the other. "This is the longest night of my life," she said. "I thought I was too old for long nights."

"Seems like you caught a few Zs," Wes said.

"A few." She leaned over stiffly, snagged the loop on her water bottle, and unhooked the cap. "I was having a nightmare about my husband."

She hadn't said much about her husband, and Wes hadn't asked, had just assumed he was someone dull, a lawyer or a corporate executive, and that Marta had taken the trip as an extreme response to empty nester's syndrome. "What was it about?" he asked.

"I'm already starting to forget it." She took a gulp and lay back down. "I'd gotten bit again. I remember that much. And he was trying to use the Stamp on me, but he kept missing the spot and burning me other places."

"That's horrible," Wes said.

"In the dream it was painless. It was just the idea of it. Knowing I was running out of time, and what would happen when it did." She shivered and clutched the blanket to her neck. "What about you? You sleep?"

"Not really," he said. He ducked his chin down, surreptitiously, he hoped, and sniffed his armpit. He was starting to smell himself already, and it made him anxious. Back home, he showered twice a day, once when he rose, once just before bed. He had, in preparation for the excursion, tried during Boot Camp to skip his evening shower, but he found himself cheating, rationalizing to himself the harmlessness of a fast five-minute scrub the way an alcoholic might argue that beer isn't the same thing as liquor. So now he was here, with no practice living unwashed, and the novelty of the situation hadn't jolted him out of his neuroses, as he had assumed it would. Worse, he was starting to feel the press of his bladder. He moved the muscles down his groin, assessing, and yes, there it was—that first faint cramp of fullness. He shifted his hips. Contracted the muscles in his groin again. The prickle. He would never be able to sleep, needing to urinate. Or knowing that he might soon need to urinate.

If he were sharing the tent with another man, he'd just relieve himself into an empty bottle. But next to Marta? Good lord, no way.

"I need to go to the bathroom," he said, understanding the absurdity of his word choices but not willing to say "take a piss" or "take a leak" in front of this woman who could be his mother (if his mother were nicer and warmer and generally more motherlike). "Is that OK? I won't be long."

"Of course," she said, switching on the lantern. Its bulb glowed cool and blue against the tent's white walls, and they both squinted.

"You'll want to run the vac as soon as I'm outside."

"I know," she said. Her voice had thinned slightly with impatience, but she put her hand on the remote to let him know she was ready.

"Okay," he said, and she hit the Open button. He wriggled out as quickly as he could, and when his second foot hit the ground behind him, the flap drew shut with a snap and the vacuum motor whirred softly. The air outside was chilly and clean; he exhaled a white cloud. Seven tents formed a circle on smooth, even ground, ground that had been worn to mostly dirt by the traffic of multiple excursion groups. The last embers of their evening fire, which Andy and Tia had built in a rock-lined depression that was sooty from previous use, were long dead, still faintly redolent of the greasy soy dogs the campers had roasted on sticks (these also from a well-used, fire-hardened stash stored in a utility shed just downhill and out of immediate sight). There had been throughout the evening an air of forced cheer, everyone in the group trying too hard to demonstrate their enjoyment, to prove to one another, and themselves, that the risk and the expense were worth it. *Look at that sky!* people kept saying. *You don't see stars like that in the zone!* And, *Smell that mountain air!* Berto and Anastasia, a married couple, both lawyers of some stripe, in their late thirties—fitness nuts (Wes realized that calling someone a health nut, even in his own head, was a bit hypocritical), lean bodies knobbed with long muscles—had started singing an old children's camp song as the group worked on pitching their tents, and it caught sluggishly on with a few of the others, Jesse Haggard pausing (while his girlfriend worked on, Wes noticed) to play his ukulele and over-sing the lyrics.

I'm a mean old man in a little old shack
With a mean little dog and a duck—Quack! Quack!
And a pig and a horse and a cow—Moo! Moo!
And a mean old wife who died—Boo hoo!

And all the while Mickey Worthington, one of the pair of pudding-faced lawyers Wes had a hard time distinguishing from each other, was still moaning from the pain of a particularly nasty bite-Stamp combo, this one on the tender flesh of his neck, just left of his Adam's apple. His buddy, Lee, who had panicked when the moment came to administer the Stamp, silently erected their tent on his own, occasionally throwing looks of guilt and annoyance at the weeping man he'd so humiliatingly let down. It had been a bad episode, halfway on the trail between the drop-off point and the campsite, and it was Andy, finally, who pushed the shocked Lee out of the way, gripped Mickey's head roughly in his left arm, as if he were shouldering a watermelon, and depressed the trigger. "You need to get a fucking grip," Andy said when he released Mickey, eyes lit with fury. It wasn't clear if he was talking to Mickey, Lee, or both of them.

"I think the itching stopped before you got to it," Mickey wailed, wiping his sopping face with a sleeve.

Andy stood with his hands on his hips, breath short. "You'll know soon enough," he said. The humor, the gruff-but-reassuring paternal pose—both were gone. He seemed simply annoyed and disgusted, and the look he flashed at the rest of them in turn was no warmer. "I'd suggest y'all wear your microsuits properly. The calf, the neck—there's no reason why these bites should have happened."

But then the anger slipped from Andy's face. "Look. I'm sorry. You've just got to understand that I've been through this more times than I can count. You can't treat every bite as cause for a nervous breakdown."

"I don't care," Mickey said. "My partner didn't do his job. It's not right." In his distress, a twang had slipped into his voice. It was like seeing him naked, and Wes flushed to the roots of his hair.

"It's probably fine," Andy said gently. "The odds are on your side. Remember that."

"It's not right," Mickey said. His face shined with tears. "You pay as much I did, you expect some things."

That had been his refrain, on and off, for the rest of the evening. He skipped dinner. As soon as Lee had pitched their tent, Mickey retreated into it. When Andy called to him irritably, "You know, Lee still needs a buddy out here," Mickey yelled, "Fuck Lee!"

Wes crept past Mickey and Lee's tent. It was silent and dark, and Wes hoped Mickey had exhausted himself into a deep sleep. He'd tested everyone's nerves tonight with his whining, Wes's, too, but you would have to be soulless not to pity him a little. To have your buddy fail you like that right out of the gate. You'd have to be soulless, and you'd have to be pretty confident in the brave stoicism of your own hypothetical future self. Wes wasn't feeling that confident.

There was a glowing gibbous moon in the sky, bright enough that he could watch his footing as he put some distance between himself and the tents. He had a pocket-sized flashlight, but he refrained from switching it on yet. Everyone was sealed up in a tent—he'd hear their door vacs if they stepped out—but he felt sheepish and exposed out here. His digestive cycle was off; he hadn't emptied his bowels in nearly two days. Andy had recommended that they answer that particular call of nature only in the daytime, unless it was an emergency, so that they could scan the area around them in full light. Good advice, of course. Wes imagined a nightmare scenario in which he'd have to try Stamping his own bitten ass or—worse—scream until someone (Marta? Good lord) could come and do it for him. But he needed privacy, and now that he was out here, this might be one of the few opportunities he'd have to get it.

He shuffled downhill another twenty paces, until the camp lights were an abstract glow without an identifiable source, and shined his flashlight on the ground in front of him. There was a rich, musty smell in the air that he'd never before experienced, a damp smell, decaying but totally alive, that rose from the layers of fallen leaves that created a soft carpet underfoot. He liked it. Not enough, yet, to make him glad that he was about to take his first open-air dump, but enough to ward off some of the despair that threatened to level him—a despair that was bigger than Wes, a despair that felt as real and risky as it did because he could sense that the other travelers were on the verge of it, too.

He stopped beside the wide trunk of a tree and looked around. Here was as good a place as any. He put the penlight between his teeth, letting the beam fall on the ground, and started clearing a circular patch of leaves. When he'd done that—no sign of ticks, not that they'd be easy to spot with these shadows—he used the edge of a small, flat rock to dig a shallow depression in the earth. Then, heart racing, he quickly swung around, unzipped the back of his suit, and dropped down on his haunches, letting his back rest against the tree trunk for balance. This was a thousand times worse than using a public toilet. A million times worse. He waited, sweat slicking his temples, his thighs and ankles beginning to quiver under the strain. He was, he realized, terrified.

Jesus Christ, he thought. *What am I doing? What have I done?*

After the spectacular failure of Virtuz, and the eighteen months of his life he'd lost to what amounted, now, to a digital garbage pile,

Wes was left feeling a little cynical. And more than a little panicked. There were rumblings among the shareholders; the little upstart virtual money co-op everyone had been dismissing just last year, Bank On It, was gaining an indie following that would soon spill over into something . . . well, not so indie. Bank On It's nineteen-year-old founding CEO, Chetna Sai, was the newest tech darling, a tattooed, eye-riveted punk pixie whose innovation to social banking was a brilliant little spin on crowd-sourcing, in which groups of people could mobilize behind a charity, or a movie project, or a politician, whatever, and do a Collect Invest, with to-the-second updates on interest gained and market trends. One Bank On It Collect Invest had earned, in a month's time, enough profits to bankroll the campaign of Compassion Party presidential candidate Guy Wiley, who was now poised to make an actual showing in the November elections. Why the hell hadn't Wes thought of this? Why, instead of screwing around with the idea of virtues, hadn't he been coming up with ways to let money do what it does best: create power? The key was to find the right vessel for that power. *That* was capitalism at work. *That* was how a person could hope to be both a good person and a successful one.

Should have, would have, could have. It was all pointless, this speculation—throwing good time after bad. And Pocketz was still on top, by a big margin, a *huge* margin. The job now was to stay there.

So, though he hadn't been lying to Marta when he told her that his breakup with Sonya had been the catalyst for this trip beyond the wall, there was another reason he was now swinging his ass over a bare spot in the ground, trying to convince his bowels to move. Wes had given in to his board on their oldest, most chewed-up bone of contention: Pocketz Corporate Collaborations. The trick for pulling off this new venture, they'd decided, was to start slow and start *smart*: whatever product they came up with had to have an emotional appeal, so that Wes's investment in it would feel more like an event, epic in scale, than a crass opportunity. But it also had to have the potential to make a pile of money. "We're not talking prosthetic legs for orphans," his COO, Sandy, had said. "More like—pharmaceuticals. But that's risky because it's so regulated, and there are liability issues out the wazoo."

"National defense? Weapons?" suggested his CSO, Cedric.

"God no," Wes said. "Can you imagine how that would play with Sai's crowd?"

"But he has the right idea," Sandy said. "Weapons, no. We don't want this getting torn apart by factions. We don't want that to be the headline. But people want to feel safe. Everyone wants to feel safe."

"Clean energy," Wes said. "What's that solar micromotor company called? I saw them profiled on *Sunday Salon*."

Sandy shook her head. "I don't think that flies either, Wes. It's political and it's boring. People see that technology as basically here already. They take it for granted."

"But it's not here," Wes said. "Not in any form that people can afford to use yet."

"That's the problem. We need something that the average Pocketz user can purchase. A grand idea with some kind of concrete form you can actually own. They want to be able to take a picture of it and post it to their feeds. You can't post a picture of a solar micromotor."

And then, like that, Wes knew. This was the way his brain had always worked, and it was a superb gift, one he tried to never take for granted.

"Protection from ticks," he said firmly. He knew from the spark in Sandy's eye that he had nailed it, and he continued, getting excited. "Sprays. Microsuits. Detectors. That sort of stuff. We present it as an investment in freedom. But we make sure the trends feed recirculates some of those old stories about the tick population growing, the projections that our Wall will be infiltrated by such and such a year. None of those products are regulated, right?"

"Nope," Cedric said. "Government doesn't touch 'em."

"Ticks have no faction," Sandy mused. "I mean, not that I know of. There's probably some group of ticks' rights nut-fuckers out there." She laughed—three bars—then grew pensive. "I guess we might get thrown into the Wall debate, though, and that's a PR loser, any way you slice it."

The Wall debate, the goddamn endless Wall debate. Build it bigger, expand the TerraVibra perimeter? Tear it down? And just as the conversation would seem to be dying out for a while, another Wall tax hike would get shoved through Congress, and the whole cycle would start again.

"But a suit—that's about individual choice," Wes said. "Wear it outside the Wall, if you want to travel. If you ever need it inside, God forbid, you've got it. I really think this might be insulated from the other debates. Or even bolstered by them."

Sandy nodded. "You may be right there. And the usefulness of all these gadgets is hard to gauge, from what I understand."

"That's a good thing," Cedric said, noticing the look of worry that appeared on Wes's face.

"Definitely a good thing," Sandy agreed. "I think it's brilliant, Wes. It makes a statement. It communicates an interest in the greater good. It hits on big ideas without making big promises. I say we do studies on the major forces in the market, put out some feelers, draw up profiles, and make an approach."

Wes, feeling like he'd ceded some essential part of himself—and dear God, there was a relief in that—had patted the conference table and stood. "Do it, then. Keep me updated."

The report had been ready in a matter of days. There were three sizable, suitable companies specializing in mass-market tick-protection products. The biggest, Circutex, had all of the Atlantic

Zone government contracts, as well as contracts with the other North American zones and several international ones, and a handful of lucrative out-of-zone corporate contracts, including the beef supplier for Burger Blitz. They specialized in industrial microsuits—spacesuits, Wes thought, looking at a sample his staff had brought him. They wouldn't photograph well at all. The next company, Field and Shaughnessy, had a product called NO-BITE, available in cream and spray forms, that touted a 95 percent effectiveness rate against miner ticks and other invasive insect species. It had been around for a long time, nearly sixteen years, and though Wes suspected the company wouldn't mind a splashy new corporate partner to bring new attention to an old standard, he just didn't see the opportunity in that for Pocketz. That was an easy pass.

The last possibility—a somewhat mysterious umbrella corporation called Perrone Inc.—was the most interesting to Wes. Its owner, David Perrone, seemed to have a lot of capital, and his investments through Perrone Inc. were all over the place, literally and metaphorically: a chain of quick-lube shops, with locations both in Atlantic Zone and Gulf; a few outer-zone factories; an upscale Salon and Spa in Raleigh; and maybe some Wall fortifications subcontracting, though Sandy admitted that the dotted lines on those were harder to trace. Perrone himself had gone over the last three years from having, astoundingly, almost no significant digital footprint—there were Pocketz accounts in his wife's and sons' names, an expired Mi Familia account, a few other weirdly vague, random hits in the feeds—to quietly emerging online and in life, forming a picture of a cautious family man with powerful ties to some of the heaviest hitters among conservative zone leadership. "I think this is a person," Sandy told Wes, "who is primed for some kind of a positive, public coming out."

It sounded almost sinister, when she put it like that, though Sandy saw this as a mark strongly in Perrone's favor.

Perrone Inc. also owned a start-up called SecondSkins, a microsuit marketed not in bulk to out-of-zone contractors but mostly in direct sales, via the web, to individuals, regular folks—well, *rich* regular folks. SecondSkins had a few bulk contracts. One was an outer-zone touring company, Outer Limits Excursions; Perrone Inc. was an investor. They also sold to some specialty shops in Gulf Zone, where tick infestations cropped up a few times a year, always causing a big panic and leading to quarantines, refugee relocations, riots. It was a strange product. People who could afford a SecondSkin Elite Microsuit (3,500 credits) were largely not the people who would ever be in a position to need one. But Wes's antennae tingled as he reviewed the report. OLE was a relatively new operation, and there were others cropping up, here and in other zones. It was natural for a kind of large-scale claustrophobia to set in once the panicked post-eradication years were behind them, mostly. People were going to want to travel. Take calculated risks.

Hell, Wes would buy one. As a sufferer from what his psychiatrist called "health anxiety," his own personal flavor of OCD, Wes was always on the lookout for ways to shield his sad sack of fallible human flesh from disease and injury.

Talk of the Wall was abstract to him. It had been there for the entirety of his lifetime, would be there, he believed—political debates notwithstanding—long after he was gone. He'd never seen it in person. Never traveled within the span of its perimeter, felt its vibration. It was like God: you took its existence on faith, mostly, and you assumed it meant you well. Or you didn't. But if the scientists were to conclude tomorrow, for sure, that it was an enormous expenditure of energy with no real environmental impact, outside of an increased rate of earthquakes and (some claimed) brain damage and hearing loss to those living and working long-term in its shadow—say they proved it, and the Greens had their way and razed it—well, these forces were beyond Wes's power of influence. They were certainly beyond the average Atlantic Zoner's power of influence.

A suit, though—your own little personal Wall within the Wall, another barrier between your body and global disaster? Well, Wes knew there would always be a market for that. Especially if it came (as SecondSkins really should, he thought) in a fashionable, figure-flattering cut, with customizable colors and patterns. This was a product Wes himself could stand behind. Could stand *in*.

And that's when the last piece of his plan had clicked into place. It was kind of mad, really—and he'd have to do a hard sell to his board and shareholders to convince them the risks were worth the reward. But what better way to make a show of solidarity with SecondSkins (Wes had already assumed his approach of the company would be successful, that they'd feel they'd won the corporate lottery) than for Wes Feingold, Pocketz CEO, to travel out-of-zone wearing one?

Oh, would he have hatched such a scheme if he weren't still smarting from the breakup with Sonya, if he didn't want a drastic change of scenery—a drastic change in himself? No. In that way, he'd been honest with Marta. But he couldn't let slip his other motives, not to Marta and not anyone else on the excursion, either. If he were to be bitten in the next three weeks (*Think positive, Wes!* he told himself, his personal "Wall" now bunched awkwardly over his bent knees), the SecondSkins partnership was a bust. Pocketz would have to find some other investment opportunity. But OLE was taking every precaution to make sure Wes *didn't* get bitten, that the deal would go through as planned and Wes would return from the excursion triumphant, ready to describe his experiences and boldly announce his intentions to invest in SecondSkins Gen2, a comfortable, attractive microsuit available at a price point (1,000 credits) even the middle class could afford.

He was almost comfortable now, thinking through the particulars of the launch, when he heard something: voices. Coming not from the camp but from the woods out beyond him.

At first he was just embarrassed, and he pulled up his underwear and zipped back into the microsuit with frantic, haphazard motions, face so hot that it felt like a giveaway, an ember in the dark. Then his instinct was to hold very still, to let the voices pass him back to the camp, so that he wouldn't risk startling them and having to explain himself.

His flashlight, still on, had dropped into his lap. He switched it off and held his breath.

There was rustling in the leaves, a broad movement of at least two bodies, then a pause. Wes peered into the direction of the noise, but his vision had been seared momentarily by staring at the flashlight beam.

"How do we do this?" Wes didn't recognize the voice. It was male, raspy.

"Fast," another voice said, and this one he knew. "I'll point you to your positions. I'll point out the tents with the VIPs." There was more murmuring, this too muffled for Wes to distinguish. "—under no circumstances. Got it?"

A high-pitched voice, maybe female: "Yeah."

The raspy voice again. "Yeah."

Maybe there was another. Wes couldn't be sure.

"Let's move, then," Andy said.

Wes could see a bit better now, well enough to distinguish the shapes of four figures. Moonlight glinted off something on one of their shoulders.

It was the barrel of a gun.

He pressed himself against the tree, biting his lips to contain his rapid breath. There had been time in his other life to wonder, with casual curiosity and even a little yearning, what he would do in one of those situations that were always cropping up on the news feeds: convenience store holdups, back-alley attacks, home invasions. There had been incidents in the last couple of years of PickPocketz, thugs with clever technology for getting past the company's complex security firewalls, even the coercion monitors, and forcing victims to authorize untraceable large-scale credit transfers. *What if that were me?* Wes had wondered when these stories crossed his desk. Was he a fighter or a fleer? He was the kind of man—diminutive, neurotic, cerebral—that people automatically assumed was the latter.

But it was not as simple as all that. For now, watching those four dark figures stride toward the corona of light at the top of the hillside, he was neither. He was an animal, paralyzed. And yet he was also his fourteen-year-old self, trying to find a logical explanation, an algorithm for creeping, weapon-wielding menaces who belonged out here in the darkness, who didn't actually mean him and the rest harm. *People from the Wall. Government. Something they forgot to tell us, some problem they're here to notify us about. That's why Andy's with them.*

He thought about earlier, when Andy's mask—was it a mask?—of gruff good cheer slipped. What was left when it did: the contempt.

Fight. With what? He reached down and retrieved the flat rock he'd used to dig his makeshift latrine. It felt utterly inconsequential.

Run. Where would he go? Andy had the food, the shelter, the maps. The guns.

And Marta was still up there.

He gripped the rock, cast his gaze around. A stick. A bigger rock. Something. *Anything.*

They were almost to the top of the hill.

Go.

He moved before he could doubt himself, hunkering low to the ground, trying to make his steps light. The damp, rotten smell of the leaves was very close now, no longer pleasant; he was dragging himself through the stuff, would probably have ticks crawling all over him, but what could he do about it?

There was a brisk clapping at the camp—sharp, but reasonable. Sane.

"Lights on, folks," Andy called out. His voice was so steady, so full of the old reassuring charm that Wes had come to associate with him, that he doubted himself for a moment. Had he seen—heard—what he thought he had?

The glow at the hilltop brightened. Wes could hear murmuring, grumbles.

"I'm going to need you all to step out of your tents. This'll only take a minute or two. Got to do a quick head-count."

Wes took a few more steps, careful to stay behind the cover of a stand of trees. He could see the clearing now. Andy and the three other figures from the woods were there. They had positioned themselves evenly around the circle of tents and slightly behind them, each wearing a mining light that blazed so brightly that the people emerging from their tents could only blink in dazed confusion, holding up their hands as if to blot out the sun. In this way, they didn't see at first what Wes saw: that Andy and the other three figures were armed with high-powered assault rifles, which were leveled at their torsos. The first to notice was Wendy Tanaka. She screamed, and Andy stepped forward and unceremoniously clocked her with the stock of his gun. Her cry was cut short, and she fell in a heap at his feet. Her brother made as if to go to her, but Andy swung the rifle in his direction, and Ken put both hands in the air in surrender. The others quickly followed suit.

"That's one," Andy said flatly. "Rest of you, line up. Get in the light where I can look at you."

The others—Tia was among them, Wes noticed, and her expression of shock was either genuine or a damn good acting job—did as he asked, hands still high in the air. Andy walked from one end of the line to the other.

"All right," he said. "Where the fuck's Feingold?" He went to Marta. "Feingold. Your buddy. Where is he?"

"I don't know," she said. Wes could see the fright in her eyes even from his hiding spot. "He got out of the tent to relieve himself. Maybe ten minutes ago."

"Check the tent," Andy said to one of the goons, motioning.

The goon checked. "Not there," he said in his raspy voice.

"Fuck," Andy muttered. He pulled a revolver out of his back waistband and pointed it at Marta's head. "Yell for him. Yell for Feingold."

She looked at him blankly.

Andy signaled to another of his goons, the woman. "That one," he said, pointing at Mickey Worthington.

"Wha—?" Mickey began.

The woman pulled Mickey out of line by the collar and forced him to his knees.

"Put him out of his misery," Andy said, and she unholstered her own revolver and shot him in the temple.

Wes jolted as if he himself had been shot, every nerve in his body sending out an electric charge. In shock—he couldn't seem to make himself move—he watched as Marta, Andy's revolver still pointed at her forehead, screamed, "DON'T COME BACK, WES! DON'T COME BACK! DON'T COME—"

"Now her," Andy said to the woman. She grabbed Marta by the arm and pushed her to her knees. Wes stumbled forward.

"No!" he said. "I'm here. I'm—" His chest was heaving now. He couldn't catch his breath to say the word.

"The golden boy," Andy said. He smiled. "The guest of honor. Violet, bring him over to our little powwow."

The woman approached, miner's light on her forehead a blinding eye. As she dug her fingers into Wes's shoulder he got a look at her, and it took every bit of what was left of his will for him to keep from gasping.

She could have been twenty or sixty. She could have been of any race. The skin on her face was taut with bands of purple scar tissue, and her neck pulled down, froglike, from a sagging bottom lip. One of her eyes was shriveled to a blind asterisk; the other, bright blue, glinted at him from under a painful-looking hood of puckered flesh.

It was the worst suffering he had ever seen in another living person, suffering beyond the realm of what he had understood was possible, and he would have been moved to pity for her if the gleam in her visible eye hadn't been so full of loathing.

"You think of splitting," she said into his ear—her breath was nauseatingly sour—"and I'll kill every person here. Starting with your old girlfriend. You understand me?"

"I understand you," Wes said.

"Gather round the fire, folks," Andy said. "I've got one more speech to make."

Part Two

The Shaman

Seven

One of Edie's clearest early memories of her father was of nighttime, a long car ride home, the blur of yellow streetlights outside her window. They—her father, her mother, Edie—had been somewhere exciting, probably to the beach or Old West Mountain; Edie could reconstruct this now because there were photos of her at about three and four, some with her bottom sunk in the sand and a plastic pail tucked between her knees, others of her riding a ski lift seated next to her mother, both of them grinning and waving to the person behind the camera, her father, who had been seated in a separate chair ahead of them. Her father was almost always behind the camera. Edie's mother, whose vision was very bad, and corrected to something slightly better than blindness by a combination of laser surgery and heavy lenses, could never take a good photo, and so the only pictures Edie had of her father were out of focus, off-center, or obstructed by a finger or some object in the foreground. In them, her father seemed more ghost than person, a mythological creature, a Bigfoot: large, brown, always in motion.

So what she had were her memories of him, like this early one, the one that began in the car, with the sense of abstract, sleepy joy, blinked out into unconsciousness, and ended when she was briefly awakened to her father unbuckling her from the car seat. He lifted her easily in his strong arms, put his handsome face close to hers, kissed the tip of her nose. "Beddy-bye, baby girl," he said.

What a pleasure, a luxury, to be carried to bed by someone you loved and trusted, someone with the physical power to move you gently and tenderly, to slide you between cool covers at the exact moment you slid back down into sleep. Edie imagined this with longing as she rushed, heart thumping in the cold darkness, to gather her few personal belongings and help Jesse collapse their tent and its vac system into a package small enough to be stowed in its custom microfiber pack. They were muttering at each other: instructions, curses, corrections. *It goes this way. No, goddammit, you've got to unfold it and refold it the other direction. Did you unlock the brace before bending it?*

"Thirty seconds," Andy shouted. "If you're not ready to move when I say move, you leave the shit behind. Leave it behind, and you sleep outside."

With a final surge of panicked adrenaline Edie was able to see what they were doing wrong, the corner they had neglected to tuck in, and she made the necessary adjustment, then shoved the tent into place and zipped the pack closed with a gasp. She shouldered it quickly because she knew Jesse wouldn't think to in time, slung the strap of her pack of personal items around her neck, and stood ramrod straight. In another situation, another life, she might have offered a sarcastic salute to punctuate her success. Now, she only dropped her hands to her sides, palms open, and kept as still as she could stand to. Mickey Worthington's body was still slumped in the shadows of the dwindling campfire, generous bottom resting on his socked heels, his head—what remained of it—cheek-down in a pool of blood. *It's not right,* she could hear him wailing. *You pay as much as I did, you expect some things.*

Andy approached her. "Hands in front of you," he said. His eyes didn't meet hers.

She complied. They were shaking; she couldn't do anything about that.

"Cross your wrists."

She did, the inside of her right wrist resting on the inside of the left, but he roughly turned her left hand over. "Like that," he said impatiently, as if she were stupid, and then he looped a neon pink zip tie around her wrists, cinching it so tightly into place that her skin was pinched, even under the protective layer of her microsuit. When he moved on to Jesse she relaxed the weight of her arms, experimenting. Let her hands drop, and the zip tie sank even more painfully into the skin on the back of her left hand. But holding her hands up, she could tell, would quickly put a strain on the muscles in her upper arms and shoulders. She wiggled her hands around, testing for give. There was none.

Jesse's shoulder brushed hers. "This is fucked," he said. She could hear the panic in his voice. "What the fuck are they doing? What do they want? Money?"

Edie peered as surreptitiously as she could at the disfigured woman who had shot Mickey. She was difficult to look at, and Edie could only imagine that she didn't like being looked at, and so Edie dropped her eyes—only to feel them dragged back upward to that unfortunate face, so riveting in its painful contortion. "I don't think so," Edie whispered. All the credits in the world couldn't help this woman, though perhaps a top-notch Atlantic Zone doctor could at least give her some grafts to make her face more pliant, or scrap that face and put on a new one, the way they did with people who were mauled by pit bulls or who walked into helicopter blades. And then, instead of this horror show face, the woman would have a slack moon-face, saggy eyes, bottom lip puckered like a newborn's. But that seemed unlikely, too. Edie guessed that this woman would rather be a horror show.

"Violet," Andy said, and the disfigured woman jerked her head around in response. *Violet?* Had Edie heard that right? Maybe he had said "Violent." Violet would be a name of almost cruel absurdity, applied to this woman with the gun slung across her chest, face singed of any of its femininity.

"Collect the Stamps," Andy said. "Check their bags."

She made her way around the circle of hostages, jamming her hand into holster-pockets and tossing the Stamps into an empty knapsack, then turning each traveler's knapsack inside out and picking through the contents, leaving some items for the traveler to clumsily repack, tossing others into the sack with the Stamps, and—in a couple of cases—keeping her find. From Wes she stole a peanut butter–flavored power bar. From Anastasia—and this could almost stoke your sympathies, if you weren't being held at gunpoint by the murderous ghoul—she took a fine gold chain with a letter *A* charm, slipping it over her head with a little smile playing at her tendinous lips. There was such childlike pleasure in her gestures that Edie wondered if she wasn't perhaps a little touched, as her mother would have put it.

When the woman reached Edie, though, and started going through her bag, Edie revised her assessment. There was too much adult efficiency in her hands—pristine hands, unburned and even lovely, faintly freckled. The hands of a thirty- or forty-year-old. The hands quaked suddenly, and the bag slipped out of them; on instinct, Edie dropped her own bound hands down and managed to catch it.

"Thanks," the woman muttered, her blue eye touching Edie's for a fraction of a second. Then she shoved the pack back at Edie and moved down the line.

"Now, wait just a minute," Ken Tanaka said as Violet collected his Stamp. He was trying awkwardly to support his sister without the use of his bound hands, and Wendy, temple swollen and bleeding, looked only half-conscious. "Wait, now, how are we supposed to protect ourselves?" It was the most Edie had heard him say at once in the entire three weeks of their acquaintance.

Violet grunted in an amused way and tossed Ken's Stamp in with the rest.

"I advise you to stick close to the group," Andy said. "Behave yourself, and one of us might Stamp you when the time comes."

Edie found herself watching with interest when Violet approached Marta, wondering if Marta had been stupid enough to pack those diamond earrings.

"Bag," Violet said through her mangled mouth. Marta handed it over, shaking so much that she seemed to be playing keep-away with Violet, and finally Violet snatched it and turned it upside down. Edie expected something good, given this display: the earrings, or a contraband phone, maybe. But there was nothing of note, nothing even worth stealing: the usual changes of underwear and socks; bug spray; ibuprofen. Violet paused over what looked like a Smokeless, still shrink-wrapped in its Canteen packaging, and seemed to consider taking it, perhaps only on principle. But in the end she left it in the dirt and went on to the next person, and there was something oddly frantic in the expression of relief that crossed Marta's face. The woman must really like her NicoClean.

They were marched out of camp in twos, Andy taking the lead, Violet in the back, the other two armed men roaming up and down the line to shout in the ear of anyone who flagged with exhaustion, or to send a warning poke with the business end of their rifles into the lower back of anyone who—what? Seemed to be thinking of escape? Edie was pretty sure that escape, at this point, was on no one's mind. Not if the person had any sense. It was pitch-black out—even the stars were obscured now behind a scrim of cloud cover—and they were heading in the opposite direction of the road they'd come in on. Unarmed, unStamped, wrists bound, they'd be completely helpless away from the company of their guards.

Jesse, beside her, huffed with exertion and affront. "I can't believe this," he muttered. "I mean, how stupid can they be? I have people. I'll be missed. This will be all over the news."

"Not for another three weeks," Edie said tiredly. It was amazing the effect that an extreme situation—a little out-of-zone travel, a bit of hostage-taking—could have on a relationship. Jesse's presence was intolerable right now—his voice, reedy with terror and steeled by entitlement; his rank fear-sweat; the way he kept veering into her, as if he had a flat left tire. She took some perverse pleasure in reminding him, "No one's expecting to hear from us for three more weeks."

There was nothing for a full moment but the sound of their breathing and the rustling of their boots through the leafy groundcover. Jesse bumped into her shoulder again, and Edie pulled roughly away from him, exhaling with a frustrated whoosh of breath.

"Shit," Jesse said.

Hours passed. Andy and his men gulped from canteens, their headlamps tilting up toward the sky, spotlighting the canopy of limbs, then dropping down to blind a parched, covetous, staring traveler. Edie learned to stop looking. She retreated within herself and half-closed her eyes. The lamps became a guiding blur. She was in a locomotive of shuffling bodies. The muscles in her calves and shoulders burned—her right shoulder, bearing the weight of the collapsed tent, was a half-numb misery—and her heels erupted with blisters in her stiff new boots. The line stopped three times at the sound of shrieking. The first time it was Tia, who'd tripped and fallen flat on her face, unable to catch herself with her wrists still zip-tied. Violet dragged her roughly to her feet. Sometime later, a Stamp was administered. Another bite was, Andy declared, not a tick. Edie talked herself out of sounding the alarm at various itches, trusting that Andy hadn't been lying about the unmistakable nature of the miner tick bite, even if he lied about everything else.

He had told her to leave, though, hadn't he? He had told her to leave, and she'd said something virtuous about wanting to take care of Jesse. Jesse, who was muttering curses under his breath with every step, just loudly enough to touch Edie's weary ears and no one else's. The weight of their gear was hanging around *her* neck, but still he muttered.

She was taking care of him, all right. Good God, it was almost funny.

Sometime during the never-ending march, the light started to change. A soft grayness crept in, defining the shoulders of the person in front of her. Feingold. Fifteen or twenty minutes later, she could read the label on the back of Wes's microsuit:

SecondSkins

"When Seconds Matter"

Made in Indonesia

"OK, stop," Andy called, the first loud noise in hours, startling most of them out of dazes. Edie nearly ran into Wes.

"Listen up," Andy said. "There's a firebreak up ahead and two vehicles. I want you in them in five minutes. Go where we point. Find a place to park yourself. There are more asses than seats, so get ready to get friendly with each other and put your crap wherever you can fit it. Questions?"

They all blinked dry, swollen eyes and tried not to attract this new Andy's notice.

"Great," Andy said. "Fantastic. If I'd have known that all it would take to shut you whiney fuckers up was a four-hour hike, I'd have done it a lot sooner."

This was bad, but Edie couldn't help but feeling a bit of hope at the thought of sitting down. Even if she had to ride the whole way in Jesse's lap. Because vehicles meant they were leaving the woods. They were going somewhere with fuel. Roads. Roofs. Right?

The vehicles, a car and a van, were ancient-looking, the metal shells barnacled with painted-over rust. One of the men waved Edie and Jesse to the van, on the heels of Wes and Marta. This man was tall and bone-thin, with olive skin and long black hair—it fell to the middle of his back—pushed back from a high forehead. Midforties, maybe. No head cover, no microsuit, just a canvas button-down shirt and pants, navy blue but cut like military fatigues. Despite his lack of precautions, his visible skin was much clearer than Andy's: a few older-looking Stamp scars on his face and neck, a few more on the backs of his hands. Edie thought she'd heard Andy call him Joe. He was, for no good reason, the one among their captors she'd deemed kindest, most susceptible to pitiable displays, despite the fact that he wielded his weapon with as much casual brutishness as the rest of them. Maybe it was because he talked the least. The big hulk of a guy wearing the bandolier—his name was definitely Randall; Edie knew because she'd heard Andy hiss the name with impatience more than a few times during their endless hike—was a yapper. Body of a Rottweiler, personality of a Yorkshire terrier. He'd be a bully and a coward, both, Edie thought, and if she could get a stolen moment with Jesse, it would be wise to warn him to stay off that one's radar. Jesse, she imagined, would be exactly the type to push Randall's buttons.

But Joe, maybe-Joe, was waving Edie and Jesse to the van, and when the travelers had assembled beside it, he slid the side door open, releasing a terrific squeal that made them all flinch. Edie and Jesse, at the back of the group, were the last to board. There were two and a half bench seats, all occupied hip to hip, or hip on hip, the floor space crammed full of packed tents and knapsacks. The interior was rank with body odor and bad breath, and Edie's optimism about the van dissipated when she scanned the expressions of her fellow travelers, hoping to find a face generous and open enough to impose upon. *Can I suffocate you with my body and bags?* They were understandably stony, hostile; they'd shifted their anger from their kidnappers to Edie and Jesse, and Edie thought of every ride she'd ever taken on the school bus, every tray of lunch she'd brought to a table in her high school cafeteria, and—inevitably—of the one time she'd flown in a plane. That was back when she and her mother moved from Gulf to Atlantic Zone, seven months after her father's death, and they'd only had the money to fly Group Economy, where the seats were first-come, first-served and the storage spaces an unregulated free-for-all, notorious for provoking fistfights among customers trying to sneak in extra carry-ons. But this was worse.

Jesse paused on the step behind Edie. "Aw, no," he said. "How are we supposed to make this work? There isn't any room left."

"Figure it out," Joe said. "Or stay here. It's no matter to me."

Edie cast a desperate look to those who were seated. "You all know we can't do that. Please don't make us do that."

"You better hurry," Joe said.

There was a pregnant moment—probably seconds, felt like much longer—when no one moved, no face twitched with understanding or even sullen resignation. Then Wes Feingold, seated in one of the narrower nooks toward the back, lifted his hands. "Here," he said. He exchanged glances with Marta, who nodded a fraction. "We'll make room here."

Which was progress, but Edie thought the declaration meant about as much as "I'm going to make this woman disappear" would have. Wes and Marta had maneuvered their packs off their backs and into their laps, an operation not easily reversed because of the zip ties. They were seated next to the Tanakas. Wendy appeared to have already fallen asleep—Edie marveled at the fact that she'd made it this far—and Ken appeared unwilling to shift over even a millimeter. His jaw was a rigid L, his shoulders set as if expecting a blow.

"Please move over," Marta said to Ken. Her tone of voice was low and polite, but steely. There was something else to it—a command, even a threat. And to Edie's great surprise—what threat could this petite woman in her fifties really pose?—Ken shifted to the left, adjusting Wendy's unconscious body so that her weight was centered on one hip and her torso rested heavily against his.

"You get up," Jesse said to Marta, and Edie winced at his rudeness. He motioned. "You sit on him, and Edie'll sit on me."

"Now wait a minute—" Wes began, but Marta shushed him.

"It's fine," she said. "It probably wouldn't work any other way."

The door rattled shut behind them. So Edie and Jesse hunched and slipped their packs over their heads, then arranged themselves in the back between Wes, Marta, and the Tanakas. The air was close and hot. The van chugged loudly into motion, and Edie, perched clumsily on Jesse's knees, straddled the tent between her legs, leaning on it for balance each time the van hit a bump in the road, which was often. Jesse weighed only twenty pounds or so more than Edie, most of it in his length, and he grunted in an affronted way whenever the bumps sent Edie's weight back onto him. *Bastard,* she thought. Her head kept knocking against Marta's, and she muttered an embarrassed "sorry" each time, but Marta patted her knee as if to say, "Don't be."

Time inched forward. The windows, which ran only along the driver's side, were caulked shut and grimed with filth, so it was impossible—from Edie's vantage point, at least—to make out where they were going, what they were passing. Trees and more trees, probably. Every now and then a wedge of bright sunshine pushed through a window to land hotly on a face or arm. Someone sniffled and hiccupped. Edie's hips and calves burned with the strain of keeping her upright, and she thought about the exercise ball she used at night (in another life) when she watched her webshows, the one that was supposed to firm up her core and better her posture.

She strained to peer over her shoulder, planning to ask Jesse if he still had his watch, but Jesse's face was slack with sleep. She caught Wes's eyes on her.

"Must be nice." His words dripped with contempt.

"Jesse can sleep anywhere," she said. Dared to say, because she knew that a sleeping Jesse was beyond the reach of her voice, beyond anything but a scream or vigorous shaking. "He's like a child that way."

She could see Wes wanting to retort to that, to take the opening she'd given him, but he only smirked. He was, Edie was beginning to think, the kind of man who wanted to be capable of greater nastiness than was really in his nature.

"He always does this before concerts," she continued. She was whispering, but the bodies around her were silent, yearning for distraction. Her words, she knew, were going into every ear. "A thousand people in the audience, and they're all chanting his name, and Jesse's flopped out on a couch backstage. Then his manager yells, and he's up, he's ready to go." She was bragging out of habit, in the way she used to do in those heady days of their relationship after the abortion, when—freed of the crushing burden of pregnancy—Edie's life shifted surreally from bartending, grieving, and suffocating worry into months of extended play: travel, good food, late-night jam sessions in Jesse's penthouse apartment, where nothing more was required of her than to lean on the arm of a sofa, consider the twinkle of the city outside the expanse of windows, and nurse a whiskey and cola, watching Jesse and his bandmates cover old folk songs, spirituals, Irish punk, weird, wonderful stuff that they would never play at a paying show. That was all done now. Those easy days were gone. She was so tired she could barely keep her head up, and Jesse's bony knees were digging into her thighs, and she was wan with the van's rough motion.

Suddenly, they stopped. The travelers started murmuring to one another: "Can you see anything?" "How far do you think we went?" Jesse came gasping violently awake, as he did in bed whenever Edie tried nudging him into a position where he wouldn't snore. He'd have dumped Edie into the floorboard if there was any empty floor for her to land upon. "Wha—?" he gasped. "What? What? Where are we?"

"No one knows yet," Marta snapped. "Be quiet."

The van's door rolled open.

The idea of walking was as appealing to Edie now as the idea of sitting had been to her mere hours ago. The van and car were parked along the shoulder of a road that, while in significant disrepair, was paved. Wooden poles, reaching a couple stories high, were driven into the earth at semiregular intervals, leaning under the freight of snarled green vines that dripped down, touched the ground, and rolled off in waves across the surrounding hillsides. Kudzu, Edie recalled. The scale of it—how much the green sea of vines had consumed—was beautiful and terrifying.

Andy, who was starting to look as exhausted as Edie felt, had merely waved his gun in a direction: uphill. The incline wasn't bad yet. The sun had risen above a mountain peak, penetrating the mist, and it was quite beautiful out, actually, almost cheering. The trees that weren't netted in kudzu, whose crowns penetrated the leafy mass and reached toward the blue sky as if gasping for breath, were red and golden—a version of the world promised on the Outer Limits feeds. People began, tentatively, to murmur to one another; to Edie's surprise, their captors seemed willing for now to allow it.

Wendy Tanaka had been a problem that led to another unexpected lightening of the tension. She couldn't walk more than a couple of steps unassisted, and Ken, with his wrists bound, couldn't do much to help her stay on her feet. A trickle of blood still pulsed from her temple, where Andy had struck her, and the captors—Edie had finally started thinking of them as such—had a fierce whispered conference as the OLE travelers watched warily on, bracing themselves for another matter-of-fact gunshot to the head.

Instead, Andy produced a pocketknife and started cutting zip ties.

"You and you"—he pointed to Ken and Berto—"see to her. If she can't keep up, carry her, or we'll leave her where she drops. Got it?"

The men nodded.

"The rest of you," Andy said. "I'll let you loose for now. Any trouble and I'll hog-tie and leave you in the vines over there. You don't want to test me on this. Got it?"

The rest of the group nodded eagerly.

When Edie's turn for release came, Andy wielded his knife quickly, grazing the back of her hand, but she could barely feel it—could barely feel anything below both of her elbows. The *pop!* of her zip tie flooded her with a pleasure so intense that she nearly collapsed. She lifted her arms, stretched, rubbed her wrists briskly, stretched again. Her fingers tingled, and her back cracked luxuriously. She unslung the tent from around her shoulder and shoved it wordlessly into Jesse's hands as soon as his were free. He grunted, slipping his head through the straps without comment. Now, she guessed, would be the time to run—but no one appeared to be up to it. Not even close. No, what Edie saw were ten slack-faced people, clad pathetically in fitted white bodysuits, each of them gazing gratefully at their unbound hands, their bruised and chafed wrists. When Andy began trudging ahead again, they all followed dutifully.

Wendy had one arm slung around her brother's neck and the other across the shoulders of the strapping Berto, whose wife, Anastasia, lagged behind the threesome, carrying Wendy's gear as well as her own. Edie, eager to escape Jesse for a few minutes, took two long steps to match her stride to Anastasia's.

"Want to pass that off for a little while?" she asked, motioning to the extra pack.

Anastasia looked at it, smiled a tiny smile. She was her husband's physical counterpart: long, slimly muscled, with the broad shoulders of a weight lifter. "Nah. Not yet, anyway. It isn't much."

"It might be down the road," Edie said. "So holler if you change your mind."

"Thanks." Their boots scuffed along the old asphalt with everyone else's. "I will."

"I'm embarrassed that we didn't really talk before," she said.

Anastasia gave her a confused look. "We talked—" She paused. "Yesterday. Feels like longer ago. But we did talk."

"At the training center, I mean," Edie said. "Well, I don't know what I mean. Just that it seems a shame now."

"Because they're going to kill us." She said this without inflection.

"What? No!" Edie hissed. "No. What do you mean?"

Anastasia crooked an eyebrow. "I guess you missed what happened to Mickey."

"Of course not," Edie whispered. "But what would be the point of all this?" She flapped her arms, trying to indicate the group moving in a sluggish mass up the old highway. "Why not shoot Wendy back there? Why untie us?"

Anastasia pointed to a figure a few feet ahead. "Feingold," she mouthed. Edie could barely hear her.

"Wes?"

"Don't you follow any of the alt-news feeds?" she whispered. "The Underground? ConspireWire?"

Edie wasn't even sure what an alt-news feed was, and she certainly hadn't heard of the feeds Anastasia had mentioned. She didn't even follow any of the regular news feeds, except occasionally Snark Park, and only that after she'd started dating Jesse. What a panicked thrill she had felt the day her picture appeared below a headline: "Jesse Haggard Steps Out with Bartender Girlfriend." The thrill had ceded to dismay when she glanced into the comments matrix just long enough to see that the biggest trending threads were "Appearance"—thousands of variations on "She's not that hot"—and what Snark Park called, charmingly, "Doability," where Edie had rated a 7 out of 10 on the "I'd FAP to THAT" meter, most of the comments animated with graphic porn snippets.

So she just shrugged. "I guess I don't read the ones you read," she said.

"Outer-zone insurgency groups," Anastasia said. "There've been rumors about them going back forever. You remember the plane crash at the Memorial to the Lost Republic, don't you?"

Barely. It happened before Edie had moved to Atlantic Zone, and there had been an information placard about the incident on her school field trip. Some nutjob in an antique Cessna. The plane came down off target, passing the central monument spire to land in the reflecting pool. Minimal damage to property. No casualties.

She nodded.

"So you know about the manifesto?"

It was like being in high school again. Pretend to have done the reading and fumble forward? Or admit her ignorance? She found she didn't have the energy to fumble. "I guess I don't."

"Wow," Anastasia said. "I'd like to move to the island you must be living on."

Edie bit back a sharp retort. "So, the manifesto? What about it?"

Anastasia dug a Smokeless out of her pack, looked to make sure Violet wasn't paying attention, and sneaked a quick puff. "He had this crude device on his plane. It worked kind of like an old cell phone. Basically, it was set up to send out one small data burst to the nearest networked device. When the plane went down, the phone grabbed a signal and shot its wad just before the crash. And then the thing got forwarded before the NSA could run a confiscation, though they did a pretty good job of discrediting it after the fact."

"But what was it?"

"Like I said, a manifesto. The guy said he lived in a village in east Tennessee. He said there were hundreds of people just in that one town and hundreds of towns just like his. He said the ticks were a government conspiracy. Cures for Shreve's had been suppressed. Anyway, he got a plane over the border somehow."

"Wow," Edie murmured.

"There are reams of intel about this stuff, all of it authenticated," Anastasia said. "There's no doubt people live out here. Probably whole communities of them. People resettled Chernobyl, after all. Whatever this is"—she waved her arms to indicate the pretty landscape surrounding them—"it sure isn't Chernobyl."

Edie didn't dare confess that she had only the foggiest idea of what Anastasia meant by "Chernobyl." "All right," she said, "but I'm still not clear on what this has to do with him." She pointed at Wes.

"The manifesto had a list of strategies for how outer Zoners would revolt. One of them basically amounted to economic terrorism, cutting off supply lines, setting fire to out-of-zone production units, that sort of thing. It happens a lot, actually. More than you'd think. A guy in my practice, he works for a biofuel company with half a dozen farms out here. They have to pay out the nose for security. Even so, there are a couple of incidents a year. Mostly just tickbit wackadoos hopping the fence and getting promptly laid out, but sometimes they do real damage. Or make off with a big haul of goods."

"So you're saying that these people are those people. The terrorists."

"They have to be," Anastasia said. "Andy knows who every one of us is. He knows what he's got in Feingold. He knows what he's got in some of the others, like the Tanakas. You know they're the Tanakas from the bioelectronics company, right?"

Edie didn't.

"She's the techie. He's a neurosurgeon. There's another brother that is a biologist or something, but he's not here for some reason."

"They're brother and sister? I thought they were married," Edie said.

"They put off a weird vibe, don't they?" Anastasia said conspiratorially. "But no. They're siblings."

"And you think these people are going to use them somehow. The Tanakas and Wes."

"I don't know what value they ultimately have as hostages, or whatever we are. The president would probably see us all dead before he opened the gates to the great unwashed, but those three have symbolic value, at the least. They're proof of a vulnerability. Or a lot of vulnerabilities. And that will scare people, which is probably the best weapon these people have got."

"They scared me," Edie admitted.

"You should be scared," Anastasia said. "Shit is getting very real. Berto and I have been bracing ourselves for this for a long time."

Edie looked over her shoulder back at Jesse, who caught her gaze, a pleading in his eyes, and lifted his chin in greeting. Something in her softened. He wasn't perfect. But he was what she had.

"What do you think we're walking into?" Edie asked.

Anastasia laughed, short and bitter. "You ever watch that show *Crater Plain*?"

"Never heard of it," Edie said.

"It's obscure. Comes out of Australia, and it hasn't really taken off here, which is kind of surprising because it's pretty good, smart but not too smart. Berto and I have a little group who comes over for viewing parties when the new episode streams." A sadness passed across her face. Edie could imagine Anastasia's house—all low horizontal lines, shiny metal, glass—and her friends, good-looking, successful. They're drinking red wine, eating little canapés, shouldering in companionably on a big sectional couch. Anastasia says, "OK, quiet! It's on!"

"The first episode starts after a nuclear war. The people who are left have all of these weird little powers. They can't make food out of nothing or draw water from a rock. Their powers don't guarantee their survival. But clumps of people complement each other. Like, the female lead can generate a perimeter of warmth. One of her love interests is resilient to radiation, so he can go foraging where others in their party can't. The other love interest is a telepath. Which has its down side, you can imagine, but it also means he can hear the thoughts of another group if they get too close, and he can tell if they mean well or not."

"OK," Edie said. Asked, almost. She couldn't tell where Anastasia was going with this.

"There are always two love interests in these things," Anastasia said. "A bad boy who's really a good boy, and a good boy with a dangerous streak. That's what makes the show addictive, and you need something, because it's just relentlessly awful, actually, people with their faces melted off and rape gangs and cannibals. There's this assumption that most people, if you strip society and its laws away, are capable of evil. I agree with that."

"That's just a webshow," Edie said.

"Yeah, maybe so." Anastasia shifted Wendy's pack to her other shoulder. "But don't kid yourself. These people shot Mickey. They didn't give it a second thought. They're herding us. I don't know what toward, but I can promise you it isn't good."

"You're so fucking casual about it," Edie said, fighting tears.

Anastasia was silent for a while. Edie could hear now the churn of arms and legs, the rhythmic rustle of pack straps against microsuits. The air, cool and moist, made her nose start to run. She could pick out a half dozen different whispered conversations. Some light talk: *How many kids do you have? Where did you grow up?* And heavier: *I'm starving. I have the shakes. Where do you think they're taking us?* Randall, who carried his gun in his hands instead of slung across his back, was holding forth to Joe, loudly, about some technical matter concerning the vans. *These old Jap cars run forever, but you can't work on them. I keep telling 'em and they keep saying yeah-yeah and not doing nothing about it. I know where we could—*

"I don't mean to be unkind," Anastasia said finally, "but I'm a realist. I don't get any comfort from pretending things aren't what they are." She looked at Edie shrewdly. "You're what. Twenty?"

"Twenty-six," Edie said.

"Well, close enough. You live in the reality you want to believe in. That's easier to do at your age than mine, what with the drugs and the fucking and all that fun shit. And hey," she said, putting her hands up in a warding-off gesture, "no judgment here. I miss the drugs and the fucking. Well, sort of." She took another secret Smokeless puff.

Edie couldn't think of a reply. She kept pace with Anastasia, wondering how she could exit the conversation politely, and then she registered the absurdity of that—of worrying about conversational politeness. So she slowed down, falling back into step next to Jesse.

"Making friends?" he asked.

"Something like that, I guess. She was kind of freaking me out."

"She has issues," he said. "She's crazy. She and her husband both. They're gun rights activists. Survivalists. Didn't you hear them talking at boot camp? Listen, if Andy and these people were going to do something to us, they'd have done it by now. You're with me. They know I have money. I have a public platform. We have value."

"OK," Edie said, tired.

"We have value."

There was something ahead, at the side of the road. A sign, large, close to the ground.

"Can you read it from here?" Jesse asked.

Edie peered ahead. "Not quite yet."

Another ten steps and the vague shapes of words fixed themselves into something faded but legible: "Ruby City Mine and Campgrounds." A half dozen meters more and she could also make out the words below that, in smaller typeface:

MINE FOR RUBY'S, SAPPHIRE'S, & MORE!!!!!
GEM CUTTING AND GIFT SHOP.
"A TREASURE IN EVERY BUCKET GUARANTEED."
CLEAN RESTROOMS & SHOWERS, LEASHED PETS WELCOME.
TURN R ¼ MILE AHEAD!

"Clean restrooms and showers." Jesse sighed. "I have a feeling that's out-of-date."

"You're probably right," Edie said.

But she was sure they'd take the turn when it arrived, and they did, onto a gravel road curving steeply downhill and around a bend, its destination out of sight. The events of the last day had taught her not to anticipate—not to hope that the next thing would be better. But she hoped anyway. She fantasized, even. Her feet, numb with fatigue, trundled forward, and she imagined being welcomed by a grandmotherly type with flour handprints on her thighs, and she's telling them that they each have rooms, and there's hot tea and warm bread just as soon as you're settled in. This was a terrible misunderstanding of some kind, unfortunate, but they'd be put on buses tomorrow and shipped straight to Quarantine.

A radio on Andy's hip crackled, making them all jump, and some unintelligible string of words issued forth. Andy unhooked the radio, depressed a button, and spoke into it: "Yeah, it's us."

They finished circling the bend and approached a break in the trees. As they advanced, the edge of a building came into view, and Edie started noticing a sound—steady, familiar, coalescing after a moment into something identifiable: moving water. By then the building, too, had revealed itself fully. It was small, one story. The siding looked freshly painted, and flowers—daisies—were blooming in clumps on each side of a bright yellow door. A sign above the door, in faded lettering, announced, "Welcome Prospectors!"

The door opened. A man moved his considerable bulk from inside to out, stooping to clear the lintel, and Edie saw that he was coarsened with age, skin the color and texture of old saddle leather, the hair atop his head and his brows and covering the lower half of his face a frizzy cloud of steely gray. He stood, she guessed, six foot five or six foot six, and he had a tall older man's hunch, broad shoulders, soft belly. He, like the guards, didn't wear a microsuit. Edie couldn't imagine him in one. Instead, his shirt and trousers were cut from the same heavy dark gray weave, softened with wear and washing, and leather suspenders framed the row of mismatched buttons marching down his front. This must be the man in charge, Edie thought—the man who would decide their fate.

When he spoke, his voice was unexpectedly soft. "Y'all be needing to go see June then, I guess," he said.

Eight

The camp stretched along both sides of a river that the tall man told them—mildly, as if he were leading a tour group rather than a collection of hostages—was the Little Tennessee. Marta noticed, as they followed the bank for a stretch, that the river was traversed by two footbridges. The first, a suspension bridge, was walled off with what appeared to be scavenged chain-link fencing, and it swayed alarmingly as a woman crossed with a large duffel bag hoisted over her shoulder. The second bridge, perhaps half a kilometer ahead, appeared newer and sturdier, engineered from something other than scrap metal and desperation.

Their guide waved to the woman with the duffel. "Morning," he said.

The woman looked at the group with undisguised curiosity. She, like their guide, wore what seemed to be the local uniform: colorless button-down shirt and trousers, suspenders. The cuffs of her pants were tight-rolled over thick, bright red socks and old-looking leather work boots. No microsuit. No tell-tale bulge of a Stamp. "Heavens to Murgatroyd, Curtis. This is them, then?"

"Seems so," said their guide.

"Huh," she said. Thoughtful, swinging her gaze from face to face, pausing, it seemed to Marta, longest on Wes's. Her own face was sun-spotted and lined, but she might have only been in her thirties—hard to tell. Rare that a person in Marta's circles made it past twenty-nine without some kind of tweak or polish. Her frizzy hair was tucked back in a ponytail, revealing a bare circle of scar tissue at her right temple. But it was an old scar, pale as milk, and Marta didn't see any others. "Well, then," she said. She dropped the duffel at her feet and dipped in a sarcastic little curtsy. "Welcome to Ruby City." The bag shifted, slumped, and a small dead animal slipped out. Squirrel or rabbit, something fluffy and brown. "Enjoy your stay."

"You know," boomed Lee from the back of the pack, the first time Marta had heard him speak since Mickey was shot, a moment that seemed distant but hadn't even been half a day ago, "that this one"—he pointed a shaky finger at the disfigured woman they called Violet—"murdered a man this morning. One of our group. No reason at all. Murdered him." Marta, along with everyone else, held her breath, aghast and impressed at his nerve. Violet's cratered face flushed dark, and her hand went up to the stock of her gun.

"Really," the woman said tonelessly. Her expression, unlike Violet's, lacked malice—but it was somehow worse than Violet's. This was a disregard that couldn't even muster passion. "Then I'd not piss her off, if I were you."

Violet laughed hoarsely.

"That's enough lollygagging," said their guide—Curtis. "See you later, Vic."

"See you tonight," the woman replied.

As they continued their walk, Marta amended her impression of the setting from "camp" to "village." A township had coalesced around what she assumed were the remains of the old Ruby City campgrounds: a cluster of a dozen or so small, cube-shaped cabins, all built with porches facing the river. The air smelled of wood smoke and crackling animal fat (the travelers' stomachs rumbled loudly in chorus). Outside one cabin, two men, shirtsleeves rolled above their elbows and aprons tied across their middles, worked in rapid synchronicity at a galvanized metal box, one turning a hand crank with sure, steady motions, the other dropping whole ears of corn into an opening at the top, the two of them creating a terrific clamor, a growing pile of shucked cobs, and a trembling pan full of kernels. They didn't pause as the OLE group filed by, but the man at the crank watched them, puffing air off his bottom lip to part the hair dangling over his eyes. In front of another cabin, a woman and man tended a huge outdoor stone hearth. This, Marta saw, was the source of the delicious aroma. The woman, using a brush with a long wooden handle, daubed a row of small pink bodies with brown liquid, and the coals beneath them sizzled as they dripped. The man hunched down, added a log to the flames, and blew through cupped hands. Behind them, a broad, makeshift table was pinned with the hides of whatever the couple were roasting. Each hide stretched in six different directions, like a starburst. The effect wasn't graphic or disturbing, even to Marta's sheltered gaze—just grimly efficient.

Beside her, Wes said, "Wow. This is a whole community. Can you believe it?"

Marta murmured an agreeable sound, but she didn't share his surprise, exactly. When she was a girl, and the news drones still flew, you heard all the time about camps, towns, even small cities hanging on between zones. There had been a webshow called *Roughing It!*, Marta remembered. Her father and brother liked it. Her brother, when teasing her, would threaten to send her to one of the smoking heaps of rubble depicted in shaky night-vision video. Glowing green outlines of humans, eyes flickering in the infrared light like coals. Satellite footage of shanty villages, not so different from this one, built along once bustling city thoroughfares, riverwalks. No, what surprised her wasn't the existence of the community but its normality, its calm. No microsuits, no Stamps. And yet, somehow—no obvious fear of ticks, either. How was it possible?

They passed a soap maker. A baker. (The sour-sweet smell of yeast—such delicious agony.) The tradespeople mostly worked out of the onetime vacation cabins, or on the lawns outside them, but there were buildings of more recent construction, too: trim, simply made cabins comprised, almost charmingly, of scavenged materials as well as new lumber. There was art here, Marta thought, evident all the more as they left what appeared to be the trade district and entered the town proper, which extended broadly along both sides of the river, joined by the newer footbridge she had spied when their walk began. Here the land had been cleared to make room for a scattering of structures, each unique, several beautiful enough to imagine they were somewhere back home, perhaps in one of the posh little eco-communities around the university. The first such building they passed was clad in multicolor scraps of corrugated metal; the windows, all mismatched, flanked a set of mismatched double doors, which were thrown wide open onto a broad front porch. Here, folks gathered—old, gray, stooped over knotty canes or games of what appeared to be checkers and chess. A dozen of them, men and women, their drab garb brightened by odd touches. One man, she noted as she passed close, wore a vest stippled with all kinds of pins and yellowing buttons—from this distance, she could read "Vote Reed" and "I ♥ ∏"—reminding Marta of the waitstaff at a restaurant chain that the boys liked back home, Looney's. (*The boys*—how her heart twisted at the thought of them. Would she see them again?) The woman by his side had her wispy gray hair tucked up into a brimmed red velvet hat, which was moth-eaten and adorned with a spray of feathers. Her lips—the upper lip was seamed with scar tissue—were painted a matching shade. She pursed those crimson lips with distaste at the OLE group. Maybe she could smell them. Marta could no longer smell herself, but she guessed that this wasn't because she had suddenly started sweating rosewater.

The building wasn't marked with a sign, but the glimpse Marta got through the open double doors revealed what appeared to be a kind of general store: rows of canned foods, piles of furs, a slumped burlap bag, near the door, with a handle jutting up out of it.

"Town grocery and supply," Curtis confirmed. It was the first time he'd spoken since bidding the woman at the footbridge goodbye. There was a note of pride in his voice, as if he couldn't quite resist showing off a bit for his captives, though he considered them beneath such effort.

"How does it work?" Wes asked. "Do you have a currency?" His face was pink with the walk and cool air, with the sun and the breeze, and he looked very young to Marta—of course he was young, a baby, really, no matter his accomplishments—and he sounded almost enthusiastic, as if he were posing a question to one of his college professors rather than speaking with a gun to his back.

Lee, from somewhere behind them, made a disbelieving grunting noise.

Curtis seemed amused. "You want to study our economy, Mr. Feingold? We do have money of a sort. June may want to explain to you. Or maybe she won't. The grocery is a co-op. Everyone in town owns an equal portion."

Wes nodded vigorously. He looked as if he had a follow-up question, or a series of them, but Marta nudged her shoulder into his, and after casting her a quick, apologetic look, he pinched his lips closed.

Who was June? That was Marta's question. But she knew better than to ask it.

"Bye, baldies," one of the old men called as the group moved off behind their guide, and the collection of porch geezers roared with laughter.

The slow pace of their progression through the village, at first a relief, had lulled Marta, allowing her exhaustion to catch up with her. Her feet, tender and slick with sweat that had worked its way down her legs, throbbed with pain. The Stamp on her calf pulsed hotly. Her stomach was empty to the point of near nausea, and she wished that David had thought to cleverly disguise a piece of candy in her Smokeless rather than the Salt, though the thought of the Quicksilver—a miracle that the hideous woman called Violet hadn't confiscated it—still gave her a small measure of courage and hope. Tiny. Minuscule, really. But better than nothing.

There was a bar of sorts—a long low building with a shed roof, doors thrown open to a dirt yard with half a dozen picnic tables. More old people, adorned with punches of color—four of them, heads bent over mismatched glasses filled with tawny liquid. If Marta hadn't seen the woman called Vic and the middle-aged tradespeople, she'd have wondered if Ruby City weren't some kind of outer-zone retirement village.

They walked on. The land around flattened and broadened away from the curve of the river, climbing gently uphill, and Marta saw where at least some of the town's younger residents were spending their day: among dozens, maybe hundreds, of long raised beds, shoulders brushing the leafy stalks of a flowering plant. She couldn't have named the plant if she tried. Gardening didn't remotely interest her. The blocks of green were punctuated occasionally by crimson blooms with black centers—beautiful, but the sight unsettled her in some unnameable way. The plants seemed swollen, out of proportion. They didn't belong, so red and vibrant on this cool autumn day.

As they drew closer to the nearest bed, Marta could hear the rustle of the stalks, the murmur of the women and men working among them. "Seen June?" Curtis asked the first person they encountered—a young man, late teens or early twenties, of a beauty as improbable as the nearby flowers. He was tan, lithe, with wide-set eyes so light blue as to be almost clear, and he was, so far as Marta could tell, utterly unmarked, as fresh and unscarred as a Zoner. Again, she wondered at this—and she wondered if Wes had also noticed. How could he not?

The young man thumbed uphill. "Number six or seven, I think," he said.

They moved in the direction he'd indicated, passing more beds, more gardeners—or maybe you'd call them farmers?—two or three of them to a bed, most youngish, around her sons' ages, and there was a general atmosphere among them of cheerful industriousness, and it occurred to Marta that industriousness—and cheer, frankly—weren't qualities she associated with the youth back home. There wasn't a tablet in sight. When was the last time she'd seen a group of twenty-year-olds without at least a few heads bent over an electronic device? And yet they were recognizable. A burst of laughter erupted from somewhere a few beds over, followed by a shushing sound, but the shushing was amused, lighthearted. There wasn't any real fear of reprisal in it. It was almost warm here, where the midday sun could hit the slope with full force, and a pretty young woman had her brown face lifted up toward that rich light, as if she herself were a flower. Beside her, another girl drew a small, scythelike blade across the chalky green flesh of a golfball-sized bulb or fruit on one plant. She made three quick hash marks, and as Marta passed close, the girl pressed the tip of her pinky to the milky liquid that had surged from one of the slits, then, eyes locked fixedly on Marta, placed the fingertip between her puckered lips. She winked. Marta looked quickly away, flushed.

What on earth was this place?

Their guide finally stopped. Andy and his armed associates, who had grown uncharacteristically quiet during the walk through the village, flanked him, turning to face the group and lifting their weapons again, though Marta doubted that any among the OLE travelers had the energy left for raising their voices, much less staging an attack or making a run for it.

"Here they are, June," Curtis said. "Andy got 'em here. He did good."

His words seemed to be directed at the back of a diminutive figure standing in one of the flower beds. The figure turned, lifting a forearm to brush hair and sweat off her forehead, revealing an almost ordinary middle-aged woman's face, the face of a woman maybe a few years younger than Marta, a woman who, in-zone, might have been tending the flowers lining the front walk of a trim bungalow with a screened-in front porch. The only thing compromising this effect was a single Stamp scar on the woman's freckled high cheekbone. The rest of her visible skin—neck, chest, bare arms—was unmarked. She had something in her hand that resembled a trowel; it was coated in maroon-colored sludge.

This, Marta supposed, was June.

"Why, yes he did," the woman said. "Well done, Andy."

"Thank you, ma'am." He lowered his gun to bob his head and shoulders toward her, nervous, it seemed, as a boy called in to the principal's office.

"And it's all of them?" she asked. She appraised Marta and the others with a more genial version of the interest those back in the village had shown them.

"All that matter," Andy said. "Along with several that don't."

"Well, that remains to be seen." She had a soft but commanding voice with a southern lilt you hardly heard any longer in-zone. She stepped up on the plank lip of the raised bed, and even those seven or eight inches didn't bring her to chin level with their guide; she was not just short but practically rendered in miniature, with narrow shoulders and wrists as delicate as a ten-year-old's but a woman's curves, a woman's laugh lines, and a woman's frizzy cloud of amber-going-to-silver hair. She wore the trouser half of the local getup—grayish brown, baggy, rolled at the ankle and cinched at the waist with a leather belt—but the shirt tucked into them looked like something that could have been purchased off the rack at any one of the in-zone department stores: red and blue plaid, soft flannel, also oversized. Cheap. Nothing special. But anomalous out here, robbed of its mundane context.

"I'm June," she said, unnecessarily. She set her trowel down carefully in a ceramic bowl at her feet, hopped down from the flower bed, and approached the group. Andy and the other guides stiffened, but she took the hand of the first person she approached—it was Anastasia—with the confidence and measured warmth of a schoolteacher or an aunt you only saw once a year at the family reunion. Anastasia towered over her. She let her hand be shaken, but the expression on her face was dazed and disbelieving. June released her hand, smiling, and reached for Berto's. He, too, consented to being touched. June proceeded to shake the hand of each of her captives, that mild smile still on her face. When Marta's turn came, her fleeting thoughts of staging some sort of protest—withholding her hand, turning her back—dissipated in the face of June's calm reserve. Her hand was cool, dry. Very small. She placed her free hand over her and Marta's grasping ones. She fixed her hazel eyes on Marta's, demanding contact.

"You look tired," she said. "That trek in is a bit much for women our age. I do apologize."

"The trek was fine," Marta managed to say. "The treatment we received wasn't."

June continued holding Marta's hand. Marta's palm prickled with sweat.

"I'm afraid," June said, "that prisoners of war don't often get the red carpet rolled out."

"What war?" Marta asked.

June shook her head and exhaled in an exasperated way. "Good lord. That you even have to ask that." She turned to Andy. "Enlighten me. What sort of poor treatment did they get?"

"We had a loss of life, ma'am," Andy said.

"Ha!" said Lee, again from the back of the group. "Loss of life! Ha!" He waved a finger at Violet. "That—that *thing* right there, she shot my friend in the head."

June pushed between Wes and Wendy Tanaka to get to Lee. The mild smile—the slight upturn at the corners of her lips—flattened. Her jaw stiffened. "What did you call her?"

Lee had well over a foot on June, but he dropped his chin and fixed his gaze on his twisting hands. "Nothing. I'm just angry. I saw my friend murdered."

"I gave the order," Andy said. "The man was dying anyway. He wouldn't have made it here."

"He was not dying!" Lee said. "That's a lie! He got bitten but we Stamped him."

"*We* didn't do shit," Andy said. "You stood around with your thumb up your ass and *I* Stamped him. But it wasn't quick enough. He had an infestation. He came and showed me the rash after the rest of you bedded down."

"That's a lie," Lee repeated, but with less fire. "You couldn't know if he'd caught Shreve's. It had only been a few hours."

"The bite was right over the jugular," Andy told June. "He'd have bled out after the hatching. We didn't have the time or the resources to patch him up. I made a judgment call."

"A good and necessary call," June said. She looked at Lee. "Mr.—"

"Flannigan," Lee said. "Lee Flannigan."

"Mr. Flannigan, my people haven't been on the receiving end of much fairness and humanity, but we're a decent sort, and I think you'll find I'm a pretty reasonable woman. Tonight you'll sleep under a real roof with food and even liquor in your belly, if you're inclined to a nip. We even have a decent little bluegrass trio that'll play. That sounds nice, doesn't it?"

He nodded, hesitantly.

She drew closer to him.

"But if I ever, ever hear you talk about Violet that way again, I will shoot you in the head myself. Do you hear me?"

"Yes," Lee said hoarsely.

The quiet mirth was back on her face and she craned her head to the left and right, taking in the rest of the group. "And you? We're all in agreement? We understand one another?"

Marta nodded along with the rest of them. Her horror, embarrassingly, was kept in check by the promise of food. Liquor. Rest.

"That's good," June said. "Well, now that we've dispensed with all that ugliness, let me show you where you can take a load off."

Nine

Ruby City had a central gathering structure built, at a first glance, in the pleasingly haphazard fashion of its other major public spaces. A second look, however—and this second look, for Wes, happened as June and Curtis led the OLE group across the river and steeply uphill, to a grassy, flattop mound upon which the building perched like a porkpie hat—revealed a more surprising, even ingenious use of cast-off and repurposed materials. The outer walls, which formed a cylindrical base for a conical roof, were log columns connected by an assembled puzzle of mulled-together windows—single, double-hung, clear-paned, stained glass. Some of the windows were open, slid up or pushed out.

"We call it Town Hall," June said, breathing easily despite the steep climb, "but it's a bit of everything for us. Meeting space, church. Dance hall. You name it. We finished the major construction work ten years ago. It took a year, and that doesn't count all of the time we spent making scavenging runs and stockpiling salvage."

"What's with the hill?" Wes asked. He sensed that there was betrayal in his interest—that his fellow hostages saw it this way—but he couldn't help himself. He was exhausted and terrified and so hungry that even those barbecued squirrels back in town verged on tempting, but he'd be truly lost if he ever gave up his curiosity about the world. It was so central to who he was, to how he'd made his fortune. And the more he knew about the place—the more he understood—the likelier he'd be to recognize a way out when he saw one.

"It was a Cherokee mound. It would have had a roundhouse structure on it similar to this one, so we decided to base our design on that."

"Fascinating," Wendy Tanaka said. Her voice was brittle.

June considered Wendy. "It is, actually. The Cherokee interest me very much. I feel a kinship with them. I'd say 'for obvious reasons,' but I suspect that they wouldn't be obvious to you."

Wendy's temple was a blue-black bruise still crusted with dried blood, so tender-looking that Wes winced an apologetic look each time his eye caught hers. She shrugged dully, apparently unmoved by June's reproof.

"You might not be surprised to learn that nearly a quarter of the Ruby City citizens are of Cherokee descent. Most of the residents on the reservation didn't get the zone vestments they were promised."

"Neither did the rest of us, for that matter," Curtis said.

"True, true," said June. They had reached the top of the mound. The Town Hall had a beautiful, almost grand entryway: large, wooden double doors, which had been sanded and oiled to a creamy luster, flanked by sidelights of a multicolored glass mosaic. Above the doors, a transom, also in mosaic glass, spelled out "Ruby City."

June ran her hand down the filigreed carving on one of the doors. "These came out of an Episcopal church in Asheville. I don't like to ransack lovely old architecture, but plenty of other people are willing to, so it becomes a matter of sifting through what's left. I hear there's a pack of folks living at the Biltmore who've more or less trashed it. Pity." She unhasped the brass latch and threw the doors open. "But we've all got bigger things to worry about now, of course."

The Town Hall from outside was impressive; from inside, it stole the breath away. Wes, filing in beside Marta, craned his head left and right in wonder at the view through the many-sized windows into the river valley and the Smoky Mountain range beyond. The Little Tennessee below them gleamed silver in the strong midday light. The fall foliage rivaled the color of the intermittent panes of stained glass, which threw rainbow light on the plank floors. Beams climbed from each log post to join high above them, and from this central point dangled a large wagon wheel hung with five unlit lanterns. It was only after taking all of this in that Wes noticed, on the far end of the roundhouse, a table laden with what appeared to be some kind of food and a large, bright orange insulated water cooler—the kind you saw at football games (not that Wes ever went to football games). His throat clenched, tacky with thirst, at the sight of that cooler.

"There's beans and cornbread," June said. "Plenty of it. Help yourself, then we'll talk. All of this'll seem more bearable on full stomachs, I'd wager."

They rushed the table as if it could disappear at any moment. Jesse Haggard made it to the cooler first and grabbed a glass with a shaky hand. He pressed his forehead against the cooler as he filled the glass, and when it had reached the brim, he took a long swig, shuddered, and handed the rest of the glass to Edie. Then he got another glass and proceeded to fill it, too. Anastasia and Berto started at the food, grabbing the cornbread with their dirty hands and piling it high in bowls, ladling in brown beans. The others—their armed kidnappers, too—pressed in behind them, grabbing bowls and spoons, postures rigid with anticipation. Wes, who had always been food-neutral—an aspect of his constitution, this lack of passionate appetite, that he saw as emblematic of, perhaps even responsible for, the single-minded focus that had led to his successes—recognized what he'd come to think of in more comfortable times, smugly, as "buffet stress." Back home, Sonya had always had a bad case of buffet stress. If they went to a barbecue or a cocktail party, she filled her plate with enough food for two people, returned to the line for seconds after complaining of being full, spent time later in the day reflecting on her choices: Should she have gone for the brownie rather than the pie slice? Why hadn't she eaten more of that great casserole? Buffet stress had even informed some of Wes's updates to Pocketz. Twice he'd invited Pocketz Prime members to an App Buffet, with all of the most popular add-on packages offered, for an hour, at steep discounts. These events were hugely popular, hugely successful. Participants filled their shopping plates as quickly as possible with cheap apps, afraid of missing out on something good before the buffet ran out, blowing credits on Line Cutz and Xtra Helpingz.

Wes would pay good credits for a Line Cut right now.

"I guess we waited this long," he said to Marta, trying to tamp down the stress, the fear of missing out. "It won't kill us to wait a little longer." They were a problematic match in this way—neither of them aggressive enough to demand their share, their partnership enabling the other's passivity.

"It could kill us," Marta said flatly.

But June had told the truth: the food and water were plentiful, and a woman, the one they'd seen earlier, with the bag of squirrels, came in with a big steaming kettle of beans when the first kettle ran low. The others had taken their food and drink and retreated to the outer edges of the building, staking out seats on the sun-warmed boards next to the east-facing windows, and so Wes and Marta were able to fill and refill their glasses undisturbed. The water was cold, with a delicious, bracing mineral quality.

His thirst quenched, he grabbed a bowl from the top of a rickety, mismatched stack. It was chipped, yellowed porcelain, with a dainty daisy pattern, and he followed the lead of those who'd gone before him, crumbling a chunk of cornbread into the bottom of the bowl and pouring a soupy spoonful of beans on top. He'd resigned himself to giving up veganism during the OLE tour, but the appearance of a pink, fatty rind of mystery meat in the bean broth made his stomach roil. It had been seven years since he'd eaten even fish.

"It's better than it looks," Marta said, noticing his hesitation. She had spoken around a mouthful.

His stomach settled by the third bite, and Wes felt then a surge of energy, a lifting of his mood. He gulped down another draft of water, then tucked into the food as eagerly as the rest of the group, spooning around the strip of meat as best he could manage. His stomach filling, he could appreciate the other luxuries of this moment: the relief of getting off his feet, of having space to stretch out his legs in front of him, of seeing Andy and the other guards put their guns down long enough to lift their bowls and shovel food to their lips. Now would be the time to make a move, if there were a hero in the group. But making a move would require movement, and what Wes wanted—and hey, no one had forbidden it yet, so why not—was to free his tender feet of these hot, stiff lace-up boots, then lie on his back and let his eyes lower to half-mast, so that only a little golden light filtered through his eyelashes. He went at his shoelaces with shaking hands, needing several tries to loosen each double knot. His bare feet were shriveled and damp and lined with the imprint of the boots' seams; his heels were stripped raw, the soles quilted with thick, watery blisters. He bent his toes, luxuriating in the pain that radiated up into the metatarsals, and groaned as he lowered himself to his elbows, then his creaking back.

The floor was hard, so he put his pack under his head. Better.

Didn't seem anyone else was plotting heroics, either.

"This is where you'll sleep tonight," June said. "You can pitch your tents as you normally would, if you're paranoid about ticks or you want the privacy. But I can't remember the last time I saw a tick up here."

"What if we don't want to sleep in here?" Berto asked. "What if we want a little more breathing room than that?"

"I'm afraid it's not negotiable," said June.

Berto nodded. "Just so we're clear. And no one misunderstands all of this hospitality you're showing us."

June had perched on the floor in the center of the large room, her boots and socks off, legs pulled into a tight pretzel and forearms resting on her knees. She looked like she might be about to begin leading a yoga class.

"I wouldn't want you to misunderstand me. You're hostages, not guests. Let's not pretend it's otherwise. Your comfort here will be contingent on your willingness to contribute to a few—well, Andy, what would you call them?"

"Operations?" Andy said.

"I was going to say 'projects,'" said June, "but I like that better. Operations. Yes. And Mr. Feingold, you're going to be especially critical to these operations."

Wes's tentative good mood fled him. He had been trying to talk himself out of the sense over the events of the last day that he was watched—noticed—in a way that wasn't true of his fellow travelers. He could guess easily enough why this would be true, in a general way, but he couldn't actually imagine what they'd demand of him—what he'd be able to do in the face of their demands. If June and her clan thought he could hack Pocketz, do any redistributing of credits, they'd be in for a bad surprise. The system—by design, by absolute necessity, by law—was protected by layers and layers of safeguards. The only account Wes could access, legally and also in practical fact, was his own. Would that satisfy them? He found that the prospect of surrendering his fortune (in fact, only a quarter of his fortune, the rest of it being tied up in property and investments) didn't bother him as much as he would have expected it to. He had never done any of this for the money.

"I'm not sure what you think I can do," he said.

June gave him her serene, yoga-instructor smile. "Don't worry. We'll fill you in soon enough. In the meantime"—she pointed to

Andy, and he and the guy with the bandolier, Randall, jumped to a stand—"these boys are going to escort you each to the privy, and then we're going to have story time."

Within a half hour, they had all visited the outhouse—a roomy, pin-neat structure with a padded seat and a single roll of toilet paper sealed in an old plastic food storage container. A mirror hung above a dry sink, upon which rested a bowl, a jug of water, and a rough-cut bar of soap the cloudy yellow of earwax. It wasn't what Wes had expected. He wasn't sure what he had expected.

Upon returning to Town Hall, they each took seats on the floor in a semicircle around June. Wes was very, very drowsy, but it was clear that an afternoon nap wasn't an option. He pulled up his legs, wrapped his arms around his shins, and rested his chin on his right kneecap. Perhaps story time would be brief.

June lifted a hand and beckoned at someone. She had her head tilted and chin tucked, her lips pulled wide in a closed-mouth smile. It was an expression of loving indulgence, and Wes sensed that this was the closest they had all gotten so far to seeing what lay under her veneer of calculated geniality.

The person who answered her call was Violet. She dropped to the floor beside June—flopped down, like a child, or a puppy leaning into a belly rub—and placed her head in June's lap. June brushed strands of long, light brown hair off Violet's scarred forehead. "Tired?" she said softly, looking down into that horrifically disfigured face, and Violet said "Yes" out of her mangled mouth.

"Where to start?" June said. She was still gazing down at Violet, but her voice, louder now, was addressing the group. "I could begin with the extermination or the rezoning. I could begin with my parents, how it was they gave up their vestments and decided to raise me out here. Or I could start with the day we founded Ruby City. They're all good stories. They're all part of the big story.

"I've been thinking about this moment for a month. Ever since Andy got me the manifest for this OLE group and told me what he knew about this excursion. Why it's special. And that very day, I imagined us all here, and I pictured what I might say to you, how I'd begin to tell our story and what I'd say to make you see why this is how things have to be, and again and again I return to Violet."

Now she looked up.

"And what I've said, each of the times I've begun this speech in my mind, is this: If you want to understand what the world is like these days, you should look at Violet."

Violet's Story

I know some of what you know about life out here. What you've been told. We have occasional feed access. There's a spot we know a few hours northeast of here, and it's close enough to a gap in the TerraVibra to pick up a faint signal. So we check in now and again, and Andy's filled us in over the years, too. Sometimes you've got to laugh about it. We sit together just like this and have fellowship just like this, and we look around at each other and ask, "Are you sure you're here? Are you sure I'm here?" Because the feeds say we're not. Or you dig a bit deeper, you go into the web's backwoods, and there's whispering—satellite footage of villages like ours posted on Chinese IPs, or maybe some agri-contractor comments on a message board that he got held up by a band of outlaws and the company hushed it up. But this is all part of the lie. A way of enabling the lie. Most people won't believe the surface story that hardly no one lives out-of-zone. Not if you've got a lick of common sense. But there's a second layer of story that'll satisfy most people, and if you don't think your government and the people who control your government shape that narrative, too, you're a fool. And the way it works is that they let slip just a bit of what's bad and scary, and they know that most people will stop there and won't want to see the rest of it. It's hard enough imagining that anyone is trying to survive out here. It's scary to think that a pack of masked men could overcome a cargo truck, that there are men enough out here to form a pack that could form a plan like that. Imagine if your people back home knew what you all know now. Imagine if they could see this town. Imagine if they could see the life we've made. They might be afraid, or even angry. Or they might feel hope. And it's the hope that's dangerous.

I'm sorry. I'm getting abstract.

I was talking about Violet. And talking about Violet makes me angry. It makes me give speeches instead of telling stories. Isn't that right, dear? You don't have to listen to all of this again, my love. You can go find Vic, if you want. Tell her she can take away the dinner things. If everyone's done, that is. Are you? All done?

There'll be a big feast tonight. Your bellies won't be empty so long as you're here. I promise you that much.

OK. Good, then. Well. Where was I?

Violet. Of course.

I gave her that name. It's been suggested to me a few times over the years that the name is an unkindness, a mockery of her. I think that says more about the people doing the suggesting than it does me, that they can't imagine a tormented child would be deserving of a sweet name. At any rate, I called her Violet because the first time I saw her—found her is what it really was—she was sleeping in a bed of purple flowers. She couldn't have been older than seven or eight, though I thought her younger at first, because she was small for her age. I was young myself. Not yet twenty. My parents and I were traveling west along what had been Highway 176, just wandering, gathering plant samples for my father's work and seeing what there was to see. It was the only life I'd ever known, but even so I'd call it a strange time, a quiet time. People lay low then. You didn't see many on the road, and the ones you saw were wary, they weren't looking to take you in or be your friend. Big groups drew the wrong kind of attention from in-zone, unless you had some special arrangement. And those special arrangements came with their own cost.

I can speak to that now firsthand.

My parents and I were camped near Saluda. I was both old and young for my age. I hadn't known other children, other teenagers. I didn't have friends. Where could I have made them? I was wholly dependent on my parents. And I was their equal. But that's its own story, as I said, and anyway, what you need to know now is that Mama and Daddy were working, setting up the mobile lab, and I'd promised to go do some foraging but what I really wanted—and I think they always knew this—was a breather from them. A couple of hours on my own, time enough to imagine a life occupied by the kinds of characters I'd always read about in books. So I'd go on my walks and I'd pretend myself a boyfriend or a best friend or a loyal dog. I'd pretend myself a purpose—a job, an act of heroism. You can be lonely without ever having known anything but being alone.

I went south. It was hot and sunny, sunny enough to set your eyes to aching. The air wasn't moving. I was thinking after twenty minutes that I might just turn around and go back, that I'd be better off napping through the heat of the day, but that's when I spotted the child in the flowers. You could see that the sun had moved as she slept and she was baking in a patch of bright light. What I remember about that first glimpse of her is the sight of her bare arm, how hot and red it was, and by instinct I rushed over to block the sun with my body. It didn't occur to me that she might be dead, and I've wondered about that since, why that thought never crossed my mind. I think it was the sleeping posture. She was on her side. She had her head resting on her crooked elbow, her thumb in her mouth, and her face was hidden by this scraggly blond hair that went down almost to her waist. Her knees were drawn to her chest. The fetal position, you'd call it. I must have stood there at least two full minutes, just staring at her. I hadn't seen a child in real life since I'd been one and looked in the mirror. Oh, I'd seen photos in old books, and my mother had some movies stored on a drive that I was allowed to watch on special days, and there were children in some of them. *The Sound of Music* was one. Have you seen it? There's this part where the children are singing farewell at the end of a party, they're ascending this glorious staircase, and the youngest one, Gretl, curls up and falls asleep. It's very sweet. I saw this child in the purple flowers and I thought of Gretl. What happened next is that I crouched down and very softly drew back that curtain of long blond hair, thinking I'd see beneath it a face like Gretl's, plump and rosy and smooth, and what I saw instead—

Well, you know what I saw.

I made some sound, some startled sound, and her eye popped open. I fell back, and my heart was just skittering away. That blue, blue eye. The color of the sky. It is lovely, and I bet none among you has been able to see that yet. Its beauty. But I tell you it's there. This suffering child fixed her one blue eye on me, and now, I look back, and I think of all the things a regular child would have done. She'd have jumped up, or screamed, or cried, or maybe she'd have clung to me and begged for water or help. But not Violet. She lay there and she stared, she didn't move, and I didn't see fear in that eye, but I didn't see hope, either. What I saw was resignation. It was an old look, an ancient look, and I won't lie to you now: I almost fled. I looked in Violet's eye and I thought, *This'll be my burden to bear.* And I wasn't wrong, but what I couldn't see then is that a burden can also be a gift.

For whatever reason, I didn't run. Maybe my legs just didn't work. I said something my mother always used to say to me. I said, "Honey, are you all right?"

She didn't respond. She didn't move. She just kept that level blue gaze fixed on me, her one eye on my two.

I said, "What's your name?" I said, "I'm June, honey."

She said nothing back.

I put my hand out slowly, like this, I was shaking like a leaf, and I touched her hot little arm. She trembled just a little. But that was it.

I said, "Honey, you're going to burn up in this sun."

She had nothing to say to that, either. And why would she? What was a little sunburn to what she'd been through already? She looked like she'd been set torch to. But still, I'd fixated on it, I'd convinced myself that getting her out of the sun was the right first step, and so what I did was scoot back on my bottom until I'd gotten to the shade under a tree, and I beckoned to her, I said, "Why don't you come over here, honey?" and when that didn't work I took out my canteen. I said, "Come and get some water, at least."

This went on for what seemed like a long time. Me waving the canteen at her, beckoning. Violet still lying there on her side, that blue eye on me, thumb in her mouth. She had on this cotton slip thing and nothing else. It had been white once—the hem came almost to her knees, and her legs poking out from under it were scratched and Stamped and scarred and skeeter-bit, and the bottoms of her feet were blacker than owl gravy. I was thinking through my options. I was wondering if I should try to leave the canteen and walk out of sight, to trick her, or try to pick her up and carry her to camp by force, or if I should run and get my parents and hope Violet would still be there when we returned. I was just about decided that I'd leave the canteen and run when she sat up—all at once, as if she was spring-loaded. Still with that just-about-unblinking eye on me. She got to her feet, took small steps my way. Stopped. Two more steps, so she was just within my reach. Then her hand popped out. Like, *gimme.* So I did, I put the canteen in her hand, and she tilted her head back, gulping until it was empty, and when she finished and looked at me again so still and solemn, I could see in her blue eye that she was mine now and I was hers, and I thought, *God help us.*

She clutched the canteen. She gave no indication she planned to hand it back to me.

I said, "You want to come with me, honey? Do you want to come to where I live?"

I don't know what I expected her to do, but it wasn't what she did. Which was to put her hands up toward me, one of them still gripping that canteen. And I hadn't seen another child before, but I guess that's a universal gesture, isn't it? Pick me up. So I picked her up. I hitched her up by her armpits and sat her on my hip, and she slung her sunburned little arm around my neck and with the other cradled the empty canteen like it was a teddy bear. She was skin and bones. I don't think she weighed two stones. I carried her the half mile or so back to my parents, and by the time our camp was in sight she'd fallen asleep again, her poor face nuzzled into my collarbone, hot breath on my neck. I called, "Y'all need to come out here right now." They did. My mother and father. They saw me with the child and they froze.

I said, "I found her in the woods."

And my father said: "You take her back right this goddamn minute."

Thank you, Vic. You read my mind. It hits the spot on a fall day, doesn't it? Go ahead, send it around. Have a swallow, all of you. This recipe came over with Vic's family on the boat. It goes down smooth. Too smooth. See how that swallow treats you before you have more.

My stories have a tendency to spring leaks. I'll think I've found a pretty clear way forward, and then I realize that I'm going to have to stop and explain something else first, and then it seems that explanation requires its own explanation, and pretty soon I don't know if I'm coming or going. Or what metaphor I started with. Leaks, right? I'm not so good at plugging the leaks.

Like now, I'm remembering that moment with my father and this dark fury he had on his face as he looked at Violet, and how I was shocked by that, because my father wasn't an angry sort of man, but not shocked, too. And to explain that contradiction, I'm tempted to explain my father to you. Of all the things I could say about him, for now, I'll tell you this: my father was a fastidious man and a brilliant man, a scientist, and he laid the groundwork for everything we've managed to do here, but he had a cowardly streak. Or maybe that's not fair. A coward wouldn't have given up an in-zone vestment to do the work he was doing. But he knew the kind of good that was within his powers, and it wasn't playing the hero. The loneliness of our lives out here was almost entirely his doing. When we saw people, we hid. We turned around and went the way we'd come. Always. Daddy saw it as his life's mission to save the world, and he was never once struck by the irony that he trusted almost no one in that world he was so bent on saving. If I'd have asked him about that—and I never did, I never had the courage to—he'd probably have said that saving the world was the only way to make people trustworthy again. And there may be some truth in that.

Either way, it meant nothing to him that Violet was a child, that she'd suffered terrific hurts, that she had no one else. "Take her back," he told me again, because I was standing there with her in my arms and I wasn't moving, I hadn't responded. It couldn't have been long, but it felt like a long time. I remember my back was aching, and I wanted so much to put her down on my pallet in the big tent, but I had this sense that if I let her go Daddy would snatch her up and throw her away.

"Take her back," he said again. I looked from him to my mother. She had an expression on her face that I could have drawn, I knew it so well. The eyebrows tilted up, like this, and her lips tight, and she was turning her hands in one another. She was the peacekeeper. She was the deciding vote, but she just about always cast her vote with my father, and in that way his word with us was as good as law. So when I said no—and that's what I said, simple and flat as that—her eyes got big and unbelieving, and she said my name, but I just shook my head, hard.

"No," I said. "I won't. And if you won't have her, you won't have me, either. We'll leave."

Daddy said, "June, you don't know what this means. You've got no idea what you're doing."

And I said, "Maybe not, but I know what I won't do. I won't leave her for dead." I was crying at this point, and I didn't even know why. Because a part of me wanted to be unburdened of her. I guess it was scary, how tempted I was to leave her sleeping where I'd found her and run. I was disgusted with myself. But also, I was disgusted with her. She terrified me. The sight of her ruined face on my collarbone terrified me. And so I dug in my heels, as if I weren't terrified and disgusted. I said, "I will not." I said it as though I didn't doubt it, so as to make it true.

My father continued to argue with me. Telling me how close he was to a breakthrough in his work, how much there was at risk. I seem to remember Violet sleeping through it, or pretending to. And next I recall, the child was on my pallet, and my mother had brought me a cool soaked rag to put on her forehead. The two of us stood there together, looking down at her, and Mama said, "She's going to break your heart."

Truer words were never spoke.

In the evening, as the sun hid behind the mountains and the skeeters were nipping, Daddy came into my tent with a lantern, and he set it on the floor near Violet's head. The child's head. She was only "the child" to me then. "She's still asleep?" he asked me. His voice was mild. All the rage had gone out of it.

I told him she'd been up for a little bit, long enough to have some water and a hoecake. Then she'd drifted off again.

He pointed at her little arms with his thick, blunt forefinger. "Stamp," he said. He pointed again, and a third time, a fourth. "Stamp, Stamp, Stamp," he repeated, and I said, "Yeah, so what?" I had a couple Stamps of my own, from long back. Both near my ankles. They glowed like white coins on my sun-brown skin. Daddy's arms were dotted with them.

So he pointed to a couple of other scars—funny-shaped ones—

on her arm again, and on the calf of her leg. "Those are from infestations," he said. "You can tell from the scar pattern. They cinched her back together like a feed sack."

And again, I was thinking, "So?" That wasn't unheard of, either. Daddy'd had an infestation before I was born, though I sometimes forgot, because the scar was on his inner thigh and so I never had cause to look at it.

But I didn't say anything out loud. I just waited for him to make his point. I knew he had one.

"All of these"—he motioned at her body—"all this I can account for," he said. "She lived with folks. Folks with Stamps, so there's some Zoner connection. And they used 'em liberally," he said. He shook his head. He was exasperated. I only had a couple of scars because Daddy had insisted on throwing the Stamps out long ago. Even before his experiments had advanced. He always said that a Stamp was a fool's cure. More harm than help. We kept our legs and arms covered, wore hats, and did regular body checks. We used a smelly salve Daddy concocted. And for the most part, that did the trick. I'd had some bites, but none of them led to infestations.

"But her face," Daddy said. "There's no accounting for it. The rest of her isn't burned this way." Then he drew more invisible lines with his big finger, this time along a curve on her forearm, then a knob along her shinbone. "Her arm's been broken," he said. "And her leg, too. That's just what I see at a glance." I saw then what he'd seen. How the parts of her had been roughly rejoined.

"Some kind of accident," I said.

And my father said, "No." He said, "No, whatever it was that happened to her happened on purpose."

I was trying to fit my mind around that level of awfulness when he said, "I want you to come with me. There's something I need to show you." He motioned for me to follow him outside, and I saw that he'd unpacked our trail bikes. They were leaning on their kick-stands in the moonlight.

"It's a bit of a ways from here," he said.

Maybe fifteen, sixteen kilometers, as it turned out, westward, with lots of hard bends and uphill climbs. A swift night ride, the air cool and fresh. It was rare that we moved at such a pace.

We approached an old green highway sign that said "Village of Flat Rock," and my father braked and coasted to a stop. I joined him, and we paused to drink some water.

"You caught your breath?" he asked me.

I nodded.

"Stow your bike," he said. "We walk from here."

We scrambled along on what had been the highway's shoulder. I realized that the road fronted a lake; the water flickered with moon-light through what had been, in another life, a chain-link fence and a line of ornamental trees, all of them now unpruned and unwieldy. The air was thick with the smell of honeysuckle. I loved the scent before that night, and I can hardly stand it now.

We could see light ahead. Not just *a* light, mind you. A haze of lights, many bleeding together, and it wasn't long after we saw them that the noise reached us, first a uniform murmur, like the ocean; then, as we drew closer, the noises expanded, separated, became distinct. Engine noise. Human noise—their shouts, their laughs. Music. Acoustic guitars, harmonica, drums.

When the trees on the lakeside ran out, Daddy stopped me by putting his hand on my arm. He looked up and down the road, and we both listened, but all I could hear was the noise ahead. "Let's cross," Daddy said, "and then we're going to get up into the woods and out of sight. Got it?"

I said I did.

"Then go now," is what he said, and we went. We scurried across the road and climbed uphill into the woods. At some point a motorcycle passed. It bore two riders, the back one a woman whose hair streamed out light-colored and long behind her. And I remember thinking, *Well, what's ahead can't be too bad if a woman's part of it.* Lord, you have to laugh. But I was young.

Now's a good time for another shot. Go ahead, Vic, send it around again. This story goes down better with whiskey.

Twenty, thirty minutes later, we were in sight of it.

"Now you listen to me," Daddy said. "If you make a peep at the wrong moment, you'll get us killed. Or worse. So don't talk. Hear me?"

I nodded at him. My heart was beating like crazy.

"Stay behind me," is what he told me. "Go where I go," he said. "I want to get you a look and then I want to get out of here."

The woods ended where a driveway curved up from the highway. And where the drive led was up to a broad, graveled expanse that abutted the edge of the lakeshore. Tall pine trees reached up at regular intervals, and among them were hundreds of RVs and campers and motorcycles, many of them parked beside pitched tents, and outside these tents and vehicles sat people, mostly men—but not all—some of them in folding chairs, others lounging on couches that had been dragged outside, or on pickup tailgates, or at wooden picnic tables set up next to charcoal grills. Mouthwatering smells rose up from those grills. I hadn't had supper that night, and my stomach growled, and Daddy gave me a stern look as if I could help it. They were drinking, most of them. Maybe eight meters from me, a man was tilting a frosty bottle back to his mouth, and his feet were extended in front of him and propped up on a cooler. Relaxed like I'd never seen the likes of. I could make out the beads of condensation on that bottle. I could see the tread on his new-looking hiking boots. He had a paper plate balanced on his knee, and he set the bottle down to pick it up and lift a hot dog to his mouth.

Daddy crooked a finger to say, *Come on.* We started making our way around the perimeter of the campgrounds at a not quite run, keeping to the shadows and hiding behind trees when there was one to hide behind. We stopped on a little wooded rise on the far side of the camp. The disintegrated remains of an old outbuilding were overrun with creepers, more honeysuckle, and its perfume wafted around me on the cool mountain breeze. Following Daddy's lead, I settled down on my belly, propped up on my elbows. The nearest camper was just down the rise from us, fifteen meters away, maybe. A group of men were congregated in front of it. Laughing. Passing around a bottle. Smoking home-rolleds, the sweet smoke tickling my nostrils.

Daddy pressed something into my hand. His fold-up binoculars. I put them up to my eyes, adjusted the lenses, and looked at the men. They were about my father's age, a couple maybe a handful of years younger. I guess, if there was something to notice about them, the first thing was that they were all big men—tall, broad, strong-looking. Like they lifted weights or did hard labor. The white guys had leathery skin that had seen too much sun, ruddy faces, deep creases around their laughing eyes. Stamp scars. But they all had on clean, new-looking clothes, button-down shirts, lightweight tan trousers, glints of gold on their wrists and fingers, around a couple of necks. I'd say now—now that I've seen more of the world, or learned more of it online—that they looked like men going out together on the town, barhopping.

Something else came into the frame suddenly. I wiped sweat out of my eyes. I took a long breath to try to steady my shaking hands. I adjusted the lenses again, but she was still there. A girl. A teenager. Lanky, knees knobby as a calf's, hair long and dark and carefully brushed out around her shoulders. She was wearing a little cotton dress cut like a slip. Spaghetti straps. Cheap little rubber flip-flops on her feet, and her toenails painted bright orange. The men had formed a half circle around her. What I could hear of their conversation, from my perch above their campsite, was unintelligible. Through my binoculars, it was a dumb show. But I gathered what was happening. The men jostled one another. Teased. One rubbed his chin, as if deliberating. Two of them checked the contents of their wallets. Finally one of the men stepped forward, raising a hand with some bills tweezed between his index and middle fingers. I noticed activity at the edge of my view and lowered my binoculars. A small person emerged from a large RV, which I could now see was idling nearby, and scampered to the man. Plucked the bills from his grasp and just as quickly ran away. I lifted the binoculars again in time to see the girl, a thin red smile carved into her sallow face, follow the man into the camper. His group of friends lifted their drinks. Cheered.

We stayed for another fifteen minutes—long enough for five more girls to come out for the men's inspection. Two of them they considered and ultimately waved off. Two were invited into the camper. Another one—she had a club foot and a long scar running down her face—well, the men chased her off, making barking sounds. A boy came out. Ten or eleven, I'd guess now. Clad in jean shorts, thin chest bare, bare feet. The men booed. One tossed his empty liquor bottle at him. "Fuck off!" a man yelled. I could hear it clear as day from where Daddy and I hid.

I got a better look at the small person from the RV, the one who collected the bills for each transaction. A child. A girl, I think, though she moved too quickly to see for sure. Grubby, also barefoot. Hair hanging in her eyes. At the RV, she'd do a little jump and get the door open and slide herself inside in one swift motion. On one trip she caught her foot on the step and fell forward. Busted her face on the door, and the men howled with laughter. How they laughed. The door opened, and a set of arms came out, took the child up by the wrists so that she was dangling—both her wrists in one huge hand—and paddled her bottom. More laughs from the men. The door closed. The RV pulled off, and the men who hadn't made a selection returned to their lawn chairs and their drinks.

After this, I turned to Daddy. I looked him in the eyes. It felt like the first time I'd looked my father in the eye. Really looked, I mean. And though he'd told me not to talk, I said, real soft, "I want to go," and he only nodded.

We made it back to the woods, to the road, to our bicycles hidden in the thicket off the side of the highway. I pedaled back the way we'd come twice as fast as I'd pedaled coming to, and my father fell behind.

Back at our camp, he talked to me as we loaded the bikes back into the wagon. He said that the campsite in Flat Rock had been there over a decade that he knew of, and there were others like it. He said that terrible things happened there. A few I'd seen. Many I hadn't.

"That child," he said to me. "The one who collected the money."

"What about her?" is what I said.

"They're usually children of the girls. Like the ones you saw," he said. He was talking about the prostitutes. He said, "They put them to work just about as soon as they can walk. The ones that child's age, they call them squirrels. What you saw—that's the least of how it can be. How bad it can get for them."

I motioned to the tent. I said, "You think she was a squirrel."

"I do," Daddy said.

"And you wanted me to just turn around and put her back where I found her."

His face got real grave. Stony. He said, "They don't let people go. And if they're done with someone, they kill them. They don't drop 'em off like puppies on the side of the road. She must've run away, and if she did, someone's looking for her."

"For a burnt-up, broke-down kid?" is what I asked.

"For their property," Daddy said. "They'll make an example out of her. So no one else will try what she tried."

I wasn't foolish. I told you that. I looked around at what we had. Our camp. The wagon with the bikes and the clean water and the changes of clothes. Daddy's lab, all that good, world-saving work he was doing. My mother—I could hear her warm voice through the tent wall, see her silhouette, her thin shoulders and long neck leaned over, a book open in her hands, the child a dark mound on the floor beside her. I could see what he was trying to protect.

But what I said out loud to him was, "I wonder at the fact that you could show me all that and expect I'd do anything but protect her."

He said, "You shouldn't. Wonder. Because you're everything to me and your mother, and that child's nothing to us." He said, "When you have one of your own, you'll understand."

I bet that's one y'all have heard a time or two. *When you have kids.*

He said, "I'd give up what soul I've supposedly got to keep you safe. Without a second thought."

I understand him better now than I did then. Because of Violet. Which is funny, if you think about it.

Well, you've seen Violet. There isn't any suspense on that account. My ultimatum stood. It was going to be both of us or neither of us—and Daddy chose both. She became part of our family from that day forward, and no one from the Flat Rock campsite ever showed up looking for her. Or not that we saw, anyhow, since we kept hunkered down as we always had, never settling in one place for long, never approaching strangers. There came a day when Violet went looking for them. The bastards at Flat Rock, I mean. But again, that's another story for another time.

You have a lot of questions, maybe. Well, so do I. I don't know how Daddy knew all that he knew about that place. I guess I didn't want to know. And I don't know everything that Violet endured there, but I'm just as happy to be spared that, too. She hardly spoke to us for a full year after we took her in. She grunted. Made hand signals. Would mumble a couple of words, saving them up for about a second shy of the point you'd decided to take her for empty-headed.

But she sure wasn't telling us her life story, and by the time she was talking on the regular, her memories were pretty spotty, or she claimed they were. We let her be.

I'll claim the last swallow of Vic's brew for myself. Talked till my throat's raw. I think I've earned it.

Even after you've heard Violet's story, there's a look in your eyes. I know it well. And all I can say to it is that what you want to hate about her—her ugliness and her meanness—you created. Yes, each of you. You're complicit in the acts of evil that made her who she is. You're complicit because you've let yourself be comforted by lies. You're complicit because all of those comforts you have in-zone come at a price, and Violet is one of many of us who've paid the bill.

You want to argue with me. But you don't. There's a lesson in this. Sleep on it tonight.

You don't argue with the ones holding the guns.

June held up a hand and Vic grabbed it, pulling her to a stand. Wes sensed that this was a performance of age, a way to humanize her, make her kindly. He suspected that June, when it counted, needed no help springing to action.

"Well," she said. "That ended on an unfriendly note." She laughed. She brushed her bottom off briskly. She pointed. "Tonight we'll gather at the river, as the old song goes. We're smoking two pigs for y'all. That's about as friendly as it comes, you ask me. You'll be able to meet our people. We're good people."

Wendy coughed.

"We're good people," June repeated more softly. "Any rate, you have the afternoon. Rest up. Keep to Town Hall. If you go off wandering, one of your minders will escort you back."

She and Vic left. The battered remnants of the OLE group—Wes, Marta, Edie, Jesse, Anastasia, Berto, Lee, Tia, Wendy, and Ken—exchanged glances, dazed.

"Not that any of you has the gumption to form an escape plan," Andy said. "But I'd advise against it. Randall and I will be right outside."

They left. Then—for the first time in what felt like weeks—there was silence. Enough quiet for Wes to hear the roar of his own blood flow. *We can't waste this time*, he thought. *We mustn't. There might not be another moment like this one. Another opportunity to talk, unwatched.*

Marta was clutching something in her fist. Staring at her hand, as if she couldn't believe what was there. Wes lifted his brow.

She opened her fingers. Just a Smokeless. Still shrink-wrapped in its Canteen box.

Ten

A gorgeous night. Brisk. Clear sky. The stars, as promised in OLE brochures, were so prevalent as to form a haze overhead, and down on Earth, lanterns strung across the footbridges made pretty reflections in the steady-flowing Little Tennessee. The residents of Ruby City numbered in the several hundred, and they settled along the banks of the river on blankets and in fold-up chairs, unpacking plates and glasses from baskets, looking, to Edie, utterly familiar—like every group you'd ever seen gathered for Wall Day fireworks or a street festival in the artsy part of the city. There were a few bonfires. A plank stage where a bluegrass trio played. The only thing missing was a hayride for the kids.

And kids, come to think of it. The youngest people in attendance were in their mid-teens, at least. Maybe the children were being watched somewhere away from the adult fun. Maybe their parents didn't trust the hostages around them.

Edie mentioned their absence to Jesse, and he shrugged. "Didn't notice," he said.

"But now that it's been pointed out to you?"

He shrugged again. "That's the least of my concern, if I'm going to be honest, babe."

There had been a few moments earlier today, after Andy and Randall left the OLE group alone in the Town Hall, when the ten hostages had tried to make a plan. To *think*. Wes Feingold kept saying that: *We've got to think!* Thinking didn't seem to be this bunch's long suit. Edie herself was just so goddamn tired. She wanted to lie down. Her head ached. Her feet and back. Two men holding guns were posted outside the only door. What was the point?

"This thing at the river tonight," Wes said. "Maybe some of us could slip off. Get help."

Jesse said, "Well, if you're volunteering, go right ahead."

Wes shook his head, mouth pursed with disgust. "Screw you, man."

Anastasia, lying on her hip with her palm tucked under the weight of her head, spoke without opening her eyes. "You're an idiot, Jesse. Have you paid any attention? Wes is the one they want. How long do you think the rest of us will last here if he takes off?"

Jesse surled up. "I was making a joke."

"You're a joke," Tia said. It was the first time, since the kidnapping, that Edie had heard their other OLE guide speak. She had wondered about Tia and her intentions—wondered if she was really as innocent in all of this as she seemed to be, or if she'd been installed among the rest as a spy, and would report their every word back to Andy. But Edie didn't think the look of wounded shock on Tia's face last night could be manufactured, nor the fury in her eyes each time Andy piped up with one of his snide speeches. "Shut the fuck up for once. I've been wanting to say that to you for three weeks now. Shut. The. Fuck. Up."

Jesse recoiled in shock, and the corners of Wes's mouth twitched.

Edie, irritated at them all, grabbed her pack and staked out a spot as far from the others as she could find. She lay on the plank floor, facing a window, letting the sun warm her face. Before she could decide to do it, she was sleeping.

Now—rested, full of food—she could recognize how stupid they had been to indulge in bickering and even sleeping when so much was at stake. There was a new set of armed guards tonight, fresh-faced in clean uniforms, but they were young and bright-eyed, like the ones who'd been tending those flowers earlier in the day, and their watch over the hostages was characterized by that same lighthearted half-attention. They wore their guns on their backs as they ate pulled pork off plates. They filled their glasses with cloudy beer from a cask, laughed uproariously at one another's stories. It wouldn't be hard to escape their notice, but to what end? Run into the woods—no water, no Stamp, no sense of direction? It would be a suicide mission.

There was a sensation—an impression?—that Edie had been mulling over since awakening in early evening, as the sun was setting. Something nagging at her. She had pretended to keep sleeping so she could think more about it. Isolate it. Make sense of it. And finally it occurred to her: admiration. Admiration for June. She'd shaken her head roughly, as if she could jar the feeling loose that way, but it didn't budge. Despite herself, she admired the small woman who commanded the guns pointing at them. She was fascinated by her.

Which was to say, despite her fears about what the people of Ruby City intended for her and the rest of her fellow hostages, and despite her suspicion that they'd squandered their one chance at staging an escape, she found herself being lulled: by the festive mood among the Ruby City residents, by the beauty of the evening. By the plate of food she held: shreds of juicy smoked pork, some kind of salad with pickled beets and a bitter green, grilled slices of squash, fry bread. The bluegrass trio—men on standing bass and fiddle, a woman on banjo—played with spirit, and Edie had to make a conscious effort to stop her foot from tapping along with the beat.

Jesse also seemed to be charmed—or perhaps he'd decided that enthusiasm was the way to ingratiate himself with his captors. He slurped down pints of the molasses-tasting beer until his face flushed red, then joined the trio onstage with his ukulele. The crowd met this imposition of his with good nature, clapping a little, and the pretty young woman on banjo moved over to give him room. They played a couple of songs, up-tempo numbers, Jesse picking along in the background. Then they took a break. The four drew together to confer. When they pulled back from their conference, Jesse had assumed the lead singer's spot center stage, and the fiddler sketched out a jaunty four-note intro before the other instruments joined in.

Jesse sang, "*I've got this feeling and I don't want to hide it.*"

Edie glanced furtively around, pink with embarrassment, and caught Wes Feingold's eye. His expression was kind; it was a relief to be spared his judgment of Jesse, to not have to do the work of withstanding it on her lover's behalf. Wes lifted his hand, waved a little. Raised his eyebrows. Edie nodded a little and beckoned him over.

He sat on the blanket beside her, legs crossed. He held a plate mounded precariously with a monster portion of beet salad, nothing else. Noticing her glance, he grinned and shrugged.

"I'm paying penance for lunch," he said. "Eighteen hours and a long hike and all my principles went out the window. I'm supposed to be vegan."

"On the bright side," said Edie, "if you're calm enough to worry about your diet, that probably means that we've made it past the primal terror portion of the day."

"For now, anyway," Wes said.

"I mean, look at Jesse. He's already found an adoring audience."

Wes peered at her in the dark.

"That's me teasing," Edie said.

"Oh, good." He stabbed his salad with a fork and pulled a huge pile of greens into his mouth. "I couldn't tell for sure," he said around the food.

"I shouldn't tease." She leaned back on her palms, watching Jesse on stage. He had gotten the trio members to harmonize with him on the chorus, giving the words "right night" a spectral quality. He looked good. Even with his shaved head, even in his scrawny white microsuit that could pass for long underwear in this light and context. Edie was reminded of all the things that had drawn her to him, not the least of which was his talent, though his talent was obscured by his desire to be widely known, widely adored. Did she love and adore him? She had tried, hard. But gratitude wasn't the same thing as love. And what he'd done for her—had it cost him much, really? What did it say about Edie, that she felt so indebted to, so unworthy of, this person who may well have been the baby's father, who had every self-interested reason in the world to make the offer he'd made to her?

But he hadn't had to stay with her. He hadn't had to publicly claim her, at a time in his life when dating a bartender at a shitty dive bar was a liability to his career, at best.

"He's a lot to take," Wes said.

"Yes," Edie said tiredly. "But there's more to him than this."

"Sure. Of course there is. And none of us is at our best right now."

"That's true, too."

Wes sipped from a glass of water. "Earlier today, at the Town Hall," he said. "That didn't go so well."

"You mean, plotting our escape?"

He nodded.

"I don't think this is a group of people who are used to collaborating," Edie said. "Or maybe there were just too many of us. Too many people, not enough time. Too much pressure."

"Yeah," Wes said. "I thought that, too." He looked around—a bit obviously, Edie thought—and leaned in. "So yeah. I want to tell you something. But I'm not sure about your boyfriend. Sorry about that. I know it puts you in a weird position."

"It does," said Edie. She was instantly on edge. She'd sensed his—well, crush was probably a strong word for it, but his notice of her hadn't escaped her own notice, nor had it escaped Jesse's, she was sure. Was he going to declare himself?

"I'm not saying you can't tell him," Wes said. "I mean, I'd rather you didn't. But I'll trust your judgment."

"Okay," Edie said. Now she was just confused.

"So what do you think?"

"What do I think about what?"

"About whether or not you'll tell him," Wes said impatiently.

"I guess that depends on what it is," Edie said. "I mean, obviously it does. How couldn't it?"

The trio (plus Jesse) finished "Right Night for You." Edie and Wes clapped a little with the rest of the audience. Edie held herself stiff, wondering if Jesse would stop singing now and rejoin her—if his doing so would mean her never hearing what Wes had aimed to tell her—but they kicked into another song, and she exhaled. "I don't want to be rude, but you need to just spit it out."

"All right. Just, you know. Discretion and all that."

Edie circled her hand impatiently.

"Marta snuck something out here. Something useful."

Edie leaned forward, thinking *phone*. Thinking, *gun*. "What, for God's sake?"

"A canister of Quicksilver."

Edie slumped back. "Quicksilver."

"Shh!" Wes hissed.

"Quicksilver. Like, pepper spray."

"It's a lot more than that and you know it," Wes said. "Or you should. It's fast and it's quiet. She said she has at least four sprays' worth."

"OK, OK," Edie said, raising her hands in surrender. "You're right. It's something. It's better than nothing. But what can we do with it?"

Wes sighed and picked at a thumbnail. "I had a thought about that. Half-formed."

Edie sensed there was something here to dread. "Yeah?"

"Marta's fifty-four. She's in good health, but she's led kind of a sheltered life, from what I can tell."

Edie waited. Wes stole a glance at her, then went back to his thumb.

"Lee—well, you know what we're dealing with there. Which isn't much. The Tanakas might be part of whatever that woman's cooking up. Like I am. So our presence here might, like Anastasia said, be some protection to the rest of you."

"You want me to be the one to try to steal off and get help," Edie said. She felt sick with fury at this realization—and also just sick. And disappointed, and embarrassed. She had thought Wes liked her. Actually, he had just been sizing her up, gauging whether she might risk her life in his place.

"Please lower your voice," Wes whispered. He was pink-faced, and still not making eye contact. Ashamed, maybe. Good. "It wouldn't just be you. Tia—I talked to Tia. She knows these woods. She feels pretty sure she could get to a Quarantine or even slip back past the Salt Line if necessary. She wants to do it. But she can't go alone. She's going to need help."

"Berto and Anastasia? What about them? God, Wes. At least they look like two people who could handle a night in the woods. Aren't they supposed to be survivalists or something?"

Wes's face darkened. "Yeah. I thought so, too. But they said no. They're all for the idea. They just don't want to be the ones to do it."

Edie shook her head, disgusted. "Well, neither do I."

"And I can't make you," Wes said. "You might not want to leave Jesse. I don't think it would be a good idea to take him with you. Or maybe it is, and my judgment's clouded by my dislike of the guy. I'm sorry. He seems like he'd be a liability. But maybe he has—I don't know—hidden reserves."

He did, Edie thought. But not the kind that helped you survive a night flight through a dangerous forest.

"If you want to do it, I think tonight's the night. There's a lot of activity. The ones with the guns are half-drunk. You and Tia tell them that you need to go pee, break off from the group, use the Quicksilver. Then you run."

"With no weapons, no food, no Stamps," Edie said. "No map. No clue. You have got to be kidding me."

"It's a huge risk, I know," Wes said. "But it's a risk not acting, too. Some of them are nice, sure. Got themselves a little country idyll out here. Bluegrass band and Town Hall and moonshine. But there's something we're not seeing, or they'd leave the zone alone. They're driven by desperation. That makes them dangerous."

"Or maybe they're driven by their ideals," Edie said, thinking about June's story. Thinking about Violet.

"That might be worse, honestly," Wes said. "Ideals make people stupid. Believe me, I know."

Edie stared at a distant bonfire until her eyes watered. She closed them. The fire printed the backs of her eyelids in neon.

"You know what I notice about all this?" Edie said.

"What?" His voice was wary.

"Tia and me. We're the disposable ones."

"I don't know what you're talking about."

"Yes you do," Edie said. "You've basically laid it out already. Everybody else is precious for some reason. Tia's the hired help. I'm the girlfriend. We won't be missed. So we walk our poor asses out into God knows what and maybe die trying to rescue the rest of you."

"That's not the situation at all," Wes said.

Edie nodded hard. "Andy tried to warn me off back at the training center. He said that I wasn't like the rest of you. I wish I'd listened."

The band had stopped playing. Jesse, seated now on the edge of the little stage, was smiling and talking to someone, picking at his ukulele in an offhand way. He laughed, his Adam's apple bobbing.

Edie thought for a few seconds about escape. Enter the woods. Exit the relationship. An extreme measure, you'd have to call it. Comical, almost.

"I apologize," Wes said. "Honestly, Edie. That wasn't my line of thought at all. It was not. But I see why you'd read it that way."

"Big of you," Edie said.

Wes gathered his plate and his glass. "It's a no. Gotcha. Please keep it quiet, though. What we've got. Will you do that?"

Edie sighed. "Of course I will."

"I admire you," Wes said. "I think you could do it. Maybe I think that because Andy is right, and you're not like the rest of us. Maybe that's a good thing, Edie."

He bobbed his head at her in goodbye, and she watched him walk away. Marta, downhill, waited for him. For the verdict. Edie was sorry to let her down. A little sorry. *Maybe that's a good thing.* Easy for him to say.

Jesse dropped to his bottom beside her. "Feingold," he said. Growled. "What did he want?"

"Just chatting," Edie said.

Jesse slung his arm around her shoulders. "Should I be jealous?" He was trying to sound like he was joking, like the idea was absurd.

"No," Edie said. "I'm not interested in what he has on offer." She took another swallow of her beer. "Not even a little."

Wes shook his head—a quick, negative gesture, imperceptible unless you were looking for it—before taking to the grass beside Marta. Her stomach twisted.

"She said no?"

"She said no," Wes affirmed. He bit his lip. "I think I insulted her, actually. Jeez. I should've thought of how it might sound to her. Like—" He shook his head again. "Anyway. It was no."

"Perhaps I should be the one. It's not fair of me to put it on someone else. I came out here. I did the training, such as it was. I'm as good a candidate as anybody."

Wes ran his fingers across his smooth scalp. There was a rasping sound—his hair, already starting to grow back in.

"But I keep thinking about my sons. I'm sorry, Wes. That's what it boils down to for me. In what scenario am I likelier to see my sons again? I think it's staying here and seeing what happens."

"I understand," Wes said.

She patted his hand. "I know you do."

"I don't want you to be the one, either. I don't feel like there's anyone else here I can trust. Not for sure."

Her gut twisted at that. Could he trust her? Her intentions by him were pure—but she hadn't told him about her real name, about who her husband was and what he'd asked her to do. She hadn't revealed to him the means by which she'd smuggled in the Quicksilver masked as a Smokeless. As for that last, he hadn't asked. Not in so many words. But the question was in his eyes. Should she tell him? She wanted to, in a way—how strange it was, at this point in her life, to feel that her dearest friend in the world was a boy not much older than her sons, a boy she'd only known for a few short weeks—but she also worried that the information could do him more harm than good.

They sat, watching the flow of the river and the flow of the villagers along its banks.

"I have no idea what to make of all this," Marta said after a while. "The people here seem happy. Don't they?"

"They *are* happy," said a voice from behind them, and Marta jolted so hard that she spilled her glass of water all over her lap.

"May I join you?"

June. Marta and Wes stared.

"That was a stupid question," June said. "I try not to ask those. What I mean is, will you join me? Or, rather, join me. Let's go on a walk."

"Where?" Marta asked. Another stupid question.

"Wherever I say," said June mildly.

They started upriver, away from the crush of activity around the food, music, and bonfires. Marta, looking over her shoulder at this, noticed that they were being trailed. Thirty feet back, maybe: three figures, armed. Hard to tell in the moonlight, but she thought that one was the big guy from their kidnapping nightmare, Randall. She had believed that he, Andy, Violet, and the other one were absent tonight. Sleeping off their rough all-night march. A foolhardy assumption. Maybe it was a stroke of luck that no one had agreed to stage an escape attempt with Tia.

They were heading uphill, back toward the flower beds where they'd first spied June. They—the beds—extended as far as Marta could make out in the starlight, a patchwork of tall, slender stems topped with heavy blooms, nodding as if in sleep, rustling eerily in an otherwise imperceptible breeze. June halted beside a bed, reached out, and grabbed a thick, hairy stalk, tilting a red flower toward them—its black eye, its crepe petals.

"This is why you're here," she said. "This flower. My father's life's work."

"Poppies?" Wes asked.

"Not exactly," June said. "It's a hybrid. Secret recipe. It's our cash crop and our salvation."

"You produce heroin," Marta said. For the first time since the kidnapping, it occurred to her with a sinking certainty that this situation was connected to David's situation. The one that necessitated her and the boys hiding out somewhere. Did June know who she was? Had David, instead of protecting her, sent her right into the camp of his enemy?

"No," June said sharply. "Heroin is an opiate. I've told you this is not a poppy."

"Some drug, then," Marta said, surprised at her own superior tone. The fifteen-gram vial of Salt, hidden in its NicoClean cell camouflage, was still in her knapsack back at Town Hall. She hadn't used any of it. She hadn't been tempted to—yet. But a year ago? A month?

And David, of course. She knew how he made his living. Some of it, at least. She knew, and still she ate the fine foods and drank the fine wine, slept between the silken sheets, walked her bare feet across the cool marble floors. She enjoyed the bounty and accepted it as her due, for having to live with a man she no longer recognized.

"There are good drugs and bad drugs," June said. "We make a bit of both, and both of them allow us to survive."

Wes ran his finger along the furred stalk. "This is all interesting," he said. Marta thought he sounded genuine. "But I don't understand what it has to do with me."

"We have distribution and a market for the drug that bankrolls our little operation. Salt. Maybe you've heard of it."

Marta stiffened. Wes shrugged.

"I can't say I'm too happy with our business partner," June said. "Our situation here is precarious. Marta, you said that people here look happy. I told you that we are."

"OK, great. You're happy," Marta said. "Let us go."

June smiled a thin smile. "Our happiness is contingent on the whims of a very bad man. It's fragile. If that man decides he doesn't like how we're doing things, or what we're doing—we're done."

A very bad man. Marta's hands started to tremble, and she hid them behind her back.

"Again," Wes said, "very interesting, very unfortunate. What's it to me?"

June pressed the Stamp scar on her cheekbone. "This is the only Stamp I've received since I was a child. I gave it to myself fourteen years ago. Not because of a bite. I haven't been bitten in a long time. Wes, I haven't been bitten in your lifetime. And it's not because I spend my days wearing fancy long johns, either."

Wes fumbled with the pull on his microsuit's zipper self-consciously.

"No. This Stamp was an act of solidarity with my people. A symbol of what we've lived with. A reminder of what we'll never again endure." Aware, it seemed, that her tone had strayed too far from its winning folksiness, she dropped her hand from her cheekbone and wove her fingers together across her midriff, as if she were about to sing a few notes from "Do Re Mi." "The upshot is that we have a cure. Or, rather, a kind of medicinal repellant. Against the tick bites."

"That can't be true," Wes said. "If such a thing were even possible with the current technologies, it would already exist. Atlantic Zone alone has spent billions on research. Everyone in the world has been working on this thing, and you're trying to tell me that the cure's been out here all along?"

"Not all along," June said. "But yes. It's here. And I tell you, it's possible. It exists already. My father spent his life hybridizing this flower. I refined the processing methods, and with the help of this community, I standardized an inoculation dosage. Haven't you noticed our young people? The ones working the flowers earlier today? Did you see a mark on them?"

Wes was shaking his head, hands on his hips. "I just—I just can't. I don't know. If you have what you say you have, I don't know why you didn't have Andy or someone on the inside notify the proper authorities."

June laughed. "The proper authorities! You're so accomplished, Mr. Feingold, that I forget how young you are."

He flushed dark red. Marta could see this even in the smeary light, and it occurred to her that this was, oddly, the first time Wes had seemed anything other than genial to her. June had triggered a threatening vulnerability in him. She'd be wise, Marta thought, to proceed carefully.

"Let's try looking at this from another angle. Wes, I've heard a rumor that you're about to make a big investment in"—she made a show of looking him up and down—"well, fashion."

The righteous redness in Wes's face drained away. "How did you—" He stopped himself and shook his head, lips pinched together.

"Don't be so shocked. Outer Limits Excursions is invested in your deal happening, and they've taken steps to make sure that your little publicity stunt goes perfectly."

"What do you mean, publicity stunt?" Marta asked.

June turned to Wes, politely concerned. "Is this a secret? Should I send her away?"

Wes rolled his eyes. "Jeez. It's not a done deal yet. Pocketz is looking to partner with SecondSkins microsuits. I came on this trip to test-run the product myself. If it goes well, we make the announcement when I get back."

David's major "legit" deal, Marta realized. So this was it. This was the reason he wanted eyes on Feingold.

"So now we circle back to my original point. You said 'if it goes well,' Wes. And I've told you that OLE is very, very determined it go well."

"OK," Wes said. "So?"

June peered at him. "I wasn't sure if you knew or not. My guess was that you did. But now I wonder."

"For God's sake. What?"

"You've been taking Ruby City's inoculation for three weeks, as part of your regular vitamin supply. You could strip that suit off now and roll around in the grass naked, Wes. No tick is going to bite you."

"Bullshit," Wes said.

June shrugged. "Nope. Not bullshit. The drug exists, and people in-zone know about it. Some of them even get to take it."

"What about everyone else on the excursion?" Wes asked.

"This is where I get a little confused," June said. "For more reasons than one. The Tanakas got the vitamin. At extraordinary cost, I'll add. And, for some mysterious reason"—she paused dramatically—"Marta Severs. That directive came down to Andy from the very top. He did as he was told."

"But Marta got bitten," Wes said with satisfaction. "I gave her the Stamp myself."

"Again," said June, "that's why I'm confused. Marta? Any insights here?"

She hesitated for a moment, but didn't see the profit in lying. "I didn't take the vitamins. I've been dealing with . . . a stomach thing. They made me sick. I had no idea what they were actually for."

"Well, that's one mystery solved. What about the other? Why you?"

Marta shrugged uncomfortably. "Your guess is as good as mine."

June smiled humorously. "I'll bet it is. But let's leave it alone for now. There's too much to discuss. There's the matter of your new business partner, for instance. What do you know about David Perrone, Wes?"

Marta's face burned. Thank goodness it was dark.

"Stop playing this out. Just tell me what you want to tell me."

"OK. I will. He puppeteers an entire economy that your Pocketz doesn't touch," June said. "Or touches indirectly. Drugs, of course. Our street Salt, for example. Illegal electronics and data mines, contraband of every possible stripe. And girls. Boys, too. Some women. But mostly girls. It might fascinate you, Wes—this shadow economy. The outer-zone camps like the one where Violet's life began still exist. The one at Flat Rock still exists. Groups like yours travel out here on vacation. The accommodations can be pretty luxe, from what I've heard." She eyed Marta now for some reason, shrewdly. "Of course, prostitution's legal in Atlantic Zone now, so these camps have to cater to somewhat"—she pursed her lips around the word—"specialized interests. OLE makes regular runs out to

Flat Rock and another camp up near Roanoke. They're booked as hunting excursions. Andy has led several of them. He tells me that hunting is sometimes involved, matter of fact."

"Oh my God," Marta said softly.

"Yes," June said.

Marta was overcome with vertigo, or something like it—a sensation like falling, but what she was falling into was the black, fetid pit of her own willful ignorance and cowardice. Oh, she'd kept the lights off—the drugs helped with that—and she'd stumbled around blindly in the dark halls of her marriage, but she'd felt around the edges of things in order to keep moving safely forward. She had intimate knowledge of the shapes in the dark.

"Last year," June continued, "a military unit out of Atlantic Zone leveled a community like ours in West Virginia. They burned it to the ground in the night as people slept. Gunned down the runners. It's an open secret that Perrone initiated that raid to settle a score with a rival crime boss out of Midwest Zone."

Marta could see that Wes wanted to protest again, to claim these things weren't possible. But he pressed his lips together, making a thin white line.

"That put us here in Ruby City on alert. But we thought we had fairly safe status. We thought we had a product Perrone wouldn't want to do without, and we thought we'd done a pretty good job of safeguarding that product, keeping it proprietary, even keeping our village's location secure. Perrone's been trying for years to get us to make a onetime deal with him. He wants seeds, plants, formulas—for the street Salt and the therapeutic Salt. Says he'll make a big onetime payout to us and then leave us alone. Sounds nice. But I'm not stupid. I know what happens if we hand all of that over. I know what he's capable of. So I've put him off in every way I know how. So far, it's worked.

"Then, three things happened.

"First, we got word of your deal. Microsuits, of all things. We've braced ourselves for all kinds of possibilities here, but I'll admit that wasn't high on anyone's list. What's the next big Pocketz investment, Wes? Aluminum foil hats?"

Wes seethed. June, unruffled, continued.

"Around that same time, some of our raw product went missing. Some seeds. Not much—it's pure luck we caught the discrepancy, because whoever took the stuff was careful. It was literally a matter of a pouch being a tenth of a gram off during a chance weigh-in. Once we knew, though, we discovered the other thefts pretty quickly. And we haven't figured out the who or the how, but we know the what. We have to assume David Perrone has them, or soon will.

"The last thing happened after your training started, and that's when I told Andy to pull the trigger and get you to Ruby City. Another community out here became a crater in the ground. I don't know the ins and outs of this one, but I have it on good authority that the community housed a lab bankrolled by private interests in Gulf Zone. Three, four hundred people, easy. I'm guessing they had their own little vitamins. I can only assume other people have figured out what we've figured out, or else they've solved another dimension to the problem, like curing Shreve's specifically. Either way, it's all gone now. And we're looking at the sky, wondering if we're next. We're Perrone's pet lab. We've got that going for us. But if he's gotten his hands on our seeds, that might not matter. He hasn't come knocking with his buyout offer again, and that makes me nervous. And if he's making microsuit deals, maybe he isn't interested any longer in getting into the business of fixing the tick problem. Maybe he's discovered that he likes the tick problem just fine."

She stopped finally. Downriver, the revelry continued. Marta shivered against a sudden breeze that rattled the weeds lining the water. A light rain started to fall, little more than a mist, but Marta sensed something heavy and ripe in the air, a coming storm.

"What is it you want from me?" Wes asked. He sounded very tired.

"First, I want you to process a hard truth. Those three or four hundred people outside Gulf Zone—that happened because of your microsuit deal. That's what this man is willing to do. That's who you've partnered with, and those are the stakes if you keep this deal with him."

I have to do something kind of bold to clench it, David had said. None of Marta's suspicions about David had prepared her for a possibility like this. But she couldn't muster enough disbelief to doubt June. Could David have done what June said he'd done?

Yes, she had to admit. Yes. He could have.

Wes's eyes were bright with dampness. "I had no idea—you have to believe I had no idea anything like that could happen."

"I do believe it," June said. "But now you know."

"So what do I do then? Back out of the arrangement? It's done. I won't do it. You have my word."

"That's something, but it might not be enough for us. Because Perrone has our seeds. I have to operate on that assumption, anyway. So here's what I propose: you make us your partners, instead." June shook her head suddenly, as if arguing with herself. "Not even partners. Partnership is more than what I'm asking for here. I'll let you have the deal Perrone wanted. I give you seeds, plants, and formulas to take back to Atlantic Zone, and you give us some kind of reimbursement to cover our losses from the alliance with Perrone. I can promise you we'll be a lot cheaper than Perrone's deal, and you'll be getting a product that actually does something." A sadness settled into her face, making her features sag. "A product that changes everything."

"You don't seem so happy about that possibility," Marta said.

"I'm not. You know why this zoning business has gone on as long as it has? Because lots of us like it this way. The David Perrones of the world like living behind walls. Me, I like living outside of them.

When Salt gets tested and packaged and distributed, and people's insurance starts covering it, that's the beginning of the end for all of this." She motioned downriver, where the glow of bonfires etched the edges of the starlit sky. "It won't be long before the zones are fighting about who owns us, which government gets to tell us when to bend and squat. But what choice do we have? I'll take a few more years over nothing. I have lives to protect."

Wes ran both hands over his shaved head, thoughtfully. It was quiet enough now that Marta could hear the dry rasp of his palms against the new stubble.

"If I do this," Wes said. "If I agree to it. You let everyone go home tomorrow."

June shook her head firmly. "No, Wes. I'm sorry. I have to keep you here until you're scheduled to report back to Quarantine 1. Otherwise Perrone's going to know something's up, and we can't risk that."

"What will you do with us?" Marta asked.

"We'll treat you like guests," June said. "We have comfortable bunkhouses. You'll all get doses of Salt—we drink it here in a tea, and it hits the system faster—and so you won't be at any risk of disease. We'll feed you well. Heck, you can spend the time doing all of the things you planned to come out here to do: hike, swim, fish. Sit under a tree and read. You won't have to use a Stamp. And Wes, I can show you how our operation works. You can gather all the information you'll need to bring back to your people."

She held out her slim, pale hand. Wes studied it.

"You know it will take years—maybe four or five years—for a drug to get FDA approval. That's a conservative estimate."

"I'm counting on it," June said, letting the hand drop. "We want the time. We need it. As long as you publicize the development of the drug, as long as Perrone knows you know about us, we might be safe. If there is such a thing as being safe."

"Jesus," Wes said. "How do I explain this to everyone else?

You've terrorized them. Us. Your"—he searched for a word—"daughter shot one of our group in the head. Whatever Andy says about that, the bite, the infestation, it doesn't matter. This is the guy who held an assault rifle to our heads and marched us through the woods all night. Why didn't you just kidnap me and leave everyone else alone?"

"Because OLE procedure would have called for a halt to the excursion and immediate return to Quarantine, which would have set off alarms. As for terrorizing you, yes, I wish it hadn't had to be that way. I wish we could have led you off kindly and been assured that you'd wait patiently for an explanation. But you know and I know that wouldn't have worked. As for the man Violet shot, I believe Andy when he says he was dying. But it's unfortunate. It wasn't part of the plan."

Marta said, "And who's to say this plan will work any better than that one did?"

"It did work," June said. "You're here. You're hearing me out. The question is: Will you help?"

Wes looked at Marta. Thinking of all she knew and hadn't told him, even now—and could she? could she confess that she was married to a man who'd done the things June was saying he'd done?—she dropped her gaze. What would she do when all of this was over? Return to that house, that bed? Resume her place at David's side?

But how else would she see Sal and Enzo again?

June was holding her hand out to Wes again. He considered it for an uncomfortably long moment, letting it hang in space. He was reaching out to take it when a cry rose up behind them, in the village, and footsteps pounded their way. Marta stiffened, startled. Her scalp prickled. She could hear the rasping exhalations of runners—sprinters—and braced herself to be leveled by a stampede.

Andy drew to a careening stop in front of them and hunched over. He put one hand on his knee and gasped. The other he pointed uphill, toward the Town Hall.

"She took out Miles and Leeda," he said hoarsely. "She's gone."

"Who?" June said. "Who are you talking about?"

"Tia." He drew fully to a stand, mopped his face dry with a rag, and stared balefully at Marta and Wes. "She killed Miles and Leeda. She disappeared. She has their weapons."

"Wait, wait, wait," Wes said. "What do you mean, killed them? Are you sure they're not just unconscious?"

Andy bum-rushed Wes, knocking him to his back, and Marta huffed out a startled little squeak that might have been funny under other circumstances. Andy slapped Wes's cheek, leaving behind a dark print. Backhanded the other cheek, streaking it, too. There was a smell in the air, iron and mud, and Marta grasped suddenly that she was seeing blood, a lot of it. Andy's fingers dragged red marks across Wes's microsuit as Randall hauled him off by his armpits, and he screamed, "She bashed their heads in, you piece of shit! She murdered them!"

Wes lay on his back, too petrified to move. Marta knew the feeling. Her knees were so weak they couldn't even knock together.

The expression on June's face was cold. Cold. "Go after her," she said softly to Andy, who was still being loosely restrained by the guards. "Get Roz. You know what to do. As for the two of you"—she turned to Wes and Marta—"well, I'm afraid this changes things."

Eleven

Within three hours of Tia's escape, the hostages, once again with wrists zip-tied, were moved roughly at gunpoint, through a driving rain, from Town Hall to a grim corrugated storage building with narrow horizontal windows positioned near the ceiling, so that only the tops of trees and a wedge of night sky were visible. A single doorway separated inside from out, and it would be guarded at all times, June promised, by an armed villager. A curtain strung up in a corner hid a waste bucket. "The facilities," June said, loading those two words with more malice than Edie would have imagined possible. The floor was oiled dirt.

The group clumped together, cold and soaked, in the middle of the room, trembling as June directed Joe and Randall to pat them each down. Their backpacks had already been confiscated. Into a satchel the shoes went. "What's going on?" Lee kept saying. "What are you doing?"

"Where's Tia?" Edie dared to ask. Afraid of the answer.

"Gone," June said. She gave Edie a shrewd look. "She killed two of our villagers and took off. A nineteen-year-old girl and a seventeen-year-old boy. Good kids. Really good kids. They were found in the woods with their heads bashed in."

Edie looked at Wes before she could stop herself. His eyes widened, and he shook his head, an anguished expression flickering across his face. *I didn't know she was going to do that,* the head-shake said. *It wasn't part of the plan.*

"Those so-called good kids had guns," Berto said.

"They weren't loaded. But that's not a mistake we'll make again."

"What are you going to do to us?" Wes asked.

"I haven't decided," June said. "I'd hoped to work this out peacefully. I had thought I could have you back on your way home in a few weeks' time. But that required some trust and goodwill."

Marta snorted. "Trust and goodwill."

"That's funny to you?" June asked.

"It's absurd to me," said Marta tiredly. "And not funny at all."

June's lip curled. "I was talking to Wes when this news came in." She was addressing the larger group now. "We seemed to be close to an understanding. A mutually beneficial arrangement. Maybe Wes will tell you about it. Maybe that understanding isn't out of reach. But I can't look at any of you right now." With that, she walked out. Randall followed her, eyeing each of them with cold amusement, and pulled the door closed behind him. A deadbolt turned.

The rain roared against the metal roof. It was a sound Edie normally loved, but tonight it felt like an assault. Like the sky was falling in.

"What's this arrangement she mentioned?" Ken Tanaka asked. All eyes shifted to Wes.

He squirmed under the scrutiny. There were red streaks marking the chest of his microsuit, and angry red blotches on both of his cheeks. June had left them with a single lantern, and it flickered wanly across his face. "It's a long story. Marta, you'll have to help me tell it."

"I don't believe it," Lee said. "I don't believe a word of it."

"You think I'm lying?" Wes asked.

"No," Lee said, "but I think you're stupid if you buy this load of horse crap. Miracle tick cure, out here in the boonies? Gangsters commanding the Atlantic Zone military to mow down innocent women and children in their beds? Use your brain. What sense does any of that make?"

"Sounds plausible to me," Anastasia said. "ConspireWire has been reporting for years on the outer-zone insurgency problem. Just last month they posted—"

"Don't even start with that conspiracy nonsense. I won't hear it. I tell you, it's horse crap."

"So why do all of this?" Edie asked him.

"Money! You heard the man. She's going to send him home with some magic beans and he's supposed to send her back a pile of cash." Lee's face was bright pink, and a thatch of iron-colored hairs sprouted from the open neck of his microsuit. *It's a wonder they didn't make him shave all that along with his head,* Edie had thought the morning they embarked—was that not even two days ago?—picturing him in a pastel golf shirt and plaid trousers, driver tipped over a shoulder. He carried himself like a man used to bossing around underlings, underlings who called him Mr. Flannigan, sir, and picked up his dry cleaning during their twenty-minute lunch break.

Wes shook his head, exasperated. "It wouldn't be as simple as that. What good does money do out here? They don't have a Pocketz account. I don't even know if they have a computer. I can't just make a transfer. They're taking a huge risk, trusting that I'd follow through on my end of the deal once I'm back in-zone. You can call me stupid, but I believe June when she says that her object is to get the drug out in some public form before Perrone can act."

"And anyway," Berto said, "so what if they're just magic beans? Let Wes give her what she wants. I'll chip in. We should play their game and go home."

"Like they're going to just let us pay our own ransom and leave," Wendy said. "She made her deal with Wes. Not us."

"I wouldn't make any deal with her that didn't guarantee the safety of everyone here," Wes said.

"Do you think she'll just let all nine of us go back in-zone, knowing everything we know about this place?" Anastasia asked. "Genuine question."

"I think," Wes said, "it's a risk she's willing to take, given what's at stake for them."

Jesse, who had been strangely quiet through all of this, finally spoke. "So it's your fault this all happened, Feingold. You're the reason the rest of us are here."

Silence fell again. Wes's jaw tensed and his eyes watered. Edie still felt the sting of his proposal, but the pain on his face was real. And she had her own dose of guilt to bear, didn't she? If she'd gone along with Tia, would those two teenagers have been killed?

"Don't start that nonsense," Marta snapped. "He couldn't have known."

"But he makes a good point," said Wendy. "The rest of us are just dragged into this, for nothing." She hid her face in her hands, muffling her words. "I can't believe it. I can't believe Ken and I paid four hundred thousand for this."

"Did you say four hundred?" Berto asked. "Ani and I only paid two."

Jesse leaned in eagerly. "Me, too. For me and Edie, I mean."

Ken cast Wendy such a thunderous look that Edie felt real concern for her, real alarm about what he might do. She was reminded again of her initial impression that the two were spouses rather than siblings. There was a strangeness between them, though maybe that was just Ken's strangeness, because he was brooding, distant. Unfriendly. Though Wendy's English was thoroughly American, even accented with the slight twang that Edie associated with the southern reaches of the Atlantic Zone, Ken, unless forced by Outer Limits procedures or the barest demands of politeness to speak, only talked to Wendy, and then only in Japanese. The reason Edie had thought them married, she had to admit to herself now, was that there seemed between them a power imbalance particular to a certain kind of couple. Though Wendy was the one who did all of the asking and engaging for both of the Tanakas, and Ken stood silently, even meekly, to the side, he gave off the unmistakable air of being in charge.

"That's interesting," Marta said. "Because Andy told June that the two of you were the only ones in the group other than Wes getting the inoculation. She didn't know why."

Wes's eyes darted Marta's way. Marta, staring at Wendy and Ken, missed this, but Edie did not.

"Wendy misspoke," Ken said softly. "We also paid two hundred thousand."

"Was there a premium package?" Lee asked. "Because I would have sprung for it."

"You just said you didn't even think the drug existed," Wes said. "You just said I'm stupid and this whole story of June's is a fairy tale."

"I said it was a load of horse crap," Lee said. He seemed unbothered by the contradiction.

"I don't know what to believe anymore." Anastasia put her head in her hands.

"If there was a premium package," Marta said carefully, almost soothingly, as though she were speaking to a skittish animal, "that's important information for us to have right now. That's information we'd need as we decide if we can trust June's story."

Wendy seemed as interested in Ken's response as everyone else in the group was, but he only shook his head. "We also paid two hundred," he repeated.

Berto huffed and rubbed his face. "OK. Say it's all a lie. What can we do about it? They have our Stamps, our shoes, all our gear. I don't even know what we're arguing about. There's one way forward." He made a jabbing motion with his hand. "Go along with whatever they want. Hope for the best."

"There's still Tia," Anastasia said. "If she gets back, gets help—"

"That's a big 'if,'" Wes said. "What's our plan if she doesn't?"

A long, empty stretch. Time to listen to the rain on the roof. Edie closed her eyes against the lantern light, watching its afterglow lick at the inside of her eyelids.

"It's on you, Feingold." Jesse again. Edie opened her eyes in time to see what she'd missed before in Jesse's eyes: his cellular-level terror. "You have what they say they want. You have the power. You believe what they're selling. Get them to let the rest of us go."

"You should at least try," Wendy said.

Wes took a deep breath. Then nodded. "Yeah, OK. I'll try."

"Or maybe Tia will get back home," said Anastasia. "Maybe help will be here soon."

Twelve

The dogs were named Tauntaun and Wampa—dumb names, Andy thought, but it was their handler's doing, some kind of inside joke, and the handler, Roz, was quick-tempered and absolutely indispensable to June and so Andy kept his thoughts about the names to himself. The dogs themselves were magnificent mongrels, littermates, both male: at least forty kilos apiece, brindled coats, big square skulls and powerful jaws, strangely long ears that hung around the dogs' block faces, making them look a bit like they were wearing women's wigs. Roz was more trainer than breeder, June had explained to Andy long ago (Roz explained herself to no one but June), but she kept about a dozen dogs, knew all of the neighborhood dogs, and was always on the lookout for what she called hill curs—muddy-colored dogs with muddled pedigrees, tick-resistant, feral but not too wild. Coaxable. She mated the dogs by instinct and whim rather than system, kept the pups she thought she could work with, gave away the ones she couldn't, drowned the rest. (June had laughed when this disclosure made Andy flinch. "You really are a Zoner, aren't you? God love you.") Those she kept she raised up to whatever seemed to be their strength, for there was ever a need in Ruby City for good trained dogs, hunting dogs especially but also guard dogs, herding dogs, and even service dogs, of a sort; after all, blind children out here stayed blind, and if you were lucky enough to get old out-of-zone, you did it without the benefit of laser surgeries and retinal reattachments and even corrective lenses, unless you could get your hands on an old scavenged pair of glasses or something smuggled from in-zone.

The one or two dogs—never more than two—who struck Roz as most versatile in their intelligence, steady, loyal, hale: these she called the princes (whether male or female), and she kept them by her side at all times. When Andy first came to Ruby City eleven years ago, there had been a different prince—Leto, that one was called—a tall, spindle-legged dog with shaggy gray fur and the narrow haunches of a greyhound. Leto had been regal, aloof. Tolerated petting, but didn't seem to enjoy it. Tauntaun and Wampa, when they weren't at work, were sweet, loving dogs, kissers, playful as pups. Woolers, June called them. "Look at 'em woolin'," she'd say, smiling her serene smile down at the dogs wriggling on their backs in a patch of hot sunlight, chortling, rolling each other.

At work now—a condition signaled to them by the leather collars Roz had buckled around their necks—Tauntaun and Wampa trotted seriously through the underbrush, Tauntaun ahead, off-lead, Wampa leashed by a six-meter rope tied off around Roz's thick waist. Her tracking process was another thing Roz didn't deign to explain to Andy—but he could gather the basics from watching her. Tauntaun went ahead, sometimes even out of sight, zigging and zagging, nose to the earth. When he caught the scent, he barked, and Wampa answered, lunging forward, slowing reluctantly at a yank on his lead and an unintelligible correction from Roz, then dipping his nose, too, to the ground. The dogs would reunite, sniff each other. Then Roz would cast off again by making some noise from the back of her throat, and Tauntaun became a brown blur, a smudge in the woods ahead.

The morning air was gray. Opaque. That it was morning, and they had only been on the trail for two hours, frustrated Andy—but Roz refused to set out at night, said she was too old and fat to go off gallivanting into the woods during a turd floater, couldn't even see your own hand in front of your face. *What do you want, for me to break my neck?* And Andy knew it would be useless to try to track Tia without the dogs. So he agreed to wait. He went to his cot in the bunkhouse, lay back with his boots still on, and looked at the plank ceiling while the cookout revelry continued out by the river, most of Ruby City's residents oblivious to the tragedy that had just occurred uphill from where they shoveled in plates of barbecue and gulped glasses of foamy beer. June's call. "I'm not laying that news at the feet of a bunch of happy drunks," she said. "They'll go after the hostages, and I'm not sure if even I could stop them. Let's see if we can bring them some good news first."

Bring them Tia is what she meant. For what purpose, Andy couldn't say. He had lived a double life for almost a decade, but it wasn't a life split neatly into halves. Most of the eleven years, for him, transpired in-zone. And even in his time spent on OLE tours, he could only escape to Ruby City for brief visits, after lights-out, stealing hours from time he was supposed to be sleeping, leading his groups on hikes and hunts the next day in a drowsy fog. A wonder that he had never shot himself in the foot or walked off a cliff. He knew Ruby City less from firsthand experience than he did from encrypted electronic correspondence with its residents and his memories of that three-month-long stay eleven years ago, when June had brought him here, shown him her world and, in so doing, showed him his world back home—the horrendous lie of it. And then she had shown him his purpose. He'd had no regrets. Not even with the sacrifices. But still, he knew only in the abstract what justice looked like in Ruby City, and as furious as he was at Tia, as grief-stricken as he was at the senseless deaths of Leeda and Miles, he didn't relish the idea of leading Tia to the gallows, or whatever fate Ruby citizens reserved for those who murdered one of their own.

I'm knocked up, Tia had said to him just before boot camp for this excursion had begun. He couldn't stop remembering her words, the look on her face. The desperation in her eyes that she'd hidden, as she always did, behind a defiant bravado. *I might be off my game.* And what he could see now, flat on his back on this cot, was that Tia had wanted to be talked out of going on the excursion or even tattled on. OLE had a policy against sending pregnant women, guides or paying customers, on excursions. Liability was too high. Andy could have gone to Larry Abrams, excursion director, and let Tia's secret slip. She might have been fired for noncompliance, or she might have been moved to an office job at a quarter of her regular salary, but she would have been safe. Why hadn't he done that? Some screwed-up sense of loyalty? Maybe. He hadn't wanted to betray her, even to help her. Distraction? That, too. What had popped in his head at her confession was, *Great. Of course.* His silent work all these years, never really knowing if, or when, his time would come—it had all led up to this trip, and so of course it was just his damn luck that Tia would come up pregnant, that Tia, whom he'd regarded, always, as a real friend—as real a friend as a man whose entire life was a fabrication could hope to make—would be assigned to this excursion at all.

But that wasn't the whole of it, he admitted to himself.

It had been crazy, half-formed, foolish, fantasy, stress-induced, exhaustion-induced—if he'd stopped for even a moment to think this impulse through, he'd have recognized its absurdity—but Andy had always liked Tia, there had been fleeting moments over the years when he'd wondered if he might more-than-like her, and he was giving up everything to serve June and Ruby City and his own ideals: his wife, his sons. (June and Ruby City and his ideals predated Beth, predated Ian and Colby, but that didn't make abandoning them any easier.) Maybe he didn't have to be so alone. Maybe he didn't have to give *everything* up. And it was the baby, weirdly, that had triggered this fantasy, because he knew what a baby would mean to June and the rest, imagined it as a beautiful sort of gift he and Tia could make to the community.

Crazy, half-formed, foolish. Fantasy. Not even a conscious plan, not anything he could register as having entertained as a possibility until now, in retrospect, in this first quiet moment since he and the others had raised their guns on the travelers—but there it was.

And Tia had made her own crazy, half-formed plan. Now she was God knows where, and two people—kids, really—were dead.

All of this was why Andy spent his first night in eleven years under a Ruby City roof not sleeping—his eyes wide in alarm, head swarming with regrets—and embarked on his hunt the next morning in that same old familiar, albeit caffeinated, fog.

Wampa was pulling now toward Tauntaun, who had lain on his belly, posture rigid. Roz had to yank twice on the leash, offering her guttural command, before Wampa's loping slowed to a scamper.

"That's Tauntaun's tell," Roz said. "He found something."

They closed the distance. Andy extended his finger to graze the edge of the trigger guard on his rifle, holding his breath. He didn't think Tia was here, or close. But he knew she was armed—though the guns were supposedly unloaded—and he no longer had a sense of what she was capable of. (She could say the same about him, he knew.) If he had been her last night, he'd have used the rain and night cover to gain high ground, as high as he could stand to get, and he'd wait, hidden, for his pursuers. Then pick them off. But Tia was not a good shot, even if she did have firepower. She'd started turning down hunting excursions after the birth of her first baby, even though he knew she could use the money. He was counting on her unease with the weapon, her desperation to get home. She wouldn't lie in wait. She'd flee.

That didn't mean she wouldn't turn and fire on him and Roz, if she saw them. In fact, he expected nothing less.

Roz scratched Tauntaun's head, slipped him a treat, then Wampa. Hunched down. "Hmm," she said. "Ain't seeing it."

"Seeing what?" Andy asked.

"Whatever it is to see." She beckoned. "Bend down here. You got young eyes. Tell me what you make out."

He did as he was told, setting his rifle carefully down beside him. Roz's gaze was fixed on the ground at Tauntaun's feet, where—Andy had to agree—all there was to see was dirt. A dried-up leaf. Some scraggly blades of grass. He could smell the dogs, their doggy smell, not perfume but not exactly unpleasant, and he could smell Roz and himself, their body odor after two hours of brisk, uphill hiking, and something else. Something unnatural but recognizable. Chemical.

"I think she Stamped herself." He looked around, grabbed a stick, and leaned in further, nose almost to the ground, pushing the leaf to the side, folding back the blades of grass. There. He picked the dead tick up between his fingers and rested it on his palm.

Roz wrinkled her mouth as if she'd bitten into something sour, and shook her head. "Good lord. Throw that thing down."

"It's been cooked in chemicals. It's harmless."

"Don't mean I want to look at it," Roz said.

A big one—almost the size of a pencil eraser. Five of its eight legs still attached. Andy turned his hand over, letting what was left of the tick fall back to the ground, and wiped his palm on his pant leg. He picked up his gun, stood. He could not remember, for a long handful of seconds, what was supposed to come next.

"Wake up, bud," Roz said. "We ain't done yet."

"I know that," Andy said irritably. He noticed Roz's dark look and allowed himself a second to enjoy it, though he knew that he shouldn't push her. The missus. What did June see in this woman? This coarse, humorless woman with her soft, shapeless body and her helmet of dry hay-colored hair? The two of them had been a mystery to Andy from the very start, though he had to say, if nothing else, that aging had hurt Roz's looks no more than youth had helped them.

Roz mumbled some order at the dogs. They took off, and she followed without a backward glance. Andy trailed after.

Andy's mother had been sixteen years old when she accepted a hardship leave from Biloxi Secondary and decided, on a whim, to go ahead and try taking the Intra-Zone Career Aptitude Exam. She got one free crack at it, it was one Saturday of her life, and she knew in her heart of hearts that she was never going to be able to come back from her hardship leave, that her entire life was a hardship and only a miracle would change it. This was what she told Andy, years later, almost to the word: *My entire life was a hardship. Only a miracle would change it.* But she got her miracle. A few moments after she hit the Finish Exam button, the proctor called her back to his office.

There's still an official review of scoring, he said, *but you did very well, young lady. Very, very well.*

How well? she'd asked.

Well enough to write your own ticket, he told her.

Like most tickets, it came with the usual list of requirements and restrictions, but write it she did. To Atlantic Zone. Full vestment. Admission to the Point, commission to the Corps of Engineers, minimum of eight years of service with the hope, said her recruiter, that she'd love the work well enough to keep with it after her required term was up. She did. Love it, and keep with it. She met her husband, Andy's father, at an officers' ball. Served twenty-five years, retired at the rank of lieutenant colonel, still young enough to launch a second career in the private sector and amass a small fortune as an executive for the Valley Corporation. The military had given her everything. It became a religion to her. (Though, a devout Presbyterian, she would have called this claim blasphemy.) She was a strict parent, occasionally distant, always busy. But kind. Loving, in her way—it was never that Andy didn't feel loved. What he found himself rejecting wasn't his mother, the person she had been to him, specifically, but everything she admired and trusted and believed in. Her smarts had gotten her out of Gulf, but she wasn't smart enough, somehow, to understand that the system was broken, something must be fundamentally wrong, that the price of her escape was twelve years of indentured servitude. She saw only her own success story. By the time Andy was sixteen—the age of his mother's miracle—he oscillated in his attitude toward her between tender pity and outright disgust. He started frequenting anarchist web feeds. After a year or so of dedicated commenting, he was invited into private, encrypted feeds that he hadn't, still more child than adult, even guessed existed.

So began his divided life. There was the Andy who existed virtually, as Sonofascist90823—the *real* Andy, he thought. He didn't know what he was rebelling against, exactly. He only knew that he didn't buy into his mother and her story of virtue rewarded. The guys on the feeds supplied him with some targets for his derision: capitalism, precious mineral mining, tablets, the space program, academia, synthetic marijuana, some strains of feminism (but only the ones that tried to hold men down in order to advance women), organized religion. Others. The encrypted feeds were more sophisticated. Rants were honed into arguments. Ideas into plans. Andy acted, twice during his freshman year at State, as a digital launderer/courier. For what purpose he wasn't entirely sure—this was by design—but his actions both times preceded big news stories about large-scale hacks on SmartMart credit holders and an alt-sexuality social feed, De Gustibus.

Offline, he was only Andy: disappointing son, lackluster communications major, dateless, depressive. The depression, so far as Andy could tell, wasn't a consequence of his disillusionment, or a cause of it, so much as its mate. He had walked arm in arm with them both as far back as he could remember. When the depression was at its most manageable, he was merely—merely?—upset with the state of the world. Angry at what he couldn't change. His gut churned with desire for the way things ought to be, his pulse raced as he stabbed out comments in forums. But every so often, for weeks, months at a time, his dissatisfactions coalesced into an impenetrable fog, so that even his anger seemed pointless and small. These fogs had happened enough times that he recognized, from somewhere outside himself, the pattern. He could, for a while, tell himself: *This will pass. This isn't you. This is some stew of chemicals and hormones in your brain, translating stimulus into despair, and if you take these meds or do this exercise or spend this amount of time a day out in the sunshine, the recipe will change, and you'll see clearly again. Wait for it. Just a little longer.*

The more spells he endured, the harder this became: Believing his reasonable self. Believing that his reasonable self was even reasonable. There was a very cheesy, very old movie Andy saw when he was a boy, *They Live*, and it was about this guy who had a pair of sunglasses that allowed him to see that all of these perfectly normal-looking people around him were actually skeleton-faced aliens controlling human minds. In the depths, Andy realized that this was his world: only in his depression did he see clearly, and there were indeed skulls behind every normal-looking face. Not because they were aliens or evil. Because they were doomed. Everyone was doomed. And nothing awaited you on the other side.

He tried committing suicide for the first time when he was nineteen. The old slit-wrist trick. Found by his roommate, a guy who couldn't stand Andy enough to share a meal with him at the student union but was willing to tie off Andy's wrists with one of his own close-at-hand oxford dress shirts, probably so he could put it on his résumé: *Once saved life of my waste-of-life roommate.* His mother cried at his bedside. *What did I do? What can I do? Tell me, Andy.* He stared ahead. He didn't have an answer for either question.

Dropped out of school. Waited tables, worked on a landscaping crew, and, for thirteen very bad months, clocked the midnight shift at a rendering plant. Even considered enlisting, but the suicide attempt was on his record, as well as a hospitalization for alcohol poisoning, and so that was out, not that he'd have actually gone through with it. Probably not.

The second suicide attempt, he was twenty-four. The old handful-of-pills trick. Washed it down with a liter of vodka. Swallowed, sent his on-and-off (currently off) girlfriend a text, *Good by*, and she called an ambulance. Got there in the nick of time, pumped his stomach, etc. Embarrassing, Andy thought, to have drunkenly misspelled your suicide note. If only you could die of embarrassment, as the saying went. The other methods weren't working for him.

He was transferred from the hospital to a private psychiatric center, bills sent to his mother. The days were long and dull. He could barely sleep, and so the nights were even longer and duller. He was denied access to a tablet; his doctor felt that web addiction was one of his sources of depression, a trigger for his obsessive thoughts. Andy stared at a thousand-piece jigsaw puzzle—"Thatch-Roof Cottage in Winter," read the box—and resolved, whenever he got out of here, that he'd ride a bus down to the Bottoms, buy a gun, and take a more decisive way out. No more of this namby-pamby, cry-for-help stuff.

Cheered by this promise to himself, he settled into life at the clinic. He knew from past experience how to play it. Couldn't be too chipper, too eager. Dr. Benik would see right through him. He started coming to Morning Group. Didn't speak, didn't respond to the therapist's questions about his goals for the day, but he listened to the others, even nodded a few times. A week in, he mentioned to his counselor that he thought the new dosage might be helping. He finished the thatch-roof cottage in winter—well, not quite, eight of the pieces were missing, but the box was empty, and he let one of the staff members, Hakim, see him surveying his work with a little smile on his face before he began to take the puzzle apart for the next user.

"You won't be letting people see your masterpiece?" Hakim asked. He had materialized to Andy's left.

"Nah," Andy said. "It was a bust. Pieces missing. I'm going to ask my mother to send me a new puzzle. Or maybe some art paper and oil pastels. I used to like working with those. You know the kind I'm talking about?"

"Indeed I do," said Hakim. "In fact, I think I could scrounge up something tonight, if you're not too particular about the quality."

"I'm wearing pajamas at four o'clock. I'm not too particular about anything." Andy smiled as he said this.

"Let me see what I can do," Hakim said.

The challenge of pretending to get better really was making Andy feel a bit better.

Hakim, it turned out, was as good as his word. He got Andy the promised oil pastels, some decent-weight drawing paper, a sketch pad, some charcoals. Andy set to his first drawing with something a bit like real enthusiasm. In the days that followed, Hakim came around, watched him, asked questions, seemed genuinely interested—not just fake, patronizing-interested—in what Andy was doing.

"Those mountains," Hakim said, motioning to the page. Andy had decimated what was left of the Prussian blue to shadow the hills in the foreground, and now he was adding a layer of dark green, smudging together the colors with his forefinger as he went. "You've been there?"

Andy shook his head. "Just seen pictures. Why?"

"Oh, only curious about why you're drawing them."

"Why shouldn't I?" Andy said. He didn't elaborate. He was disappointed that Hakim was going to psychoanalyze him or whatever. He'd given him more credit than that.

"I only ask," Hakim said, "because I have. Been there. You capture them well."

Andy stopped and gave Hakim his full attention. "Really? You have?"

"I have," said Hakim.

"What for?"

"I worked at the infirmary for V&M Logging for six years."

"No shit."

"No shit."

Andy set his crayon back to paper and bore down. "Guess you were glad to get this gig and get out of there, huh."

"It wasn't such a bad gig," said Hakim. The word "gig" sounded funny in his mouth, like something new he was trying. "The money was good. The food was excellent. Pretty scenery, lots of quiet. I read many books. If I'd had a companion, I could have stayed there indefinitely. There aren't many women in a logging camp, though."

Andy huffed. "That's a recommendation, far as I'm concerned."

Hakim smiled big, revealing very straight, square teeth. "I suppose it can be. Though you miss them. Women. Not even just for the—well, you know."

Andy was charmed by Hakim's delicacy. He laughed. "The fucking? You can say it to me, Hakim. I'm not that fragile."

"I don't think you're fragile," Hakim said.

"You're the only one."

Hakim shrugged. "May I be honest? What you say is unimaginative. Egotistical. As if we're all in agreement about Andy. The world had reached a verdict on Andy." He mimed striking a gavel. "Fragile. Send in the next case."

"That's all well and good," Andy said. "I like what you're doing. It's very tough-love of you. But the world—enough of it—decided I needed to be here. Whether I want to be or not." He tossed the dark green roughly back into its plastic tray and pawed around for a lighter hue.

Hakim, who was sitting across the commons-room table from Andy, leaned back in his chair and rested his crossed hands on the tabletop. "Fair enough."

"Being in here makes you egotistical," Andy said. "It makes you feel like everyone's watching and judging you. Because they are. You are. You're like the rest of them. Don't get me wrong. I like you. In the real world, I'd go have a beer with you. In here, though . . ." He trailed off.

"You wouldn't have a beer with me," Hakim said.

Andy laughed again. "Well, I will if you're offering."

Hakim smiled his brilliant smile again. "I can offer you soda pop."

"Soda pop! Hot damn. I'll pass, H."

He leaned forward, smile tightening. "I can offer you a purpose, Sonofascist90823."

What Andy would remember most clearly about this moment, later, was how Hakim pronounced his screenname: *So-No Fascist.* He'd been embarrassed, for them both, at the butchering of his cleverness.

He stopped the movement of his crayon. Tried to steady his breathing.

"My intent isn't to alarm you," Hakim said.

"Who said I was alarmed?" He carved at a smudged line with his thumbnail. "I don't even know what you're talking about."

At the edge of his vision, Hakim's hands shifted position—left on top of right, ring finger winking gold. He had huge hands, pale fingernails that had been smoothly and evenly clipped. A snail of scar tissue slivered across a knuckle.

"Ah," Hakim said. "I know how this dance goes. How about this? I talk, and you indulge me for a moment. Then I'll walk away and leave you alone. Sound OK?"

Andy kept coloring.

"Yes. OK. First of all, what I'm saying here? All of the risk is mine. None of it is yours. And the risk for me is significant." He tapped the gold band with his thick forefinger. "You could ruin me. I am about to give you the ammunition to ruin me, if that's what you want."

Andy chanced a quick glance at Hakim's face. It was a handsome face of indeterminate age. He could be thirty or fifty, though something in the eyes seemed to place him on the older end of that spectrum.

"No one in this hospital knows about So-No Fascist. No one here wants to know. And if they did know, they would only be required to report you to the authorities if they thought you planned to cause harm to another person. So-No Fascist has never talked of harming people."

Well, that wasn't precisely true. There had been talk, in one forum, about—hypothetically, that was all, as a kind of intellectual exercise—the possible rewards of assassinating the president.

"Your mother," Hakim said. "She—"

"Wears combat boots? I've heard that one before." Jesus, Hakim really was a cliché if he thought getting Andy to talk about his mother was going to crack him.

Hakim laughed his hearty laugh. "Well, yes, Andy, I suppose she did. I was going to ask about that. She was recruited out of Gulf Zone for the military? This is correct?"

"This is correct," he said, mimicking Hakim's funny intonations.

"What you could think of this," Hakim said, "is that you scored well on a test. And I'm a recruiter. Here to offer an opportunity."

"I never took any test."

"You can't sign up for this test." Hakim leaned forward. He had not whispered in all this time; he seemed to have a knack for pitching his voice just low enough to blend into the mild racket of midday in the rec room. "You've been watched, as you say. Noticed. But this isn't bad. There are people who appreciate your ideas, your perspective. People who could help you do more than think about these things, who *need* you to do more than think about these things."

"What things?" Andy said. "I still don't know what you're talking about."

"Let me try this another way," said Hakim. "What are you doing after you get out of here?"

Andy shrugged.

"Job?"

"No." He'd quit the rendering plant three weeks before his little exit attempt. Had been living on his meager savings, the proceeds from selling an old tablet and easy chair, and credit.

"You still have an apartment? Place to live?"

This Andy couldn't even bear to answer. His mother had told him that he'd be staying with her. That's how she put it, last time she visited: "You'll stay with me and Dad. Until you get back up on your feet." An order disguised as a kindness.

Hakim, registering that Andy wouldn't fill the silence, said: "You have a woman? Friends?"

Now he was just being cruel. If Hakim knew that Andy was Sonofascist90823, he'd surely glanced at the visitors log and seen that Andy had received only two callers, his mother and father. "Tons of them," Andy said. "Women and friends." He lifted his arms, palms to the ceiling, and swiveled in his chair, face falsely alight, as if basking in his bounty. "You're never alone if you're at Brightwater Healing Services."

Hakim accepted this patiently. "But you won't be here much longer. Two, three weeks."

Andy traded crayons, pressed down again. "That's my understanding."

"Are you glad?"

"To leave? Sure," Andy said.

"Because out there is better than in here?"

This was an interesting question. One Andy hadn't quite posed to himself. Was it? Better? "Out" was a direction, a change. Like being born. And therefore was something to anticipate.

"Out" was where the guns were.

"Out" was where an out was.

"It's no worse," Andy said finally.

"Here is a thing for you to think over," Hakim said. "If the best you can say about 'out there' is that it's no worse than 'in here,' perhaps you are a man with nothing to lose."

"Oh, OK," Andy said. "I see what test I passed. We must be a real select bunch. The cream of the crop. I can't wait to hear what my great purpose is. Does it involve some kind of wired vest and a trench coat?"

"Far from it," said Hakim. "What I'm asking of you is scarier. It would require you to live your life."

Andy laughed through a quaking sensation that had rooted in his midsection.

Hakim tapped the page on the table—the shadowed mountains. "You could go here."

"I thought you said I'd have to live my life."

"There's life to be lived out there," Hakim said. "There's a life for *you* out there. The doctors tell you your problem is here." Hakim tapped his temple. "That what you feel is abnormal, and you must take a drug to fix it. They're wrong. What's wrong with you isn't here." The temple again. "It's here." He swirled his finger vaguely, indicating—well, the world.

"No offense, but you seem to be in the wrong line of work."

"I'm in the perfect line of work," Hakim said. "There are ill people in here. People who don't understand reality and make themselves miserable, thinking they are fat, they are dying of diseases, they are persecuted. We help them. Or at the very least, we keep them from hurting others or themselves. I know the difference between them and you."

"And what's that?"

"You do understand reality and make yourself miserable."

Andy found himself grinding his thumbnail between his teeth.

"I don't think there's any nobility in misery," Hakim said. "There's certainly no nobility in suicide. I was once like you. I saw the world and grieved. I didn't see any reason for it. For existing. So much pain and so little point. Yet I had a life! This was a fact. It would one day end. This was also a fact. And I could end it whenever I wished. This was my reassurance. 'I can always end it tomorrow,' I told myself. And then I discovered something."

"Oh, hell," Andy said. "This is where you start talking about Jesus, isn't it?"

"Ha! No, this isn't. Weeding, Andy. This is where I start talking about weeding."

"Weeding."

"Yes, my friend. This was when I lived at the logging camp. There was a large garden on the premises and helping with it gave me something to do. When I despaired, I weeded. I lost myself in the physical process, the repetition. I pulled and pulled, and one day I pulled myself out of my sadness."

"So that's my purpose," Andy said. "Weeding."

"There are all sorts of ways to weed," Hakim said.

And that was the beginning of things. Each day he could opt to not yet take his own life. Pull a weed. First one, then another. There was always another. Do this instead of thinking and maybe, eventually, the thinking wouldn't hurt so much. Hakim was right about one thing: Andy had nothing to lose.

Hakim made some calls. Upon his release, Andy started working for a man named Jude, who owned a franchise location of Southern Farm Supply Co. The store, it turned out, was a front for several kinds of criminal activity, most of it connected to out-of-zone smuggling. Jude received several shipments a week of fertilizer, mulch, and topsoil. One in every half dozen or so of these shipments included extra cargo: recreational drugs, mostly, but also random illegal goods from other zones and countries. Once Andy was tasked with unearthing a hundred boxes of Kawaii sneakers from a mound of compost. Another time it was boxes of Lil Bums Diapers, sizes newborn and one. Once he pried the lid off a crate to find a dazed, light-blind woman and two children, a flashlight, a bucket of eye-wateringly ammoniac urine, and a few empty gallon jugs of what he assumed had been water. "See if she and the kids want something from the vending machine," Jude had said. "And throw that piss bucket in the Dumpster."

He'd been working at the store six weeks when Hakim came by to check on him. "The time has come," he said, "if you're ready."

"Ready for what, exactly?" Andy asked.

"To meet your purpose," Hakim said.

He was shown his own crate, his own piss bucket, his own (full) plastic gallon jugs. The truck would travel four hours before stopping off at an organic waste facility outside Statesville to pick up a couple dozen barrel loads of compostables collected from area utility customers: food scraps and yard waste, mostly. "It's gonna smell god-awful," Jude warned him. Then another two hours to the Wall, and an hour for weighing and inspection. ("Keep your mouth shut and everything'll be fine. They care more about what's coming in than what's going out.") Two more hours to the composting station, and then another thirty minutes to what Hakim called a "transfer point." "You'll be out of the crate," he said. "Smooth sailing from there on." His journey would end at Ruby City, "and then you're going to understand what all of this is about, and your whole life is going to change for the better," Hakim said. "I promise."

This was another promise Hakim kept. Andy spent eleven hours in his crate before emerging to see the sun, and he thought, getting into the ancient Jeep Wrangler with the quiet man named Curtis, who offered Andy little more than an apple and a grumbling hello, there was nothing in Ruby City that could compensate for the time he'd just spent in hell, and he'd sooner find a knife to slit his own throat than repeat this horror in three months. But then he met June. And the people of Ruby City. He saw how they lived, what they had achieved, their harmony and (cheesy, but he couldn't help thinking this) their purity. For the first time in his life, he contributed to the making of his own food, pulling literal weeds now along with the metaphorical ones, loading a gun, taking aim at squirrels, deer, rabbits. He slept hard at night, his eyes popping open at first light. Mornings, he stood on the bank of the Little Tennessee and watched the sun burn the mist off the tops of the Smoky Mountains. He had never been as alive as this. He murmured thanks at night to a God he didn't believe existed—his mother's God, a white-bearded, benevolent king—for this chance. "Thank you for not letting me kill myself," he said.

Jude and Hakim covered for him back home—with his mother, with Brightwater. Hakim had even promised to send emails to Andy's mother from Andy's account, and Andy got a kick, during quiet moments at Ruby City, imagining them: *Hello, Mother. I am doing very well. This job I hold is most stimulating. And how do you fare?*

But the plan was never for him to stay. He'd known that from the start. "What we have here can't last," June said, "unless we have some help on the inside. That's where you come in. You and a few others like you. Will you help us, Andy?"

He would.

It was better, in a way. This was what he told himself as he climbed into another, smaller crate—more of a casket than a box—for the journey back in-zone. He had his memories of Ruby City. He had his instructions. And he had a goal, a dream: to save the little community out in the mountains, away from the corruption and consumption that characterized life in-zone, and then, eventually, to take his rightful place among them. He knew that tending the dream, keeping it hidden away like something precious, would probably be, for now, better for him than living it. But maybe, with time, he would heal enough to enjoy his reward.

They hiked another two hours. The trail, thankfully, had abruptly stopped its uphill climb, swerving north. There was a tense twenty minutes when they crossed a creek and the dogs were in disagreement about how to proceed on the other side. Tia must have waded down or uphill. Roz speculated that she might have circled and retraced her own steps back to some point they'd missed, and Andy was cursing as they cast yet another twenty feet downstream, sure that all was lost, when Tauntaun barked twice, decisively, and ran off ahead. Wampa strained against his leash to follow.

"Looks like they know something," Roz said.

Damn you, Tia, he kept thinking. *Goddamn you, Tia*. He wanted to shake her. Hit her. He wanted to hug her tightly and press his lips into the ruffle of black hair behind her ear. He was afraid they wouldn't find her. He was more afraid, in a way, that they would. Roz called for a halt, took a long drink from her canteen, and mopped her brow with a handkerchief. Andy sipped some water, too. He had some knots of jerky in his knapsack, and the time would soon come to choke one down, but he couldn't stomach it yet.

He played through scenarios in his head, flickering through them almost too quickly to register. Tia on higher ground, perched on a rock, raining bullets down on him and Roz. Tia waiting, resigned, with her hands raised in surrender. Tia unconscious. Tia dead. Tia, having disguised her scent in some ingenious way, hiding behind a tree and watching them pass. And then there were all of the versions of their return to camp, Tia coming along voluntarily, gratefully, having exhausted herself and her resources in the woods all night. Tia fighting them, and Andy having to use the zip ties again. *Why are you making me do this?* he asks her. *Don't you know you're doing yourself more harm than good?* Tia swinging from a noose as the Ruby City villagers cheered. (Would they do that? Were they those kind of people? How was it that Andy didn't know?) Tia incarcerated some way. He pleads to June on her behalf, tells her about the pregnancy. That child—it would mean everything to June. June wouldn't take the life of a pregnant woman, especially now.

Then he imagined—daring himself with this thought—pointing his gun at Roz. Taking her gun. Escaping with Tia back to the zone, to his wife and his sons. It wasn't too late to reclaim his old life, was it? It depended, he supposed, on the fate of the other OLE hostages. They'd eventually implicate him, if June allowed them to go home. (Would June allow them to go home? Andy didn't know. He hadn't had the courage to ask.) If Tia escaped back to the zone, June would have less reason to keep them alive. She'd have the marines descending on her. Or worse.

He couldn't believe he was even thinking this stuff. If Tia escaped, if he helped her, went to the authorities with her and turned on his friends, he'd be to blame for all of those deaths—almost five hundred souls.

But the boys. His boys. God, he knew it was going to hurt, leaving them. But he'd left them lots of times, each time he'd gone on an excursion, and he'd counted on the familiarity of that pattern to get him through the worst of the grief at their loss. By the time the six weeks passed and forever started, he'd thought, there would be distance enough to dull the ache. For all of them. But there had been moments on this trip when understanding rained down on him—*I'm holding a gun on these people! This is happening! I'm never going to see Ian and Colby again!*—and his chest got tight, his airways seemed to narrow. June had told him: *Live your life. Be normal, whatever that is.* She'd said: *You can't put yourself on hold for us. For this. Because I don't know how long the wait will be. I don't know exactly how we'll need you. Your job for now is to keep your head down and keep us in your heart. That's what I ask of you. Keep us in your heart.*

He had. He had. But when he'd become a father, his for-now life had become a real life.

He could convince Tia not to go to the authorities back home. They'd go to Quarantine with some story. He drank more water, feeling a second wind. A road gang, marauders. You heard about them. He and Tia barely escaped with their lives. Everyone else dead, they presumed. Tia had lost nothing so far, really. And she had blood on her hands. She'd back him up. It would be like none of this had even happened. He'd quit the OLE job and be there for his boys. Ruby City could hang on a while longer—not saved, maybe, but at least not leveled by marine firepower—and if June let the hostages go, well, Andy would cross that bridge when he came to it. There might be time enough to get Beth and the boys and flee somewhere.

It could work.

Later, he would wonder: Would he have really gone through with it? It seemed, for a few moments, that he would. Relief had flooded him. His knapsack felt lighter. He wiped his sweaty palms on his jacket, first one, then the other, maneuvering the gun carefully and then resettling his fingers around the pistol grip and hand guard. He registered a flicker of pleasure at the thought of disarming Roz—gruff, know-it-all, dog-drowning Roz. (Could she sic Tauntaun and Wampa on him? He would shoot them if he had to. He, too, could be cruel, if left no other recourse.) He thought about what Hakim had said about showing him his purpose. This was, he'd think later, the tragedy of his life, if *tragedy* wasn't too strong a word for the sadness of a man like Andy: if not for Hakim and June and Ruby City, Andy would probably have killed himself years ago. If not for the dream of his secret life, Andy wouldn't have been around to meet Beth. And even his and Beth's first date, their courtship, their marriage—did he not owe Ruby City its share of credit for the success of their relationship? Ruby City had been his ace in the hole, his mistress. Beth had been intrigued by his distance, he knew. More certain she wanted him because she was less certain she was wanted. He told himself this each time he felt his guts twist at the thought of all the lies he'd told her.

But the boys were innocents. Ian, seven years old with a lighter shade of Beth's sandy blond hair and Andy's broad feet and blunt toes, sensitive, still young and sweet enough to hold his mother's hand at the grocery store. Five-year-old Colby, Andy's little look-alike, who crawled into Andy and Beth's bed during thunderstorms and slept with his sweaty cheek against Andy's chest, knees tucked up against Andy's rib cage. How could Andy have thought himself capable of abandoning him? Even for the sake of a village? Even for the sake of the world?

Tauntaun, just out of sight, howled. Wampa answered with a yank so ferocious that Roz nearly toppled over, and Andy had to take a hand off his gun to steady her.

"Must be the girl," Roz said. She went after the dogs at a trot, swift despite her bulk, and Andy, seeing his moment, raced ahead. He had no plan. He only knew that he had to reach Tia before Roz closed in—look her in the eye, then make a decision about where to point his gun. Tauntaun hadn't stopped barking, and there had been no gunshots. Maybe this was a good sign.

He scrambled, with feet and hands, over a washout of rocks, topped a rise, saw the dog first. It paced off a half circle, stopped to keel back on his hind legs. Barked. Then paced another half circle back in the opposite direction. Its attention was directed at the base of a tree, and Andy, letting his finger slide into the curve of his gun's trigger guard, made out the figure of a person. Head against the tree, a few feet above the ground. Dark, short-cropped hair. Not moving. He drew closer. A dozen meters. Ten. She wasn't flinching when Tauntaun barked. No reaction at all.

He pulled up his gun and sighted her, close enough now to make out Tia's sprawled legs, the scattered contents of her pack. The shape of what he thought had to be her gun, on the ground a few inches from her right hand.

"Tia," he called. No response.

Tauntaun, noting Andy's presence, stopped his pacing, sat, and barked sharply again. Behind him, Wampa answered the bark, and Roz yelled, "Tauntaun, to me." A bag rustled—the dog's jerky treats—and Tauntaun cheerfully obliged. Then, to Andy, Roz said in her coarse, thoughtless way: "What's she doing? Dead?"

Andy didn't answer.

A few feet away from the figure slumped under the tree, he thumbed on the gun's safety and slung it over his shoulder. Her eyes were wide open, unfocused. Mouth slack. A tremor of grief gripped him, and then—

She blinked.

"Tia," he repeated breathlessly, dropping to his knees beside her. He cupped her face in his hands, and her staring eyes filled with liquid. "Oh, jeez," he said then, understanding dawning on him. "Oh jeez, oh jeez." He touched her neck, and her pulse pounded madly under his middle finger—such frantic, determined life. Like there was another creature inside this still, dead skin, squirming to burst free. And the smell of her, too. Her unwashed body, the two days' exertions, sour, yeasty, again so goddamn scarily *alive*. He had heard about Shreve's so many times. He had never seen it for himself. The horrors he'd be warned about didn't prepare him for the reality.

Close enough now that he could kiss her, if he were to lean forward, he could hear her faint, shallow exhalations. *Hih. Hih. Hih.* She blinked, and the tears made matching trails down her cheeks, cutting through a skim of dirt.

He took her hand, and it spasmed in his grip.

"Well, there you go," Roz said from behind him. "I guess she won't be bashing any more heads in."

"Shut the fuck up," Andy said. There was a sob inside him, wriggling toward the light, and he bit his lip against it.

Roz made a grunting, displeased sound, then that clicking that signaled the dogs. They retreated, out of sight. Maybe back to camp without him. Andy, for now, didn't care.

He sat beside Tia, still clutching her hand. The fingers twitched again in his. He couldn't tell if this was an act of Tia's will or some automatic response, unknown to her. He thought, for some reason, of the office tower where OLE headquarters was housed. How the building started to clear at 5:00, as all of the eager clock-watchers fled, the parents with children in daycare, the coworkers with the weekly pub trivia night. That pub—Andy knew it well. Once a month he had to don a shirt and tie and attend a day's worth of meetings at the office tower, and his reward at the end of it, the only thing that dragged him through the handshaking and vigorous nodding, all of the assurances he had to offer to men in well-cut suits who talked of "traveler satisfaction quotients" and "extra-virtual entertainment experiences," was the promise of a sweaty pint of ale at the Artillery Arms. Occasionally Tia joined him. One winter night, they'd taken a window seat, complained about the day's many absurdities, and watched the lights in the building go out one by one, until only one—eleventh floor, third office from the right—remained.

"I think we should wait him out," Tia said. "As long as it takes. We go home when he does."

"Or she," Andy said.

"Or she," Tia agreed. She raised her empty glass until the bartender spotted her, smiled broadly. Held up two fingers.

"Man, Tia, I don't need another. Beth's going to be climbing the walls if I'm not home soon."

"Blame me," Tia said. "Thad and Berry are at Thad's mother's tonight. I'm having another beer."

He'd wondered, nursing his third pint, watching the last lit window in the tower, if that was a hint. An invitation. He didn't really think it was, but he thought that Tia had maybe known he'd parse her words this way—that there was, for her, the faintest illicit thrill in imagining the course his thoughts had taken. Instead of feeling manipulated, he felt tenderly toward her, and very warm and cozy in this dark wood and gilt pub, and he thought, *Don't go out, light. Don't go out.*

In another twenty minutes it did.

Now, her hand stiffened in his, then went slack. But the shallow breaths kept going: *Hih. Hih. Hih.* She must have been here for hours. One light going out. Then another. The brain, he thought he remembered, continued for a long time to function normally. She'd be thinking of Berry and Thad. Maybe, as he held her hand, she wished with all her being that she could snatch it out of his grasp, pick up the near-at-hand gun, and put *his* lights out. He couldn't blame her.

"I'm so sorry," he said. He added in a rush, "I know how it looked. How it seemed. I know why you did what you did. But I want you to know your life was never in danger." He wasn't sure this was true, but he continued, anyway. "I wouldn't have let anything happen to you, Tia." Why was he telling her this? Stealing what might have been her only reassurance—that she had no choice? "I just don't want you to think I'd have done that to you. That I'm that sort of person."

Well, there it was.

"And . . . I'll make sure Berry has everything she needs. That she wants for nothing." An even bigger lie. With what? Ruby City's largesse?

"I'm sorry," he repeated. He looked into her eyes, hoping to see—forgiveness? Absolution? They watered again, blinked. Another set of twin tears ran toward her chin.

"Can you close your eyes?" he asked her. He thumbed the safety on his gun back off. "If you can, you might want to close them."

Thirteen

There were three body-shapes laid across the smooth plank floors of Town Hall.

"I wanted you to see for yourself," June said. "I wanted you to know what she did, and I wanted you to know what we didn't do." She sighed and motioned to Andy. "Show them Leeda and Miles first."

He hunched down and peeled back the muslin covering the first body-shape, then the second, making neat rolls of the material down to the figures' waists. The arms were slim, smooth-skinned. The boy's were tanned, thatched with curly dark hair. The girl's were milky-pale and freckled. A spill of light brown hair had been brushed neatly around the girl's shoulders. The head above that spill of hair was a chin and lips and a beak of nose with a red wet crater opening above the nose. The boy still had a visible eye. Open. Edie couldn't make out the color from here.

She remembered them both from the barbecue by the river. The girl had offered to hold Edie's beer while she went through the line for food. She had slung her gun over her back to extend a free hand. "I can get that for you," she'd said.

"Jesus Christ, cover them up," Lee Flannigan said.

Andy looked up at June. She dropped her chin in acknowledgment, and he rolled the muslin back up.

"Andy found the young woman from your group this morning, several kilometers east of here. He and another of our group tracked her with trained dogs. The dogs first landed on what turned out to be the contents of her ejected Stamp. Then they found her. She was—well, you should tell it, Andy."

"Paralyzed," he said hoarsely. "Propped up against a tree and breathing, but that's it."

"Shreve's," June said, as if this wasn't already clear. "I warn you that there's a gunshot wound. Andy didn't want her to suffer."

Edie waited for the sarcastic, doubting retort to that—from Lee, or even Jesse—but no one spoke.

Andy hunched down at Tia's side and rolled the cloth sideways this time, so that most of her body was exposed. Her head had rolled to the side, so that the bullet's exit wound was mostly hidden from sight. Andy slid his fingers gently under the body's shoulder and arm and tipped it in the same direction, turning it so that the body was slumped three-quarters of the way to prone, hips hovering awkwardly in space. Edie could see now that Tia's microsuit, which was blood-soaked, had been cleanly cut down the middle of the back. Andy folded these flaps open, revealing the ragged deep wound they'd seen in the video on that first day of boot camp, saucer-sized, positioned almost exactly between the shoulder blades. Bone—her spine, it must be—winked from the churned red meat.

Andy stayed hunched, with his back to them, for a strangely long time. Edie realized he was crying.

"So that's that," June said flatly. "Three dead. For nothing."

"Four dead," said Lee. "Your girl shot Mickey."

"Mickey was going to have a goddamn hole in his neck just like that in another six or ten hours," Andy said roughly. He repositioned Tia's microsuit, rolled her flat, and covered the body again with the muslin. "We did him a kindness. Just like I did Tia."

"Two of yours. Two of ours," June said. "So here's my question: Can we put an end to this?"

"There's a big difference between your dead and ours," Wendy Tanaka said. "You caused this situation. We didn't. This isn't even our fight. Everything you told Wes about your situation could be true, and that doesn't change the fact that no one here is that Perrone guy."

June closed her eyes and made a temple of her hands, pressing the index fingers between her eyebrows and inhaling deeply. "I am asking for a few weeks of your time. Weeks. Weeks you planned to spend out here anyway. I am offering you protection during that time. So this"—she pointed at Tia—"can't happen to you. And you don't have to use a single Stamp, and you don't even have to sleep in your tents if you don't want to. I'm asking you that in the name of four hundred sixty-eight innocent people." She stopped. "Four hundred sixty-six. We're not an army. We're not bad people. We gave teenagers guns because we didn't have a better option. I made a call, and it might have been the wrong call, but it was the best I knew to do at the time, and I'm asking you now for some understanding, for some humanity. Wait three weeks. Andy will take you to Quarantine 1 on the scheduled date. The end."

"May I speak?" Wes asked.

"Please," June said tiredly. "Go ahead."

"I believe you. I sympathize with you. With everything you said. I'm willing to stay; in fact, I want to stay. Send the rest back. Do it as a gesture of goodwill. If Perrone wants his Pocketz deal so badly, he's not going to blow you up while I'm unaccounted for."

June shook her head. "No. I send the rest back, and as soon as they're over the border, and they're getting asked, 'Where's Feingold?' they spill everything. And then Perrone's the least of our concerns. Then we've got the Atlantic Zone cavalry charging, and I know how these people work better than you do. They shoot first, and then they burn the bodies. They don't ask questions. They don't investigate."

"What if we just promise to tell them Wes wandered off, got lost?" Anastasia asked. "We say that's why we came back early."

June faltered, looking down at the bodies. Edie felt for her now not just an intellectual sort of sympathy, impersonal, hypothetical, but something more acute than that. And the thing was: she was out here now. What did she have to get back to in such a hurry? Jesse's apartment, where she tried to make herself unobtrusive and small, so he would like having her around, so he'd never tire of her, so he'd not get to the point of saying: *Maybe it's time you found your own place.* That? Or her grief? Or the job she quit, because she thought she hated it, and she no longer needed it, only to discover that hate is relative—that when you have no money of your own, no outside force shaping your days, you might long for even some low-wage drudgery?

"I'll stay," Edie blurted out. "I'll do the three weeks."

"Jesus Christ," Jesse said. "Are you nuts? Why would you say that?"

She hadn't even thought of him, honestly—she hadn't thought of what her intention to stay would mean to him or require of him. When she gave Jesse the go-ahead to book her on this excursion, it had occurred to her that the trip would fall during what would have been her due date. It was one of the reasons she'd decided, *Fuck it. I'll go.* A strange impulse—she knew it even then. Was she trying to distract herself? Punish herself? The baby might have not been Jesse's, and he had never, probably, done the math she had done, the counting forward of squares on a calendar; there was no reason he'd have known to mark the day when it came, and he probably wouldn't have understood, even if Edie tried to explain it to him, how she could be both gloriously relieved, and grateful, and free of regret, but also . . . something else. The abortion wasn't the great loss of her life, but it would probably always be the greatest mystery; with no other choice could Edie imagine a drastically different parallel version of herself, an Edie catapulted into a radically different future with its own joys and miseries.

"I'll stay," Edie repeated. "But Jesse goes back. And you'll know he'll stick to any story you want him to because you'll have me here."

"Fuck no," Jesse said. "I don't agree to that."

Berto put a hand into the air. "Me, too. Same deal. I stay, Anastasia goes back."

Anastasia blanched. "No, Berto! No, I stay, too. We don't split up, ever." Tears spilled down her cheeks, and Berto grabbed her, pulled her tawny head close and buried his face in her neck—a rough embrace, Edie thought at first, but then she saw that he was whispering something in her ear, and she kept shaking her head, and then she finally stopped and just leaned on his chest, shoulders quaking.

"I'll have to think about this," June said. She was looking at the bodies on the floor, but she seemed to be seeing through them, or just short of them, her mind working on an equation, carrying the one, moving the decimal.

"I don't agree to it," Jesse repeated. His jaw moved, and he shot Edie a look of anger like she'd never once seen from him. There was no threat in it; that wasn't what rattled her. He seemed gutted. Like she'd betrayed him. Like he was realizing, suddenly, that he didn't know her at all.

"Take them back to the shed," June told Andy, still off in her own head. "I need to consider this from every angle." Her pale gray eyes sharpened as she looked up, and she seemed to direct her last words right at Edie: "Sounds like you all do, too."

That night, the hostages talked around the lantern for hours, circling the same handful of worries and hopes, reaching no new conclusions. Finally, exhausted, they doused the light and retreated to the shed's corners, as far from one another as the small space would allow. Togetherness had accomplished nothing, Edie supposed. So now they were planets, flung away from the warm center, alone and committed to their own solitary orbits.

Edie was no longer sure if she and Jesse shared an orbit, but she followed him to the spot he'd staked out near the door, and she slid into the sleeping bag behind him, pressing her chest, her stomach, her thighs, against his back, his legs. He held himself rigid, all bony shoulder and hip. Making a wall of himself.

She wriggled up, so she could put her mouth near his ear. "Don't be mad at me," she whispered.

He pulled his shoulder roughly forward. "What do you want from me?" He wasn't keeping his voice very low. "I'm supposed to leave you here? Or you want me to stay, maybe. Say I'm going to stay with you. Or maybe you want me to volunteer in your place. Maybe that's what you've been angling for."

"You know that's not true," Edie hissed. "That doesn't even make sense."

He sighed, and his back softened slightly. "I don't know how to do the right thing here. You've put me in an impossible position. I don't even know what the right thing is." He was whispering now, too, at least. Though Edie didn't doubt that anyone in the room who wished to follow the conversation could.

"You go home," Edie said. "In a few weeks, you pick me up from Quarantine. That's what you do."

"That's not what will happen and you know it," Jesse said. "You trust these people. Why? What have they done to deserve that from you?"

"Nothing," Edie said. "I just feel like this is the right thing to do." What she actually felt, saying this, was absurd. She had always scorned people who made statements like this: claims about their gut, their instincts. And what she felt, the impulse she'd acted on, it wasn't even anything so sophisticated as an act of the gut. She'd simply acted, thoughtlessly. And for some reason, she didn't regret it.

"Or maybe this is about me," he continued, as if she hadn't spoken. "Maybe you want rid of me so bad you're willing to risk your life."

"Don't be ridiculous," she said. "No, that's not it at all." She hugged him as fiercely as she could, one-armed, awkward. "I love you, Jesse," she said, and she found that she meant it—she did love him—he was a good and flawed man who had given her a reason to keep living when she'd despaired of ever finding one. "I do."

"I have a feeling, too," Jesse said. "You know it? I have a feeling that we do this, and we never see each other again. That's what I think. You and I split up, and that's the end."

"No," she repeated. She rubbed her nose against the back of his neck, left-right, in refutation. "No." She slid her hand forward, grasping the zipper of his microsuit, and worked it down as quietly as she could, though the noise was still humiliatingly loud in the little room, and Jesse jolted from the surprise of it. Still, though, she proceeded, his zipper, then hers, and he rolled onto his back, and she climbed atop him and leaned forward and whispered "No" into his ear again. The air in the shed was hot and close, the nearest person maybe half a dozen paces away, but she needed with all her heart to tell him this loving lie, and to make herself believe it, and so she said "No" again, this time in his other ear, and they moved quickly together, and Edie's insides rang with the unexpected thrill of it, the audacity of it, and in this way they said goodbye to each other for good.

For now, Edie amended, lying beside him, catching her breath. Goodbye. For now.

Fourteen

Some Sunday mornings, when most of the villagers were gathered at Town Hall for the church service, June and Roz stayed home and had their own sacred ritual. Once a month, they cut each other's hair.

Well, June cut Roz's. When June's frizzy curls crept past her shoulders, she'd take a turn on the stool as Roz *snip-snip-snipped.* But that was an easy job, one blunt pass across the length, no trick to it. Took only five or ten minutes. Roz's hair, on the other hand, was straight and fine, and she, unlike June, was particular about the cut. She liked a kind of fade (the best June could manage without electric clippers) from crown to nape, then some longer layers on top and in the front. Utilitarian without being outright severe. It took a lot of work and skill to give Roz her signature look, and it struck them both as funny that June was the one who seemed, with her halo of feminine fluff, to be the half of the couple who made an effort.

But it was a pleasure, cutting Roz's hair. A little music on the crank-charged Lily Pad—June had an extensive cache of digital audio files, though she found herself returning again and again to country singers from a long-gone age: Loretta Lynn, Hank Williams, Johnny Cash, Conway Twitty, Tammy Wynette—a pot of their daily dose of Salt tea, the window open to catch a breeze, weather permitting. They had their most important conversations this way, with June's fingers running along Roz's scalp, measuring, comparing lengths, and the whisk of the scissors just audible over the soundtrack of steel guitar and fiddle. This Sunday, June was talking her way around the situation with the OLE group, and what had happened to Leeda and Miles. Rambling, really. She'd said a lot of this before, but Roz was listening carefully anyway, offering affirmations in the right places, and the princes were snoring amiably at their feet.

"There are the rare people, like my daddy was, who live their beliefs. Crazy people, usually. Like Daddy. He was brilliant but crazy. He gave up his vestment, his whole way of life, and moved out here, because he thought it was the right thing to do."

"So did your mother," Roz said.

"But she wasn't crazy." June combed Roz's bangs up, tweezed them between her right forefinger and middle finger, and did some expert quick cuts with the scissors pointed at the sprigs of hair. She was good at this. She took pride in it. "Mom went along with it. I guess that's a kind of crazy. But it wasn't her vision."

"All right," Roz said. "I'm following."

"Daddy was a good kind of crazy. Useful. Then there's the bad kind of crazy, like the fundamentalists, but those are two sides of a coin. Anyway, the ones who actually live what they believe are the rarest."

"Thank goodness," Roz said.

June laughed. "Yes, maybe so. The rest of us in the middle—what we think and do's trickier. We're trickier. We trick ourselves. We convince ourselves that we're living according to our beliefs when we aren't. Or we change our beliefs so they line up with how we live. Or we don't believe anything."

"Or don't give it any thought one way or the other."

"Oh, sure," said June. "Which is maybe the same thing as not believing." She swatted Roz's shoulder. "Stop drinking for a minute. You're moving your head too much."

"Garsh, sorry."

"Take me. I'm not like Daddy. I don't have that kind of genius, and I don't have that kind of crazy. I'm out here because I was raised out here. I don't kid myself that I'd have been a crusader if Mama and Daddy had given me a life in-zone the way they could have."

"Well," Roz said, "I give you more credit than you give yourself, then."

"You shouldn't," June said. "What I'm saying is, I don't hold it against them, the Zoners. How they live. There's a gift in not getting. You're never asked to give it up. You don't have to decide if you're going to live with your hypocrisy or make a sacrifice that no one else around you's willing to make, just as a symbol. That's what we're up against." She combed her fingers down Roz's neck, grazing gently, thoughtful. "I never saw myself winning those people over with just a sad story. But I thought our sad story might make them trust our good intentions long enough to get us to the next step."

Roz leaned her head back into the motion of June's fingers, sighing.

"Those deaths have been wearing on me," June said. "Even that woman, Tia's." She paused, her finger pads resting on Roz's head. "I'd hoped it wouldn't come to that. Shreve's is a terrible way to go."

"Andy was tore up about it," Roz said. "It made me wonder if something was going on between them."

"Maybe there was. I wouldn't have thought less of him for it."

Roz made a dubious grunting sound.

"We've asked a lot of him. Everything of him. And he's delivered."

"I suppose that's true," Roz said.

"What went wrong wasn't on him. I can only blame myself for that."

Roz twisted on the stool to turn and give her a hard look. June used her hands to firmly turn Roz's head facing forward again. She'd finished cutting, more or less—maybe shy of a few corrective touches—but she liked the feel of Roz's close-shorn layers under her fingers, and she liked talking to the back of Roz's head about this stuff more than she did meeting her eye. "I was stupid. I told myself I could work with them. I told myself I needed to treat them with respect if I had any hope of getting Feingold's cooperation. But the truth is that I didn't have the stomach for what needed to be done." June dropped her chin to the crown of Roz's head. Roz leaned back, and they kissed softly. "I still don't, Roz. But we're in it up to our eyeballs now."

"What needs to be done?" Roz said. They were still face-to-face, Roz craning her neck back, June hunched over. June could smell the bitter earth of the tea on Roz's breath. Instead of answering, she kissed her again.

By 10:00 a.m. it was hot. Summer hot. Second half of October and you couldn't stand to be out unless your shirtsleeves were rolled up. Each year June allowed herself to be lulled by the occasional runs of seasonally appropriate days into thinking: well, it's not so bad, maybe. There's hope yet. And then she'd see steam wafting off the kudzu, or she'd forget to wear her bonnet and come home with her neck sunburned again, and the despair would settle on her once more. The flowers thrived in the heat, though. There was that. As she so often did, June thought, as she passed the flower crop to the village, about how the world offered its cures in its diseases, and its diseases in its cures. The hotter climes that the ticks liked so much? They extended the growing season, making it possible to produce enough Salt to bankroll Ruby City and inoculate its residents against tick bites. June had been tempted over the years to see harmony in that. Proof of some bigger, elemental force of balance. Divine planetary engineering. But she knew better.

Especially these last few years, when she could no longer deny the evidence right in front of her. The last birth in Ruby City had been three years ago. Hap Hollander, Mose and Ivy's youngest. Even before him there had been cause for worry, but these things were clearer in retrospect than they were in the living, as so many things are. The birth rate had been slowing for years before Hap marked the onset of its standstill, but in a community of fewer than five hundred people, a couple hundred of them women in their childbearing years, fewer than that number paired off, much less actively trying for children—theirs was a world, after all, where plotting parenthood required some magical thinking, or dogged unthinking—this hadn't seemed so strange. For a long time, it hadn't even registered as something to notice.

The first to notice was Harold Owle—"Doc," everyone called him. Not that he was really a doctor, though what qualified as "real," really, in this day and age? He'd supplemented some passed-down folk knowledge with a lot of self-education—his house was full of old medical books and encyclopedias, some literature and digital files (including a bank of video tutorials) smuggled from in-zone. June, through her connections, could get her hands on certain medicines, pieces of equipment, and Harold and his two apprentices put these items to use fairly successfully, though they were never going to be able to administer chemotherapy or an MRI out here. Harold's chief roles were sawbones and midwife, and, as he told June nearly two years ago, he was not getting as much practice at the latter as he used to.

"You know, I was checking on Marianne Worth the other day, and her older boy—the ten-year-old—he was out in the yard playing with the Ventry twins, the girls, and I had this funny thought. I thought, those kids are all going to be trying to fool around with each other in four or five years, and how're we gonna handle that? Getting ahead a myself, like I do. Thinking we're going to have to start teaching 'em sex ed. Trying to smuggle rubbers out a the zone. God help us. 'Cause you know, there was that bumper crop of them. The Worths, the Ventrys, the Redferns' three, Mary Sue, Terry's girl, whatever her name is, the Pullman boy with the harelip, the Esquillo twins, and them's just the ones I could think of off the top of my head. Seemed like there was a couple years there where I couldn't just about put my head down at night without someone pounding at my door, yelling me to come out and catch another one."

June, remembering this time, had smiled. The baby boom had been a morale boost in the camp, evidence of Ruby City's legitimacy. Life out-of-zone was hard, but they'd made a sweet little town for themselves, and what better testament to that—to their hopefulness—than babies?

"But you know, my next thought after that was—well, gosh, I can count on one hand the number of births in the last five years. Well, OK, maybe that's normal, I think at first. You know, a crop of little 'uns is born, then everybody has their two or three and quits it, and the original settling group had a lot of twenty-some-year-olds in it. So you have to grow the next generation up before there's another boom. Even so, it don't add up."

They were in Harold's little house, at his kitchen table he'd built with boards he'd planed and sanded himself, and he patted a sheet of paper on the tabletop. "Skootch on around here," he'd said, and June had dragged her chair over to his side. "I got some numbers from Curtis and did some figuring." He ran a forefinger that looked like a gnarled twist of tobacco down a column of numbers. "Here on the left is years since settlement. Then there's number of live births, number of deaths, and over here I'm keeping a tally of total population. Then there's the percentages: birth average, death average, total percentage of increase. Now, don't hold me to all this, exactly. I haven't gone through to double-check my work. But you're going to get a rough idea.

"We finished the first year at two hundred seventy-eight people, more or less. Course there was some flux that year, a few packs broke off, I think we ended up bringing in another group right before Thanksgiving, but two hundred seventy-eight's the number Curtis took down in his books. One birth, twenty-eight deaths. That was a rough time. Death average was about ten percent, birth average not even half a percent.

"The next year was a little better. Two births—that jumps the birth average up to point-eight percent—and eighteen deaths, which brings the death average down to seven-point-two percent. And the numbers level out quick from there, then they switch, like they're supposed to. By our tenth year, the number of births jumps up into the high teens. There are two years when it tops twenty, almost five percent, and the mortality rate goes down to eight, or about two percent. Not bad, considering what we're working with here. I mean, you got me cutting melanomas off a people, and there were still a fair number of tick bites happening then.

"But then, here"—he motions to Year 11—"something starts to change."

June let her eyes drift down straight to the bottom line scribbled out in Harold's shaky hand.

"Now if you were going to chart this out some way, it'd look a little like this," he said, and he drew a line across the sheet under his chart. It was a lopsided mountain: a gentle but steady rise on the left, a peak—and then a sharp downhill slope.

"I can already tell you that this year'll be half that, assuming the two who's pregnant carry to term."

June stared at the page, rubbing the furrow between her eyebrows with her middle finger. Harold drew a line through the mountain peak, made a little arrow. Under it he wrote, *Year 11*. "I guess I don't hafta tell you what happens here," he said. "Or maybe I should say, what happens about nine months before here."

He did not. That little peak and the sharp slope that followed it marked a couple of Ruby City's most exciting years. That was when they had made their deal with Perrone for large-scale distribution of recreational Salt and standardized their own inoculation through regular consumption of the seed tea. They broke ground on Town Hall. A group of children put on a Christmas pageant, and June had laughed until she cried when little Meera Ouaka had abandoned her mark on the stage, where she had been praising God on high along with the other angels, to meander over to the manger, toss the doll baby Jesus roughly to the side, and climb in herself, tucking her thumb into her mouth and slipping effortlessly into a deep sleep. *We are not just a camp,* June had thought. *We are not just a mite clinging to the back of civilization. We are a community. We are a* town. She had been able to declare, at the annual New Year's Eve gathering, that there had been not a single tick bite all year, and a big cheer went up in the crowd.

"The Salt," she said hoarsely.

"Aye," said Harold. "The Salt."

"But this doesn't really prove anything, does it?" She looked at the numbers again. "The percentages are scary, but we're talking only a handful of births' difference a year, really. We're such a small community that the standard measures just might not apply."

"Like I said, that occurred to me. It may still be true. But I can tell you that I've had three different women come to me in the last year asking for advice about getting pregnant. One of them said she's been trying for almost two years. The other has had three early miscarriages."

"Still—" June began, but Harold raised a hand to hush her.

"Hear me out. There's more. I got to thinking and looked over my journals. Now again, this ain't scientific, and God knows how many other factors come into play, but it gives you pause. I think I'm safe saying that I'm seeing more cases of female troubles altogether. Irregular periods, late-onset periods, endometriosis. I'm also seeing lactation problems among the newer set of mothers. I don't have the know-how to really study this thing, June. If I had an ultrasound machine—"

"I know, I know," she said. "I've been trying, Harold."

"This ain't blame-laying. I'm just telling you how it is. Something's going on, but I don't really have a way to tell you what it is."

"So what are you saying? Do we stop taking the Salt?" She imagined how that would go over. What kept Ruby City stable—and the worst they'd weathered in their sixteen years as a community, extraordinarily, were some thefts and some fistfights, one serious enough to result in death, and a couple of cases of domestic violence—were luck, June's leadership, and the Salt. The Salt was a powerful incentive for good behavior. It was, June thought sometimes, a miracle drug, and not just because it kept the ticks from biting. The Salt gave Ruby City its economic power, and it cohered them to each other. You couldn't grow, harvest, and process a crop alone. It took a village.

Without Salt, would Ruby City survive?

Without babies, she knew, it surely wouldn't.

"I'm not saying that," Harold said. "For one thing, you got to look at the number of deaths, too. That keeps dropping. We stop taking our dosage, who knows?" He reclined in his chair, grabbed a leather bag off a little shelf by the wall, and started unpacking his pipe and tobacco. "Remember Mike Ventry."

How could she forget? Mike, eight or nine years ago, had become convinced that his Salt dosage was responsible for his heart palpitations. For that matter, maybe it had been. But the upshot was that he stopped taking it, after years of regular usage, and a month later he was tick bitten down by the barns. His bad luck must have been saving up for that day; he contracted Shreve's and died eighteen hours later.

"People are going to want to stop taking it when they know," June said. She flicked her eyes up to Harold's, quick, and dropped them again. "When we tell them," she added, though the word in her mind was *if*, not *when*.

Harold seemed to sense this. "So far as I can tell, it's not *people* who'd have to stop it. Just people who want kids. And maybe just women, at that. I can't know that men aren't also having fertility issues, but I'm not seeing them come in with other symptoms." He sprinkled a pinch of tobacco into his pipe bowl, packed it. "Even so, who's to say if it would matter? The damage might be done."

"My God," June whispered.

"This was always going to be a problem," Harold said, adding his third pinch of tobacco to the pipe bowl and packing it tight with his yellow-stained forefinger. "We started small. We were going to have to bring in some outsiders no matter what, or else start inbreeding." He stuck the pipe stem between his teeth and lit a match, then touched the flame to the bowl, tasting the smoke with what appeared to be deep satisfaction. "The current situation just—you know—underscores the problem."

"Well, it does more than that," June said. She tried to imagine some new order, where women—some women—stopped taking the Salt in the hope of getting pregnant. What a choice. To live with all of that fear and uncertainty again while your man kept bopping along on his merry way? An image flickered across June's mind: all-male hunting groups, all-male fishing and scavenging groups, the women hanging back at the hearth, venturing nervously out into the village, maybe, their worlds suddenly very small, their existences defined by one hope: a baby. It was not a course of action June would have ever taken herself. She had known, even before committing to Roz eighteen years ago, that children weren't in the cards for her, that caring for Violet was the only parenting she ever wanted to do. And there would be others like her, others content to forgo motherhood. But she recognized what was at stake. She recognized how betrayed the women would feel, this done to them without their knowing, without their approbation. And June might be forgiven if ceasing the dosage eventually restored a woman's fertility, but if it didn't? And what about the girls, the ones who'd gotten their first exposure to Salt through their mother's milk? What would this mean for them?

And there was another problem: David Perrone. If David knew that regular consumption of Salt caused infertility, would he keep buying from them? What about that big, onetime deal he kept offering? And if this killed any hope of a deal, what were the chances that he'd simply leave them alone?

"Tell me what to do," June said. "What's the right thing here, Harold? We call a meeting tonight and show them what you just showed me? Leave it up to the individual to keep taking the dosage or not?"

Harold shrugged. "Maybe. But we don't know anything for sure yet."

"What, then?"

"Well. We could quietly try some things first. See what effect there is, if any."

"What things?" June said. Her throat was very dry. It seemed to stick to itself when she swallowed.

"Leave that to me," said Harold. "I'll put out a feeler or two. I have some ideas."

"We can't risk this getting out. There'll be a panic. People'll say I kept it from them."

"Like I said, I have an idea. The less you know about it, the better."

Once a few years back, Roz had gotten word from a villager who'd been out hunting that there was pack of abandoned wolf pups trapped in a crevasse on the other side of the mountain. "Thought you might have some use for 'em," he'd said, and Roz, who'd always hoped she might breed a little wolf into her princes, had gotten downright chipper, which itself was quite a sight. June, amused by Roz's excitement, had accompanied Roz and the hunter back to the puppies, and what she'd seen when she looked down into the hole had made her very nervous about Roz's rescue plan. There were seven of them: one dead, two close to dead, lying on their sides, stomachs fluttering. The other four, who had been eating the dead pup, looked up at the three humans not with relief or even indifference but a wary desperation, muzzles red.

"Goddammit, Billy, those are coyotes," Roz had said. "I can't believe I dragged my ass a half hour up a mountain for a pack of goddamn coyotes."

Anyway, after only a couple of days' incarceration, the nine hostages looked a bit to June like those four puppies had. The room smelled nauseatingly of their unwashed bodies and old urine.

They'd left the coyote pups where they found them, June remembered.

"Here's what I've decided," June said, without preamble. "I'm sending five of you back with Andy. He'll drop you within walking distance of the Wall. You'll be given a story about the group getting separated during a hunting party. You'll say that Tia was leading your half of the group and was killed in a bad fall, and her communication devices went down with her. You'll say you found your way to the Wall through pure luck. Andy's going to make an emergency call to report the separation, and he's going to try really damn hard to convince the folks in-zone to let him complete the excursion as planned, once word comes through that you five are safe in Quarantine. That's where Feingold's microsuit deal is going to help us, I hope."

"Sounds risky," Ken Tanaka said.

"It is," June agreed. "You've left me no better choice. Unless you're all willing to stay. That offer still stands."

"Offer," one of them snorted—the man who'd called Violet a "thing." Lee, was it? "Well, my answer's no. To your *offer*." He sneered around the word.

"Which five go?" the singer asked. June stabbed the air at him with her left index finger. "You," she said, noticing that a flash of relief passed across his face before he could reconfigure his features into the anger he wanted others to think he felt, or maybe even wanted to believe he felt. She turned to point to the other four. "You, you, you, you": Lee; Wendy Tanaka; the woman with the long blond hair; and Marta Severs. She had consulted with Andy. Splitting the pairs was a no-brainer. Keeping Feingold, ditto, and the two who'd already volunteered. But the other choices were trickier. June wished she could have held on to both Tanakas—and she trusted Wendy Tanaka, with her purpled forehead and cheek, to keep her end of the bargain least of them all, maybe—but she'd recognized that uneven treatment would cause a panic, and she knew from Andy that Ken Tanaka was already wise about the Salt, had purchased a top-secret Elite excursion package with its "bite-free guarantee." That, she hoped, would make him compliant.

"I don't want this," the blond woman said. "I don't want to leave my husband."

"Don't be stupid," her husband snapped. "We've talked about this. *Go*."

Wendy Tanaka looked from her brother to June and back again, as if checking his reaction before forming her own. "But why are you even willing to do this? Why not hold us here by force?"

"It's the best compromise I could hope to reach with you," June said. "We need time. This seemed like the surest way to proceed with your cooperation. And we want your cooperation." She cleared her throat, thinking about Roz's face this morning in the mellow Sunday light. The love in it, and the understanding. "We're not bad people."

"When do we go?" Lee asked. He seemed calm now, even content. He was going home, and he was leaving no one here to worry about. Good riddance, June thought. She was glad to be shed of him.

"This afternoon," she said. "Eat lunch. Say your goodbyes. Andy will be here with a van in two hours."

Half an hour later she was sitting in her favorite spot down by the creek, watching a school of minnows throw darts of light and thinking about how this day would end, when she heard someone approaching from behind. Joe. With Marta Severs. Marta walked across the grass in her sock feet, wrists bound behind her, Joe steering her elbow with one hand and his other poised near his holster. If this had been Randall, Andy, even Violet, June's reaction would have been exasperation. An assumption that her will was being thwarted, however well-meant the thwarting. But Joe was a rare man: steady, slow to anger, slow to action. Careful without being timid. If Joe was bringing Marta Severs to June's quiet place by the creek, he had a reason.

"What's this?" she asked him.

"She had something to say that I thought would interest you," Joe said.

June nodded. "Cut her loose. I don't think she's going to run for it. Are you?"

Marta shook her head.

Joe took a pocketknife from a pouch in the quilted fishing vest he always wore, drew it open, and sliced through Marta's zip tie. Marta rubbed the insides of her wrists across her hips.

"You can sit," June told her. She indicated the grass beside her. Marta peered at the ground, then lowered herself gingerly to her bottom, drawing her knees up and sitting rigidly, balls of her feet lifted, back arched.

June laughed. "You may as well stand if you're that uncomfortable."

"I was bitten on our way out here, sitting on grass just like I'm doing now. I don't want to repeat the experience."

"Fair enough," June said. "Let's make this short, then. What's on your mind?"

"You should keep me here," Marta said. "I'm not saying to keep me instead of Wes. Keep us both. But don't send me back."

"You like it here that much?"

Marta took a deep breath. Swallowed. "I can help you. I'm useful to you. More than you realize. More than Wes, maybe."

June waited.

"My last name isn't Severs. It's Perrone."

June had a meager electronic dossier on David Perrone—some information Andy had been able to turn up for her (photographs, birth records, real estate transaction records, a portion of a medical file indicating that Perrone was being treated for Addison's disease)—and she now realized what had been nagging her about Marta Severs. There was one photograph in the dossier, taken at long range with a telephoto lens, of David Perrone, his wife, and their twin sons. They were at the funeral of David's predecessor, and so June could be forgiven for not putting the face from that image—mid to late thirties, lips a pop of bright red, high cheekbones framed with a glossy near-black bob—together with the fifty-something, shorn, unmade woman before her. But yes, June could see it now: the cheekbones, the full lips, the severe brow line, and the dark eyes.

"My husband is David. Our sons are Salvador and Lorenzo. They're in England right now, and the only demand I have is that no one touches them, ever."

"Done," June said softly. Though that was rich, really. The idea that June could order hits on people living in England. Or protect them. "So what is this? You're here to spy for your husband?" She tried to make sense of how that would have worked. How could Marta have known she'd end up here? Did that mean Andy was working for David Perrone?

"No," she said. "I don't know how to convince you of that. Well, the fact I got bitten because I didn't know to take my vitamins. That's something, maybe. But other than that, you'll have to take my word for it. David sent me and our boys off because he said something big was happening. That he was making some kind of move. He owns shares in OLE, so he said this would be a safe bet. I thought I was going on a camping trip, nothing more. The rest is coincidence." Something passed over her face.

"What?" June said. "You're leaving something out."

"He wanted me to keep an eye on Wes, get to know him. He didn't tell me why."

"Well, the suit deal," June said.

"I can see that now," Marta said, somewhat testily. "I'm just telling you he didn't explain himself when he sent me off. He never explains himself."

A crow cawed. The sunlight was golden, warm at their backs, and a broad yellow leaf detached from a branch above them, spun, then landed in the water and was carried off toward the Little Tennessee. June felt her love of this place powerfully and painfully—a love made larger and dearer because it seemed borrowed. Ephemeral. She was willing to sell her soul to protect this thing she had built. But what if even that wasn't enough?

"What are you proposing?" she asked Marta.

"I don't know, exactly," Marta said. "You could let my husband know you have me. That might give you some leverage. Or not. The truth is that I don't know my value to him. Our marriage is . . ."

"What?"

"Complicated," Marta said. "I feel safe saying that he's possessive, if not loving. He won't like that you have someone who belongs to him. It will get his attention."

June, who knew the self-spiting way that David Perrone's possessiveness had played out in the past, wasn't encouraged.

"Or maybe I have information about him you can use. I'm not being cagey when I say maybe. I just don't know. Question me. I'll tell you everything I can tell you. I've lived with him for almost thirty years. I don't know his secrets, but I know his ways."

"Like what?" June asked.

"Like, you were right about one thing." Marta held June's gaze. "If he thinks you pose a threat to his deal with Wes, he'll make you go away. That's how he handles problems. And even if you make the deal with Wes the way you've planned . . ." She trailed off. "I don't know. He holds grudges. And he has ambitions back home. Political ambitions. He won't like loose ends."

"Political ambitions," June repeated with scornful wonder.

"I can tell you everything I know about it. Some campaigns he's donated to, politicians he's done deals with—backroom or otherwise. Who he's been working with. There's a woman on his staff now who'd been on the president's staff. She—"

June held up a hand. "OK. Stop for now. I need to think about this," she said. "Where to go from here." She looked up at Joe. "Take her back to the others. Let Andy know she's staying with us. The rest go as scheduled."

"Thank you," Marta said.

"Don't thank me yet." June considered the creek, the minnows. She let her mind go out with them, along the current, around the bend, over the rocks to the Little Tennessee, its course steady and true. Marta had no idea how radically her own course might have diverged. "We'll talk," she said. "Later."

Fifteen

They rode silently in the van's middle two bench seats, blindfolded, wrists bound, Anastasia and Wendy up front, Jesse and Lee in the back. Andy had expected questions, demands, protests, complaints. Requests for a bathroom break. Chit-chat among themselves to pass the time. Three hours on the road, though, and nothing. The occasional cough or sniff, some gas passing odiferous enough to eclipse, briefly, the smell of body odor, but silence ruled, and it was a relief to Andy after the frantic pitch of the last few days.

Following June's instructions, he exited the old I-40 corridor at Morganton. The road here was in very bad shape. Potholes abounded. Whole sections of the pavement had sloughed away. The biggest craters had been leveled with gravel at some point, and the bridge over the Catawba was in good enough repair to traverse (heart lodged in throat), but Andy was giving the shocks on the old van a workout, and the vibration through the steering wheel was strong enough to make his arms go numb from elbows to fingertips. Soon, too, there was the other vibration, the one coming off the Wall, and as usual—as many times as he'd made this approach, from one side or the other—Andy was struck by a sense of deep unease, of *wrongness*. The Wall bothered some people more than others. Tia had claimed to hardly notice it. "I had it worse when the muffler on my car came loose," she said once. For Andy, the vibration was insidious, alive, and he found it hard to think clearly when he was operating within the Wall's shadow.

"You took us off the interstate," Anastasia said, raising her voice to be heard over the noise of the van's progress.

"There's a smaller gate into the zone through Lenoir," Andy said. "Video surveillance along the route isn't as extensive. I can get you closer before leaving."

He drove another five minutes, ten. Checked the map June had given him. As she'd indicated, there was a parking lot ahead on the right, and the remains of an L-shaped building with a red metal roof. He pulled in, shifted to Park. Shut off the engine.

"You can take off your blindfolds," he told the four.

They did—more tentatively than he would have expected—and squinted against the late afternoon sun.

"This is where we part ways," Andy said. "Go on and get out of the van. Then I'll clip your wrist ties."

They hesitated. Andy exhaled loudly and grabbed his gun from the passenger seat where he'd tossed it. "Jesus Christ. Don't make me wave this thing around anymore. Do you want to come back to the village with me? Christ."

Jesse Haggard moved, hunching over to pull the door handle, awkward with his hands still bound, and slid it open. Oh, he'd had no trouble leaving his girlfriend behind to return to the land of milk and honey. Made a big show of kissing her goodbye. Didn't even offer to trade places with her—Andy had thought him capable of that much—and hopped into the van as if they were heading out on a field trip to the water park.

Lee followed. Then the women. When they were all out, Andy grabbed the duffel bag from the passenger floorboard and joined them, sliding the revolver into his holster.

"Wrists," he said, brandishing his knife. They offered them to him. Four *pops*. Four neon-colored plastic ties left on the ground where they'd dropped. They did their dance, now familiar: wrist rubbing, stretching, craning their necks left, right, cracking their backs.

"Your boots and Stamps are in that bag, along with some water and energy bars." He pointed up the road. "The checkpoint is about three kilometers ahead. Follow the road. You'll walk right into it. Don't expect them to roll out the welcome wagon for you. Be polite, be agreeable. Do as they say. Yes sir. No sir. Let them know you're unarmed. When you're into Quarantine and they've confirmed your IDs, you'll get treated like VIPs again."

They looked down at the bag, then up the road.

"What are you waiting for? Kiss goodbye?"

Anastasia eyed him with loathing, hunched down, drew the drawstring on the bag. She rooted around, drew out a pair of boots tied together by the shoestrings, checked the tag in the tongue. Tossed them to Jesse Haggard, who sat on the rotten old cement and started to pull them on. Stamps followed boots. Water and food followed Stamps. Andy waited until the bag was empty, its contents transferred to the four men and women with stubbled scalps and grimed microsuits, and then climbed back into the van. He pressed the automatic lock button as soon as he'd done so.

"Good luck," he said through a crack in the window.

Jesse Haggard threw up his middle finger. Andy laughed.

"See you around," he said, and he started the engine.

He drove back southeast on Highway 18, moving his visor to block the red ball of sun ahead on the right. He'd noted the turnoff when he passed it, but he had a hard time seeing with the light in his eyes like this, so he slowed to a crawl much earlier than he probably needed to.

Here it was. State Road 1430.

Going maybe fifteen, twenty kilometers an hour, so he could refer to his map but also because this asphalt here was in even worse shape than Highway 18's had been, Andy watched for Highland Road, then Nick Road, making a right both times, passing a half-buried old sign marking the Turtle (or was it Tuttle?) Educational State Forest. Less than a kilometer south of the intersection was the turnoff June had marked on the map with a star: Cannon Town Road. *Comes to dead end,* her note said. *Park at house.*

He checked the van's digital clock: 4:48. They'd been walking maybe fifteen minutes, so he still had plenty of time.

The road here—dirt, with two wheel tracks defined by new gravel in the spots that would get muddy after a rain—climbed uphill, then leveled, and this was where Andy found the promised house. At first glance, you wouldn't mark it as special. It seemed to be in perhaps marginally better repair than the houses Andy had passed coming up here: brick ranch homes with metal carports and large rusting septic tanks, the roofs decaying, window glass shattered, kudzu sinking its tendrils into the rotting mortar. At this house, glass glinted behind the boarded-over windows. The roof, though very old, seemed to be intact. But as he exited the van and approached, Andy's eyes lit on other evidence of recent use, even upkeep. The nail heads fitting the old boards to the windows were untarnished. A steel plate had been affixed to the front door, and a new-looking padlock dangled from the hasp, its shank a good centimeter thick. Andy had the key June had given him on a string around his neck. He pulled the string out from under his shirt, fitted it to the keyhole, and popped the lock loose.

He'd known what to expect, but still, how strange it all was.

It was as if he had stumbled into an abandoned newsroom, or campaign headquarters—some space where clusters of people worked at computers in close proximity and downed cheap coffee by the liter. The living room's perimeter was lined with couches and desks, scavenged and makeshift, the floor between them a spider's web of intersecting power cords all leading to the place where a chimney might have been, once, but now sat a large, hulking piece of equipment with its own cords trailing up and through a hole in the ceiling. The solar generator. What was being powered were a handful of computers: four older, out of date by five or eight years, but one absolutely state-of-the-art, even by in-zone standards, with a beautiful two-hundred-centimeter TI Dimension-Tech display that depicted, in rest mode, an eerily realistic small waterfall finishing in a churning foam so detailed that a beam of sunlight slipping through the boarded-over windows picked up droplets of digital mist.

"There's a porch off the back of the house," June had told him. "You'll find what you need there."

He made his way through the kitchen. It was dusty but tidy, smelled of mothballs. A mousetrap rested unsprung on the tile floor, pellet of food untouched. The door to the back porch had a plastic sheet hanging over it; Andy pushed it to the side, slid three different deadbolts over.

The porch had been screened in once, but most of the screens were missing, or damaged, big rough-edge holes marking the passage of raccoons, rats, nesting birds. Moldy latticework boxed the railing in now, curtained with vines. A camera sat on a tripod, its eye pointing through an opening in the lattice.

Andy hunted for its On button. Pressed it. A red light blinked. Inside, he'd been told, the fancy computer was now recording. He'd need to download the video to a thumb drive and bring it back to June.

He glanced at the camera's display screen. It showed the time—5:07—and a crisp view of the place where Nick Road intersected with Highway 18 and Atlantic Zone had built its Lenoir substation, a broad, gray cinder-block structure that blocked the old road, angled back with two long wings, and connected to a razor-wire fence eight meters tall and God only knew how many kilometers long. Behind the fence, eight smokestacks rose like turrets, emitting a steady gray trickle of foul-smelling smoke. This was an older section of the Salt Line, the new "waste repurposing ramparts" still creeping up this way from the south, eight years from projected completion. Not even Andy had known about this entry point. Not until yesterday, when June explained the day's plan to him. The little house on the rise took advantage of a gap in the TerraVibra—the constant vibration had been proven to degrade power-generating facilities (a significant risk when dealing with some unsteady materials, some nuclear)—and so a Ruby City tech crew was able to grab a signal here from Atlantic Zone feeds. What's more, the house offered a perfect location from which they could, undetected, monitor the comings and goings of Big Sky Fine Meats and V&M Logging, two of David Perrone's biggest smuggling fronts.

And it was where, in a few minutes' time, Andy was going to watch what happened when Jesse, Anastasia, Wendy, and Lee approached the Wall.

There was a red plastic outdoor chair propped against the house. Andy moved it over beside the camera, swept some leaves and dirt out of it, and seated himself. Not bad. Comfortable, almost. He couldn't tip it back—the legs were too flimsy—but he raised his feet and propped them up on the porch railing. He was self-conscious. Aware that he was putting on a performance of some kind—coolness, indifference—which was strange, when he had only himself as audience.

It took another ten minutes. Then they came into view. They walked side by side, in step. They'd linked their arms to form a line, following Andy's instructions, following the road.

When it happened, it happened in a second. One moment they were walking; the next, they were on their backs. Through the little display screen, it was nothing. The rapid crackle of rifle fire, which traveled loud and clear from the Wall over to where Andy sat on the porch, was the most visceral part of the experience, but even that was muted. Nothing that would haunt him at night. He didn't think so, at least.

He didn't move right away. He waited to see them come out, and soon they did. Six people, dressed in gray fatigues, face masks, some kind of sheer micro-netting over their heads. Two stretchers. Two trips.

Through the camera's little display screen, it all seemed very small, very far away. Very unreal.

He turned the camera off. Inside, he woke up the computer with the beautiful display, entered the username and password June had given him, and pulled the camera recording onto his thumb drive with a little beckoning gesture. The display's prediction/intention hardware was excellent; he got the right file on his first try.

Part Three

Vimelea

Sixteen

Wes realized that his eyes had passed over the paragraph—again—without processing its content. He went back to the top, shook his head briskly, and widened his eyes.

> *Mrs. Touchett was certainly a person of many oddities, of which her behaviour on returning to her husband's house after many months was a noticeable specimen. She had her own way of doing all that she did, and this is the simplest description of a character which, although by no means without liberal motions, rarely succeeded in giving an impression of suavity.*

He didn't much like novels, never had. He couldn't easily care about made-up people. (Not that he didn't have plenty of issues connecting to real-life people, as Sonya would no doubt attest.) And the handful of novels that had managed to interest him over the years—a couple of political thrillers, a sci-fi series Sonya had talked up—hooked him mostly through their incorporation of interesting facts and ideas, so that they pleased Wes no more (and usually less) than a good biography or instruction manual might. But he had, in the last week, already exhausted the meager supply of nonfiction in his shared holding cell: a biography of Benjamin Franklin (now *there* was a man with whom Wes felt some kinship); an old pop-psychology book called *Parenting on the Spectrum*, which was a weirdly intriguing look at how autism disorders used to be regarded and treated, an era Wes was grateful to have missed. There was a great book about a series of ritualistic murders, never solved, on the Cumberland Plateau in Restoration-era Tennessee, *That Evening Sun Went Down*. A very outdated and funny (so funny for being so outdated) guide to Linux. That was it. So then he slogged his way through one of the shorter novels, *Ethan Frome*, enjoying the smell of the brittle yellow pages more than he did waiting for the obligatory big reveal about Ethan's accident, and now he had this big book in front of him, the kind of important book he always thought he'd read if he were in jail or on a deserted island or something, and now he was in jail, and he still couldn't focus on it. What he'd give to have his tablet right now! His tablet and a shower and a canister of fiber and one of his power juices, something to clear out the cement works his goddamn colon had become, not that fiber would fix his anxiety about shitting in a bucket with only a thin sheet separating him from Edie and the others.

At least there were fewer *others* to share this cramped space with. In the couple of days before June sent back Wendy, Lee, Anastasia, and Jesse—well, it had gotten bad. Wes came close to hyperventilating more than a few times, so excruciating was the feeling of having so many other hot, smelly bodies competing for space with his own, and even the more easygoing among them—Edie, Berto—were snapping with little to no provocation. If Wes had been a different kind of man, he and Jesse would probably have come to blows at some point. (Wes felt somewhat consoled by the suspicion that Jesse, too—no matter what else he tried to project—was not that sort of man, and was happy enough that Wes hadn't waved a fist at him.) He didn't think he was alone in finding Jesse intolerable. From his whining to his weird bursts of cheer, when he'd undoubtedly take that goddamn ukulele out and start picking out a grating kid's song or folk song or (worse) one of his own songs, Jesse had amplified every annoyance and indignity, to the point that the tension relieved palpably the moment he left, cheerfully abandoning his long-suffering girlfriend—a girlfriend saintly enough to send him back home with not just forgiveness but sex—sex!—sex that Wes, and everyone else, had spent fifteen endless minutes pretending miserably to sleep through.

Speaking of Edie, she sat in a corner of the room in a shaft of light from one of the opposite windows, reading a book that Wes himself had summarily rejected, a collection of the complete works of Jane Austen. She had her back against the wall, knees drawn up, book spread open across her thighs. She'd been working on the book for several days now, reading almost constantly, and appeared to be halfway through the volume. "I've never been much of a reader," she'd confessed to Wes over one of their now-common bean-and-cornbread suppers. "I work too much now—well, I mean, I did—until Jesse—you know, touring with him and everything, and then this trip." She looked embarrassed. "And I just took alt-texts in high school, like everybody but the nerds." The corner of her mouth turned up, and she stabbed at her beans with a tarnished silver spoon. "But I'm kind of enjoying these novels. I didn't think I would."

"Yeah, me, too," Wes had lied. Then, feeling guilty: "Well. To be honest, I'm not much on fiction. But reading again—that's been fun. I never have time back home to just sit and read. I mean, unless it's on my tablet. My feeds, articles, stuff like that. Sitting with an actual book slows the heart a little after . . ." He trailed off, but Edie nodded.

"All of this."

"All of this," Wes agreed. Before could stop himself, he blurted out, "I'm sorry, Edie. I'm sorry for asking you to go with Tia. Knowing how it all turned out, what could have happened to you—" Goddammit, he was close to *crying* now, and he swallowed hard against the sensation. "I can't bear it. I've done so much damage, and it doesn't even matter that I didn't think I knew any better." That village of three hundred that June had mentioned. Was that real? Or was that just a cruel manipulation tactic? "Anyway," he continued, "I just want you to know that I didn't ask you because I thought you were disposable. Berto and Anastasia wouldn't do it. I didn't think Marta could. I'd have gone, but I knew they wanted me, and I thought that taking off would be more harm than good."

Edie patted his knee. "I overreacted. I know that's not what you meant. And a part of me wishes I'd done it. Maybe those two wouldn't have died. Maybe Tia wouldn't have. She didn't have a buddy to Stamp her in time. That's on me."

"No," Wes said. "It's not."

"Well, I guess we both need to give ourselves a break. For now, anyway."

"OK. I'll save it for my therapist."

Edie smiled in that crooked, rueful way she had, revealing one dimple. "You do that. You'll have plenty of material after this."

Embarrassed—*Was that weird, mentioning a therapist? Doesn't everyone have one?*—Wes motioned at her Austen book with his spoon. "So it's good? You're liking it?"

"Maybe it's just because there's nothing else to do," Edie said, and Wes felt her snapping shut against him, drifting back to that secret, inward space that seemed, so much of the time, to be her habit and solace. He'd ended up choosing the Henry James novel to read because the painting of a woman on its cover reminded him of the painted woman on the cover of Edie's Austen collection, and he'd thought that this might be the book she would want to read next, and then, maybe, they could talk again. She would talk to him, confide in him, again.

To be fair, there were a few other things to do in the shed, other than read. They'd been given a crude chess board, carved and painted by hand, and Marta and Ken had been playing a long, mostly silent tournament, every now and then switching off with one of the others. (Wes was quite good at chess, but playing it stoked his anxiety, so he usually begged off.) There was a deck of playing cards. Some scrap paper and pencil stubs. With these Wes had found himself staying up late last night, after the others had turned in, and making a list by moonlight:

Why do I think I like Edie? What is this about REALLY?

1. Because she is pretty? That's shallow . . .
2. I hate her boyfriend and want to best him in caveman sort of way? Also shallow, immature.
3. We are trapped together in life-threatening situation. Members of group most obviously matched in age. Probably some instinctual/primal urge to plant seed before murdered.
4. Lonely?
5. Rebounding from Sonya?
6. She is nice and smart. But lots of people nice and smart.

And then, as was typical for him—he wished he had a tablet so he could organize his digressions—he was off on another tangent.

True? Lots of people nice and smart?
Or lots of people actually raging lunatics in shithole world?
Virtuz for nice and smart people and Virtuz tanked.
Pocketz is for a shithole world.
What does that make me?

He knew the list was silly, but he couldn't stop himself. What someone like Sonya wouldn't have understood was that he wasn't as literal-minded as the list suggested; he didn't actually go around making life decisions or reaching conclusions about the meaning of life based on bullet points. But writing the list, giving physical shape to his thoughts—the act actually unlocked in him something freer, more abstract. It forced him to face what he might otherwise turn away from. Like what he'd written on the back of the scrap of paper:

1. Why would she like me back?
2. What does it even matter? We're going to die.

We're going to die. The thought kept coming to him like a radio transmission, something his receiver would randomly pick up depending on how he tilted his head or where he moved in their holding cell. He saw it in the pages of the books he tried to read. In the eyes of the rotating crew of Ruby City guards. In a slant of light coming through the windows, in the red-orange leaf that pinwheeled off a tree limb and plastered itself against the glass. He saw it despite everything June had told him, despite the fact that he actually continued to believe most of what she'd told him. But he didn't see his certainty reflected in his fellow captives. On Monday, the morning after Andy had left with the others, Berto had awakened from a sound sleep, yawned, stretched, cracked his neck with a satisfying grunt. "Knowing Anastasia's out of here makes all the difference," he said. "Whatever else happens, I can deal with it. She hadn't even wanted to do this trip, really. I talked her into it. I couldn't have lived with myself if they'd hurt her."

Berto had glanced apologetically at Edie, seeming to think that his chivalry must reflect badly on Jesse. But Edie was staring off into the distance, lost in her own thoughts.

"I feel good. I feel hopeful," Berto said. "As long as you're here, Feingold. I'm sticking to you like glue."

"Stick away," Wes said with weak humor.

Wes himself felt good about one thing: that Marta had somehow managed to return her ticket, if only—selfishly—because he would have been so lonely without her company. She had been mum about how she'd pulled it off. All Wes knew was what the others knew: she had whispered something to one of June's henchmen, been escorted out of the building, and returned maybe fifteen minutes later. When Andy collected the group a couple of hours later, she remained seated—and none of June's people told her to come along. Wes didn't even know why she had wanted to stay, if it was out of loyalty to him (a stab of guilt at that), or if she had also felt uneasy about the sudden offer of freedom—or what. He was looking at her instead of *The Portrait of a Lady*, mulling this over, when she lifted her face from the chess board she was studying, caught his eye, smiled. He waved back.

Marta, who'd also sneaked in the canister of Quicksilver, was full of surprises, he was finding.

She said something to Ken, then came stiffly to a stand and stretched. She crossed the room to join Wes.

"Who won this one?"

"No one yet," Marta said. She leaned down, touched her toes. Bobbed a little, then put her palms flat on the plank floor. "I called a break. I needed a rest."

"What are the stats so far?" Wes asked.

Marta stretched out beside him, taking his pack, with an unthinking familiarity, to use as a pillow. "I have eight wins, and he has ten."

"Not bad. Isn't he a doctor or something?"

"Neurosurgeon." She lowered her voice. "I could beat him more often if I cared more. He's a very fierce competitor. He needs to win."

"You don't?"

She shrugged. "Obviously not." She put her forearm over her eyes. "Ken reminds me of my husband. My husband is a very good chess player. He taught me to play. And my husband needs to win, like Ken does. So I have a lot of practice losing. I am an excellent loser."

"Your husband sounds . . ." Wes searched for a word. "Intense," he decided.

Marta nodded from under her arm. "That's a good word for David. A perfect word."

"What does he do?"

"What does he do, what does he do," she murmured. She rolled onto her side and propped her head up on her palm. Her eyes met his—and there was a frankness there, an intimacy that almost embarrassed Wes. "Wes, what if I told you that my husband is a very bad man?"

Wes waited for her to go on, lost. He shook his head slowly.

"Your would-be business partner. David Perrone?"

"He's—your husband?"

She nodded.

"What? Wow. Wow." He rubbed his temples. "Was June telling the truth about him?"

Marta nodded, a dropping of the chin so measured that he almost missed it. "Probably. I haven't let myself think much about it over the years. I guess that sounds awful. I don't know what he's done. But what June said didn't surprise me much."

He tried to make sense of this, to make it fit with this kind woman, this mother figure, whom he'd come to trust and admire so much. How—why—had she hidden this from him, even after everything that June told them?

"He owned a garage when I met him. He wasn't a mechanic himself. But he had business instinct. He always seemed to sense what was in the wind. He'd bought a garage and a few months later the new inspection legislation passed. The money rolled in. Well, it seemed at the time like big money. We got a three-bedroom house on a half-acre lot. He paid cash for it. We both had cars." She stared at the ceiling, smiling a small smile. "*That*—" She jabbed at the air. "*That* was the sweet spot. I didn't know it then, though. David was always saying, 'Onward and upward.' As directions go, that sounded good to me. So I followed him. He had more good instincts. And then we were very wealthy, and I had the boys. It's easy to live in denial about your world when you have children, Wes. Maybe you'll see that firsthand someday."

He hadn't thought much about kids. He shrugged.

"But I'm giving myself a pass. The truth, Wes, is that my husband's one of the reasons we're hostage here. And I guess that makes me responsible, too."

"You know that's not true," Wes said. "I mean, if you want to lay blame, lay it here." He tapped his chest. Despite his breezy comment to Edie about saving it up for his therapist, what Wes couldn't stop thinking about for the last several nights, as he tried to sleep, were all of those lives lost outside Gulf Zone. The crater in the ground. The massacre that happened simply because he had gotten greedy and insecure and come up with a bright idea, a shiny new money-making scheme. He hadn't known, could never have guessed in a million years this outcome, but was that any excuse? He could no longer deny to himself the truth: he'd seen the gaps in the reports his people gave him on Perrone. He could read between the lines. His COO Sandy had made herself indispensable to Wes, in part, by shielding him—from underlings, from petty concerns, from annoying details, from inconvenient truths. If David Perrone were everything Marta and June seemed willing to agree he was, then Sandy knew, or knew enough. And she spared Wes this knowledge. Wes, so full of Virtuz, had gladly let her.

"I don't think David was like he is now when we started dating," Marta said. "In fact, I'm sure of it. Which makes me wonder. About me. Our marriage sure didn't stop him from changing. For all I know it helped him along his way."

"So you told June who you are," Wes said.

Marta nodded.

"Why?" Wes thought about it. "You could have gone home to your sons. You could have warned your husband about what was happening out here."

"Could I?" Marta said. "I'm not so sure." She threw a pointed glance toward Ken, who was still studying the chess board, and lowered her voice. "He isn't like Berto. He isn't happy or relieved, I mean. He seems sad. Lost. Like he's in mourning."

"He's always seemed like that."

"Not like this. Not quite."

Wes ran his thumb along the pages of *The Portrait of a Lady*, releasing another puff of that good old book scent.

"At any rate," said Marta, "I made a quick decision. Maybe it was the wrong one, but I don't think so."

She put out her hand, which was closed around some small object, and opened her fingers to reveal a NicoClean refill canister.

"What is that, another Quicksilver canister?" Wes asked.

Marta shook her head. "I thought when I brought it out here it was fifteen grams of street Salt. David gave it to me along with the Quicksilver."

Wes processed this oddity. "Why on earth would he do that?"

"You flatter me," Marta said. She smiled thinly. "Or else you see me as too old to party. Not that I ever partied, really. But I did this stuff. For years. It's an excellent high. I have to give June and her people credit. It's like . . . a gondola ride. Steady and smooth. I quit about a month before boot camp started, and David never knew. Hardest thing I've ever done."

"But it's not the Salt?"

"Oh, it's the Salt," Marta said. She unscrewed the cap on the vial, turned it over on its side, and tapped the contents into her left palm. A fine white powder. She rubbed it with the pad of her right forefinger, a longing, almost sensual touch. "Look inside the vial. At the very bottom."

Wes did, angling it toward the light coming in from the window. "Is that . . . some kind of microchip?"

"I think so," Marta said. "Well, I wouldn't know, actually. I figure you'd know better than I do. But I think it's a tracking device. I think he sent this with me to keep tabs on me. Or on you, through me." She ran a thumb over the chip, thoughtfully. "That's more likely, actually. He told me to stick close to you. Get to know you. I didn't know why. And Wes, that's not what I did. I mean, I got to know you, but not for him. I did it for me. I hope that's clear."

"Hey," Wes said. "Don't sweat it. I believe you." He did. "And you just happened to find it," he mused. "The chip."

Marta cupped her hand and shook the powder back into the vial, then wiped her palm briskly on the leg of her microsuit. "Oh, I thought about blitzkrieging on it. By the second night in here? Oh, I thought hard. I didn't. But it was close."

"So he's tracking us," Wes said. "He already knows where we are."

Marta nodded.

"I don't know what to do with that."

"I don't either," Marta said. "Well, I'll say this—if our people made it back to Quarantine, David knows. Whatever stories they've told, whatever promises they've kept. He knows."

"Unless they didn't make it back."

"Yes. Unless that."

"You think they might be dead," Wes said. A wave of sorrow passed through him. He hadn't cared much for Lee. He'd loathed Jesse. Anastasia, Wendy—they were fine, he'd liked them fine, but he felt no special kinship with them. You couldn't endure what this group had endured together, though, and not ache at such news. How hopeful they'd all been, gathering their meager belongings, heading out to the van with Andy.

"I think," Marta said, "we have to consider that possibility."

"Oh, man." Wes pinched his tear ducts. "Man. Wow."

"We can't trust her," Marta said. "I'm not saying I don't sympathize with the situation here. It seems like there are some good people. June might even have their best interests at heart. But there's some piece of the puzzle missing. Something June hasn't told us. And she hasn't started dosing us with the tea, either. Not even you. Or letting us roam free like she promised."

"Even Berto's had trouble explaining that one away," Wes said. "It's been days."

"We have to assume the worst of them, and we have to look out for ourselves."

Wes swallowed hard. Then bobbed his head in assent.

"I just want to be with my sons again. I can't see any further ahead than that." Marta sighed and rubbed her middle fingers along her sharp, high cheekbones. "I need to make sure you know that about me. My motives are selfish. Everything I do—it's going to be a calculation. Whatever I think is likeliest to get me home to them. Whatever it takes."

"I understand," Wes said. "So what do we do? Do you have a plan?"

"Ha. Not as such."

"What then?"

"I play it like I play chess," Marta said. "June will come to me. She'll want me to do something, or she'll want to ask questions about David. Maybe she'll kill me and send him my head. I don't think so, though. Not yet. So right now, I wait and see. When I know her move, I'll start thinking about mine."

Seventeen

Violet has three distinct memories of the time before she escaped Flat Rock.

The first is of her mother's death. She'd had a baby in her belly, she'd explained to Violet (though Violet wasn't Violet then; Violet's very young, very well-meaning mother had saddled her with the name Alexandria Magnificent—Alma, thankfully, for short), and the baby had hurt her bad coming out and then ended up dying after all the trouble it had put her through. Violet's mother was laid up after the birth in their camper, thin under a thinner blanket, and a red bloom had suddenly appeared down where her tummy was, the size of a saucer and then, in seconds, the size of a dinner plate. "Alma," she'd said, face white as bone and lips the faded blue-gray of a winter sky, "you got to run and get Big Mama right this instant." And Violet (Alma) had. She had dragged Big Mama, muttering and cursing, to the camper by her index finger. But Violet's mother was dead by the time they returned. "Mommy," Violet had said, jabbing the body. "Mommy. Mommy, wake up."

Big Mama had slapped her jabbing hand. "Quit that. Your mumma's dead. Go lay in your bed and hush up before you give me a headache."

The second memory of that time is from some summer night.

Wall Day, maybe, and there were fireworks over the lake, and this man (his face was a blank to her now, but he'd had a mustache) had made her go with him, she had been very scared, this hadn't happened before, and Big Mama had said to her, "Put your big girl britches on. It'll be over before you know it." So she had expected something very bad, but the man had only hoisted her to the top of his camper, held her hand while the black sky was fissured with gold and green and red, and she hadn't liked his sweaty palm much, or his loud, stuttering respirations, but he was nice, he didn't hurt her, and he'd even given her a soft brown sweet square that melted on her tongue. The most extraordinary thing she'd ever tasted.

This is a good memory. Violet is grateful that one of the three is.

It would be inaccurate, really, to say the third memory is "distinct." It lacks form, it lacks narrative. But it makes up for these lacks in its intensity, a story told by sensation—a pain so large and long it nearly blots out every other sense. The pain is

ROOOOOOOOOOOOOOOOOOOOOOOOOOOOOOOOO
OOOOOOOOOOOOOOOOOOOOOOOOOOOOOOOOOOOO
OOOOOOOOOOOOOOOOOOOOOOOOOOOOOOOOOOOO
OOOOOOOOOOOOOOOOOOOOOOOOOOOOOOOOOOOO
OOOOOOOOOOOOOOOOOOOOOOOOOOOOOOOOOOOO
OOOOOOOOOOOOOOOOOOOOOOOOOOOOOOOOOOOO
OOOOOOOOOOOOOOOOOOOOOOOOOOOOOOOOOOOO
OOOOOOOOOOOOOOOOOOOOOOOOOOOOOOOOOOOO
OOOOOOOOOOOOOOOOOOOOOOOOOOOOOOOOOOOO
OOOOOOOOOOOOOOOOOOOOOOOOOOOOOOOOOOOO
OOOOOOOOOOOOOOOOOOOOOOOOOOOOOOOOOOOO
OOOOOOOOOOOOOOOOOOOOOOOOOOOOOOOOOOOO
OOOOOOOOOOOOOOOOOOOOOOOOOOOOOOOOOOOO
OOOOOOOOOOOOOOOOOOOOOOOOOOOOOOOOOOOO
OOOOOOOOOOOOOOOOOOOOOOOOOOOOOOOOOOOO
OOOOOOOOOOOOOOOOOOAAAAAAAAAAAAAAAAAAAA

AAAAAAAAAAAAAAAAAAAAAAAAAAAAAAAAAAAAAAAAAA
AAAAAAAAAAAAAAAAAAAAAAAAAAAAAAAAAAAAAAAAAA
AAAAAAAAAAAAAAAAAAAAAAAAAAAAAAAR

a thing that keeps happening, that she participates in, it is outside of time, somehow, so that what Violet remembers of her agony might only be its first few shocking seconds, or minutes, or of all the weeks that followed them. There is the pain, the primal enduring roar of it, and a handful of other sensations that flare across the roar like—well—fireworks. Blinding light, then a dark blot moving across it. Screams. A brief dimming of the pain when something cool and thick touches her neck, and the odd sticky, crackling sound the cool stuff made. Like river mud when it sucks at your boots. This is a comparison Violet can only make now, because she didn't have boots when she lived at Flat Rock, and she'd never seen a river. Only the lake, the lake so expansive from Violet's brief glimpses of it that it might as well have been an ocean.

Violet can remember other things about her years at Flat Rock, but what she remembers are amalgams of many moments and many days. Her walk from home to Fat Daddy's camper. Shaquoia—she was the one who took Violet (Alma) in after her mother died—frying fish patties on the camper's little hot plate, and the accompanying smells of oily tinned fish and hot old grease.

A flicker here, at this memory. A very bad thing. But Violet doesn't pursue the thought, has no desire to follow it where it goes.

There was a game she would sometimes play with the other squirrels, if no one needed them, and they kept very, very quiet. Duck, duck, goose. She remembers how it felt to whisper-giggle, needing to laugh but never sure what the laugh would cost you.

There were many hurts. Violet doesn't remember breaking her arm or her leg, she doesn't remember any one of the hundreds of hits or bruises—but she has a composite memory of Fat Daddy's furious face, Big Mama's long-suffering face, a composite memory of the hits and bruises, of the way a bruise starts deep purple and fades to yellow. She has a composite memory of being afraid. Constantly.

Violet doesn't remember why she was burned. This is partly because she never knew and partly because there is no why. If a hypnotist or witch doctor were to make Violet remember what immediately preceded the roar, Violet would be able to tell him that Shaquoia was cooking the fish patties, like she did at least once or twice a week, and that Fat Daddy had come over. She would be able to tell him that she was sitting on the floor in what Shaquoia called "the den," which was really just the open middle space of the tiny camper, putting together a puzzle that had belonged to Shaquoia's son before he died. She could tell him about an angry shout, and how she'd looked up in the shout's direction. That was it. One second her eyes were fixed on the puzzle. Mickey Mouse hugging Pluto. A piece was missing, right at the bottom of Pluto's tongue, and each time Violet (Alma) took apart the puzzle and put it back together, she harbored the vague hope that the piece would suddenly appear, though it never did. The next second she looks up. Then the roar.

What happened is that Fat Daddy got angry at Shaquoia. There is no why here, either. Fat Daddy got angry a lot. Fat Daddy was missing some essential piece of his humanity. He got angry, and before he could even register his intention, he was grabbing the hot skillet and flinging its contents at the child.

Then the roar.

Violet doesn't remember exactly how old she was that night—which was seven, barely, her birthday passing just a few days earlier without her or any other living person's knowing—or how long the formless, all-encompassing pain lasted after the burn: months. She doesn't know that Shaquoia spent her meager savings paying one of her regulars, a logger named Teddy, to steal some burn salve and antibiotics from his company's infirmary, how she did her best to scrub Violet's (Alma's) wounds clean, the way Flat Rock's harried med-tech instructed her to, but the child's screams threatened to draw down on them Fat Daddy's wrath all over again, and so an infection set in, and that was why Violet lost her eye. She doesn't know that the salve ran out, and there was no money to get more, and so the healing tissue grew hard and contracted, and Shaquoia despaired because there was nothing to be done, short of slathering the child with lard, and Fat Daddy and Big Mama kept telling her to just let them put Alma out of her misery (as if the two of them knew how to do anything but create misery), and she had just about resolved that this was the right thing, the kindest thing, when Teddy offered to get the child out of camp and hand her over to someone who could help her.

Violet doesn't know that Teddy, who'd acted in offering to help Shaquoia on a vaguely well-meaning impulse—he was a devout Pentecostal, had always felt guilty about patronizing the Flat Rock camp, though not guilty enough to stop—panicked shortly after smuggling Violet out. What on earth was he going to do with her? Why hadn't he thought this through? So he'd given her one of his night-night-sleepy-time pills (there went five credits down the crapper), driven a few kilometers off his path back to the logging camp, and walked the child into the woods a little, to a nice, quiet spot where no one would bother her. Like many people who derive their sense of goodness from their religious affiliation rather than their actions, Teddy was able to soothe himself with the belief that this was part of God's plan, and if the child were meant to survive, God would protect her. If she didn't—well, paradise would be her reward.

Violet, since moving out of June and Roz's place eight years ago, kept a bed at Central Bunkhouse. She had at least a decade (close to two, in some cases) on the building's other seven habitants, who all worked the flower crop during the growing season and spent the off-seasons on production. Violet was treated by this group with reverent disinterest, like a dotty old aunt who kept changing the names in her will. This was fine by her. The bunkhouse's list of occupants changed over time, but its attendant passions and dramas did not. They fell in and out of friendships, in and out of one another's beds (tipsily cavorting in the early a.m. hours under the bedsheets, as if a thin layer of cotton soundproofed their fucking). Eventually, they fucked around enough to start thinking about settling, then paired off, moved out, and some new seventeen- or eighteen-year-olds would take their place. The bunkhouse had slept as many as twenty at a time. Eight, the current number, was as low as Violet had ever known it to be.

Still, she preferred the bunkhouse to June's place—she was too old, had long been too old, to keep playing the child, the daughter. June had offered to build Violet her own little cabin—even up in the woods a bit, if what Violet wanted was some privacy and distance—but Violet had turned her down. She wasn't good with other people. Other people weren't good with her. But she couldn't function alone, either. Couldn't sleep. Couldn't turn off her mind. Her parade of bunkmates—young, unblemished, caught up in their absurd romances, their petty grievances—were harmless. Sleeping among them was a bit like sleeping among one of Roz's litters of pups. They were loud and messy, liked to roll each other, liked to get into pointless tussles, but they didn't know how to inflict real hurt. Not even when they whispered things that Violet could overhear (*"Shh, you'll wake up ol' Candleface"*). They seemed to assume that her ears didn't work because she was missing an eye. Or that her brain didn't work. Violet wasn't motivated to change their minds. She used them, hid behind them. A wall of good fortune. Nothing could reach her through them.

Wednesday morning, she rolled over, turning her back to the others, and listened as they rose, dressed, heated the teakettle to whistling. There was a rustling behind her. "Violet, I'm putting your tea over here on the table. OK?" Meg, it sounded like. A nice girl. The oldest in the bunkhouse, after Violet.

"OK," Violet said. "Thanks," she remembered to add.

"Are you sick? Do you need anything?"

"I'm fine," Violet said. "Just another headache. I'll be up soon."

"All right," Meg said. "Find me if you need me."

Violet didn't reply. In a few more minutes, the bunkhouse cleared and she finally had some quiet.

She rolled onto her back and stared at a water stain on the ceiling, blinking until its familiar shape (like a four-fingered hand) came into focus. The vision in her eye was weakening. Slowly, but noticeably. What would she do if—when—it worsened?

No. She wasn't going to think about that right now.

She waited.

Twenty seconds. Sixty. Two minutes. *There.* It happened again. She hadn't dreamed it.

The sensation was both intimate and distant. It was like a single piano note in a large, empty auditorium. A flare of light across a night sky. A crackle of static across dead air.

Her baby. Moving.

She never smiled. A smile sat stiffly and uncomfortably on her face, pulled at the tendons of her neck. She felt lit from within, though: a secret smile, one that touched her eyes if not her lips. *My baby. Mine.* She had been walking around for the last three months in a daze of disbelief and terror that occasionally verged into wonderment, though never for very long. Her first clue hadn't been morning sickness—she'd not once thrown up. Her breasts had knotted like fists. Then, shortly after, she noticed a funny twisting sensation in her abdomen, as if hands were gently but firmly wringing her insides. Doc Owle had made her wait another full week before giving her one of his precious supply of pregnancy tests, and the results had been decisive. As soon as her urine traveled up the stick, the pregnancy indicator line blazed bright purple, darker than the control line.

Owle had let out a halting laugh. "Well," he said. "Look at that."

Look at that. She did. She looked and looked, a thrill racing through her body and setting her heart to pounding. Still, it didn't sink in. It didn't sink in then, or each of the times she came to Owle's house so he could check her blood pressure and question her about how she was feeling. Only this morning, when she first felt that distant chord getting played deep within her, did she trust what Owle insisted was happening to her. Her body—her abused, broken, pain-racked body, this body she had spent most of her lifetime hating—had done something good. Her baby. She had done this.

"Hello in there," Violet said, more terrified than ever.

She rose, slipped her tunic over her head, drew up her trousers. They pinched her waist; she would have to let them out again soon. Before leaving, she took the chipped white mug of tea Meg had made for her, walked to the front door, and peered out. No one around. She dumped its contents in the dirt. She had forgotten a few times, and once, Meg noticed. "You missed your Salt dose this morning," she said, motioning to the full cup on Violet's nightstand. A fly floated in the cool brown liquid.

"Oh. Yeah. I remembered later, at Vic's. So I had a cup then."

"Cool," Meg said. She had taken the cup, grimacing at the fly, and flung the tea out the door.

Violet had thought, for a long time, that fear was something she would no longer feel. *Would*, yes: it was an act of will, this relinquishing of fear, because her poor brain insisted on it long after she had nothing, or close to nothing, left to lose. She lived on, through the loneliness and constant pain, for June's sake. Out of love for her. Which made her hate June sometimes, and she had wanted more than once to say, "If you really cared about me you would let me go." The problem, though, was that June *would* let her go. If Violet put it that way. And then June would have to live on with the guilt of letting her go, of the consequences of such letting go, and Violet wanted, despite everything, to spare her that.

Long back she'd started regularly using Salt—in grain form, taken orally—for pain. Owle dispensed it to her. If the initial trauma of the burn had been an all-encompassing, months-long *ROAR*, and her day-to-day baseline now was like trying to have a conversation with someone while some other person at your side shouted nonsense, the Salt sent the shouter across the room, sometimes even across the house. On the rare occasions when Violet had shot up, the shouter was banished entirely, leaving behind a calm so eerily perfect that Violet knew the risks of indulging more often, knew that to do so would be as good, ultimately, as firing a gun into her own skull. She had lived with pain so long that its absence seemed a kind of death.

Still, she'd come to depend on her low-level dosage—both the reprieves it offered and the anticipation of a reprieve, which gave her hope, something to aim for, a way to muddle through even when the medicine wasn't in her system. Owle's plan, then—his offer—had stopped her cold.

"I'd have to do without all of it?" Violet had asked. They were sitting at his kitchen table—the same table where Owle had outlined for June the full scope of Ruby City's fertility problem only the previous week. "Not just the tea but the pain meds, too?"

"All of it," Owle confirmed.

"And there's not even a guarantee?"

"Nope," said Owle. "That's the whole reason for even trying this, Violet. We have to know if the contraceptive effect stops when you stop the Salt. And even if it does, there still aren't guarantees. You're what, thirty-six?"

"Around that," Violet said.

"It's not your fertile prime."

"Then why are you fucking asking me, then?"

"Because I trust your discretion," said Owle. "I know you wouldn't want this getting out and causing June trouble. And because I thought you might be interested."

It was true. She had come to him a year earlier asking—haltingly, unable to meet his eye—if she might be going into early menopause or something. She hadn't had a period in over six months, she said, and normally she'd just say fuck it and good riddance, but in the back of her mind—way back, far off, just a hypothetical, mind you—she'd wondered if maybe, someday, some way or another, she might think about having a child. Owle had looked at her in a way she hadn't much liked: shrewdly, pityingly.

Now, she asked—unable, again, to meet his eye—"Who'd father it, then?"

His turn to look away. "Me, I guess, though I'm most definitely not in my fertile prime. I'm not talking about laying you down on a bed of roses, either, so don't worry about the old man trying to romance you. We'd do it with syringes. That's assuming you start menstruating again, of course."

"If there is a baby," Violet said. "We—what? Share it?"

Owle shook his head emphatically. "No, ma'am. I'm not interested in that. I'm too old to start daddying, and I'm too busy doctoring. If you have some other candidate in mind, that's fine, but I'm operating on strictly a donor basis."

Hell of a proposal. Stop your medicines, both the one that saves you from deadly disease and the one that saves you from constant pain. Wait an indeterminate amount of time. If, *if* your period returns, come in a couple of weeks later for a syringe of old-man spunk. Repeat. Repeat. Wait some more. And at the end of it all, maybe you'll have a baby to raise. Out here. Alone.

"I'll do it," she said.

It took eight months for her period to resume. Eight months with the pain shouting over her shoulder, eight months having to keep up with her regular responsibilities—for June could not, must not, know what she was trying—without the protection from tick bites. Doc Owle got her a jar of NO-BITE and a Stamp; she had to use it four times. "You need to make some excuse to June to stay closer to home," he kept telling her, and Violet kept refusing. If June thought that something was wrong, that anything had changed, that something was happening in Violet's life without her knowledge or approval, she'd go into lockdown mode. June hated anything she couldn't control. She would try to stop Violet. She would pressure and cajole and lay down guilt trips on Violet until Violet capitulated to her demands, because after all, she'd be right, wouldn't she? What business did Violet have trying to become a mother? What child would want to nurse at her breast, look up into her ravaged face?

Still, she persisted. Even after Owle started murmuring doubts, suggesting that it might be time to give up and resume the inoculation, she persisted, and finally she was rewarded with the familiar aches, tenderness, the sight of blood on a washcloth. Owle celebrated with a slug of whiskey. "This is good news," he said, his hand shaking. "This is reason to hope. You did good, girl."

Getting pregnant took another year, over which her menstrual cycle started, halted, sputtered, started again: 36 days, 21, 62, 23. Timing her fertile days became its own job. She grew intimately familiar with Owle's house, the tick of his windup clock, the smell of his pipe smoke, his curtained-off "exam room," his attempts at professional courtesy and efficiency: like the clean sheet he made a show of removing from a drawer and laying out on the exam table, even if he was only taking her temperature. People probably either thought they were lovers or that Violet was dying of some terrible cancer.

She persisted through another five tick bites, too, though she did finally allow Owle to feed some story to June about Violet having a nutritional deficiency that was affecting her energy levels and compromising her immune system. Best if she stayed near camp for the foreseeable future, he said. Another sacrifice, because the work

Violet did for June, for Ruby City—it gave her days shape, purpose. She didn't like milking plants alongside her bunkmates, or helping Errol with the bread baking, or any other job that forced her to spend her day with people, their yearning need and barely masked disgust.

Then finally, three months ago: two lines.

Owle had wanted to go right to June with the good news. "Absolutely not," Violet said, and she only shook her head when he demanded to know why, what could possibly happen, what was she afraid of. When Violet came to him three weeks ago and told him of her intention to accompany Andy back to the OLE camp to help with the hostage taking, he was livid. "This has gone on long enough," he said. "It doesn't just affect you. The whole village has a stake in this. I can list four women for you off the top of my head who'd want to stop the Salt this second if they knew what we know. You can't risk going out there and getting yourself killed."

"I've risked everything," Violet said. "Me. Not you, not June, not anybody else. People aren't as stupid as you think they are. I live in the bunkhouse. They know what's what. They chug that tea like it's beer, trade partners once a month. If the rest haven't put two and two together, it's only because they don't want to face it."

"That may be true," Doc Owle said. "But there's still no good reason for you to go join that group. I thought you wanted this baby. I'm starting to wonder now."

"You have no fucking idea what's going on inside of me," Violet said. "Not in my body and not in my head. I have my reasons, and I swear to God, Owle, you tell June before I decide to and I'll slit your throat. You don't want to test me on this."

He blanched and backed away a step. "Fine," he said. He grabbed his pipe and chomped down hard enough on the stem that he couldn't hide a wince of pain. "Do what you want. I'm officially out of it."

That wasn't what Violet wanted. She'd come to almost like Harold Owle—it certainly didn't hurt to almost like the father of your unborn child—and though she knew to not expect partnership from him, didn't really want a parenting partner, it had been nice to have someone to go to, confide in, consult for advice. Almost like having a friend.

But she didn't know how to smooth things over and still have her way. So she nodded, stood. Left.

She was out of the bunkhouse at 10:45, in time to collect the hostages' lunches and bring them over to the warehouse. She was supposed to have put in a couple of hours this morning at the flower beds, but she was content, on occasion, to exploit her status as June's adoptive daughter. No one seemed to miss her company much, anyway.

From Vic's cabin she retrieved a crate loaded with a steaming crock of green beans and potatoes. "Errol has the biscuits this time," Vic told her. "How're they doing on water?"

"Don't know," Violet said. "I haven't been over there yet."

"You might want to check on that. They're probably running low." Vic shook her head with frustration, or maybe despair. "Lord God, I'll be glad when this is over. Those two poor kids. Dead and gone. They didn't have no business with guns, and I'm not afraid to say so." She seemed afraid, though. She kept wringing a dishtowel. "Your mama said to you what the plan is?"

"June does what June wants," Violet said. "She sure don't answer to me."

Vic grunted and wiped her forehead with the back of her wrist. "Nor to me. Well, she ain't steered us wrong yet. But I'll be glad when this is over. That's for sure."

At Errol's, Violet was greeted by a cloud of flour dust and the perfume of rising yeast. Errol, his back to the door, lifted a hand from a mound of dough and pointed it at one of his work tables. "Bread's in that basket. Tell them it's all they're getting today, so save some back if they want any with dinner."

Violet's stomach rumbled audibly. Her appetite over the last eighteen weeks had been fickle; her one consistent desire was for bread and sweets.

"Want a roll?" Errol asked.

"Sure," Violet said.

"They're by the stove."

She set the crate on the table by the basket of biscuits, walked over to the cooling pan of rolls, and plucked a golden one from the edge row. A runner of steam spiraled into the air when she tore it open. She sunk in her teeth, transported for a few seconds by its buttery richness.

"You been looking better," Errol said. He was using a broad handle of wood, sanded to a fine edge, to fold the dough over on itself. He flashed a quick glance at her. "Not so scrawny."

Violet nearly dropped what was left of her roll in surprise.

"No offense. I just meant you should eat what you want. You got room to grow."

"OK," Violet said, too startled to be annoyed. "Thank you."

"Anytime," Errol said.

She set the basket of biscuits on top of the crock and lifted the crate again, letting some of the weight press against her stomach. So it was starting to happen, then. Her secret would come out. How shocked they'd all be if they knew, she thought with a kind of pleasure. What she had said to Harold Owle was the truth: no one understood what was inside her.

The baby moved again, as if in agreement.

It was a cloudy day. The warm snap held—it had to be close to seventy out—but rain spit in a fine mist. Violet hunkered under her hood, head dipped over the crate, and hurried toward the warehouse, where Cedric sat with his back against the door, taking what shelter the roof's overhang offered. He looked up from the book he was reading. "Hey, there. Got lunch?"

"Got my hands full."

"Oh, right," he said, jumping up. He slid the paperback into his back pocket and picked up the gun from where he'd laid it on the ground beside him. The door was stopped from opening out with a heavy wood bar, which Cedric lifted. Then he fitted a key into the padlock.

"I need to check the water supply," Violet said. "So keep an eye out."

"I always do," he said, patting the gun's stock.

Violet was struck first by the barnyard smell of the storage shed's interior. The five remaining hostages looked up and just as quickly looked away, as if her face were a cause of shame in them. Except for the very pretty one, the one who'd caught the knapsack Violet dropped the day they had taken the OLE campers hostage. This one looked at Violet, then the food, then at Violet again. "Need help?" she asked, careful not to leap to a sudden stand as Cedric had done. He was standing in the doorway now, gun pointed into the room.

"You can clear a space on the table there," Violet said. "I've got to see how you're doing on water."

"Less than a few liters left," the tall, muscular one said dully.

She looked herself just to be sure. There were maybe a couple of centimeters of liquid at the bottom of the insulated jug. "I'll send Vic over here," she said—more to Cedric than to the hostages. She unpacked the crate—biscuits, a chipped set of dishes and mismatched forks, the ceramic crock, its glass lid beaded with condensation—and loaded the dirty bowls and spoons from breakfast. "The bread's all you get today. Save some if you think you'll want it with supper."

Only the pretty one—Edie—seemed to be listening to her. The others were lining up at the table, using their forks to transfer, slowly and awkwardly, beans and potatoes to their plates. This wasn't the staring Violet had become so accustomed to over the course of her life, though. It was curious, and frank, but the curiosity penetrated her scars. And then Violet realized a strange thing. Edie wondered about her. Her motives. Most people turned not just their eyes away from Violet but their minds; their curiosity only extended as far as, *How did that happen to her?* This deeper consideration was new, uncomfortable, inconvenient. It was also such a relief that she wanted to cry.

This was the one. If Violet were to go through with this, Edie was the one.

At the door, she said to Cedric, "If you see Vic before I do, tell her I'll deliver dinner tonight, too."

"Got it," Cedric said. He squeezed the padlock closed, barred the door, and removed the paperback from his pocket. "See you then."

Roz was outside with the princes when Violet approached the house. She had a hank of rope that the dogs took turns tugging, both of them growling softly with excitement, and Roz barked laughter, transferred the grip end to Tauntaun, and let them wrestle each other. "Vi," she said. She beckoned roughly with her now-free hand and drew Violet into a fast hug, pounding her twice on the back, firmly, and smacking the side of her head with a kiss. "You'll make your mother's day."

"I can't stay long," Violet said awkwardly.

"Oh, sure. We understand. Just do what you can do."

She hadn't grown up in this house—Violet was in her teens by the time June and their small group had settled what would become Ruby City, and the house was built another year after that—but it was as close to a home as she'd ever known. It was small, plain, but cozy: the front door faced a staircase that went up to a half floor; this is where Violet used to sleep. A door to the right of the entry went to June and Roz's bedroom; and the great front room, as they always called it, with its fireplace and three south-facing windows, was to the left. The kitchen took up the house's back half, and a porch off the back of the kitchen faced Piney Gap Branch, which made a pretty racket after a good rainfall. Violet, when she was sixteen or seventeen, had dragged a fallen tree over to traverse the branch, and she'd spent more hours than she cared to count now sitting on it, legs straddling a knot that was shaped a bit like a saddle horn, letting her bare toes graze the water's surface and dreaming hopeless dreams about love and romance, the miracle surgery that would fix her face, or the boy who'd want her exactly how she was, and she'd thought about sex, felt the same confused stirrings as the procession of oversexed kids in the bunkhouse felt but no way to satisfy them. Or not the ways she wanted.

June, through all of this, was a force—a strong and tireless leader, selfless to a fault, visionary, brilliant, intense; when she loved, she loved fiercely, and only Violet and Roz lived behind the protective barrier of June's devotion, and that barrier sometimes felt more like a holding cell. For Violet, at least. How did you thwart the will of the person who had gathered you up from where you had been abandoned to die and accepted you as her own, in a world of people who regarded you as monstrous, disposable? How did you rebel against that person? How could you bring yourself to disappoint her? The answer, most of the time, was that you didn't. Violet had chosen two battles: moving out of this house and down to the bunkhouse was one. The other, sixteen years ago, was when she ran away back to Flat Rock for two weeks to kill Fat Daddy and Big Mama.

Violet found June in the great front room. She had been dozing in the rocking chair and startled when Roz let the door bang shut. "Oh," she gasped, sitting up straight and widening her eyes, then rubbing her face briskly. "You scared me half to death."

"It's lunchtime," Violet said, taking a seat on the big old sofa with its tattered upholstery and blown springs. She remembered the day it had come in on a scavenging trip. *I'll take it if no one else's interested,* June had quickly said, and of course no one had expressed their interest after that. "What are you doing sleeping?"

"The usual. Up late worrying. And my sciatica's been bothering me."

"She don't do her exercises like she's supposed to," Roz said. She'd gone to the kitchen, and she came back with the teakettle in hand. "You going to want some, Vi?"

"No," Violet said. "Thanks," she remembered to add.

"Lunch? We're having cheese sandwiches."

Violet thought about it. "Just the bread. And some water."

"Ask her if she wants one of the cookies Loti made," June said.

Roz threw June an exasperated but amused look and turned her head pointedly at Violet. "Do you want one of the cookies Loti made?"

"Sure," Violet said. "Two of them."

"And the bread, too?"

"Yes," Violet said.

June was rocking now and kneading her palm into her hip. "What a lunch. Bread and cookies. I hope you still brush your teeth morning and night, Violet. The last thing you need on top of everything else is an infection in your mouth."

"I know," Violet said. "You've said that before."

"I've said it a million times. It's still true."

Violet shrugged and scraped her thumbnails against each other.

"I don't know how you're supposed to get over a nutritional deficiency when you just eat bread and cookies for lunch."

"The cookies were your idea," Violet said.

"I guess it's better than nothing." June stopped rocking and peered at Violet. "Are you sick?"

"Huh? No."

"I heard you didn't make it to harvest this morning. I almost sent someone in your place to fetch the lunches."

"I guess you can't keep a secret around here," Violet said, savoring the irony. "I had a headache, but it's better now."

"It looks bad for me when you skip out on your part of things. I can't seem to treat my own daughter differently than I expect everyone else to treat theirs. People are sensitive right now. Especially after Miles and Leeda."

Violet bit back a sharp retort and said instead, "Well, that's what I'm here about. I'd like to take on more of a role again. I've been talking to Doc about it, and he agrees I'm doing better. I've put on some weight."

"I noticed," June said.

Violet cleared her throat. "Anyway, whatever it is you're planning with the Zoners, I want to be a part of that. I want to help."

June stopped rocking. "Why?"

"Because I've always helped."

"Close to always," June said. "If I'm going to be honest, you haven't been quite yourself lately."

"I came through for you getting the hostages here, didn't I?"

June's gaze sharpened. "I guess that's true."

"And I let you use me as a prop to tell your story. Your 'saving Violet's life' story."

Now June dropped her eyes. "That, too."

"I'm telling you I want to help now. So let me. What's the plan?"

"All right," June said as Roz came back in with a tray and handed out plates and glasses. On Violet's were two thick slices of Errol's sourdough bread, buttered, and two big oatmeal cookies. This was one of those times when Violet wished she could smile. She loved Roz a lot. She wasn't sure Roz knew it, or that she'd done a good enough job of letting Roz know it.

"Andy got back last night, finally. The thing I'd thought might happen—it happened. For better or worse." June bit into her sandwich and chewed.

"We saw the footage," Roz offered while June swallowed and sipped some Salt tea.

"I had asked him to stay and monitor the feeds for information. So I knew not to expect him back right away. But I've been climbing the walls."

"No pun intended?" said Roz.

June gave her a sour look.

Violet peeled the crust off a bread slice and tucked it into her mouth, processing all of this. "What now, then?" she said finally.

"That's what I spent the night mulling over. All of this hinges on something we can't know, and that's what they did with the bodies once they had them inside. If they followed procedure, they dumped them into the incinerator and filed a report, and it'll take weeks before that info should trickle down to Perrone. If it ever does. And even then, it shouldn't mean anything to him. There's no reason for him to expect that four people from the excursion would break off and end up shot at the Wall.

"But there will be video surveillance. And maybe one of them would have been recognized. That singer. Andy says he's on a popular webshow. I never once thought about that."

"And Andy didn't think to mention it to you until it was too late to do anything about it," Roz said irritably.

"If someone saw him, knew his face . . ." June shrugged. "Well, the situation might be real different. Andy didn't see a big news story, and that's good, so they'll have kept it hush-hush. But that doesn't mean anything when David Perrone's involved. Anyway, there's an argument—a good one—for leaving it like this and seeing what happens. We follow through with Feingold like we talked about and have Andy take them back to Quarantine on schedule."

Roz was shaking her head, lips pressed together.

"I know," June said. "My father was a wait-and-see type of man, and it cost him. Besides, we have Marta Perrone. Do you realize how extraordinary that is? All along I thought Feingold was the ticket, and then Marta Perrone is dropped in our laps. And I wouldn't have even known it if she hadn't told me."

"Why do you think she told you?" Violet asked.

"Because she's no fool. She bought herself some time."

"How much time?

"I don't know," June said. "Still, I think I'd be inclined to wait if not for the stolen seeds. That's what keeps me up at night. More than the Pocketz deal. Even more than what he did to that other village. We've been so goddamn careful, and he got to us anyway." She leaned forward and scooted her chair toward Violet. Took her hands. "Your beautiful hands." She ran her fingertips along the tendons, knuckles. "I've always loved them. You have elegant hands. If you'd have been born in a different time you could have been a surgeon or a musician . . ."

This was another thing Violet had heard many times over.

June stopped, frowned. Turned Violet's hand over. "What is this?" She touched one of Violet's most recent Stamp scars, a grayish-red weal on the inside of her wrist that had slipped into view out from under her sleeve. "Violet?" Her eyes were wide and frightened. "Is this a Stamp?"

Violet jerked back her hand. "No. I did it when I was helping Errol with the baking a few weeks ago."

"Are you lying to me?"

"No, goddammit!" Violet shouted. "Why are you like this with me? For God's sake, I'm thirty-seven years old! You make me fucking hate myself!"

She wasn't even sure why she said this last thing. It burst out of her. And it wasn't precisely true, though it circled some truth, some even darker thing Violet couldn't dare to name, even to herself.

June pulled back. Stood. Very deliberately, she tucked her cloud of frizzy hair behind each ear.

"June," Roz said warningly, and June held up a stopping hand.

"I'm sorry," she said, but her voice was cold. "So you want to help. That's why you're here."

Violet, not meeting her eye, nodded.

"I think I'm decided. We'll take Marta Perrone to the Lenoir house tomorrow morning. We'll have her contact her husband and see what that buys us. If we tell him we're ready to take his deal, let him have the credit and the money for Salt, maybe he'll leave us alone. We hold on to Feingold as collateral. If he won't work with us, he's not going to be able to fall back on the microsuit deal." She paused. "But I don't see why he won't do it. We're not asking for much."

"You're not asking for anything at all," Violet said. "Except not to be killed."

"And you think that's nothing?" June asked sharply, her pale gray eyes flashing.

Violet snapped her head Roz's way—a gesture she paid for when the scarred skin around her neck pulled painfully. "Do you agree with her? Roll over and play dead?"

"Yes, I do," Roz said. "I trust your mother. I always have. We have four hundred sixty-six lives to protect, and the most valuable thing we've got is this town. So yes, if we get our lives out of the bargain and nothing else, I'm fine with that. Thrilled with it, in fact."

June peered at Violet. "Do you have something to say?"

Violet thought. After a few beats, she shook her head.

"You sure?"

"Yes," she said.

"You still want to be part of the group going to Lenoir tomorrow? Are you up for it? Honey, are you behind us?"

"Yes," Violet said. "I want to go. And yes, I'm behind you."

"I'm glad, honey," June said. She looked to Violet, briefly, like an elderly version of herself. "I'm glad."

After lunch, Violet returned to her bed at the bunkhouse. She was tired, so tired. Afternoons were the worst for that lately—around 1:00, 2:00, she started to feel as if she were not walking but wading, and her limbs ached dully from the effort. The bunkhouse was empty, the others still out at the fields, probably eating their packed lunches now, perched in the shade of the flowers, brown young legs tangled up together. The thought didn't make her angry, or wistful, as it once it had. She begrudged them nothing. Not their youth, not their beauty. Violet had something else, something better.

She lowered herself to her mattress with a sigh and nudged off her boots, toe to heel. It was sweet to lie down. And she needed to think hard about what was to come, but first a nap. She drew a light blanket over herself, nestled into her pillow. Sunlight printed hazy dots against her closing eyelids.

Before she drifted off—by habit, by reflex—she put down her hand and wormed her fingers under the fitted sheet, nails catching the edge of the slit she'd carved into the mattress about a month ago. She pushed her fingers in, flexing until her middle finger touched it: the edge of the seed pouch. Reassured, she withdrew her hand, rolled to her right side, and slid one arm under her pillow, the other around her growing middle. She wouldn't risk having this baby out here, losing it, dying in a bed of blood the way her own mother had.

She wouldn't.

Eighteen

Edie had barely begun the final novel in the fat Austen compendium, *Persuasion*—"A few years before, Anne Elliott had been a very pretty girl, but her bloom had vanished early"—when the door to the storage shed opened. She didn't know the time, but the slant of light through the narrow windows told her that this was earlier than usual, perhaps by as much as half an hour.

The one who entered—for the second time today—was Violet. Odd for her to tend to this task more than once in a day; odd, too, that she was early.

"Her," Violet said to the person manning the door now. Randall. Edie hated Randall the most of the guards; though, actually, she didn't really hate the others, even Joe, who struck her as decent people driven by desperation to actions even they weren't entirely comfortable with. Not Randall, though. He was—she could tell—a bully and a blowhard. She hoped there never came a day when she was left alone with him.

Then Edie noticed where Violet was pointing. On reflex she touched her chest in the universal gesture of "Who, me?"

"Her?" Randall replied in disbelief. "Are you sure you don't want to just watch the door while I go? I can haul it without any help. Or at least take the big guy."

"I didn't ask you to do it, and I didn't ask for the big guy," Violet said sharply. "You," she said to Edie. "Grab the water cooler. You're going to the well with me."

"I don't have any shoes," Edie said.

"You won't need them. It isn't too far."

Doubtful, but excited about the thought of fresh air and sky, Edie folded her book open and facedown on the floor, stood, and dusted off her bottom, which must be so grimy by now as to make such an effort pointless. Wes looked at her with wide eyes. Edie shrugged.

"Come on," Violet said. "Grab a handle."

She took one of the cooler handles and followed Violet out of the shed; it swung between them, banging awkwardly against the door as they went.

"We're going this way," Violet said, indicating upriver with her free hand.

For a few moments they plodded forward in silence. The ground was damp, and Edie's feet were quickly soaked, but still, she didn't mind. The air had a fresh, after-rain summer smell, and the lowering sun brindled the river. God, it felt so good to walk, to really extend her legs. She drew some odd looks from the few villagers they passed this far upstream, but no one asked Violet about her. No one said much to Violet at all. A nod, a "hidey," a small wave. And Violet herself made no reply.

They reached not a well—or at least the stone-lined ring in the ground Edie had pictured—but a large galvanized hand pump with a poured concrete base. "Get the lid off and the lip under there," Violet said, adding, as Edie complied, "They're all dead."

If Edie thought anything in the ten bewildered seconds she spent trying to process this statement, it was, vaguely, that Violet was as crazy as she was scary. Then she looked at Violet's face—into that startlingly blue eye, the white so damp and fragile surrounded by such ravaged flesh—and the half-formed thought drifted away.

"What?" Edie managed.

"Your people. The four June sent back home, supposedly." She started cranking the pump and a gusher of water rushed out. "They were shot by border guards trying to cross over. June knew it might happen. She sent them knowing it might." Violet cleared her throat. "Hoping it might."

Jesse. Tears spiked her eyes and she rubbed them fiercely away. *You and I split up, and that's the end,* he had said. And he'd been right.

"But why?" Edie said.

Violet watched the cooler fill. "She's in over her head. She didn't know what to do with all of you, and she knew she couldn't make you all cooperate." It was hard to read Violet's scarred face, its limited range of movement. "She wanted the problem to fix itself."

How could that diminutive woman with the kindly aunt's fluff of hair have done such a thing? That woman Edie had come so goddamn close to admiring?

Edie, not caring about ticks or about Violet or what anyone else might see, sat, put her head between her knees, and wept. She hadn't cried throughout this whole ordeal. Not once. But now, she gave in. She cried for Jesse and the others, and she cried for herself. Because a person who would do what Violet was saying June had done was a person who would do pretty much anything.

"You need to pull it together. If you come back looking like you've been crying people are going to ask questions. Here." Violet pressed something into Edie's hand. Cool, damp. A rag she'd run under the well water. Edie held it against her eyes.

"Why did you tell me?" Edie asked, words muffled against the cloth.

"So you'll listen when I ask for your help."

It took Edie and Violet twenty minutes to haul the cooler back to the storage shed. They progressed in units of a dozen or so shuffling steps before one or the other had to stop and catch her breath. At least it gave Edie an excuse for coming back with her face damp and her breath hitching, though the efforts made it difficult for her to think ahead, to plan how she was going to break this news to Berto and Ken. Especially Berto. She remembered Anastasia's flat certainty that they'd all be killed by their captors. Had she really believed it or was it bravado? The four had, if Edie understood Violet, all been within sight of the Wall when they were taken down. So close—if they'd harbored doubts, they must have been on the verge then of believing. Which was cruel, but maybe also better. Maybe it had all happened so suddenly that they didn't have time to change their minds again. There was hope—and then there was blackness.

But this was still nothing she could explain to the others. To Berto. There had been Anastasia's flippant fatalism on the walk to Ruby City, but there had also been the dogged hope of a woman injecting herself with fertility drugs in a bathroom in the godforsaken out-of-zone wastes, a woman who believed enough in the future—one possible future—to do that to herself again, and again, and again.

"Look at you two. I don't know why you didn't just let me do it," Randall said as they approached. He came forward, rifle pushed around to his back, and grabbed the cooler before they could muster the breath to protest—though not as easily as he'd expected to, Edie noted. He bounced it a little, setting off the contents to loudly sloshing, to save face. "Get the door for me, Violet. I'll take it from here."

Violet gave him a look of disgust that Randall missed entirely. Then she went to the door and drew her key out from where it was tucked under her shirt.

"Like your little walk?" Randall asked Edie.

"Sure," she said dully.

His face was reddening, but he bounced the cooler again and took a deep breath through his nose. "Violet must like you." He said this loud enough for Violet to hear. "Violet doesn't usually like anybody."

Edie, whose mind was full of the things Violet had told her, just stared ahead, waiting for the door to open.

"Well, go on in. Ladies first," Randall said.

The others looked up at her with relief, then curiosity. Edie turned her gaze to the floor, afraid of what her expression might give away or what their expressions might set loose in her.

Randall slung the cooler back up on the table with a grunt. "H-2-0," he said. "You're welcome."

Violet hadn't followed them inside. When Randall left, the door closed, and the OLE travelers were once again alone. Edie saw that supper had arrived in her absence. A platter of tough-looking pieces of meat. More beans and potatoes.

Edie sat by the door and peeled off her muddy socks. No way to clean them. Her bare feet were cold and shriveled, and she drew them together and grabbed her toes, feeling the question no one had quite yet dared to ask: What happened?

Finally: "Are you OK?" Wes.

She nodded mutely.

"Did something happen? Did she hurt you?"

"No," she said. "She didn't hurt me. But—" She swallowed, her throat tacky and dry. "She told me some things. I don't want to be the one to say this. I guess I've got no choice, though."

"What?" said Ken. "Say it."

She looked up at Berto. He seemed genuinely baffled.

"She said the others are dead. Anastasia, Wendy, Lee. Jesse." Her breath hitched. "She said that June sent them to a part of the Wall where she knew they'd probably be shot on sight, and they were."

"Bullshit," Berto said. "You believed her? Why would you believe her? She's the one who shot Mickey. She's obviously some kind of psychopath." He was shaking his head fiercely, and he got up and started to pace. Ken stared ahead, expressionless. Marta scooted forward and grasped Edie around her shoulder, then pulled her close. Edie turned her head by instinct, some muscle memory from earliest childhood, and hid her eyes against Marta's soft neck. It felt wonderful. Wonderful to be held, wonderful to finally let go, and she did, and Marta rocked her a little, humming and rubbing circles on Edie's back, and she whispered, "I know. I know. I know."

"Bullshit!" Berto said, getting loud now, and Marta said, not raising her own voice, "You need to stop. I know you're hurting. But you need to stop before that man out there hears you."

"What do I care if he hears?"

"Stop," Marta repeated with gentle firmness.

He did. When Edie pulled back, she saw that his eyes were streaming, chest heaving, the planes of his face cut with anguish.

"Thank you, Berto," Marta said. "Thank you. OK, Edie. Listen to me. Tell us everything she said."

"She said—she said that June's going to come to you tomorrow." Edie said this to Marta. "And maybe also Wes, but you specifically. You're going to go to a house they have near the Wall. She's going to have you contact your husband and make him some kind of offer. She said your husband is someone important. Does that make sense to you, Marta? Do you know what she's talking about?"

Marta exchanged a glance with Wes, then nodded.

"She said that you need to demand that we all go. Say you won't do it if we're separated. If she threatens you, stick to your guns. She said June will give in because you're too important."

"OK," Marta said. "What then?"

Edie relayed Violet's instructions, though there wasn't much to them, nor were there many reassurances. *I don't know how many guards there'll be,* Violet had said. *It's going to be dangerous, no matter what. And I don't want June killed. Whatever else happens, I won't see her hurt.*

"Why is she going to help us?" Wes asked. "She's pretty much this woman's daughter, isn't she? What's her angle?"

"She's pregnant," Edie said. She turned to Berto. "She's pregnant and she wants to have the baby in-zone. She wants us to get her across the border with us."

Berto laughed sharply. "Wait a minute. Didn't you just say people going up to the Wall get shot on sight?"

"I asked her about that, of course," Edie said. "And the truth is, she doesn't know for sure. She said there are some other entry points. Some other things she knows we can try. But she was pretty straight that she couldn't guarantee anything. It's a risk."

"It's more than a risk," Berto said.

"But what choice do we have?" asked Ken.

The five sat contemplating that question in silence.

That night, after a meager dinner that she all but choked down, and more talking and planning (and fretting) with the others, Edie stole to her pallet to be alone. It was too dark to read; she didn't think she'd be able to focus on the story, anyway, though she had not, despite everything, stopped longing to know what would happen to Anne Elliott in her long-ago time so different from Edie's own.

Marta had given her not just a spare pair of socks but a fresh, unworn pair, still wrapped in its little cardboard sleeve with the Canteen logo. "I was saving these for a day when I really needed a pick-me-up," she had said, smiling a little. "I think today's the day."

Edie took them, lifted them to her nose. Unblemished cotton. A hint of the perfume Marta must have been wearing the day she bought them. Edie was probably supposed to argue with Marta, try to give back this gift, but she didn't have the energy. "Thank you," she said.

"Try to get some sleep tonight."

She lay back now, slid her finger under the lip of the cardboard sleeve. The glue separated with a satisfying little rasp. She unfolded the socks. It was a shame, in a way, to sully them on her disgusting, unwashed feet. Nonetheless, she rolled one up over her toes, heel, ankle. She could just about melt with the pleasure of it. Then the other foot. These were the socks, she promised herself, that she was going to find her way home in. It was a comforting thought.

She allowed herself, then, to think about Jesse. She was an old hat now at grief, but this was a different sort of grieving than she'd done—was still doing—for her mother. That was the grief of the routine, the everyday, grief that leveled Edie as she toweled a dish dry or when she caught the scent of honeysuckle on an evening walk. This grief for Jesse was the grief of mystery, of having the story suddenly halt but not really end. Would they have stayed together? Married? Would they have chosen one day to have a child, a child conceived not in self-destructive anguish but love? She would never know now. She'd never see his slim hands pick out another song on the guitar. She'd never rake her fingertips through the dark curls on the nape of his neck, or bristle at his insecure bluster, or groaningly cover her head with a pillow when he cued up his tablet in the dark of night, writing down the dream gibberish that may or may not eventually become a song.

She was restless, not sleepy at all, so by feel she packed what was left of her belongings, sliding the book into the bag, too. There was no way to know what would happen tomorrow, where she'd finish the day, how much living she had left to do. But she'd like, if possible, to finish *Persuasion* before her time was up.

Nineteen

They loaded, as they'd done a couple of weeks ago, in two vehicles: June, Violet, Randall, Edie, and Berto in the lead car; Joe, Andy, Marta, Wes, and Ken following behind. The hostages, once again, were zip-tied, and June didn't bother to offer an explanation, make an excuse. Marta, wrists chafing against the neon orange plastic, view obscured by a blindfold, passed the time by imagining a zip-tie general store: Ruby City Old Country Zip Ties. After today, God willing, she would never again wear a zip tie.

What would her boys think if they could see her now? Would they be scared for her? Proud of her? They'd not yet grown into the men she hoped they'd be. They were spoiled, no doubt about it, and Sal had picked up on his father's habit of speaking to her with harsh impatience, and Enzo—maybe this was a consequence of being the younger twin?—had a frustrating vagueness, a lack of initiative or direction about everything from what he wanted to eat ("I don't know, Ma, anything's fine") to what he wanted to do with his life ("I don't know, Ma, anything's fine"). But they were hers. She loved them. She would love them no matter what they did or who they became, and yet she also believed that goodness resided in each of them, and someday, perhaps, she would help them access that goodness. If Marta could make it through this experience, then she had the courage to face her husband, and she could finish the work of raising her boys to be decent men.

It had not been as hard as she'd feared it would be to convince June to bring all of the hostages along. "The only way I'm going to be certain they're OK is if they're in my sight," she'd said this morning, after June came to her with news of the journey east to contact David, exactly as Violet had told Edie she would.

"What if we just bring Feingold? Will that be enough?" June asked. "I hate to take two cars. Gas is precious for us out here."

"No," Marta said. "We all go, or I don't go."

June had stared at her for a silent few seconds that felt like much longer, probably biting back some threat that she really didn't have to make, flanked as she was by armed guards. In the end, she shrugged. "Fine. Violet, let's bring Joe and Randall, too. Will you go get them?"

"Anyone else?" Violet had asked.

"No. I think five and five should be safe enough. We're all friends here."

Yes, a guard for every hostage certainly seemed safe enough, especially when each of those guards was toting a semiautomatic rifle. Marta, contemplating this, hoped that Violet knew what she was doing, because she certainly didn't know the group she was depending upon to execute her plan. Berto—well, he was strong enough, and his grief could maybe be channeled into a useful rage, but for now Marta just hoped that he wasn't in the lead car sobbing, as he'd done throughout most of last night. Ken, to her right, was bouncing his leg so hard that Marta kept having to touch his thigh in a friendly(ish) stopping gesture. He would stiffen, stop—and then, a few minutes later, start again.

The car slowed and veered right—Marta was pushed into Wes—accelerated, slowed again, and swung left, pushing her into Ken. Then the terrain got very bumpy. She lifted her bound hands to tweeze the bridge of her nose, fighting the rise of her gorge, and Andy snapped from the front passenger seat, "Don't touch your blindfold! I see you back there."

She dropped her hands back to her lap. "I wasn't—I'm sorry."

Wes's shoulder pressed into hers. She returned the gesture. *Please let him get through this,* she thought. *This dear, extraordinary young man. Please let him be safe.*

An endless time later, during which the terrain seemed only to worsen and worsen, the vehicle slowed again, made another left, then twisted and turned uphill enough times that Marta lost any remaining sense she had of the shape of their travels. Soon gravel was grinding under their wheels.

"Almost there," Joe said.

And finally, the car stopped. The engine died. Marta waited.

"You can come out of your blindfolds now," Andy said.

She pulled hers off and squinted against the sudden brightness of the day. When her eyes adjusted, she peered out Wes's window, then Ken's. They were parked in front of a ranch house with boarded-over windows and faded tan siding. It sat atop a little rise, on a clearing skirted in pine trees. The other car was parked ahead of them, the doors already open and passengers climbing out. Joe and Andy exited, then opened Wes's and Ken's doors. Marta scooted out after Wes.

"Go stand over there," Joe said. He waved with his rifle stock at Berto and Edie, who were leaning against the front of the house. Marta, Wes, and Ken did as he said. Violet seemed to be the one tasked with watching the hostages while June ordered the men around, and Marta studied her carefully, hoping for some look or signal or sign of reassurance—a reminder, now that she was behind a gun, that she remembered whose side she was really on—but she wore the same stony expression she always had. It was enough to make you doubt, well, everything. Even Edie. Maybe she'd misunderstood. Confused something Violet said. Maybe Violet was manipulating them, testing them, setting them up—

June strolled over. "This is a little satellite of ours. We're close enough to the Wall here to be able to scan feeds from in-zone. Andy, get the door, would you?"

Andy popped the padlock.

"Let Randall through first. He has his hands full."

Randall, arms straining with the weight of a large square plastic cooler, said, "Where you want this?"

"Kitchen," said June. "Through the door and to your right."

So Randall had never been here before, Marta noted.

Violet followed, then the hostages. June, Andy, and Joe brought up the rear. Marta, entering the dark living room, took in its contents with surprise. She wasn't sure what she'd expected, but it wasn't this—especially that huge 3D display playing the waterfall animation. How in the world had they gotten that kind of technology out here? Those monitors went for ten thousand credits in-zone.

"First we eat," June said. "Then we get down to business. Sound good?"

Knowing what she knew now about June, Marta was more disgusted than ever with June's little shows of joviality. She didn't bother to react. She accepted her sandwich with her bound hands and dropped down on the ladder-back chair Violet indicated. The sandwich was folded in a faded, almost transparent square of cotton: some of the excellent Ruby City sourdough (though she'd had enough of it in the last couple of weeks that she was sick of it), a salty slice of ham, some bitter greens. The usual fare. They were all given a couple of skins of water to share.

Marta, chewing through a pasty bite, found herself staring at Violet. Yes, there might have been a thickening around her middle—hard to make out, given the baggy local uniform. If Edie had told her anything else about Violet's motives—that she wanted revenge on June, that she wanted in-zone to get her face worked on, that she simply wanted to see how the other half lived—Marta probably wouldn't have believed it. A baby, though: that she bought. When Marta was pregnant, she'd read in one of her baby books that DNA from the fetus could migrate back into its mother, so that the mother didn't just carry her child, she became changed by him—or, in Marta's case, them. Pregnant, she had merely seen this as interesting trivia. In the years after Sal's and Enzo's birth, however, she'd come to understand both the wonder and horror of such a concept. She had felt the impact of that reprogramming. It called her home even now, even if home meant returning to David, his mansion, his rules, his rule. If she could make it over to London, or get the boys back from London, she'd have some options. Until that time, she had only the one.

Violet, perhaps, was also answering a call.

As if hearing this thought, Violet looked over at Marta, piercing her with that bright blue eye. The look lasted only a second, but Marta's doubts dispelled. They were in this—whatever *this* turned out to be—together.

"OK, it's time," June said. "Let's make the call."

Things got to a rather humdrum start with an argument over technology. Joe and Andy disagreed about the best way to transmit information through the feeds without being traced. Andy wanted to ping off an IP in Gulf Zone, then worm through a back channel in the dark web; Joe wanted to "hitchhike" on an automatic signal burst from the Lenoir substation. They also disagreed about how to best set up the TI Dimension-Tech display and cameras before at last remembering that one of the cofounders of Tanaka Industries was in fact stowed on a nearby couch, and then Ken, offering the caveat that his sister had been the product engineer (a slip of tense that the Ruby citizens seemed, thankfully, to have missed), gave them his recommendations, which seemed to satisfy them and settle the matter.

Andy consulted a nearby laptop screen. "Looks good," he told June.

At last Marta was positioned within the wings of the display, so that her field of vision was occupied by app icons and the waterfall wallpaper, and the conversations happening behind her were muffled with the soft roar of churning water. Andy snipped the zip tie binding her wrists.

"You ever used a display like this?"

"Not much," Marta admitted.

"Your script will appear on screen. The adaptive software's good," Andy said, "so the text document will adjust to your vision, and you can look beyond it to see your husband if you want to make eye contact or whatever. Try to stick to the talking points. If you're not sure about what to say, ask June. The big no-no is anything about Ruby City: what we've got, how many we are, hints about where we're located, or where this house is located. If you start trying to be sneaky, if you start saying stuff to him we don't understand, we'll have to stop you. Do you understand what I'm saying?"

"Yes," Marta said. Yes, his meaning was perfectly clear.

"And you say he always answers calls?"

"In my experience, yes."

"We've labeled the trace-code Marta Severs, so that should create some urgency. You ready?"

Marta craned her neck around so she could see her captors, her fellow prisoners, the cramped, dark room where the rest of this would play out. Wes, seated in a recliner by what had been the fireplace, lifted his hands in a little wave.

"Yes," she said.

Andy typed in the trace-code Marta had given him—the one that went to David's most private line (or at least the most private one she had been allowed to know about). The waterfall desktop vanished;

in its place, an animated fishing pole cast out a line toward a distant vanishing point, splashed softly, tugged, and then reeled in, accompanied by the appropriate winding sound effect. Marta's heart beat harder as the sound grew louder, and the animated spool fattened with line. A beautiful big fish burst out of glassy water and flapped on a bright golden hook.

"Connected," the screen flashed.

And then, there he was. It was probably around 1:00 p.m., and she hadn't been sure where they would catch him—out for a martini lunch at Lupo's, or maybe in Patrick's filthy office over the flagship garage location. At Jane's. But he was at his home office, the one attached to their bedroom, tie knotted, hands folded across his desktop. As if he had known she would call. Where was his shock, his confusion? How could it be that he seemed, as ever, unsurprised, even in control?

"Thank God, Marta. I've been worried sick. I hoped I would hear from you."

He didn't look sick. Or even ruffled. But she accepted the concern with a nod. "Thanks. Thanks for answering." She chanced a glance toward Andy but couldn't make out his form in the darkness beyond the bright left wing of the display. "Why have you been worried? Why did you think you'd hear from me?"

There was a shuffling behind her. Something hard pressed against her side, and she stiffened, though she'd expected as much.

David's mouth tilted almost imperceptibly—a flash of mirth across his mask of solemnity. "Well, I don't know what you know. What you're supposed to know. But you can tell your captors that I got the message they left at the Lenoir substation."

"What message?" Marta dared to ask, and the screen suddenly darkened, and the hard pressure against her side became a painful jab.

"Get on script," Joe hissed. "You get one warning here. This is it. This is the one."

"What message is he talking about?" Marta asked again. She wasn't sure why she pressed Joe, except that there was a petty pleasure for her in it. The pettiest. Four people were dead, after all. If she hadn't been able to wholly believe it before, she couldn't deny it now.

"Do as Joe says," June said from behind her. There was a dangerous flatness to her tone. Marta, afraid to say anything at all, simply bobbed her head.

After a moment, the screen relit, David's face coming back into sharp focus.

"Ah," he said. "There you are. Are you OK?"

"I'm OK," she said. "I'm not hurt. I've been treated . . ." She searched for a word. "Fairly."

"Am I allowed to ask who has you?"

She read from the script: "I've been the guest of one of your valued business partners. Due to recent events, your partners wanted to reach out to you and reassure you of their commitment to supplying you with a quality product. They would like you to know that they're ready to have a conversation with you about your offer of a onetime buyout of Salt."

David leaned back in his chair. "Oh. How thoughtful of them." He fiddled with something out of range of the camera, then pulled a cigar to his mouth. He struck the flint on a silver-plated lighter fixed with a single small ruby in the cap. Marta had given the lighter to him early in their marriage, a significant expense to her then though nothing of great value now, and she'd never imagined he still possessed it or used it. She found herself unexpectedly touched.

He brought the flame to the end of the cigar, took a puff, exhaled. "Though, I must say: this is a strange way to accept my offer. I could have come up with some nicer ones. They have Feingold, too, I have to assume. Unless they killed him." He seemed to be thinking about this. "That would probably have been the smartest play, actually."

Marta consulted the script, wishing she could know what was happening behind her. "Wes Feingold is also a guest. He is getting to know the operations at your partners' camp, and he's excited about shifting his Pocketz business from SecondSkins to Salt, if such a deal goes through."

"What makes them think I'm still interested in buying them out?"

Marta scanned the script for an appropriate response. There was a rustling to her right, and new text expanded on the screen, dominating her field of vision, almost too large to read without moving her head left and right. The language was first person now, the pretense of dinner-party cool stripped away, and Marta read it awkwardly, stumbling over the typos and the missing words. "They" had become "we." As if Marta were one of them.

"What we're pro-proposing would be only good for you. All we ask is be—to be—left alone. Feingold returns to zone with seeds, some plants, and our formulations. Both rec-recreational Salt and medical. Medicinal. We can continue to run production for you, we have the . . ." She took a breath and backed up, reading the comma as a period. "We have the infrastructure. Nobody could do it cheaper."

"I could have had that deal years ago if I wanted it," David said.

A new sentence materialized on screen, and this one sent a chill along Marta's spine: "We didn't have Feingold years ago, or your wife."

"Feingold was still shitting his britches then," David said. "As for my wife"—this was strange, as if Marta herself had become an automaton, or the speaker at a fast-food drive-through—"are you planning to keep her there forever? What do you think will happen if you send her back? Or kill her?"

Even after all this time—after all she'd learned about her husband—his casual tone wounded her.

More furious typing.

"We are asking so little. You'll lose nothing by letting us be."

"I don't gain anything, either," David said.

No typing now. Marta waited, darting her eyes over the existing script, wondering what was expected of her. She risked a look to her right and could make out in the dimness beyond the screen Andy, his hands poised over the keyboard, back hunched.

"I wonder," David said, drawing Marta's gaze back to the display. "I wonder if Feingold knows about the drug's side effect."

"What side effect?" Marta risked asking. No one bothered to nudge her with a gun this time.

"Infertility," David said. "That, and a bunch of other problems. Birth defects. Ovarian cancer. What my mother would have called 'female troubles.' Yes, I know all about it. I've known for a long time. If I thought I could get the drug past the FDA and on the market, I'd have done it already. But there's no way. Not even for me. Not for what I'm willing to invest. I've set my sights elsewhere. I don't need your drug."

Another endless pause. Marta looked around, scanning the faces—Andy's, Joe's, June's, even Randall's—for some clue about how to proceed. Finally, June whispered in Andy's ear, and he started typing again. Marta read: "That's not certain. Drug still—is still valuable. Can be tested and refined. Rec-recreational Salt is still lucrative business."

David shrugged. "It's OK business. But there are lots of ways to get high. Lots of ways to make money off people getting high. You haven't cornered the market."

More typing.

"Hope of a cure could be good for your political prospects."

David put the cigar into an ashtray and folded his hands on the tabletop. Something in his eyes shifted, and he was seeing her again, not just seeing through her. "You've been talking, Marta." He made a *tsk*ing sound. "But no, that's OK. You did what you had to do. I'll do what I have to do." She didn't like the sound of that. Not at all. "Besides, listen. I've learned some things this last year. I've been educating myself. And you want to know what I've figured out? Fear sells better than hope. In business and in politics. So yes, again, thanks but no thanks. No deal. Not now. Not ever. So. Where does that leave us?"

Typing. Marta, voice shaking, read the words. "Can you mount a political campaign while trying to explain how your wife died west of the Wall?"

There was a murmur, a shuffling, and then Marta felt the barrel of a gun against her temple. She pinched her eyes shut against the image of David's calm face, his dark, empty eyes. Her mouth started to move, shaping the words of a prayer that she was hardly conscious of making.

"You think that touches me? Scares me?" she heard her husband say. "As far as all of the documentation shows, Marta traveled to London with our sons. If anything happens to her, it happens over there. An accident, or an incident of random street violence. There are a lot of different ways to make it look right. All of them would only help me if I ran for office."

"The boys would never go along with that," Marta blurted out.

"You have no idea what the boys would do for me," David said.

She was saved from contemplating *that* by a sudden, ear-splitting crack, and a heavy thud to her left. A smell wafted up in the wake of this double boom: acrid, but also coolly ozone.

Marta, surreally aware that she still had a head, still had a brain, opened her eyes. She was left staring at not even the waterfall animation or the app icons but three ordinary panes of smoke-colored glass. A nickel-sized hole in the left pane marked the center of a spider's web that expanded across the width of the display, but the trifold shape still somehow held. Marta froze, hands vibrating against each other, afraid to turn around.

"Violet?" June's voice. "Honey, what on earth is this?"

Marta risked a look behind her.

Violet had her rifle trained on Andy, who was still seated in front of the laptop, hands up in the air. Edie also had a gun—a handgun, the one Violet had said she would try to bring along—and she was pointing it at Randall, who had his palms raised halfheartedly in front of his chest. Berto, Wes, and Ken were standing but unmoving, their wrists no longer bound by zip ties. Joe was slumped on the floor beside Marta.

"Big guy," Violet said, not taking her eyes off Andy. "Get Joe's gun."

Berto did as he was told.

"Point it at June."

He did that, too. He looked, in fact, like he wanted nothing so much as to pull the trigger.

"Andy," Violet said, "I want you to take off your gun by the strap. Just the strap. Move slow. I'll shoot you, too, if I have to."

Andy snagged the strap in the web of flesh between his forefinger and thumb, lifted it, and wove his head out from the loop. The gun dangled at the end of it.

"Lay it on the ground. Slowly."

Slowly, he did.

"OK, that one's yours, Feingold."

Looking almost embarrassed, Wes took it, drawing the strap over his own head and shoulder.

"Point it at Andy."

Wes did.

"What are you doing?" June asked again. "Talk to me, Violet. Look at me."

"Randall, your turn. Just like Andy did it. Move slow and put the gun on the floor."

"Violet, for God's sake. I'm your mother."

Randall dropped the gun roughly to the carpet and kicked it out of reach, making Marta wince.

"That's mine?" Ken asked, and Randall snickered.

"It is," said Violet. "You're going to point it at Randall. Randall knows you're probably not as good a shot as I am, but he also knows you're a lot more scared than I am, and that makes a sudden move very risky. Right, Randall?"

"Violet. Violet! Why won't you talk to me? Why are you doing this to me? I don't understand any of this." There was real anguish in June's voice, and Marta couldn't help feeling a reluctant kinship with her. "I love you. Roz loves you. We've done everything we know to do for you. What do you want? Why are you doing this?"

"OK. Now you, Marta," Violet said.

She jumped in her seat a little.

"June's gun. You take it." Marta spotted it on the couch cushion by June's hip. She darted forward quickly, grabbed it, and shouldered the strap, disturbed by the rifle's cool, heavy weight against her chest.

"There's a bedroom in the back corner that has one window. Go and make sure the door is unlocked."

"Now?" Marta asked.

"Yes."

The room was dark and close, the couches and chairs arranged around a scattering of pieces of electronic equipment and snarls of cords. June, Andy, and Randall were all closer to Marta than any of the others; she would have to squeeze between Andy and Joe's dead body to get to the doorway to the back part of the house. She moved carefully, choosing her footing, and still she caught her toe on something and plunged forward, barely catching herself before she fell onto Joe's body, and she couldn't stop herself before expelling a disgusted sob. Why Joe? she wondered. He was the one who'd listened to her the day she asked to speak to June. Randall, she knew, probably wouldn't have. It might have been odd for her to care about this man's fate—this man who had done nothing but harass her from the safe side of a weapon, who might have shot her had Violet not intervened—but she did. The smell of his blood filled the air, warm and flat, and her eyes fixed on a grayish piece of tissue—bone or brain matter, something that had been inside him only moments before—snagged on a loop of the green carpet.

And then, beside that: a tick.

"Oh my God," she said. "There's a tick in here. On the floor."

"Check the back room, like I said!" Violet barked.

"I don't think we packed a single Stamp," Randall said with false remorse. "That's too bad."

In a fog that she registered, from somewhere outside herself, as protective, as saving her from an all-out panic, she found the corner room. The door was cracked, and Marta pushed it open the rest of the way. The room was empty, save a scrim of dust on the hardwood floors. "It's unlocked," she called.

"Drag three chairs in there from the kitchen. Be quick."

She made two trips, dragging the chairs by their back rungs and banging the hell out of the walls along the way. She deposited them all into the middle of the room and returned to the where the others still stood, with their raised hands and raised guns.

"I don't know why we don't just shoot them like you did the one guy and leave," Berto said. "She killed my wife."

"If you shoot her, I'll shoot you," Violet said. "You don't touch her."

"Violet—" June tried again.

"Shut up!" Violet yelled at her. Sorrowful, petulant—Marta remembered this tone of voice from her sons when they were teenagers, when their passions and furies hadn't yet found subtler modes of expression.

June pressed her lips together. Her eyes were bright and damp.

"Big guy, you're going to watch her while we take care of Andy and Randall. You aren't to hurt her. Can I trust you?"

"Yeah," Berto said dully.

"You two." She swung the end of her gun between Andy and Randall. "To the bedroom, slow. Sit in a chair when you get there. Put your hands behind you."

The two men, paced by Violet, Edie, Wes, and Ken, with Marta bringing up the rear, walked slowly to the bedroom. Randall pointed to a chair and made an exaggerated shrugging gesture, lifting his eyebrows as if to say: *This one?* He still had that amused light in his eyes, as if he knew something Violet and the others didn't; he'd pressed a secret call button, stashed a secret weapon. Marta was almost certain this wasn't possible, but it made her even more uneasy.

"Just sit," Violet said. "I wish you'd have been the one with the gun on Marta. I wouldn't have felt a bit bad about taking that shot."

"It's not too late," Randall said.

"That's a fact." Violet drew a bundle of zip ties from her pocket. "Andy, take the other chair."

"Can I speak?" he asked.

"You can say whatever you want," Violet said. "Marta, tie their wrists. Pull them really tight. Don't worry about hurting them. Really dig in there."

Randall's arms were thick and pale and fringed with coarse black hair. He made fists as she pushed his hands into position, the tendons on his forearms popping. She wasn't even sure the tie would span his wrists.

"I have a proposal," Andy said.

Violet poked her gun into Randall's shoulder. "Relax your goddamn arms."

Marta got the tie around and managed to thread the end through the loop on the fourth try. She pulled two rungs, three, four. Straining, she managed to get the loop past a fifth rung. Violet came over and yanked to test.

"Good job," she said.

"Do you want to hear it?" Andy asked.

"What?" she hissed, finally looking at him.

"You want to get across the Wall? You're going to need me."

"We don't need shit from you."

"Wrong," Andy said.

"Do you want me to go ahead with the tie?" Marta asked Violet.

"Yes," Violet said.

"And that's cool, that's fine," Andy said, thrusting his arms out helpfully behind him. "Tie me up. Leave me tied up. Just take me along." Marta bound his wrists, remembering his hands on her own wrists back at camp, the way he'd yanked the tie, the way he'd looked at her: as if she were contemptible, worse than contemptible. It felt good to do this. She muscled an extra rung through the loop.

"Look," Violet said, "just stop. If you don't try anything, you'll be able to go with my—with June back to Ruby City. I shot Joe because I had to. I'm not looking to shoot you. I don't have a problem with you."

"I don't want to go back to Ruby City," Andy said. "I want to go home to my kids."

"Too bad," Violet said. "We don't have room in the car for you."

"You're going to all get yourself shot like the others," Andy said.

"I think we should listen to him." Edie had lowered the revolver halfway.

"Big guy!" Violet called toward the living room. "Bring June in here."

"Maybe we should hear him out," Wes said.

June stumbled into the room, Berto following closely behind her. She went to the third chair without Violet's asking and put her arms behind her. Marta tied her. The skin on June's arms was translucent, banded with raised bluish veins. One of her fingernails was missing, long gone, and the others were neatly trimmed.

"Let me tell you all about Andy," Violet said. "Andy who wants to see his kids so bad. Andy's been sneaking over to Ruby City for ten years. June had him recruited out of a mental institution. Andy's had a thousand chances to change his mind about helping us. Andy could have sold us out before you ever got on that bus to the Salt Line."

"It's all true," Andy said. "And worse. Worse than that. I betrayed my best friend and got her killed. I did that, too. You're still going to need my help."

"Roz was right about you," June said. She sounded tired and resigned. "She never liked you. She said it wasn't even a matter of trust. She said you're weak. She said you're just looking for a crusade and it doesn't matter what it is."

"I guess you should have listened to her," Andy said. "What did she say about Violet?"

June looked at Violet with unmistakable love. "She said Violet was a gift. She was right about that, too."

Violet, Marta noticed, was making a concerted effort not to meet June's eyes. "So you just changed your mind about everything," she said to Andy.

"I thought I could do it. I thought I could leave them. But I can't."

"But you did," Violet said. "You're here. You were doing what June asked of you. That's why you're sitting in that chair with your arms tied."

"Yeah, I'm a cowardly asshole. I'm an opportunist. I still want to go home."

Edie said, "I believe him."

"Me too," said Ken Tanaka.

"Do we vote?" Wes asked.

"Do we vote? Jesus Christ," Violet said. "This isn't a goddamn club."

"I say we take him," Edie said. "We can put him in the trunk."

"Sure! Put me in the trunk," Andy said.

"Let's take him," Ken said. "We can always dump him later if we have to."

Wes actually raised his hand. "Yeah, I say we take him."

"I say we shoot him," Berto said. "Or are the rest of you forgetting who drove off with our people? My wife? This piece of shit. I say we shoot him, then we shoot the other two, and then we figure out how to get back ourselves."

"No one is shooting June," Violet repeated. "That isn't negotiable."

"Marta," Wes said. "What do you think?"

She stared at Andy, trying to have an opinion. Fatigue had settled upon her now that the flood of adrenaline in her system had begun its retreat. Maybe Andy was lying about knowing a way to get them home. Actually, he hadn't even made that promise, had he? He'd just said that they needed him.

Maybe they did. Only time would tell.

"I say we take him," she said. "If he's willing to go in the trunk."

"I have experience traveling in tight places," Andy said. "As June knows." He seemed almost cheerful. "Let's do it."

The OLE travelers looked at Violet, who sighed. "Fine. Get him out to the car. I'll finish up in here."

Even with Andy in the trunk of the car—a mongrel four-door sedan with a front passenger door that had to be tied shut and overlarge patchwork tires—things were going to be tight. Berto, by far the biggest of the group, agreed to drive. By unspoken consensus they saved the front passenger seat for Violet; Marta wasn't sure if this was an act of gratitude or deference rising out of some residual fear of her.

Their boots hadn't been restored to them. They stood on the gravel driveway gingerly in their sock feet (Edie's feet, clad in Marta's spare pair, were comically white), heads cocked for activity from within the house. Berto stood behind the car with his gun resting on the roof, pointed toward the front door. Though, if Randall were to somehow best Violet and escape, she imagined he would steal out the back. That, or aim Violet's gun between the boarded-up windows and pick them off as they ran.

"I can't believe we're not shooting them," Berto said again.

"We made Violet a promise." This was Edie.

"You made Violet a promise," Berto said. "I didn't promise her anything."

"It's her mother," Marta said. She was leaning against the hood of the car. Today was November 1, she thought. She'd seen that on the computer's task bar just before they called David. (What must be going through David's mind now?) "I'd be more worried about traveling with her if I thought she was a person who could kill her own mother."

"No one said that she had to be the one to pull the trigger."

"We have to have some honor here," said Edie, "if we're going to trust each other long enough to get out."

Berto shook his head, disgusted, and clammed up. Marta remembered her first conversation with him and Anastasia, back at the OLE training center. They were lawyers, they'd told her—lead partners at a firm specializing in commercial litigation. Anastasia was thirty-eight, Berto, forty-one. No children. "Maybe after we get back in one piece," Anastasia had said with a laugh. They had beauty, money, early success in their chosen profession, a profession they both seemed legitimately to enjoy. They had each other. Funny how much you learned in a month of intense acquaintance, but how little you really knew, still. Marta had learned Berto's first dog's name—Luther—and that his beloved father died two years ago of cancer of the esophagus. She'd learned that he and Anastasia met during law school, when they were both part-time baristas at the campus Starbucks. She'd learned that their politics were conservative, their zone loyalties fierce, and a lot of what motivated them to do the OLE tour was their belief (or Berto's—this had felt more like Berto than Anastasia) that very bad days were ahead, apocalyptic days, and they had to train for every exigency. She'd learned that they had been doing weekend training retreats for a full year before the three-week mandated training, and they considered themselves experts now on all sorts of matters: how to kill and dress game, which fungi of the eastern Appalachians were edible, the quickest way to start a fire, the best brand of portable water-filtration system. Lots of other things. And yet: they'd been cheerful, warm—more like people engaged in a satisfying hobby than people who truly believed that their acquired skill set was the only thing standing between themselves and the loss of everything they held dear. And yet: when the day came that they might have tried to stage a heroic escape, take Marta's Quicksilver, and steal off with Tia toward home, they'd declined.

And so Marta didn't know if Berto could really shoot someone—as an act of rage, even as an act of defense—or if he just really wanted to believe that he could. She suspected he didn't know, either.

The front door opened, and Violet strode out, businesslike. "Let's go," she said. "It'll take them a while to get out of there, but I want to put plenty of miles between us before then."

Berto started, "Why don't we just—"

"Enough," Violet said. "Enough. Have you ever killed someone?"

Berto's jaw clenched, but he didn't respond.

"Because I'm up to four now. No more." She threw open the front passenger-side door, and it emitted a squeal so sharp everyone winced. "Who's driving?"

"I am," Berto said.

"Good. Let's go."

Marta, Wes, Ken, and Edie crowded into the car's backseat. Violet dug a set of keys out of her pocket and selected one. "Here," she said to Berto.

He started the engine.

The noise of tires on gravel was very loud, the car's motion choppy. Marta twisted around to watch through the back window, a part of her certain that the door was going to fly open and out would come Randall, firing some gun he'd found in the house. Then the drive curved, and the house disappeared behind a row of trees. In another few minutes, they were back on the paved road, or at least the crumbling remains of it. "Left," Violet said. "You go right and you'll drive us right into the Lenoir substation."

Berto turned left.

They drove for ten minutes, fifteen. Marta only realized how tightly she had been gripping the handle over her door when she relaxed her hold on it. Her palm was hot, the fingers aching.

"We did it," Ken said disbelievingly. "We got away from them."

Marta nodded a little. He reached for her hand and gripped it. She smiled, squeezing it back.

"Is that right, Violet?" Wes asked. "Are we clear?"

She threw a glance back at him. "Yeah. Yeah, it looks that way."

"OK," Wes said. "Then please find a safe place to pull over, Berto."

"What?" Berto said. "You need to take a piss or something?"

"Not exactly." He pushed up the sleeve of his microsuit and held out his right forearm. On the plump healthy skin just below the elbow was a taut red bump, about the size of a mosquito bite. A little dark spot, like an apple seed, was visible under the surface. Around this bump were three smaller red dots. Wes dug into these welts with the fingernails of his other hand, leaving pale grooves, and Marta, cold with fear, grabbed his hand to stop him.

He tensed in her grasp, shuddered. His temples, she now saw, were beaded with sweat.

"I got bitten during our little showdown," he said between gritted teeth. "I didn't want to say anything. I mean, I didn't want to be a distraction."

"Oh, Wes, no," said Edie.

"So pull over, please," he said. "I don't know how quickly these things will burst."

Twenty

The sun was setting when they finally emerged from the room. Of all the people Violet could have left her with, June wished it hadn't been Randall, though she doubted that Joe or Andy could have managed as quickly as Randall did to come out of his zip tie (Randall half-sawed, half-pried his off using a crooked nail head on one of the boards over the room's one window), or to wriggle the pins out of the door's three rusted-over hinges. In the hours it took to do this, Randall cursed and raged, and June sat watching him uselessly, hands still bound because he didn't bother to free her after he'd freed himself. "There's the nail head," he said, face slimy with sweat. "Have at it." She tried with no luck. It was too high for her to reach at any kind of a workable angle, and she couldn't get her balance if she stood on one of the rickety chairs.

"Their asses better be gone if they know what's good for them," Randall kept saying. "I will slaughter them. I will bash their fucking skulls in."

June, for the first time in twenty years, was mute—afraid to contradict him, afraid to pose a suggestion. A couple of zip ties, a tiny room, a nailed-shut door: and suddenly she had no power. Had Violet known it would be like this? Surely she hadn't.

At last he'd pulled the door free, almost growling, with a terrific screech of the hinges and a crack as the wood along the nailed side splintered. The board that Violet had propped under the knob as she left clattered to the floor.

Randall walked out without looking behind him to see if June would follow.

He went to the front window and peered between the boards. June hung back, watching him.

"They took the Prowler," he said, more to himself than to her. "But they left the other car. If they didn't cut the brake lines or something."

"I don't think they would," June said. It was the first thing she'd said in hours, and her throat cracked with thirst. "I think Violet wanted us to be able to get back to the village."

"You obviously don't know the first fucking thing about what that bitch wants," Randall said. "Who the hell would've had sex with her? That's what I want to know."

June retreated to the kitchen, found one of the water skins on the counter. She nosed it to the edge, mouthed the nozzle, and pried the cap off with her tongue, guzzling down as much as she could before Randall could find her and stake a claim. He had driven the lead car in; he had the keys. Violet and the OLE group had taken all the weapons. Satiated, she backed up to the counter and opened a drawer as softly as she could, hoping to find something, anything: a knife, a screwdriver, a goddamn fork. The room was on the east side of the house and dim. She was working blind, anyway. She twisted her shoulders until the bones popped and reached her bound hands as far back behind her as she could without pushing the drawer shut with her bottom. The pad of her middle finger caught a splinter, nothing else. *Kill him with a splinter,* she thought senselessly. She leaned forward again and scooted to the right. Eased open another drawer.

"What are you doing back there?" Randall yelled from the living room.

She debated whether or not to answer him. Her fingers fumbled against something smooth. Cool and metal. Gritting her teeth, she leaned back and was able to close her hand around it. "Trying to get some water," she called back.

His heavy footfalls thundered toward her. She hurried back to the counter and stood beside the drained skin just as he entered.

"You have better saved me some," he said. He picked up her skin and tossed it down, throwing her a dark look. She bobbed her head toward the cooler.

"There's more in there. I promise."

He threw the lid open and found a full skin, dipped his head through the strap and mouthed the nozzle. His throat worked. Then he exhaled, pawed around in the cooler some more, and found a second skin. This, too, went around his neck.

"I'm going to go see if the car will start."

"Are you planning to leave me here?" June asked.

He stared, his eyes getting a faraway look that she assumed was his version of deep thought.

"I should," he said finally. "Look what you got us into. That crazy bitch you call a daughter, my God. Murdering Joe. Leaving us here to help those Zoners."

"I wonder how everyone would react if you came back without me," June said.

"If I told them you was dead and Joe was dead and Violet split crazy, I reckon they'd be grateful I made it back alive."

"Maybe," June said. "Or maybe you overestimate how much you're liked back home."

He considered this. "Maybe. Or maybe you do, June. Maybe you're the one who has it wrong."

Violet's parting words came back to her: *I love you, but I can't live with you. I'm sorry.*

"You could be right about that," June said.

"I always thought you didn't have it in you to do what needs doing. Sometimes I wanted to just say"—he looked left and right, miming bewilderment—"are you seeing what I'm seeing? Is this our . . . I don't know, our fucking mayor or president or whatever? Our dictator, more like it. But why? Based on what?"

He waited for her to respond to this. When she didn't, he shrugged. "Anyway. I'm checking the car. I might be back. I need to think about it."

"I'll wait here," June said pleasantly.

"You do that," Randall said.

When the front door slammed shut, she thumbed the box-cutter blade and popped the zip tie; it took seconds. Which was good. She needed every moment she could get. She peered through the boards over the picture window. Randall had reached the car, opened the driver's-side door. He was leaning over the steering wheel instead of sliding in behind it—also good. If he decided right now to turn the ignition, lock the doors, and take off, there wouldn't be a thing in the world June could do about it. The chances she'd find a car out here that would start were one in a million, maybe one in a billion. But she didn't think that Randall would take even that chance. No, if he was bent on returning to Ruby City without her, he'd kill her first.

He turned the engine off, stood. Looked at the house.

June's heart, always doing its silent, mostly unnoticed work, made itself known now. She'd felt this before—this exhilaration and terror, this bodily response to some deeper call, some instinct in her marrow. She had more experience than Randall would guess at doing what needs doing.

He drew the water skins off from around his neck, moving as deliberately as he'd done with the rifle when Violet held her gun on him. Tossed them into the car's passenger seat. Leaned behind the wheel again, and the trunk popped open. *Get the tire iron, Randall,* June thought. *Let's finish this.*

She didn't like being on the road at night. With no streetlights to penetrate the darkness, she was forced to rely on the car's weak headlights, which, even set on bright, picked up the craters in the road maybe seconds before June would have to swerve to miss them. So she went slowly. Maddeningly slow. What she wanted more than anything was to walk into her house and into Roz's arms, and when she'd done that—when she'd been restored to the one person in this life that she could count on—she would find the words to explain what had happened today, and she'd try to make sense with Roz of how Violet had done what she had done, and why, and together they would decide what came next.

What came next. What came next? They no longer had Marta Perrone or Wes Feingold. If Marta made it back in-zone, she'd be able to tell her husband everything about Ruby City. Violet could draw him a map right to their Town Hall.

Violet wouldn't do that. Would she?

Randall had been right about one thing: June had no idea what Violet was capable of.

Pregnant, she thought again, shaking her head in wonder.

It had been the parting blow. "I'll finish up here," Violet had said, and the OLE group had left the house with Andy hauled between Wes Feingold and the big olive-skinned man, the pretty young woman following with a gun pointed to his back.

When the outside door had slammed shut, Violet turned to June. She engaged the gun's safety and slid it over her shoulder.

"Is this when you explain to me why this happened?" June asked. "Because I really want to know, Violet. I really want to know what I did to make you hate me so much."

"I don't hate you," Violet said. "I love you, but I can't live with you. I'm sorry."

June, confused, had said, "Honey, you don't live with me. I don't know what you're talking about."

Violet hunched down to June's level. She touched June's knee, then drew her hand quickly away. "I have something to tell you. It's the reason I'm leaving. But it's also good news. Good news for you to take back to the village."

June waited.

"I'm pregnant. Doc Owle can tell you more. He can explain the details. But it's possible if you go off the Salt. That's what I want you to know."

Randall, seated with his back to June, laughed uproariously. "You're—oh, Jesus. Oh, that's definitely not what I expected to hear today."

Violet's face twisted.

"What?" June asked. It was as if Violet had told her she'd sprouted wings or traveled through time. It made no more sense than that. "What—but how, Violet?"

She shook her head in a disgusted way. "How do you think?"

Randall said, "Who's the lucky guy?"

"Oh, Violet," said June. This was—but how could she ever explain this so that anyone, even Roz, would understand?—even worse than she had imagined. Violet was her daughter. *Hers*. She hadn't given birth to her, but fate had put Violet in June's path, and June had chosen her, had taken on the privilege and curse of loving her, and that was more profound than any biological bond. More profound than whatever Violet felt (or thought she felt) for this baby, this product of her victimization, and if this could happen to her in Ruby City, what did that mean about Ruby City? "Violet, who did this to you?"

"No one did this to me," Violet said. "Why do you assume it was *done* to me?"

"That's generally how it works," Randall said.

"I just mean—" June began, her head filling up with unsayable things. *I just mean that someone used you. And that matters, even if you didn't know that's what was happening. And I was supposed to protect you, but somehow I failed you. So this is the price I have to pay, and that's OK. But what price are you going to pay?* "I just mean it's so sudden. You never even told me you were—with somebody. You never told me this is something you want."

"I'm thirty-seven. Why would you assume it's not something I want?"

June had only shaken her head.

"This is the way it has to be," Violet said. "I'm sorry about that. I'm grateful to you. I hope you'll tell Roz that I'm grateful to her. But I'm doing what I have to do to give my baby a chance."

"Your baby would have a chance in Ruby City," June said. "Just like every other baby there has had a chance. Better than a chance. We have a good thing."

"Ruby City is a pipe dream," Violet said.

"So are the zones. For people like us."

"People like you," Violet said. "You don't know what's possible for a person like me." She stood again. "OK. I'm going."

And in a few seconds, that's what she had done.

At almost midnight, June estimated, she took the exit off I-40 onto the old Highway 74. It was dangerous being out like this—dangerous for June, whose headlights made her a target, and dangerous for Ruby City, because she could lead a stealthy pursuer right to the village if she wasn't careful. She slowed to a crawl on a straight stretch and tried turning off her headlights. At first she could see nothing. Then, as her eyes adjusted, she was able to easily find the moon—a full moon, bright overhead—and she could differentiate enough between road and shoulder to keep the car going, so long as a deer didn't cross her path. She went a few kilometers like this. Then she slowed more, rolled down her window, and listened hard, but it was impossible to tell if anything was happening beyond the radius of her own running engine, so she came to a full stop and stilled the motor.

The night was cool enough for the air to fog when she exhaled. June had left her jacket in the Lenoir house. On the back of a kitchen chair, she recalled. She hadn't had time, when she left, to think ahead—or she hadn't bothered to take the time. Her only thought had been getting out of the house and on the road. She would not spend the night in that house. Not with Joe's and Randall's cooling bodies. Not for anything. And so she'd fled without her jacket, without food (her stomach had started growling loudly after an hour on the road; lunch seemed a lifetime ago) or Salt tea, without much concern for what would happen the next time she needed to use this house. She'd left behind a mess, and the TI Dimension-Tech was blown, but there was still some valuable equipment that they couldn't afford to chalk up as a loss, not to mention the house itself. She should have at least dragged the bodies down to the tree line. No use bellyaching over it now, though.

Crossing her arms tightly across her chest, she exited the car. The box cutter, wiped carefully of Randall's blood, was stowed in her pocket.

Silence. Oh, there was the wind rustling a nearby copse of pine trees, a distant hooting owl. The chirp of some insect, though June had thought it too late in the season for crickets.

She looked up the road. Then down. Nothing.

She walked to the copse of trees, chose a spot between trunks, and unbuttoned her pants. She never did this—still—without thinking about the ticks, only to marvel again at the fact that she no longer had to think about the ticks if she really didn't wish to. Crouching, she looked southeast, in the direction of home. Maybe another hour until she reached the old barn where they stored their vehicles. Then, a thirty-minute walk to her front doorstep. Roz would be startled, perhaps frightened. The group wasn't due back before tomorrow.

Wait. What was that light?

It was very faint, just visible above the tree line. She had missed it at first because the clear sky was starlit, but there it was: a glow. Like the lights of one of the old cities. Once, when she was a little girl, June's father and mother had led her up to the top of a hill to watch the sunset; then, when all of the light had gone out of the sky, they'd crossed to the other side of the hill, and her father had pointed to a yellow haze, and he'd said, "That's Charlotte. That's where I lived when I was your age."

"I want to go there," June had said.

"We can never go back there," her father told her.

She knew. Immediately, she knew.

Oh, she tried to talk herself out of it. As she raced back to the car, as she started the engine and turned on the headlights. She tried to talk herself out of it even as she laid down on the gas pedal, the car bounding with a trembling groan over every pothole, shocks wheezing, and any moment now she could blow a tire, delay her return by hours, but this sane talk had no effect. She tried to talk herself out of it even when she started to smell smoke. She tried to talk herself out of it even as the faint glow became brighter, and brighter, and she could distinguish peaks and valleys, mountains of hot light, and the air around the car warmed noticeably, and she started to cough so badly that she had to slow, pull over, and vomit into the grass.

She stopped trying to talk herself out of it when she saw the dogs. The princes. They burst from the forest at a gallop, hides smoking, Tauntaun a few paces ahead of Wampa, and they passed within meters of June without stopping, fleeing up the road she had just traveled down, disappearing.

Twenty-One

Berto turned the car into a driveway so ravaged by weeds that they strummed the car's undercarriage, making a sad sort of tuneless music.

"Drive around to the back of the house," Violet told him. "Where we can't be seen from the road."

"I don't know if I'll be able to get the car out again."

"We'll worry about that when we've got to."

So Berto did as she instructed, bringing the car to a stop under the yellowing strands of a weeping willow. Wes, cramped between Edie and Marta, took a panicked breath and pressed against Edie's shoulder, unable to restrain himself. "I need—I'm sorry—"

She threw the door open and scrambled out, and Wes nearly tumbled to the ground after her. He jumped to his feet—the last thing he needed was another bite—and backed away from the car. He yanked his sleeve up. In the moments since he'd last looked, a new red bump had appeared, this one above the bend of his elbow. Jesus. Jesus Christ.

"What do we do?" Edie said. The others had gotten out of the car now, too, and they exchanged—it seemed to Wes—almost angry looks. And could he blame them? *We were* this *close,* those looks said. *We should have known we couldn't be so lucky,* those looks said.

And Berto—was he imagining this? Berto's look seemed to say: *Let's leave him and go.*

"Ken?" Edie said. "Is there something you could—I mean, could you, I don't know, cut into it or something?"

Wes, trying to decide if Edie's suggestion was cause for panic or hope, wasn't left in suspense very long. Ken shook his head. "I could take his whole arm off"—Wes flinched—"and it probably wouldn't make a difference. Not for Shreve's. It hits the bloodstream too quickly. And as bad as a hatching might be, it's not going to be any worse than some backwoods amputation with a dirty knife."

"Wes passes on the backwoods amputation with a dirty knife," Wes said dully. He felt exhausted, as if he'd just run sprints.

Marta touched his sweaty forehead. "How quickly will we know if he's in the clear? What's it Andy said? A couple of days?"

"That's the wisdom on it, but I'm not an expert on Shreve's." Ken, who was leaning against the back of the car, slapped the trunk. "This one probably knows more than I do."

A thump sounded from within the trunk. "What's going on out there?" emanated softly from it.

"OK," Violet said. "Let him out, Berto."

Berto began, "Do we really—"

"Let him out!" Marta said.

Berto, jaw clenched, leaned through the driver's-side window and popped the trunk. Andy, blinking, sprang up to sitting.

"That was quick," he said.

"Make me glad I took you along," Violet said. She pointed at Wes. "Show him."

Wes bared his arm.

Andy sucked air through his teeth. "Oh, man. Sorry about that, dude."

"Is there anything we can do?" Edie asked. Wes registered, through the intensity of itching, a surprised pleasure at how concerned about him she seemed.

"*Do?*" Andy shook his head. "No. Not really. Just wait and see."

"Wait for how long?" Wes demanded. The itching had become accompanied by a sensation that was, if this was possible, even worse—a kind of slow crawling, all over, even in his head. Was it in his head? That is, not the tick eggs, on a sprint from his arm to his brain by way of a vein, but something he was imagining? This wasn't as reassuring a thought as it ought to have been. Because it seemed to him that even this imagining must be a product of the infestation, that something malevolent had invaded him, a dark, accursed thing, and for the first time in years the name of that old demon from *The Shaman and the Salt Line*, the picture book he'd so feared as a child, popped into his mind: Vimelea. *He who consumes is consumed.* Was that how the line had gone?

"The ticks hatch in twelve, maybe fourteen hours. That's reliable. Signs of Shreve's are more varied. It can happen fast. Or it can take a while. We always say within forty-eight hours, but I've heard of it taking longer, over fifty. But I think it's usually faster than that. The vomiting, at least. Like, eight or ten hours? Thereabouts."

"Thereabouts," Marta echoed.

"Look, I wish I had better news. But do you really think we'd live in the world we do if there were easy answers to this thing?"

There was a rusted-over metal chair on the house's rotten back patio, and Wes fell into it. Eight hours? At the soonest? He was—well, he had been kind of a hypochondriac in his regular life, though he kept it in check with medications. It got worse in times of stress. When he was going through that nonsense over his honors thesis, those bullshit plagiarism accusations, he spent a few months convinced he had leukemia. Then, when Pocketz launched, Parkinson's disease. When Virtuz got shit-canned? Stomach cancer. His shrink, who Wes was convinced was good for little more than prescription-writing, told him that the only cure for hypochondria was getting an actual disease. Hell of a cure, he had said.

Hell of a cure, he thought now.

"Chances are in your favor, Feingold," Andy said. "You've got to keep that in mind."

Silence fell. The air had chilled considerably since morning, and everyone but Wes stood with crossed arms, shifting from one foot to another.

"I have a suggestion," Andy said. "I mean, I think it's the only good option, actually."

"Let's hear it," Violet said.

"The OLE chalet," Andy said. "I can lead you to it. I have all the passcodes. There's showers, food, real beds. First-aid supplies. Power."

"I'd completely forgotten about the chalet," Edie said, her face softening with hope.

"I say we go hunker down there and make a plan," Andy said. "I have some ideas for getting back over the Salt Line."

"What kind of ideas?" Berto asked.

"I'll tell you all about them when I'm safe in the chalet," Andy said.

Violet went to the trunk, sliced through Andy's tie with her pocketknife, and offered him a hand getting out. "How long will it take us to drive to it?"

"Three or four hours," Andy said.

"Where's he going to go?" Ken asked, indicating Andy. "We're already on top of each other in the backseat."

"And no offense, but I don't want to be trapped in a tight space with Wes when those things come out of him," Berto said.

"What exactly are you proposing?" Marta snapped.

"Stop. Stop," Wes said, holding up a weak hand. "I get it. I'll go in the trunk."

"No, you'll do no such thing," Marta said. She looked at Violet, as if Violet were their leader now and hers the final word on the matter. Wes wasn't so confident this was the case. "We can't put him back there. We won't know how he is, we won't be able to hear him if we need to stop. Let me sit in the front seat with you. We're both small."

"I'm not OK with that," Ken said. He looked at Wes apologetically. "I just can't risk it. I hope you understand."

"It's fine, Marta," Wes said. "The trunk's fine. I can lie down. I'll be more comfortable if I'm not worried about hurting someone."

"Are you sure?" she asked doubtfully.

"Positive," he said. Though that trunk ranked just above the Ruby City storage shed in places Wes wanted to be right now.

"I guess we're decided, then," Violet said. "Let's get on the road. Maybe we can reach it by nightfall."

It took almost five hours, and Wes spent them with his arms and legs braced against the confines of the trunk so he wouldn't go slamming into one end or the other each time the wheels jostled over another divot in the road. He didn't throw up, but he felt for most of the ride like he was just about to. And if he did, would it be carsickness or the earliest signs of Shreve's? How would he be able to tell the difference?

The itching in his arm, the crawling in his head—they continued, worsened. He supposed, lying in the dark, that there was a sort of gift in not being able to see the state of his arm, though he found himself compulsively rubbing the fingers on his left hand over the rough terrain, counting the little raised places. Eight. Eleven. Nineteen. And then, after a while, there were so many that he couldn't tell where one left off and the other began, and so instead he measured the distance from the edge to his wrist and the other edge to his shoulder, and by the time the car finally and mercifully stopped, the raised places formed an interrupted band all the way around his arm.

The trunk lid popped open, and a rush of cool air swept in, hitting his sweaty skin and setting Wes to shivering.

"I tried to get them to stop," Marta was saying, her hands on his hands, tugging him. Blood rushed to his head, and he swooned, gripping the car's side for balance. "I told them you'd need a break. I'm sorry."

Wes came to a shaky stand. "It's OK. It was probably better to just get it over with. I don't know if I'd have gone back in if you let me out."

"Was it that bad?"

"It was rough," he admitted.

Edie joined them. "How's the arm?"

"I don't know." He rolled the sleeve of his microsuit gingerly over his forearm. There was a lot of swelling, and the skin now seemed tight and full of heat, so this wasn't as easy to do as it had been five hours ago. They all pulled back from the sight of it, grimacing. If Wes could have detached his arm and thrown it over the edge of a ravine, he'd have done so with barely a pang of regret. "So much for SecondSkins," he murmured.

"That looks . . . bad." Edie winced.

"But no other symptoms?" Marta asked hopefully.

The others gathered around them. Berto, Wes noticed, kept some extra distance between himself and Wes.

"Nothing so far. I didn't throw up." He wiggled his fingers, wiggled his toes in his boots. "Everything's still working."

Andy came over for a closer look. "Yeah, that's on schedule. It's been, what? Six and half hours?"

Wes nodded.

"At least it's your arm. It could be worse."

"It could be better."

Andy turned around and pulled up his shirt to expose the flesh on his lower right back. Here, instead of the uniform Stamp scars, was a hand-sized scar with irregular edges and texture, striations that reminded Wes of tree bark. "Listen, when I say I know how you feel—I know how you feel. It's shitty. It's about to get shittier."

"Can we get inside now?" Ken asked wearily.

This was cause for more negotiation. Wes had thought himself immune to spoiling, prided himself on how well he'd handled his early fame and success: he didn't do drugs or drink; he didn't sleep around; he donated a generous portion of his Pocketz profits to a variety of worthy causes; and he lived simply, keeping a modest apartment (and, OK, a modest beach house, little more than a shack, really), a compact car, a wardrobe of mostly blue jeans and fleeces and whimsical canvas sneakers. But it had been a long time since he'd been denied anything. Even in his gawky, geeky early teens he'd not been ostracized or bullied so much as left alone, and that had been fine with him since he did his best thinking alone and could find company in *Land of Shadows* if he really needed it.

But being Wes Feingold, Pocketz creator and CEO, came with perks that had become nearly invisible to him now: how quickly people accommodated him, ceded to his opinion. More than that—how often his needs and wants were anticipated. He never had to apologize for choosing the vegan restaurant when he went out for a business lunch. He never had to feel self-conscious when he entered a meeting in yesterday's fleece and jeans. When he was dating Sonya, she complained once about the lighting in his office and his apartment. "Are you a vampire?" she'd asked. "Do you have some kind of light-sensitivity disease? Are you developing film? I can't stand how dark you have to have things."

"I don't have to have things dark," Wes said. "I like it that way at home, but the office—I mean, that's the office managers. I didn't have anything to do with it."

"Ha!" Sonya said. "Keep telling yourself that, bud."

One tick bite, though, and he wasn't Wes Feingold anymore. He was toxic.

"Doesn't bringing Wes in compromise the chalet?" Ken asked. The chalet was built into the side of a mountain, an elegant, mod structure of horizontal lines and spindly structural pillars, with a broad bank of windows that glowed brilliantly in the sunset. They had approached the entry—a small door built, like something from a fantasy novel, into the hillside. The chalet loomed out maybe twelve or thirteen meters above them, and Andy had told them that this door was the single access point. "The only way you're getting in from up there is with a wrecking ball or a missile."

"Each room has its own vac seal," Andy said now. "So the answer is, I guess, 'Not exactly.'"

"What happens when the ticks come out?" Berto asks. "Do they just . . . crawl off?"

Wes felt faint, and again he wished he could just separate himself from the arm. Ken's talk of amputation didn't seem so ghastly all of the sudden. It seemed, in fact, like precisely the thing to do. His body knew this with as much certainty as it knew that it needed water when it thirsted, or sleep when it dragged with weariness.

"Pretty much," Andy was saying. "One thing you can do is what they call a water birth. You submerge the hatching site, and when it happens, they kind of float off and it contains them—"

But Ken would want to set up an operating room, probably, scrub his hands up to the elbows the way the doctors in the webshows were always doing, boil the knives and stuff—

"—assuming, of course, that there's only the one hatch site—"

Wes's instincts screamed at him, suddenly, to just GET IT OFF. But how? How—Violet. She had a knife. She had—

He staggered toward Violet and grabbed her arm. "I'm sorry," he said, not recognizing the strength that suddenly powered him. There the knife was, tucked into a pocket on her utility belt. He snatched it with tingling fingers—

"Grab him!" Andy yelled.

"Man, I don't—"

Wes twisted in the hands that were suddenly gripping him, trying to turn the knife toward his right arm, but he was using his stupid hand, and he couldn't—quite—get there. He wasn't capable of actually cutting the arm off, probably (stupid to think he could, he thought, sweating and grinding his teeth), didn't have the strength, probably he'd pass out, but if he could just dig the blade tip into the swollen part and let off some of the goddamn pressure—

"He's trying to cut himself!" Marta cried.

He went down on his back, hard. Breath knocked out of him. As he struggled to inhale, something came down on his wrist and his hand popped open. The knife was removed from his still-grasping fingers.

"He's gone fucking nuts!" someone—Berto, he thought—said.

His cheek flared with sharp pain. "Hey. Hey." Now the other cheek. "Hey. Dude, snap out of it."

Wes blinked. Rasped another few shallow breaths. He focused his eyes in time to see the hand coming toward him again and flinched away.

"Jesus Christ!" Yes, that was Berto. "He's going to try to fucking kill us! No way in hell he's coming in with us. No way."

"He's not trying to kill anyone," Andy said. He touched Wes's face with surprising gentleness and peered into his eyes. "You calm now?"

Wes shrugged. Then nodded. "I—I don't know—"

"I know you don't," Andy said. "This can happen," Andy said, raising his voice for the others' benefit. "There's a psychological term for it, probably. I can't remember. But a frenzy sets in. I've heard of guys hacking their own legs off."

"Jesus." Edie this time. Softly.

"So no knife for you," Andy said to Wes.

"I don't feel it now," Wes said. He didn't. That other desire seemed so alien and distant now that it had felt like being possessed.

"You probably will again," Andy said. "And worse, as the hatching gets closer. That frenzy—I felt a version of it. Not something that caused me to try to hack myself to pieces, thank God. But I would have clawed my back to shreds if I could have."

"Great," Wes muttered.

"We need to get inside," Ken said. "It's getting dark. I need something to drink."

"Wes comes, too," Marta said firmly.

"Hell, no," said Berto.

"This could be any of us," Edie said. "You can't treat him like that. He's a human being."

"Yeah, and so am I," Berto said. "And so is everyone else here. I don't see what putting all our lives at risk will accomplish. He just needs to stay out here until we know what's up."

Edie's dark eyes were flashing in the diminishing light. "We don't have any camping gear. We don't even have a blanket. You just want to leave him down here alone with nothing over his head, nothing to protect him?"

"You can stay down with him if you want," Berto said. "And we can probably find some things in the chalet. Bring him down food and water, a sleeping bag, whatever he needs. I'm not saying he can't have some of what we've got. I'm saying he doesn't bring that fucking diseased arm of his into the one safe haven we've got."

"I agree with Berto," Ken said.

"You are monsters," said Marta.

"And you haven't lost anyone yet," Berto said. "So shut up."

Wes felt the moment coming when he'd have to do the decent thing again, the thing he could live with, even if it meant not living. A sleeping bag out here wouldn't be so bad compared to the car trunk. It wouldn't even be so bad compared to the shed in Ruby City. At least he'd lie there in the knowledge that he could get up and walk twenty feet if he wanted to. And then twenty more, if he wanted that.

(All the way to the Wall. Where he'd be promptly shot.)

But still.

"He goes up with us," Andy said.

"I don't think that's up to you," Berto said.

"Actually, I do." Andy had his big scarred arms crossed and a little smile on his face. Though his action was on Wes's behalf, Wes nonetheless registered a flash of uneasiness. This was the man who had driven Wendy, Anastasia, Lee, and Jesse to the Wall to be shot, after all. "I have the codes for this door. And the upstairs door. I know how to get the generator running. I know the codes to the supply pantries. You want access to any of it, you need me."

"Why would you do that for him?" Berto asked.

"Because I can," Andy said. "And because I don't like you."

Twenty-Two

The chalet, though modestly appointed by the standards of most OLE travelers, was paradise after the last week. The living room, dining area, and kitchen were all one open space, lined on both sides by windows offering panoramic views of the east and west, the west now singed by the very last of the day's light. Long, broad sofas formed a U around a huge stone fireplace. Gas logs, Edie saw. Wouldn't want an open flue in this place, of course. The coffee table was huge—a rough-hewn timber base topped with a giant stone slab. How on earth did they get that up here? she wondered. It made her tired to think of it.

Upstairs, the hallway opened into five rooms, each with four single beds, and two bathrooms. The bathrooms were tiny and identical: small metal sink bowl underneath a cloudy shatterproof mirror; a small toilet that vacuumed away waste like an airplane toilet; a cramped shower stall that a plus-sized person wouldn't be able to fit into with the door closed. But the water was hot—even for Edie, who drew the last turn—and she wept with joy for most of her fifteen minutes under the stream, lathering twice, a third time, with the rosemary-scented soap, switching the sprayer to the massage setting and letting it pound her neck, then her lower back. Finally, the suds gathering around her toes were white. A few minutes after that, she shut off the water and folded herself into a clean white robe that smelled a bit musty, of storage, but still felt luxurious.

Andy had given them each a little toiletry kit from one of the locked pantries. She brushed her teeth with the fresh toothbrush and paste, flossed. She clipped her toenails and fingernails, rubbed a thin greasy lotion into her face and the backs of her hands, rubbed a tube of ChapStick over her dry lips. The microsuit she'd been wearing for the past week was—thankfully—in the incinerator. A new one awaited her in her room. Well, the room she was sharing with Marta. Her underwear and sports bra were in the washing machine, mingled with everyone else's to save time and water. Which was a little strange, though there wasn't much left to hide from these people, for good or ill.

She passed Berto in the hallway heading back to her room. He looked almost absurd in his white robe, which barely reached his knees, tall as he was—like a bodybuilder stopping by the sauna after a tough workout. "I guess you're happy," he said. "You got your way."

"I don't think there's a lot in this situation to be happy about," she said. "But yeah, I'm glad that we didn't leave Wes out all night to go through this alone."

"You don't even know him, really," Berto said.

"I don't know you, either," Edie told him.

He looked like he was thinking of saying something else. Instead, he sighed—huffed—shook his head a little, and went to his room. Edie thought he probably would have slammed the door shut behind him if that had been an option, but instead the door snicked softly closed, and then the vac seal engaged.

In her own room, Marta was stretched out on one of the beds, head nestled against a pillow. She raised up sleepily when Edie entered.

"Didn't mean to wake you," Edie said.

"Mm. Just dozing." Marta rolled onto her back and stretched, the crack of her back and toes audible even across the room. She rubbed the bottoms of her feet against the sateen duvet. "Bed. Pillows. You would think it had been years and not days."

Edie crawled under the covers and exhaled. "Yep."

They lay there several minutes more, not quite asleep and not quite awake, drifting enough that Edie thought she heard Wes calling for her from down the hall, and then she roused enough to realize that she hadn't heard him, that she wouldn't be able to hear him even if he shouted, because his room was vac-sealed.

"I want to go in there with you," Edie said. "You're going to need the help. And he's going to need the support."

"No," Marta said firmly.

"But why would you—"

"I'm not trying to martyr myself," Marta said. "I'm being absolutely practical here. You're the only one I trust on the other side of that lock. Not Andy. Not Ken or Berto. Not even Violet. If you're not out here, I don't know that they'll open the door after the hatching."

Edie nodded. She hadn't thought of this. But she recognized the truth of it, and she realized, with that recognition, what a grave responsibility had fallen on her. If it came down to it—Edie against four—she would have to find a way to act. She would have to do it for her friends.

"Besides," Marta said, "I don't think he'd want you there."

"Why?" asked Edie, wounded a little.

"Because he's going to be at his worst. And he won't want you seeing him like that."

She recognized the truth of this, too, though it hadn't occurred to her before.

"Tell him . . ." She hesitated. She had no idea what she wanted Marta to tell him. "Tell him I'm worried about him. And—and that I was willing to come with you to help him."

"I'll tell him," Marta said kindly.

Edie looked at the ceiling, thinking. At first what she saw didn't register, and then it did: a water stain. There was a water stain. And she wasn't shattered or even surprised by that, but it was proof, if she needed more of it, that there were no impenetrable fortresses, out here or maybe anywhere. Maybe even in-zone.

She had wanted away from Ruby City. Out of that storage shed. But what now? Where now? Jesse was dead. She couldn't return to the set of rooms he kept at the Hilton or to his little apartment on Savoy. Her old workmate, Inez, would probably let her crash on her couch until she could find somewhere more permanent, but Edie could eke out only a couple of weeks that way, a month at most. She didn't have a job. She didn't have any family left. The absence of her mother . . . God, that ache was still so fresh, even after all of this. As long as she'd had Jesse to take care of, his whirlwind lifestyle to emulate, she could keep the grief at bay. But now?

"Is it weird that the thought of getting back home makes me feel almost nothing?" she asked Marta.

Marta didn't answer right away. Finally she said, "I don't know. For me, getting back past the Wall means seeing my sons again. Well, and showers and a soft bed like this one. That, too."

"Yes, that," Edie said, smiling a little. "Beds are good."

"But if my children were on the moon, the moon is where I'd want to be. If they were in hell, hell is where I'd want to be."

"I don't know if I should be jealous of you or sorry for you," Edie said. "That's heavy stuff."

"Both? Neither? I don't know. Do you want kids?"

"No," Edie said. "I mean, I'm pretty sure I don't."

"Well, you're young yet. You may change your mind."

"Women your age always say that."

Marta laughed. "That's true." She rolled to her side to face Edie. "May I ask why not?"

Edie closed her eyes against a flood of tears, glad that the room was too dark for Marta to see her. She swallowed until she thought she could speak without her voice warbling. "My mother was this tiny dynamo. Mexican and Filipino. Hard and sweet, like rock candy. She worked at an industrial laundry after my daddy died. When we moved to Atlantic Zone."

"How did you pull that off?"

"Death benefits. Daddy worked out here for a timber company. Died of Shreve's."

"Oh," Marta said.

"I was eight. We left everything behind. Her family, Daddy's family. Never saw any of them again. Well, we messaged, you know, but I never got to sit in my *abuela*'s lap again, or hold Granddaddy Emilio's hand. But they understood, because it was a no-brainer to them. You find a way to get into a good zone, you go. Whatever it costs, or whoever. Say goodbye. Hold them in your heart."

"That must have been hard," Marta said.

"A little hard for me, but I was eight. I went to school, I made new friends. My mother, she worked and took care of me. She got the laundry job. Paid the rent. She did it alone. She didn't date. She didn't remarry. She was like you, Marta. She had no other purpose in life but keeping me alive. Then, you know, she got cancer, like everybody does, and she got the treatments she could afford to, and there might have been enough money to save her if we'd stayed in Gulf. But we didn't. So she finished up in terrible pain, and what she has to show for it at the end is a daughter who waitresses at a bar."

"I can guarantee you that she was proud of you," Marta said. "You're a wonderful girl. Any mother would be lucky to have you."

"Oh, she was proud," Edie agreed. "I'm not trying to say her sacrifice was pointless or that I'm ungrateful. I'm not entirely sure what I mean, actually." She thought. "I'm trying to explain why I don't think I want kids. It probably sounds like I'm going to say I don't want to sacrifice the way my mother did. That's not it, though. I'm willing to sacrifice. I just don't know if a child is what I want to do it for. For one person. Or even a couple. And everything you do is for them, and then they have children, and everything they do is for them. If I had a child, I think I'm the kind of person who would live in this world in a really narrow way. I would only want what would make my kid happy. And fuck everything else. That's not how I want to be."

Marta stared at her long enough that Edie started to feel uncomfortable. "I'm sorry if I offended you," she said finally. "I'm only talking about how I see myself."

"No, you're right. I don't disagree at all."

Edie waited to see if she'd say more.

"You saw my husband. The kind of person he is."

Edie shrugged a little, nodded.

"I called Berto and Ken monsters. I've been lying here thinking of how unfair that was. I've been married for over twenty-five years to a monster. A real monster. But he's good to our sons, and he gives them a good life. I've never been willing to think past that. I've never had the courage to."

"I think you have courage," Edie said. "I think you're one of the bravest people I've ever met."

Marta reached across the little space of floor between their beds, and Edie met her halfway. Their fingers linked.

"Well, I don't know about all that. But I've already broken one promise to Wes. I told him I'd do whatever I had to do to get back in-zone. Locking myself in a room with a young man having a hatching probably isn't the best way to go about it."

"We could switch places."

"No. This is how it's supposed to be," Marta said hoarsely, voice thick with emotion. Edie wondered if she was thinking about that thing her husband said just before Violet shot Joe. About her sons.

There was a buzz at the door. Edie rose from the bed to open the vac seal.

Andy. "I checked on Wes. If you still want to go in with him, I think now's the time."

Marta and Edie exchanged looks.

"Yes, I still want to go in," Marta said. "Show me what to do."

A couple of hours later, Edie sat in the downstairs living area with Violet, Andy, Berto, and Ken. They had been drawn in unspoken consensus not to the couches by the fireplace or the formal dining table but to the bar stools around the kitchen island. Andy made a pot of coffee. They rummaged in the pantry and freezer and pulled out a random assortment of snacks: butter cookies, pretzels, some kind of weird unrefrigerated cheese product that didn't smear on crackers so much as collapse onto them, dates, mini-quiches that heated up quickly in the convection oven. They ate in silence at first, ravenous; it was at least 9:00, and they'd had nothing since those sandwiches back at the house in Lenoir. Andy had set up a camera in Wes's room—it worked on an old-fashioned wireless system—and they watched the stream of video on a tablet, muting the audio when Wes started groaning with pain. It was strange to surveil him and Marta like this. Shameful, even. And yet it was the only way to know how and if the situation had progressed, and Edie wanted to be able to spring to action if Marta needed her. To outrace the others to the door if she had to.

"This is going to sound weird, but you know what this reminds me of?" Andy asked, finally breaking the silence.

"What?" said Berto.

"Waiting for my boys to be born." He unwrapped another foil wedge of cheese and bisected it with a cracker. He took a big bite, a shadow passing over his face. Served him right, Edie thought. He probably didn't deserve to get to come back to his family, to reenter their lives as if he'd never planned to leave them forever. Would someone sitting here rat him out? Edie didn't plan to—she wasn't interested in meting out justice—but she couldn't imagine Berto staying silent, especially after Andy insisted on bringing Wes into the chalet.

"Yes," Ken said. "It does."

"You have kids?" Edie asked, shocked. He'd never once mentioned them.

He nodded. "Four." He didn't elaborate.

Violet set down her coffee mug with a sigh, stood.

"You OK?" Edie asked.

"Yeah," she said. "Just going to stretch my legs."

When she'd wandered off toward the fireplace, Berto leaned in and lowered his voice. "So getting back over the Wall," he said. "What's the plan?"

"Well," said Andy, "I'm of two minds about that. So I'll tell you my ideas, and you all tell me what you think."

"Spit it out," Berto said.

Andy frowned, made a show of refilling his coffee, doctoring it again with sugar and powdered creamer. "The first option is to use the satellite phone in this house."

For a pregnant few seconds, no one knew what to say. Then, Berto exploded: "A phone? In this goddamn house?" Edie thought he was going to fly over the island and start pummeling Andy, but he seemed to remember at the last moment that Andy held all of the passcodes to the storage closets and safes. Trying for calm—though his face was blotchy-red with anger, or maybe excitement—he said, slowly, "Is there a reason we're not placing the fucking phone call—I don't know—four hours ago?"

"Yes," Andy said, "there's a reason. For one, our pal Wes is still doing his thing upstairs."

Berto shook his head in disgust. "I wish I knew why you have such a hard-on for that guy."

"I wish I knew why you don't have more of a hard-on for him. I mean, if we place that call, who do you think is likeliest to get the good guys here to help us on the double? You?" He pointed to Violet and whispered: "The scarecrow over there?"

"Ken's a big shot in his own right," Edie said.

"That's true," Andy said. "And yeah, if Wes dies, it's a good thing we got Ken. But better for us if they're both alive."

"Why?" Berto asked.

"Because the rest of us aren't worth the fuel it'd take to get us."

"I don't know if that's true," Berto said sorely, but he turned his attention to folding a foil wrapper. A little bird formed in his big hands. "I have the money to cover that. OLE was going to airlift us out in case of emergency, anyway."

"That's the claim, but I don't know if it's true. It's never once happened. Which leads me to the other option. And I guess all of this depends on how cynical you are. Or paranoid. Me, I'm a lot of both."

"Let's hear it," Edie said.

"If you're inclined to doubt how much our government's willing to risk for us, after everything we've seen—even for Ken here, and Feingold—then you might think it's less of a risk to sneak in on our own. I know some guys who worked for my old boss. They got me out here the first time. They'd smuggle us in for the right price."

"How much?" Berto asked.

"You were just saying you could afford an evac."

"I know what I'm getting with a government-sanctioned evacuation."

"OK, ballpark? A hundred thousand a head."

Edie laughed. It was all so predictable. "Well, that's it for me. And Violet. Andy, I guess I know how much you're charging for your contact."

"Maybe you don't," Andy said. "Maybe I'm charging three hundred thousand."

"How do we even get the credits to them?" Ken asked.

"They have the tech out here for a transfer."

"I think the way forward's pretty obvious," Ken said. "We use the satellite phone. And if they don't come to get us after a few days, we use your contact, Andy."

Andy smirked. "It don't work like that, bub."

"Why not?"

Violet spoke up from across the room. "Andy. Can you turn the lights off for a moment?"

"Lights? Why?"

"There's something outside I'm trying to get a better look at."

Andy went to the wall plate and tapped the screen. The lights lowered, leaving only a dim band around the room's baseboards, reminding Edie of the aisle in a movie theater.

Violet was standing in front of the western bank of windows, and now that the lights were out, the object of her gaze was clear: a bright blaze of orange light. How far away it was Edie couldn't guess. It might have been a very big light very far away, or it might have been a smaller light quite close. She joined Violet at the windows and peered out, trying to fix on the source. She felt the others gathering close, doing the same.

"What is that?" Berto asked.

Violet's voice was dull. "Home," she said.

"Ruby City?" Andy said. "Jesus. Yeah. Yeah, you're right."

"How do you know for sure?" Ken said.

"It's the right direction," said Andy. "We're about an hour northeast of it here. Jesus, it looks like a bomb went off."

Ken again: "What does this mean?"

"It means I vote for getting smuggled in," Violet said. Her eye was very bright in the low light—damp with tears that she roughly wiped away. "If someone's willing to pay my tab."

Twenty-Three

Perhaps an hour passed before Marta regretted turning down Edie's offer of assistance. When one of the frenzies, as Andy had called them, set in, caring for Wes became a job for two—or a job for one person with more strength and wherewithal than Marta possessed. He paced, ground his teeth; tears leaked out from the corners of his pinched eyes. He hadn't made a violent move toward Marta (yet), but he was keen to hurt himself, at one point throwing his infested arm against the wall over and over, so that Marta finally broke down and gave Wes the first two tranquilizers of the stash of ten Andy had given her. Were there more pills? He'd been cagey. "Ten should be enough. Give him more than that in a twenty-four-hour period and you might do him more harm than good." But how long would this go on? A day? Three? If she ran out, would someone come and bring more? Would they do it if Wes were trying to gnaw his own arm off through the biceps?

Now he was resting on one of the beds. Marta dipped a washcloth into the large basin of water Andy had filled for her and blotted Wes's sweaty brow with it. He let out a shuddering, slow breath. His eyes were still closed. Now that she'd showered, Marta was uncomfortably aware of Wes's stench—the smell made worse by the wild tang of his sick-sweat. She rolled her chair back, putting some distance between them, and tore the wrapper end off an energy bar with her teeth, bolting down a few fast bites and finishing with a slug of bottled water. Just enough to quiet her stomach's rumble.

"Would you like some water?" she asked Wes.

His mouth twitched. "Maybe," he said finally. "Hold on." A few minutes later, he sat up and propped his pillows up behind his back. "OK, I'll have some now."

She handed him a cup with a straw in it, aiming the end of the straw at his mouth. He took it from her irritably. "I've got it," he said. His Adam's apple bobbed. He moved to set the glass down on his bedside table, and his hand shook so badly that the rest of the water went all over him. "Fuck it all," he muttered. It was the first time she had heard him curse.

"If there's anything I can do," Marta said, "please tell me."

"I don't know why you're even in here," Wes said.

"Because you shouldn't have to do this alone."

He shrugged. "I'm doing it alone either way. Now I've got to worry about hurting you."

"You're not going to hurt me," Marta said firmly, though she wasn't convinced this was true. "I'm here to help contain things when you—you know. So if it helps you feel better, think of it as protecting the others."

His eyes fluttered shut again, and he winced. "I feel them. Like this army on a march inside me. And I hear their voices. Yeah, I know. Ticks don't have voices. I don't suppose they have thoughts, either. But I hear them. In my head."

"I'm sorry," Marta said. "That sounds awful."

"If I get through this, I'm going to stop talking and let you complain to me. For as long as you want. I guess I owe you a few weeks' worth at this point. Don't I?"

"You don't owe me anything," Marta said. "You're my friend, Wes."

"Friend," he mused. "I've never really had one, Marta. Not really.

I'm glad you're my friend. It was worth all of this, maybe. To make a friend."

"For me, too," she said. She took his hand and squeezed it. He returned the squeeze . . . and then he bore down. She felt the bones in her hands moving, popping, and she yanked free of him with a little yelp of pain and confusion. His face was bleached of color. The tendons in his neck surged outward as he threw his head back against the pillow, grinding his sweaty crown against the Egyptian cotton pillowcase, and silent tears rolled down into the cups of his ears. Under the thin sheet covering him, his entire body stiffened so hard that Wes emanated a vibration.

"Do you think it's happening?" Marta asked. She was terrified.

He nodded—one quick dip of the chin.

She moved as quickly as she could. First the restraints. Andy had tied off rope to the bedframe on three ends, and Marta looped each of Wes's feet, executing the tight figure-eight knot Andy had shown her, then his left arm. "I'm sorry I have to do this," she kept murmuring. She shook two more tranquilizers from the bottle. "Open," she said to Wes, wondering if she'd have to sink her fingers into his jaws the way you did a dog's, but he accepted the pills, and the straw, and his throat worked, and he coughed.

The water bath was a large plastic storage container filled to the brim and sudsy with dish soap. Positioned beside Wes's bed, it reached just high enough for him to dangle his arm over the side and fully submerge the tick hatching site. "But he's going to be bucking and shucking, and so you'll have to keep a close eye on it. Hold it underwater if you have to. They can't swim. The babies'll attach and feed, so there's some risk if they carry Shreve's, but they can't burrow. But I don't think they could attach to you through the water, anyway."

This didn't exactly inspire confidence.

Still, it was a risk Marta would take over the option of watching hundreds of tiny miner ticks scatter into her locked, vac-sealed room.

"OK, I changed my mind," Wes gasped.

"About what?"

"About this all being worth it. It's not."

Marta laughed through her tears and gripped his hand. "OK, fair enough. But I think it's going to be over soon. One way or another."

"Thank you," Wes said.

"You're welcome," Marta told him. She looked at his arm—at the biggest pustules around where the burrowing had occurred. There was movement under the blistered surface of the skin. First she thought this was a trick of the eyes—the lighting, her exhaustion, the intensity of her concentration. Then it happened again. And again. Now there were lots of little movements, and the blisters rippled as if they were boiling, and finally the center pustule oozed open, secreting a yellowish-red fluid, and a small, black, many-legged thing scrambled out.

Marta plunged Wes's arm into the water.

He screamed, and the water bloomed crimson, and a strange smell filled the room: blood and metal but something else, almost sweet, like raisins, but on the edge of rancid. Wes convulsed in her grip, straining against his restraints, but she managed to keep his arm underwater, bearing down hard with both hands, her face only centimeters from its churning red surface. She had no idea how long this went on. Only a few minutes probably, though it seemed endless. Her arms ached, and her back and thighs ached with the strain of keeping her balanced (so easily she could fall into the water headfirst, and she kept bracing herself for that eventuality).

At last Wes collapsed, and his arm went limp. She pulled it from the water and winced at the raw, ravaged flesh, which made a band around the meat of his forearm and stretched in a wet red mouth from the forearm's middle to mere centimeters from his armpit. She turned the arm, searching it frantically, and saw a furious black scurrying thing scrambling over the crooks and crags of the wet flesh. With a little wail of disgust she brushed it off into the water, and then she wrapped Wes's arm in the clean white towel she'd kept nearby for this purpose, and then she looked her own arms over, feeling ticklish feet where her eyes told her nothing moved. The tub of water was pink with a yellowish scrim on the surface in which floated little black specks, too many to count. Marta scanned the floor, Wes's bedsheets. She saw nothing. In the time it took to do these things, the towel around Wes's arm soaked red.

"Wes. Wes, are you all right? Can you hear me?"

He nodded wearily.

"I need to clean and dress your arm. I think it's all right to give you another pill. And I have some ibuprofen. OK?"

"OK," he whispered.

She slipped the pills between his lips, fed him some water. Then she gingerly peeled the wet towel back. His poor arm—it looked as if he'd held it in a tank filled with piranhas. She shook the canister of antiseptic spray and depressed the nozzle, coating the wounds. He bore this all with a grimace. Then she opened a package of antibiotic gauze and unwrapped it around the arm, overlapping the edges. She finished with dry gauze and a sling Andy had makeshifted from a spare sheet. Wes's face was ashy, his lips the same color as his skin, his under-eyes bluish-green. She helped him up and led him to one of the other beds, nestling him between clean sheets.

"It's over," she said, patting his knee through the sheet. "Lie back. Try to rest."

"It's not over," Wes said. "I'm not in the clear for Shreve's. Not for days, yet."

He rolled onto his left side, ruined arm nestled against his chest, and went to sleep.

She waited until the rise and fall of his chest was deep and even, then drank a bottle of water, finished her energy bar, and rose wearily to give the room a final once-over. The room was—by strategy, she supposed—all white: white tile flooring, white-painted walls, white linens. She put the lid on the storage container of soapy water and ran microseal tape around the edges: once, twice, three times. Andy had told her that miner ticks can live underwater for days, and their safest bet would be to wait a week before trying to dispose of the dirty water. Then she went to the bed where Wes had lain during his hatching, pulled the covers smooth, turned them back, peeled off the fitted sheet. Nothing. But she threw all of the linens into one of the thick plastic garbage bags Andy had given her and pulled the chemical seal. She did this with the linens on the other two beds, too, just to be safe. She turned the mattresses off the frames, pulled them to the side of the room away from the door, and stacked them. Then she walked the floor in concentric circles. She saw a dark speck that turned out to be an oat flake from her energy bar. Another that was a piece of leaf off one of their shoes. Nothing else. Satisfied, she went to the monitor. "We're good in here," she said. Then, just in case, she made the OK sign with her hand.

Now was the moment of truth. Would they come?

So quickly she didn't have time to waver with doubt, the vac seal ran and the door slid open. Edie stood there, smiling.

"Get some rest," she said. "I'm on duty."

Twenty-Four

Saturday morning. White light pours through the window blinds, illuminating the weave of his thermal blanket. Smell of coffee. Sweet dough and cooking oil. Downstairs his parents have a tablet cued to the Dawn of Pop music feed, those old-timey songs Wes can't help but tap his foot along to, and he lies there for a few moments just savoring it all: the sunbeam, the mutter of rhythm guitar, the promise of a good breakfast, the promise of an unstructured day. Had he been a good son? Probably not. He hadn't appreciated his prickly parents, had been too caught up in his own thoughts, his theories, his *Land of Shadows* campaigns, to consider their feelings. He hadn't cared for hugging, so he hadn't hugged them. He hadn't cared about hearing "I love you," so he didn't bother to say it. They didn't nag like other parents, or lay guilt trips, and so Wes assumed they didn't need these gestures from him, valued them as little as he did, but now he wondered. They were alive and well in Atlantic Zone, divorced, living separately on generous infusions of Pocketz revenue, and Wes got together with each of them maybe once a month, for dinner, usually, or a few rounds of golf with his father. He didn't fight with them. They didn't fight with each other. Everything was perfectly mild, and amiable, though this mildness itself seemed a sign of something: a critical lack. But if he ever saw them again, Wes thought—from wherever he was now, this limbo, this whitewashed world that was turning out to not be Saturday morning in his childhood room—he'd thank them for the music and the pancakes, for loving him enough to leave him alone, and he'd hug them, even if it made them uncomfortable. *You were good to me,* he'd say. *I realize that now.*

He opened his eyes all the way. Edie was sitting beside him in a cushy chair he didn't remember from the previous night—something that had been brought in from downstairs, he guessed. Her feet were propped up against the bed frame, and she had a book spread open across her thighs: the Jane Austen she'd spent so much time reading back in Ruby City. He lowered his eyelids and watched her through his lashes for a little while, hoping she wouldn't notice he was awake. The stresses of the last week had etched her brow with new lines, and her eyes were puffy—from lack of sleep, maybe, or crying. These little imperfections were a relief; they made her easier to look at, taking the edge off her astonishing prettiness. He had left his list about Edie back at Ruby City. Perhaps someone had found it already, was having a good laugh on his account. That was OK. Her eyes darted left and right, left and right, and she turned a page, and as she did so she looked up and caught his eye, and she sat up straight and folded the book closed over her finger.

"You're awake!" she said.

"Yep. I guess I am."

"How do you feel?"

His arm throbbed from shoulder socket to fingertips, but otherwise, he felt like himself. Rested, even. He said so.

"You've been out cold for ten hours," Edie said. "It's nearly been twenty-four hours since the bite. It's a good sign that you haven't had any symptoms yet. Not a guarantee, but Andy said it's promising."

Wes stretched his legs and his left arm, wiggled his fingers and toes. He held his free hand in front of his face, noting the clarity of the whorls on his finger pads, the pores on the back of his hand,

and the curly tawny hairs that sprouted from them. His vision was as good as it ever was. He felt, minus the arm, as good as he ever had.

He felt like he was going to be all right. But he was far too superstitious to voice this thought out loud.

"I guess I owe Andy big-time," he said instead.

Edie made a sarcastic blowing sound, spraying spittle. "Save your gratitude for Marta. Andy's already figured out how you can repay him."

"And how's that?"

"By footing the fee to get him smuggled back in-zone. Probably Violet's fee, too. At least, I hope you'll cover Violet's. Berto and Ken have been pretty vague in their offers of help. And I don't think Marta has it to give. Not in her own name."

"What about you? Do you have it?"

She shifted her gaze to the cover of her book and traced the raised lettering with her thumbnail. "No," she said. "But it doesn't matter."

"Of course it matters," Wes said.

"No, it doesn't matter. Because I'm not planning to go back."

"What?" Wes pulled awkwardly to sitting position. "What do you mean, you're not going back? I have the money. It's not even an issue, Edie."

"That's not it." She lay the book on the floor and leaned toward him, making such intense eye contact that Wes felt light-headed. More light-headed. "I knew as soon as I realized it was an option that it was the right thing. I felt a weight coming off me. I didn't want to be in Ruby City. But I didn't want to go back in-zone, either. That's not home to me. It's not where I belong."

"So you belong out here? Have you seen my arm?"

"No. And you can spare me the reveal."

Wes shook his head, exasperated. But there was something to the exasperation—something he wished he could sort out in a list, make sense of. Like, why would she be so stupid? But also: Why would she choose here? Knowing I'll be there? But also: Why is it such a given that I'd be there?

And then, a tangent: What's waiting for me there?

Well, that one was obvious. His parents. His company. His apartment and beach house.

"Explain to me the appeal," Wes said. "What's out here?"

"My dad worked out here. And he died out here. I thought he did it because he had no other choice. I've lived my whole life making a saint of him, but I think now that the truth was more complicated than that. I think he lived so much of his life out here because he loved it, despite the risks. Or maybe he loved the risks, too." She shrugged. "There's a way to live out here, Wes. A cure. It exists! June didn't always do the right thing, I know that, but you can't deny that she built something good. She built something good, and that could be done again. It *must* be done again." Suddenly downcast, she traced a circle on her knee with her middle finger. "I think the zone's a bad place in some ways. Lots of ways. I don't like the price we have to pay to have its protections. And if that man—Marta's husband—if he really can climb to power . . . Well, that terrifies me. Worse than ticks."

"You heard Perrone. You heard the cost of the cure. June didn't deny it."

"I heard," Edie said. "Infertility. I can live with that."

"He said cancer, too," Wes said. "So maybe you can't."

"My mother died of cancer. Cancer is everywhere. Cancer's in-zone. It might already be inside me somewhere, waiting to come out."

"And it has to be you out here, saving the world? Why?"

Now Edie looked exasperated. "Why not?"

"Don't—don't hear me wrong. Or give me a break for saying it wrong. You, Edie: you can do anything. I believe that. But how are you going to do it all alone? Why would you want to do it all alone?"

"I don't want to do it all alone," Edie said. "I mean, I will. If I have to. But if anyone wanted to stay with me—well, they could. I'd welcome that."

"You'd welcome it," Wes repeated. *Goddammit,* he thought. *Goddammit it all.*

Her eyes skittered away again. "I value your friendship and your smarts. What you've done with Pocketz, I think it could be done in a different, more meaningful way. You understand people better than you think you do. What's in their hearts. Not just what's in their accounts."

"Their Virtuz," Wes said wryly.

"Well—I guess," Edie said, clearly not hearing the word with the *z* at the end.

"You say you value my friendship," Wes said. "Do you understand what I'd be hoping for?"

Edie seemed to think about it. Then nodded.

"And you'd still welcome me? Knowing that?"

"It's a selfish fucking thing to do," Edie said, "but yes. I would. As long as you understand what I'm capable of offering."

"Which is friendship."

"Exactly."

"Exactly," Wes repeated. He smiled. He couldn't help himself. He'd faced worse odds.

That afternoon, still symptom free, Wes requested a tablet. Edie brought him, apologetically, a sheaf of paper and a pen. "The chalet's tablet is the control hub for the house systems, so Andy didn't want you tying it up. Hope this is OK."

"I'll manage," Wes said.

And he did, barely. His writing hand was attached to his bad arm, so he worked slowly and uncomfortably, trying to get the numbers clear enough to read, double-checking his work. He wrote by hand so infrequently in his regular life that his print had the sloping insecurity of a child's. But he supposed it would serve. He put his signature at the bottom, not sure if the gesture would mean anything—but it couldn't hurt.

After he'd finished, he felt well enough to join the others downstairs in the kitchen. They were having another makeshift meal at the counter, and they clapped awkwardly when he entered, made little exclamations over him: *Oh, hey! There he is! Looking good!*

"Coffee?" Andy asked after the little hubbub had died down.

Wes nodded. "Please."

Andy poured him a cup. "There's junk to eat. Plenty of it. And I fried some deer meat I found in the deep freeze. It tastes like salty shoe leather, but it's better than soy dogs."

"I'd pay a thousand credits for a cup of OJ," Wes said, sipping the coffee. "That was my treat food back home."

"That's neither food nor a treat," Edie said.

"It has a ton of sugar," said Wes.

Marta favored him with one of her serene, knowing smiles. "I don't suppose you're going to find much OJ this side of the Salt Line."

Wes blushed, feeling watched by the others. So Edie had told them.

"Is Edie for real?" Berto asked him. "You're staying here?"

"Yeah." He pulled a veggie crisp from an open bag and crunched down on it. It was stale and tasteless. "I am." He exchanged a look with Edie, who favored him with such a pleased smile that his resolve halted its wavering.

"You're both out of your minds," Ken said.

Violet, nibbling the edge of a piece of the burnt deer meat, asked, "Did Edie tell you what we think happened to Ruby City?"

"She did, yeah," Wes said.

"And you still want to be on this side of the Wall?" Berto said.

"I think," Wes said, "that it's more a reason to stay than it is to go back." He felt the truth of this as he said it aloud.

After a moment, Andy offered: "I say it's cool. Admirable. The revolution's going to come from outside the zones. That's a fact. That's why I was willing to do the things I've done."

"So are you staying, too?" Berto asked.

"Hell no," Andy said. He slowly unwrapped a chocolate-flavored Moon Pie and held it up to the light. "Goddamn, these are good." He downed it in three huge bites, then licked his fingers and thumb.

They decided to part ways at first light. Andy, Berto, Violet, Marta, and Ken would take the car an hour east to the fertilizer plant where Andy's old smuggling contacts worked. Edie and Wes would stay behind at the chalet and make their own plan for what came next. The world—even between zone borders—was vast, the possibilities endless. There were ticks. But there were also, perhaps, the remnants of Ruby City, some vestiges of the drug operations there, perhaps even survivors. Wes wanted to stop in Asheville to see if he could find the house where his great-great-grandfather—the professor of sociology he'd told Marta about when they were first bused over the Salt Line—lived and died. Edie had said that sounded like as good a place to begin as any.

Late, as each of the others yawned and stretched and left to go upstairs to bed, Wes and Marta lingered. At last it was just the two of them. It was midnight, according to the clock—thirty-seven hours since Wes's bite.

Marta was sipping whiskey, part of the stash Andy had told them a million years ago was hidden away somewhere as a special treat. They had turned on the gas logs, though it wasn't very cold out, still. High fifties, even with the sun down.

"I'm going to cut right to it," Marta said. "What in the hell are you doing, Wes?"

Wes sighed. "I don't expect you to understand."

"For the first time, you sound like one of my sons. That's not a compliment." She peered at him. "Tell me you aren't doing this for a pretty girl. Because if you are, Wes, you're going to regret it. I like Edie. I like her almost as well as I like you. But she came out here with a man."

"Jesse—"

"He died a few days ago. I'm well aware."

"What I was going to say is that they were basically done before what happened to him."

"Maybe that's wishful thinking on your part," Marta said. "Or maybe they were, and maybe she's madly in love with you—"

"Jeez, stop."

"—and maybe this is the start of some grand romantic adventure. It will end badly. This is a bad world, Wes. I think it's bad all over, but some parts are worse than others."

"What about you?" Wes said. "What's next for you?"

"You know what's next for me."

"You go back to your husband."

Marta laughed shakily and took another sip of her whiskey.

"He might have been the one to do that to the village. Just like June was worried he would."

"Oh, there's no 'might have been' to it," Marta said. "It was him. I saw his eyes before Joe put that gun to my head." She looked up, her own dark eyes reflecting firelight. "And the tracking device I showed you—I left it behind at the storage shed. He had an X to mark the spot."

"So, to quote a wise woman I know: What in the hell are you doing?"

"He is the only way to my sons," Marta said. "All roads to Sal and Enzo pass through David."

"But he isn't," Wes said. He pulled the papers he'd been working on all afternoon from his back pocket, leaned forward, and spread them flat on the huge stone coffee table. "Listen, OK. Hear me out. Will you do that?"

"Yes," Marta said. "I'll do that."

"What's here—well, it's a mess is what it is. But I think it's enough. I've written down account numbers, verification codes, keys, passwords, answers to security questions. Everything I have except my retinas and my fingerprints, and those have to stay with me. Sorry about that."

"Wes."

"You said you'd hear me out. Anyway, do me a favor and make sure not to leave this lying around, OK? Anyway. On another sheet's a kind of legal document, or the best I could come up with. I'm handing over my assets to my parents' protection. If I'm not back in five years, it goes to them permanently. I've made similar arrangements for operation of Pocketz and its subsidiaries.

"Over here. This sheet." He pointed. "This is an account I hold under another name. Untraceable. Make the transfers to get you back in-zone through this one. There should be credits enough to cover you and Violet. Let Berto and Ken foot Andy's bill.

"About two seconds after you set foot back in-zone, I want you to call this guy." He licked his finger and peeled back another sheet. "Gio Slattery. Give him these papers. I trust him. Only him. He can get you clean new documentation and a validated passport to London. He can get your sons clean documentation."

"They'll never do that. They love their father. More than I even realized, apparently."

"I can't say one way or the other about that. They're your sons. You know them, and I don't. But don't make the assumption. Have you ever sat them down and told them about your husband? All of it?"

"Of course not," Marta said. "How could I do that? He's their father. They idolize him."

"Maybe because they need to know? *Because* he's their father and they idolize him?"

Marta shifted uneasily on the leather sofa.

"I've instructed Gio to set you up an account under the new name with enough credits that you shouldn't have anything to worry about for a long time. Let him do it, Marta. Let me do this for you."

"I can't accept all of this," Marta said. "It isn't right."

"You can accept it, and it is right."

"David will find me. He'll never let it happen."

"David thinks you're dead. Doesn't he?"

Staring into her glass, Marta nodded. Then she knocked it back.

"So he won't know any different until it's too late for him to do anything about it."

"Let's say I do this," Marta said. "Let's say I let you help me, and I go to London and find my boys. That's not the same thing as what you're doing. You're setting me up as if it is, but it's not. You have a life. You have family. Your parents will be worried sick. You have a company and influence and money. You'd be a damn fool to walk away from it all for a nice girl you barely know."

"It's not only for her."

Marta made a snorting sound.

"Well, gosh, it's partly for her. And I probably am being a damn fool, on that count, at least. But I have a penance to pay, Marta. Ruby City, that other village June mentioned. Lee, Anastasia, Wendy, Tia." He cleared his throat. "Jesse. They'd all be alive if I hadn't made that deal with your husband, if I'd stuck to my values instead of trying to make a quick buck. I want to try to put some good into the world, and that medicine could still make a difference."

"I wished I believed that. I really do."

"There's another thing. Maybe this will be a more compelling argument for you."

Marta lifted her pale eyebrows.

"Your husband. Will he let me come back and not take his deal? Knowing everything I know?"

Marta flipped through the sheaf of papers, though Wes didn't think she was actually seeing any of the words or numbers on the pages. At last she stopped. Tapped them against her thighs to neaten the edges. Refolded them along the old creases. The she tucked them against her middle and crossed her arms over them protectively.

"All right, Wes," she said. "Let's be fools."

The next morning, the chalet was shrouded in fog, the view outside the two banks of windows nothing but white and white and white. The group, Edie and Wes, too, went downstairs for the first time since their arrival and gathered beside the car. Berto and Andy argued about the best way to pack the trunk with the supplies they'd pilfered from the chalet's stores. Edie felt something building inside herself like bubbles in a champagne bottle. She was scared. But she was also ready to see the others leave. She was ready for the life that awaited her and Wes after the others' taillights had vanished downhill, into the mist. She was ready for midday to come, so that Wes could pass the forty-eight-hour mark and they could both believe, for real and true, that he was in the clear for Shreve's.

But first, goodbyes. Dutiful hugs and well wishes. Edie was reminded of long-ago Gulf Zone Christmases with relatives she only saw once or twice a year, those imposed physical intimacies, unwelcome but required by shared blood. And this group all shared blood now, didn't they? Or shared bloodshed. Edie wouldn't miss Andy, Berto, Ken. But she could put her arms around each of them, feel their hearts thudding against her own—proof that they all lived, still. Was that the point of a hug? Two human hearts thudding together, testifying? This made a sort of sense to Edie.

She hugged Marta fiercely, and Marta kissed her cheek. "Take care of yourself," Marta said. "Be smart."

Edie promised that she would.

She withdrew so that Marta and Wes could exchange their goodbyes, understanding that there was something special between the two of them, a bond unlike any the others on this excursion had shared. She was jealous of them, in a way. But there was no replacing her own mother. Not with Marta, not with anyone else in the world. Edie had been loved, and lucky, and the loss served only to underscore these facts, to remind her of their preciousness.

That left Violet. She hung at the edge of the group, arms folded tightly across her chest. Edie didn't even try to go in for the obligatory hug.

"Thank you for what you did," Edie said. "You saved us."

"I saved my baby," Violet said. "And I got the rest of them killed." She dug into her jacket pocket and pulled something out. "Here. It may be all that's left."

Edie took the offering: a paper pouch. Whatever was inside it made a fine rustling sound in the transfer, and Edie peeled the flap up to examine the pouch's contents.

"The seeds," Edie murmured.

"Yeah. It turns out I won't need them."

Edie nodded and folded the flap back down, then rolled it down a second time for good measure. She slid the pouch into her Stamp holster.

"Drive safe," Edie said. It was the only parting sentiment she could come up with. "And good luck."

Violet nodded, then hurried to the car's front passenger seat. Andy was behind the wheel. He put the car into reverse, waved; the other men followed suit. Marta, seated by a window, pressed her hand to the glass and smiled. Violet, staring off in some other direction entirely, did nothing. In another moment they were gone, even the rumble of the car's engine, swallowed by fog and distance.

The silence they left was very, very loud.

"So," Edie said.

"So," Wes agreed.

"Upstairs? Look at some maps, make a plan?"

"Sounds good," Wes said.

"But I'd like to finish *Persuasion* first. If that's OK. I only have twenty pages left."

Wes agreed to that, too.

She'd tell him about the seeds later, over the maps and lunch, and they would have to worry and strategize: Where to plant, and when? How to process them once they'd grown? Seeds tied you down to a square of soil. Seeds made your world smaller. And yet, they each contained a world, too, didn't they? For a couple of hours, the seeds would be Edie's secret: these hundreds of worlds, this pocket full of possibilities.

Epilogue

She Is Consumed

Bedtime is always an hour-long ordeal, but it is a sweet ordeal. Mostly. There's the bath, the anointing with oils and lotions—Ali's eczema is very bad, and the skin on her chest is sometimes almost as angry a red as Violet's own. The fresh diaper and pajamas, the books—*Sweet Pea Sails the Sea*, *Chicka Chicka Boom Boom*, *Where Is the Bear?*, and, oddly, *The Shaman and the Salt Line* are all current favorites—the songs, the noise machine, the rocking chair. Finally, the breast. This is a habit Violet needs to break, Ali's nursing to sleep. She's almost twenty months old, and the midnight comfort feeding keeps Violet from ever getting a solid night's sleep, which she desperately needs, working the schedule she does. But it is so hard to let it go, for both of them. As they rock tonight, Ali's eyes are still open; they glitter, reflecting the star-shower pattern circling on the ceiling above her. Violet lifts the baby's bare foot and mouths it playfully, rubbing her lips against the perfect pearl toes, and Ali smiles around her nipple, pulls off, and says, "Mama eat."

"Yum yum yum," Violet says. "Tasty toes. Mommy is so hungry for toes."

Ali bops her foot against Violet's mouth and latches on once more. Her eyes flutter closed.

Several minutes later, when the motion of her mouth has stopped,

Violet pulls her breast loose and tucks it back into the flap of her nightgown. She rises, and the rocking chair creaks loudly, but Ali is heavy and motionless in her arms, out cold—for the whole night, Violet hopes. Her alarm goes off at 5:00 a.m., which usually gives her enough time to shower, dress, and drink a cup of coffee before Ali's soft cries emanate from the nursery. The bus that passes by Ali's daycare gets to the stop near their apartment at 6:00, then again at 6:15. If they miss the 6:00, Violet still has a chance of getting to work on time. If she misses the 6:15, it's call a cab and spend a few hours' pay on fare, or get fired.

After she's laid Ali in her crib and drawn a light blanket over her, Violet goes to the projector. As she does every night, she runs her fingers over the gold chain dangling from a nearby lampshade—it glimmers in the shifting light—then rubs the gold *A* charm between her index finger and thumb. For luck. The necklace is the only fine thing in this apartment. She hopes she never has to pawn it.

They live in one of the upstairs units of an old carved-up house on the outskirts of Greensboro. The house was built fifty or sixty years ago, when there was still talk of a train route being run out to this part of town. Fat chance of that. Now, most of the residents are like Violet: low-skill workers in one of the city's hotels or malls or restaurants, people who wash clothes and sheets and floors, slap meat onto griddles, drop potatoes down into vats of hot oil (a job—the one—that Violet had avoided, one of the only ways that the ruin of her face has empowered her), treat sewage, collect trash. They had settled into subdivisions like Violet's, living three or four families, even five, to houses that had been built for one, though how one family had put so much space to use is beyond Violet's comprehension. The houses in Meadow Glade Estates were all the same originally—tan siding and brick veneer, four bedrooms and a downstairs office, two-car garage, shallow front porch with grand white columns and a two-story entryway—though they've all been adapted over the years, resulting in a haphazard but creative architecture reminiscent for Violet of Ruby City. Meadow Glade is bearable only for the small ways it reminds her of her old home: the people, who are mostly decent and hardworking, though there is a crime element here, no doubt about it, and all of Violet's windows have bars, and her doors triple-lock; the thriftiness and ingenuity; the sense of community, of the importance of protecting one's own. As she emerges from her daughter's room, she can see that her downstairs neighbor, Sally—who has a key to Violet's rooms, just as Violet has the keys to hers—has left her a square of pound cake on a beautiful chipped old plate. It sits in the middle of the coffee table with a doily under it—Sally has a sense of occasion, even when there is none—and a glass of milk next to it. There's a scrap of paper with one word written on it, etched in Sally's ornate script: *Enjoy.*

Violet settles down to do just that. It's 9:30. The new episode of her favorite show, a half-hour comedy out of Britain called *Cheek*, dropped today, but before she cues it up on her tablet, she checks the news feeds—a masochistic act, one guaranteed to drain some of the pleasure out of this precious quiet time. But she can never stop herself.

David Perrone is the lead story again. Another big rally, attendance in the thousands. More speculation about whether his popularity will hold out until the primaries next year. The pundits say no, but Violet knows better. His platform has been securing the border, keeping out the illegals—like Violet. But she understands. No one understands the misguided dream of a Wall more, she thinks, than a person who'd sacrifice everything to traverse it.

She closes the news and syncs *Cheek* to the used monitor she picked up at a rummage sale. There's a crack in the corner of the monitor, but you don't even see it when the show is playing. It's amazing what people in-zone toss.

This half hour is hers. Then to bed on the pullout sofa, then work, then a few precious hours with Ali, then bedtime. And then she does the whole thing over again.

She has just taken her first bite when there's a sound out in the hall. Redford going to his rooms, she assumes, so she chews and swallows on her right side (she has a bad tooth on the left, is still saving to get it pulled), then takes another bite. But the footsteps stop outside her door, then creak. Violet pauses her show, annoyed, and waits for the knock. "Sally?" she calls.

There's another creak. Then more steps, this time moving in the direction of the stairs, and then Violet doesn't hear anything anymore.

She rises, uneasy, and sets her plate back down on the coffee table. At the door, she looks through the peephole. Sees nothing. She presses her ear to the door. Nothing.

She thinks about messaging Sally downstairs, but Sally's the nervous type, and Violet doesn't want to rile her up over nothing.

So she returns to the door, loops the chain in the slide, and turns the three locks. Opens it. Quick look to make sure no one is hiding to the door's left or right, or crouched down below the view of the peephole. Then she closes the door, unhooks the chain, and opens it wide enough to stick her entire head out.

The hall is empty. But there's something on the floor.

An envelope, folded from creamy paper, and—again—one word in a hand she recognizes: *Violet*.

Not Sally's hand, though.

Her heart starts thumping hard. She looks out into the hall again, walks to the top of the stairs, peers down. Then back to her room. The apartment is on the house's back half—none of the windows faces the front door—but Violet looks out the window anyway, and she sees nothing there, either, no dark figure moving away in the night.

Hand trembling, she slides a finger under the envelope's seal. There's a sheet of paper, and Violet unfolds it.

Violet,

I think about you all the time. I hope you found what you were looking for over here. I am still on the hunt myself. I have a debt to collect. Another visit to pay.

I think all the time about the Salt, too. Why it cost us our babies. And the conclusion I reached was that we don't deserve to be here. We're not supposed to be here. And if the ticks don't finish the job, the cure will. But I'm glad you got your baby, Violet. I hope to meet her. It gets me through a day to imagine it.

Love,

June

From the bedroom, Ali cries out. Normally, this would be cause in Violet for exhausted resignation, even despair, but tonight she goes to her daughter gladly, grateful for the excuse to snuggle her close. Maybe Violet will just sit in the rocking chair, hold her all night long. There will be no sleep for her now, anyway. She can only rock and hold her child and think about her mother—the woman who stood silently outside Violet's own door, then chose to pass over it.

Acknowledgments

To my agent, Gail Hochman, and editor, Sally Kim: thanks for sticking it out with me through three books and for not turning tail when I told you this one would be about killer ticks.

Thanks, too, to Danielle Lavaque-Manty and Leah Stewart for the early feedback and encouragement. "Trust the tick," Danielle said when I was wallowing in self-doubt. I tried to do that.

You hear a lot about how motherhood makes writing difficult, and I'll agree that finding the time and motivation to work is a challenge. But I couldn't have figured out what this book was about without my children. My first pregnancy began shortly after I started drafting *The Salt Line*, and my second child was born a few weeks after I submitted the final line edits. Becoming a mother to Selby and Raina helped me figure out the novel's *why*—but more than that, it taught me that I have to write to please myself, or else the time away from them isn't worth it.

I ended this book with Violet and a small act of kindness that gets her through a hard day. I've been shown so many of those kindnesses in the last four years. I am lucky to work at an institution with a generous maternal leave policy, and I'm lucky to be supported by so many good people. To my parents: thank you for taking such joy in my children, and Mom: I couldn't have survived those weeks after Raina's birth if you hadn't been here holding my hand. Risa

Applegarth and Matthew Loyd: you are family to us, and we love you and your sweet girls so much. Erin McGraw, there will never be enough thank-yous for all that you've done. The list goes on: Jennifer Whitaker, Amy Vines, Juliana Gray, David Roderick, Rachel Richardson, Jen Feather, Audra Abt, Tony Cuda, Katherine Skinner, Amanda Weedman, Tita Ramirez, Drew Perry, and Rhett Iseman Trull—whether you were dropping off food or hand-me-downs or sending me a funny text, you've each done more for me than you probably realize.

As ever, the last and biggest thank-you has to go to my husband, Brandon Jones. Our first date was twenty years ago, hard as that is to believe, and I can only marvel at how good those years have been, how lucky we are. You make me laugh, and you make me feel hope. As you wrote back when we were both still basically kids: Next time I see you, I'll be hugging and kissing on you.